COLLEEN A. PARKINSON

This novel is a work of fiction. Names, characters, places and events are products of the author's imagination or are used fictitiously. Any similarity to persons living or deceased is purely coincidental.

All rights reserved. No part of this book may be reproduced or transmitted in any form or by any means, electronic or mechanical, including photocopying, recording, or by any information storage and retrieval system without the written permission of the author.

Reviewers may quote short passages. All others must request permission in writing from the author.

© 2020
By Colleen A. Parkinson
SEPIA TREE PUBLISHING
ISBN (Print) : 978-1-09830-584-0
ISBN (eBook): 978-1-09830-585-7

1

Quinn tugged with a metal rake at the moist green weeds, released them from the dew-dampened earth, and used his brown calloused fingers to deposit them from the tines into a pile near his right side. He repeated this action many times until the dirt lay bare and the weed pile at his side was as tall as his waist. Satisfied for the moment, the boy wiped back-handed at his nose where a bead of sweat tickled him. He wiped the sweat on the seat of his jeans and glanced up at the sky as a cawing crow circled and alit on a branch. Boy and crow acknowledged each other with that silent eye-to-eye connection shared only by the most intimate of friends. The crow cawed and lifted skyward, dived and disappeared in the trees behind the top of the slope. The boy resumed his labor. He sang or sometimes talked to himself as he worked.

He was tall, thin, with sinewy muscles. His hair was so pale blond it appeared almost the color of mid-day sunlight. His face was long, yet slightly square-shaped, with a softly rounded chin—a very handsome sixteen-year-old boy of Scandinavian stock. He had a light tan, which he acquired over the past week as spring melded into the delightful dawning of early summer.

He continued with his task, his forehead shimmering with sweat and flecks of dirt. The metal tines of the rake scraped something hard. The boy stopped and stared at the patch of gray granite. He abandoned the rake off to his side and dropped to his knees in the dirt, bent and used his hands to uncover his discovery.

It was an old headstone. The name and date were faint, eroded by time and the elements. He scrutinized the words and numbers.

Patrick H. Fitzgerald. Father. Born 1837. Ireland. Died 1885.

A gratifying shiver went up his spine. His suspicions confirmed, and the rumors laid to rest, he chuckled to himself. "Well, sir, I bet you're happy someone has finally found you. It's about time someone gave you all a nice tidy place to rest. That's all I'm doing, mister."

A familiar vibration raced through his body, tingled every muscle, every internal organ, every inch of his skin. It raced up his spine and rose into his brain with the sensation of warm water rising into his head. The water was full of a million sparkling stars.

Quinn knew what it meant. He was seven years old when the first one came to call. There had come many others since then; they no longer frightened him.

His inner radar told him what direction to look, and he looked, his expectation verified. It was *her* again. She had appeared every few days or so since he began working to clear the old graveyard. She was a very young woman, the wispy form of her body short and slight of figure, dressed in a long sapphire blue gown—the height of early 1900's fashion. Her dark hair was neatly piled in loose curls framing an insipid face that had likely garnered few compliments during her lifetime. Yet, the young woman radiated underlying effervescent humor that produced a far deeper attractiveness. Her intense blue eyes possessed the energy of endless stories and experiences tragic and joyful. She carried one of her stories in her arms, a tiny motionless baby wrapped in a white christening gown. She cuddled it tightly to her bosom as if she feared someone would take it from her as she gazed pleadingly at Quinn.

Because she was standing less than ten feet away from him, Quinn stayed put. He didn't want to frighten her by suddenly rising to his feet. He grinned at her and amusedly remarked, "Well, you're definitely not Mr. Fitzgerald."

She stepped back to widen the distance between them. As she backed up, a branch of the bush behind her penetrated her right shoulder. It was apparent to Quinn she didn't feel it and was not aware of it. One corner of her mouth lifted with a responding smile to him.

Quinn persevered in a friendly tone of voice. "Are you going to talk to me today?"

She brought her right hand to her mouth, pressed her fingertips gently upon her upper lip, cocked her head to one side apologetically.

This was her fourth visit to him. Four visits, and still no words. Quinn finally understood.

"You're mute? You can't talk?"

She nodded slowly.

He said, "I don't know how to help you if you can't tell me what you need."

She snuggled the baby securely with her left hand, pointed with her right to a spot far off at the edge of the cemetery. Quinn looked to where she pointed, an area overgrown with weeds and littered with a thick covering of last winter's spent brown maple leaves, broken twigs, and wind-carried acorns. Beneath that mess lie the detritus of many decades. He assumed there were graves there, just a few among the many forgotten resting places in this secluded little glade. He estimated it would take him a few weeks to work his way over there; for now, it was inaccessible. He turned to her to tell her this, but she was gone. Although disappointed, he assured himself she would come again, and this gave him hope he would be able to help her cross over. Thoughts of her preoccupied him as he resumed uncovering Mr. Fitzgerald's grave.

Footfalls crushed dry leaves in the cluster of forest nearest the road.

The boy shot to his feet, startled by the unwelcome intruder. "Who's there?"

A female voice, young, called out, "Hello?"

"What do you want?" Quinn demanded suspiciously.

A bush moved, a sandaled foot emerged, a hand moved a branch of the bush to the side, and then a second sandaled foot stepped into view. Finally, she emerged, her dark eyes inquisitive but also cautious. The girl was pretty in a plain sort of way. She had fair skin, an oval face, and big brown eyes full of intelligence, humor, and tenderness. Quinn thought her lips were pretty, not too plump, just plump enough to be inviting. Her hair was dark brown, straight, shoulder-length, parted on the left side. She had a petite build, yet firm muscles that belied her small-boned fragility. She was dressed in rose color cotton trousers and a sleeveless yellow blouse with pink stripes. She had tied the hem of the blouse so it exposed her belly and her navel.

"I didn't know anyone was here." She stopped in front of the bush and quickly scanned the area with her big dark eyes. "Wow! What a great camping spot."

"It's not for camping," Quinn said, retrieving his rake.

"So, what are you doing here?"

"Cleaning up."

"Cleaning up what?"

"The graves."

She paled just a little. "Graves? This is a graveyard?"

"A very old one." He pointed to the stone he had just uncovered. "See?"

She approached him cautiously and looked where he was pointing. "Wow! That's old."

"And it's probably not the oldest one in here." He smiled at her smugly, because she was impressed with his finding.

"Are you part of a cleanup committee or something?"

"Uh-uh. I'm just doing it because it needs to be done."

"Are you doing this all by yourself?"

"Yep."

"Are there lots of graves in here?"

"That's what I'm gonna find out." The whole time he didn't look at her, lest that would encourage her.

"You must have a lot of time on your hands."

He grimaced at her comment; he didn't know why it bothered him.

She smiled and offered her hand in greeting. "My name's Stephanie. I just moved in a couple of weeks ago. I live over that way," she pointed behind her toward the main road, "Where the old grain silo is. You can see it from the road. Mom said it hasn't been used in decades, and there used to be a ranch there, but it's not really a ranch anymore; it's mostly just the house that's left."

He thought she was quite the motormouth. At the same moment he had that thought, a frown crossed her face as if she knew what he thought, and it insulted her. Whether or not she had read his mind, the very possibility of it spooked him. At once, he regretted hurting her feelings if he had done so. With this in mind and wanting a quick save, he referred back to her comment about her house. "Oh. Down the road. Mrs. Tarantino's house. That place is older than the dirt it sits on."

"She was my grandmother on my mom's side. Did you know her?"

"Not very well. We talked a few times when she was out at the mailbox and I was walking by. She was a nice lady. I liked her."

"Oh. Well, she passed away."

"I know," Quinn said.

The girl continued over his remark, "My mom inherited the house. We just moved in."

"Is it just you and your mom?"

"Yeah. My dad died last year. He was a fireman."

"I'm sorry to hear that."

"Like I said, my name's Stephanie." She offered her hand again. "What's your name?"

"Quinn." Hesitantly, he shook hands with her. Her fingers and palm were warm and slightly damp. The warmth he didn't mind. The dampness, her sweat, he found repellent. Without considering how it would look to her, he wiped his hand on his jeans the moment they released each other.

She smiled, embarrassed, and wiped her hands on the hips of her trousers. "Sorry."

"It's okay."

"Are you a germophobe?"

He laughed. "No. I'm sorry."

"That's okay. I was hoping there'd be someone around here my age."

Quinn pointed his thumb casually over his shoulder. "I live in the house up the hill. You can see it from your place."

"The Victorian-style house?"

"That's the one. My dad owns the sporting goods shop downtown. Vanderfield's Sports and Outdoors Supplies. It's right off the freeway."

"Yeah, I saw it. It's got a big yellow rowboat on the sign, right?"

"It's a speedboat, not a rowboat." He resumed raking up the weeds.

"We used to live down in L.A. area. Before Dad died my mom worked in television as a sound editor. Did you ever see *Knights of Red Dragon*?" She didn't wait for Quinn to reply, although he nodded that he had seen the program. "That was the last show she worked on. She couldn't stand the city anymore, too rushed, too congested, too much crime, too many memories. When Gram died, she thought it best we move up here to the country. I bet it's boring here, huh?"

"Not really. Once you start school here, you'll see."

"So, why aren't you out having fun with your friends?"

He took a long pause and thought before he answered. "This is more important to me."

"Why?"

"They have no one."

"I don't think they care. They're dead."

He clenched his jaw in a determined manner. "Well, I care. No one should be forgotten. What if your dad was buried here?"

A sad gleam came to her eyes, and Quinn thought at first she was going to cry. She didn't cry. Instead, she raised her chin and looked at him directly, bravely. "I suppose… well, yeah… good point."

"My family was one of the first to settle in this town. Another reason this is important to me."

"Are you related to anyone buried here? Ancestors?"

"I'm sure some are here, but I haven't found them yet." He feared he had already said too much. He continued working, hoping she'd get the hint and find someone else to bother.

She observed him for a few moments and then offered casually. "I can help if you want."

He didn't like that idea and quickly aimed to discourage her. He gestured at her sandals. "Not in those."

"I've got hiking boots. I can go home and get them."

He couldn't believe her audacity. "I'm just about done for today."

"Are there a lot of spiders?"

"Of course. Big ones. All kinds."

"What else?"

"I spotted a few mice."

"Oh."

"Are you scared of mice?"

"I used to have a pet rat. She was white with pink eyes. I'm allergic to cats, so..."

He continued raking and spoke to her over his shoulder, hoping to dissuade her. "You have to be careful of the rocks, too. There are also a few holes." Then, hoping this would scare her, "Snakes. There are a lot of snakes."

"I'm not afraid of snakes."

Shit. How can I help that dead girl if this pest starts hanging around?

Quinn sighed impatiently at her persistence. "There're a lot of hazards here. Some of the stones are broken, and some have fallen over or been pushed over. Most of them are hidden under all this overgrowth. You can get hurt. Break your leg or something. Thanks, for the offer but I'd rather do this myself."

She made no effort to hide her disappointment. "Okay, then. So, what do you do for fun in this town?"

"I don't know. It depends on what you like to do."

Stephanie persisted, "When I lived in L.A. I had passes all summer for Disneyland. When I wasn't at Disneyland, I went to the beach and hung out with my friends. There's no Disneyland and no beach here, and my friends are five hundred miles away. What the hell do you do for fun around here?"

"There's the lake up that way," he pointed, "Boating, fishing, even an arcade out there. You should check it out. The joint's jumpin' all summer."

"Is it far?"

"A couple of miles." Quinn slid weeds off the tines of his rake, began to gather his other yard tools. "I have to go now."

"Do you go there?"

"Not lately."

"How come?"

"Because I'm doing this."

She laughed darkly. "This is your summer project, huh?"

"What's wrong with that?"

"Nothing."

He suspected she was a blabbermouth like most girls. He gave her his full attention to be certain she would hear his message and take it seriously. "Listen... Don't tell anyone about this place. I mean it."

His stern tone seemed overly austere to her. "Why?"

"If the word gets out it'll attract vandals and partiers, that's why."

She nodded. "Okay." As both an afterthought and an apology, she added, "I don't usually talk this much."

That sent a dull chill up his spine. "Who said you talked too much?"

She glanced at the dirt, shoved her hands in her pockets. "You're the first person I've met since I moved here. I tend to come off like a steamroller when I meet new people."

"It's okay." Quinn was an expert at expressing sincerity while lying.

She gave him an empathetic half-smile. "What's your name again?"

"Quinn."

"It was nice meeting you, Quinn."

Quinn gathered his tools as she walked away, tried not to be obvious he was watching her as she left, watching the girl and wondering about her, wondering if she would keep the secret. The more he thought about her as he carried the tools to the brush enveloped oak beside the footpath that led up the hill to his side yard, the more he suspected there was something special about her, and maybe he should have been a little bit nicer. He leaned the rakes and the shovel carefully and neatly against the tree along his fence, his mind replaying their conversation; his mind's eye recalling her face, her very sad eyes, her obvious loneliness. Yet, it seemed to him there was something else about her; it wasn't all tragedy. Lightness. Yes… her sadness didn't weigh her down. Her spirit was light, despite her grief.

In sharp contrast to me… Quinn whispered.

* * * * *

Stephanie crossed the road after a vehicle passed, kept to her right on the dirt shoulder and down the slight incline. She turned left through a wide-open white iron gateway that led to her home. It was an old farmhouse, two stories high, with a sloping shingle roof. An inviting porch encircled the entire structure. Her mother had the house repainted a bright white before they moved in. The shutters were green, as were the borders of the four front gables. The windows in the front were very large, a contrast to those on the upper floor, which were small and square.

Large potted plants and flowers, bright green wicker furniture with coordinating colorful pillows and cushions decorated the porch. Her mother had hung a wreath of artificial pansies and greenery on the front door behind the screen door.

A warm breeze rustled Stephanie's hair. She stood still for a few moments, enough to savor the serenity and enough for her to smell the accumulated scents of hay, grasses, flowers, and pollens before it all drifted past her and continued on its way. It was quite a change from the incessant noise and exhaust-laden smog of the L.A. Basin.

Her mother pushed open the screen door. She was of average height, small-boned like her daughter, and slightly overweight. Her faintly lined face, pale from countless hours of lost sleep and too many hours spent indoors, enhanced her deep chestnut eyes. Her hair, dark at the crown and blonde down the length of it, curled at the curve of her shoulders. The color clashed with her skin tone, which only added to her appearance of chronic exhaustion. Just this morning she had been contemplating dying it to the original dark brown color inherited through her Italian lineage. She wore dark red trousers and an oversized white t-shirt. Barefooted and carrying a large clear plastic pitcher of water, she stepped out to the porch. "Did you have a nice walk?"

"I sure did. If you give me the pitcher, I'll water the plants."

"Thank you, dear." She took the chair beside the doorway where there was an unobstructed view of the property. With an appreciative glance at the blue crystalline sky and the puffy white clouds, she remarked, "What a beautiful day!"

"Say, Mom?"

"Hmmm?"

"Did you know there's a cemetery up the road?"

"Oh, yes. It's been there for over a hundred years. So, you found it."

"Is any of your family buried there?"

"Not as far as I know. There might be somebody. I don't know for sure. All my mother told me about it is that it was a pioneer cemetery, and it hasn't been used in over a hundred years. That's why she and grandpa are buried over at Oakview."

Stephanie nodded, recollecting Gram's funeral there, and recollecting her dad's funeral in his family plot down the hill in the same place. Per prearrangements, the funeral home flew his body north to Masonville and then shipped him by cargo van the rest of the way northeast to "if-you-blink-you-miss-it" Providence. There he joined his predeceased parents and older brother in the manicured plot near the manmade stream in Oakview Memorial Park. Stephanie didn't get much of a look at the place; she could hardly see through the steady flow of her tears.

Her clearest memory was of when they began to lower the casket. She thought of him reposed inside it wearing his only suit, trapped there in the eternal darkness. The finality of it was more than she could bear. She sobbed silently, her lips stretched and quivering with her effort to remain quiet. As a grieving moan threatened to escape her throat, she forced it back down and diverted her attention to the grass at her feet. There was a ladybug struggling among the blades. Stephanie stared at it through her tears, stared at it so hard, she forgot about her misery, concerned that after all was done and over someone would step on that poor ladybug. She bent and gingerly picked it up, let it rest upon her fingertip. Its wings trembled and spread. It alit and flew off to live another day. Observing its flight reminded her of what her mother assured her: the dead leave their body behind and fly away in spirit to Heaven. Still, she could not watch his casket descend. Instead, she convinced herself he had come to her as the ladybug to tell her goodbye, and she had set him free.

"I'd prefer you didn't go in there, Steph."

"Huh?"

"That old graveyard."

"Why not?"

"It's untended. Mom told me there are snakes there, too."

"There's a boy cleaning it up. He just took it on himself to do it."

"No kidding?"

"His name's Quinn."

"Oh!" The woman smiled broadly, revealing her flawless white teeth. "The Vanderfield boy. When you were three, you and he played together when we visited here. When I was a girl, I had a crush on his dad, John."

Stephanie gushed in surprise. "No!"

"Yes, indeed. John Vanderfield was quite the looker—a blond Adonis. All the girls were after him. Bernice Talmadge finally landed him. Not surprising; she was a looker, herself."

"Were you jealous?"

"No. I was off at college by then, and your father was my main squeeze." Her eyes glinted with happiness at the recollection. "Your father was something special. My god, you should have seen him when he was young. So slender and muscular… He got a football scholarship, you know—and smart as a whip. I sat at front at every game, and sometimes he would steal a glance at me as I cheered him on. He had a smile that could melt the paint off the walls. It certainly melted my heart."

"I miss his smile."

"So do I."

"I miss his laugh, too. That yuk-yuk laugh of his." Stephanie grinned, yet her eyes were moistening.

Her mother draped her arm over the girl's shoulders. "We'll see him again someday. It's all right. Really, it is. Our love will never die, right?"

"Right."

"Please don't cry. You'll make me cry. It's too beautiful a day to spoil with tears."

They sat in silence for a few moments, until Stephanie spoke. "Would it be okay if I invited Quinn over?"

"That'd be fine, honey. We'll invite John and Bernice, too. How about this weekend?"

2

The big den inside the Vanderfield house was masculine in every way with its black leather furniture, and a large executive style desk, bookcases, and tables all made of gleaming polished cherry wood. The lamp bases upon the side tables at each end of the sofa were ceramic hand-painted drakes in simulated flight topped by ecru lampshades. Paintings of hunting dogs and ducks adorned the walls, which were painted Hunter Green, and the wainscoting Deep Burgundy. John Vanderfield's books crowded the bookcases, books about hunting, nature, American and World History, biographies of famous politicians, businessmen, and philosophers. He kept a collection of movies and documentaries in a cabinet below the giant flat screen television attached to one wall across from his recliner. An elaborate stereo system that played every available format of music dominated the surface of the cabinet, the system's lights flashing different shades of colors according to the bass and treble vibrations emanating from the speakers.

On the sofa, Quinn bobbed his head to the wild rhythms of John Coltrane. Modern music held no attraction for the boy. Quinn was a jazzer, a throwback to a distant time of American innocence that ended the day Kennedy died in Dallas, and persons of forbidden sexual tastes were scratching at the doors of their closets.

Quinn would not have heard of John Coltrane or any of the other music giants who preceded him had it not been for a long-dead trumpeter named Buzz Lester who had visited him when Quinn was ten years old. Buzz had died on Valentine's Day 1947 while playing a gig at the Gadfee Lake Ballroom a few miles up the road. During a break between the band's third and fourth sets he ambled out to the pier for some cool fresh air and welcome silence. He noticed a young woman in a mink coat smoking under the light on the pier. Her sniffles and sobs indicated she was crying as she gazed off into the darkness beyond the lake. Hearing his footsteps as he approached her, she turned and glared at him, at first mistaking him for her inconsiderate date. Her expression changed once she recognized him as one of the musicians, and she apologized to him. Buzz, very drunk and feeling flirtatious, said and did all the wrong things that provoked her ire. Appalled, she struck him with her purse, which contained a handgun. As the weight and hardness of her concealed weapon made violent contact with his temple, the image of the gun in his mind was his last conscious realization before he toppled off the pier, cataleptic from a concussion, into the black water. His band mates, thinking he had passed out in his car after the third set (for this was his pattern), never bothered to look for him until they found his car vacant after the ballroom closed for the night. Police finally recovered his body at sunrise.

Buzz was an expert on everything to do with music from the 1920s through the early 1960s, "…until those damned Brits came over with their mop-heads and guitars and ruined everything." He was full of stories, full of music. He could transmit his favorite tunes to Quinn telepathically, and this is how Quinn got his "dust web covered, moldy-oldie music" education. Enraptured, Quinn exhausted his weekly allowance in thrift stores on well-preserved shellac and vinyl. The boy's collection took up three tall shelving units that fully covered two walls in his bedroom.

Buzz was a frequent visitor for many years and one day Quinn asked him why he had not crossed over.

"I'm havin' too much fun!" The slender, mischievous-faced man said with a roar of laughter.

"But, don't you wanna go see God?"

"Ha! Does God wanna see me?"

"Well, aren't you supposed to go to Heaven after you die?"

"When I'm good and ready, kid."

"But, won't God be mad at you for staying behind?"

"I look at it this way, kid: God gave us a sense of humor, so he must have a sense of humor, too. I bet he's okay with it. I'll go soon."

"Maybe you should, Buzz. I'll miss you, but you gotta leave here sometime. Are you afraid to leave because you were drunk when you died?"

Another roll of laughter. "Oh, hell no."

"Are you mad at that lady who cracked your skull with her purse?"

"Hell, I don't even remember what she looked like."

"Then, what's really keeping you here?"

"Fun!"

"This world sucks. There's nothing fun about it."

"To you, kid."

"Not just me; most people."

"More for you, kid. I can't make the world better, but I can give you something to make it more tolerable. Maybe I've done my job. Do you want me to go?"

Quinn gave this a lot of thought before he answered. "I want you to go because I want you to have peace. Don't worry about me."

"Your mother's goin' soon, Quinn. I wanna be here for you when that happens."

His mother had been sick for a long time and had been at death's door once already. Still, this news hit Quinn hard. "How soon?"

"A couple of years, maybe less. She already got the shine on her."

"The shine?"

"God's ready for her. He got his shine over her to make it easy for her when the time comes. Aw, shit… Don't start bawlin.'"

"Can't God change his mind?"

"It's predestined, kid. My time was predestined. I've been cheatin' this whole time. Your mom ain't gonna cheat. I like that about her. You'll see her again someday. Till then, you gotta be strong."

"Will she come visit me like you do?"

"I got no idea. I ain't no expert on that stuff." Buzz waited a few moments while Quinn sniffled and wiped his tears. Once the boy gathered his composure and looked him soberly in the eye, Buzz said, "That's one of the things I meant when I told you I'm leavin' you things to make this world more tolerable. Well, not things, exactly. The only thing I got to give you is what made me happy and kept me sane through the bad times. You got the music now. That always soothed me when times were bad. It's all I got to leave you. I got nothin' else except a liver fried by booze and a brain ringing from that lady's right hook. So, maybe you're right I gotta go – and I'm ready to go, but I wanna delay a while longer in case you need me after your mom passes."

"It'd kill me if you both went at the same time. I can't handle that."

"Do you want me to go now? Are you sure you won't need me?"

"My dad will be here. We'll help each other through it. Till then, I wanna give what time's left to Mom. I think that's what I gotta do. You understand, right?"

"I do understand. Yeah, this is for the best. He's been pullin' at me lately—y'know, God." Buzz chuckled to himself. "Hopefully, he'll be in a good mood when I get there."

"Yeah. It'll be okay, Buzz. I bet he's already got a gig lined-up for you."

"Keep your chin up, kid. You got the gift of seeing what others don't, for whatever's that's worth. And, to tell you the truth, you gave me a purpose I never had before. I suppose it's time for me to go. I'll always remember you, Quinn."

There were many days when Quinn longed for Buzz's company, especially these days when he felt so miserably alone in the world.

* * * * *

Soon the patriarch John Vanderfield returned home. Quinn shut off the music and vacated the room as John claimed the recliner, but not before saying hello and exchanging meaningless pleasantries. Once comfortable in his chair (which Quinn called, "The King's Throne"), John thumbed the TV remote for the evening news. This evening's lead story was something about President George W. Bush and the health of the economy. John paid close attention to the broadcast. He barely acknowledged their housekeeper and live-in cook Maria as she served him his customary mug of French Roast coffee with a dollop of whipped cream and a shot of whiskey. In the meantime, Quinn set the table for dinner while Maria filled the expensive Royal Doulton serving dishes with her culinary offerings. This was the routine most nights.

The grandfather clock in the hallway struck nine, and Maria emerged from the kitchen with a tumbler of whiskey, which she set on the table beside John. He didn't look up from his book as he mumbled his thanks. Her plump fingers interlaced upon her stout belly, she lingered in front of the recliner and finally said to him, "A letter came from the school today."

He finally looked at her. "What did Quinn do this time?"

She removed the envelope from her apron pocket and handed it to him.

He took it reluctantly, with an air of consternation, and quickly read the letter. The bad news did not surprise him. "Where is he?"

"He's upstairs doing his homework."

"Tell him I want to see him."

Without replying, she headed up the staircase.

John read the letter again, a gleam of fire in his dark blue eyes. His cheeks reddened, and his blond mustache twitched and spread with the changing position of his lips as he pressed them together. "Damned kid…" He slammed his book shut and dropped it on the side table where it made a soft thud as it landed. The lampshade over the flying drake trembled. "I don't need this shit."

The dread on Quinn's face when he joined his father in the den was no surprise to John. He motioned at the sofa. "Have a seat, son."

"What'd I do?"

"Just sit down." He waited until Quinn sat. He observed the boy's face that closely resembled Bernice. Quinn had inherited most of Bernice's traits; they even had the same rolling laugh. His son seldom laughed these days; he was aloof and secretive, and he spent too much time alone. John worried about him and was frustrated with his behavior. The letter from the school was just another example of the boy's downward spiral. Wishing to be done with it, John gently commenced, "I have a letter from your principal. I'm tired of this. I've got a lot of worries right now."

"Those guys jumped me. I didn't do anything to deserve it!"

John knew better. Quinn was a habitual smart mouth with an overly defensive attitude. Additionally, the boy's increasingly hostile behavior consistently made him a target for his schoolmates since junior high.

"It says here you called someone a... *rectum*?"

"That's bull."

"Quinn..."

"Well, maybe I did. But I don't remember."

"How many times have we been through this? How many times have you come home beat up? How many times has our front yard been t.p.'d? When are you going to learn?"

Quinn stared at the beige carpet.

His father continued. "I'd put you on restriction, but you never go anywhere, anyway."

Quinn did not raise his eyes to his father's face.

"If I had the extra money, I'd send you to private school. Do you know that?"

"Uh-huh."

"You're all I have, Quinn."

At this, Quinn finally looked up, met his father's eyes, which were full of hurt. He forced sincerity into his voice as he uttered softly, "I'm sorry. I'm sorry."

"Is there something you want to tell me?"

He knew where this was leading. "No."

"I'm not a fool."

"I never said you were."

John crinkled the letter into a ball in his hands. "It's time for bed. From now on, watch your mouth."

Quinn rose quickly and with much relief. "I will. I promise."

He watched his son cross the hallway toward the staircase, the boy moving quickly and with a bit too much resentment in each step. As soon as he was out of hearing range, John whispered to himself in a defeated and mournful voice, "Shit..."

* * * * *

Quinn was glad his father was too tired and just inebriated enough not to want to deal harshly with him over his bad behavior. Although Quinn felt a small satisfaction at being let off the hook, a part of him felt frustrated at the man's lack of concern for him and at his willingness to simply let it go as if it was too much trouble to delve into the problem and solve it. He decided his father had given up on him a long time ago, had accepted the fact Quinn would never be the ideal son any father would be proud of. That hurt more than anything. John Vanderfield, being a high school jock and one of the *popular crowd* in his day, had no idea what it was like to be laughed at and picked on. He had no idea what it was like to do daily battle with the four boys, who Quinn dubbed, "The Fermented Four," who had made his life a living hell since first grade.

The Fermented Four: Harry Richter, Marcus Stanley, Bruno Ruiz, and Farley Larson had targeted Quinn since grade school because he was the smallest of the boys in his class, effeminate in his manners, highly sensitive, and cried easily. The *cried easily* part was due to the fact the dead often appeared to him at school, and they were usually miserable people suffering psychological aftereffects of the way they died. At such a young age, Quinn was powerless to help them and could only react to their suffering as if it was his own. To make matters worse, some of the dead were angry and dumped their pain into him out of just plain desperation. All of this made it difficult for Quinn to control his emotions and there were many times at school, both in class and on the playground, that he blurted, "Leave me alone!" to tormentors only he could see. As a result, most of his fellow students avoided him while some targeted him as an object of great fun, the Weird Kid who yelled at people that weren't there. The school psychologist deemed him highly imaginative and assured John and Bernice Vanderfield their son would eventually grow out of his minor neurosis once he adjusted to the social aspects of public school. As time passed Quinn learned to silence his outbursts and ignore both the dead and the bullies as best he could. However, children have longer memories than adults credit them for, and once labeled, the Fermented Four would not and could not leave Quinn alone. Quinn's rage increased. He used the only thing he had to get back at them: his mouth. To him they became Hairy Rectum, Morbid Standard, Bruno Ruin, and Fartly Largely. His alternate names for them aroused much amusement among his fellow students, and the Fermented Four were incensed. So the battles continued.

Standing in his bedroom doorway, thinking about it, remembering it, re-experiencing it, Quinn's face tightened and flushed red. Anger filled his eyes. His hands trembled. Although he wanted to slam his bedroom door, he reminded himself the noise would bring his father upstairs. The resulting confrontation would only result in a yelling match that would end badly with a stinging slap across his face. Instead, he took a few moments to compose himself. He shut the door gently and decided he would vent his frustration in his usual manner. He went to his small pine desk against the wall where he took a little book and pen from the drawer. The book was full of lined pages, many of which had graceful cursive writing on them and too many that contained heavy angular block capital letters he had written during rages.

He sat back in his chair, drew in a deep breath and contemplated revenge for all they had done to him through the school year. Finally, after taking a few more moments to calm down and conquer his shaking hands, he found the blank page that awaited the point of his pen. He dated the page with only the month and day and then wrote:

"Tomorrow is Sunday, one more day of peace. I can't wait till school is over. I hate them all."

Quinn shut his journal and returned it with his pen to the desk drawer. The three sentences were not enough to purge his tension, and he turned in the chair and searched the room for another distraction. The room felt claustrophobic. Maria had shut all the blinds again to block the day's heat. He hated it when she took it upon herself to change things from the way he liked them. He liked light and fresh air during the day, and fresh air drifting through his windows at night. He fully raised the horizontal blinds and opened the window beside his bed. The cool night air carried the sweet aroma of mown grass and his mother's rosebushes into the room. He closed his eyes and took a deep breath of it.

Across from Quinn's window, the cemetery lay blanketed under weeds and the remnants of winter's spent leaves and rotted acorns. He could see a portion of it in the clearing below the slope where two digger pines toppled during a fierce wind and rainstorm two years before. The clearing was pale silver-white under the moonlight, yet seemed to Quinn it was lit from within. He imagined a silver-white heart lay below the soil. That heart radiated its purifying light into the sacred earth and the precious deceased who rested there.

Sometimes Quinn imagined the illumination there on nights such as this was the spirit energy of those long-forgotten souls; spirit energy trapped by their sadness and loneliness.

No one should be forgotten.

Stephanie said the dead don't care.

Oh, yes they do. They do. I know they do.

He regretted telling her about it. In retrospect, he felt he should have told her nothing except it was private property and to stay away. But, no… he didn't think of it at the time; she had surprised him and he was not prepared.

An owl hooted. Quinn could not tell if the sound came from the cemetery or somewhere beyond. If the owl was among the graves, posted high on a branch watching for careless rodents below… well… Death will visit there again.

He pulled away from the window and sat at the edge of his bed. His mother's portrait on the nightstand drew his attention as it did every night. Her eyes were the same amber as Quinn's, an unusual color, her hair the same pale blond, and the shape of her face identical to his. Her expression was at once loving and sadly contemplative. Quinn kissed his fingertips and brushed that kiss to her lips.

"I miss you so much."

She would have laughed about him calling Harry Richter "Hairy Rectum."

3

The air was cooler than it had been the previous day, and it smelled like rain. Puffy, smoke-colored clouds hugged the mountaintops in the north, and a few stray corpulent white clouds sailed languidly above the southern valley, occasionally casting shadows upon the earth as they crossed in front of the sun.

Quinn made his way down the foot trail that led from the side of his house and straight through the little forest of oaks and digger pines into the cemetery. Once in the clearing, he laid his rake and his leather gloves on Mister Fitzgerald's toppled headstone, and he took a few minutes to observe the sky and the behavior of the birds. The birds were not aloft. They were in the trees or pecking for grubs in the soil. They were quiet except for a call or chirp now and then, for to them it was a typical day with no threatening conditions imminent. This told Quinn the storm would stay up north, and if there were to be any rain in the valley, it would only be an intermittent light sprinkle. The breeze gently tickled the back of his neck and scented the air with grasses and floral perfume. It was a perfect day to work here.

He put on his gloves and set about yanking the tall weeds out of the soil, tossing them into a pile. Within an hour, he had uncovered six more graves, only one of which—that of a baby—contained an upright headstone. It was a small headstone, only three feet high, and it had a little lamb chiseled expertly on the curved crest. He dropped to his knees, dug some remaining weeds from the stone's base, and read the inscription, "Our Baby, 5 March 1885 – 6 March 1885." The surname on the stone read, "Beckett." The infant's parents and two of its siblings rested in peace in the same row. Their stones were toppled, laying flat, both cracked corner-to-corner. Quinn brushed dirt, debris, and spider webs off the stones. The year of death on the mother's stone was 1902, which indicated she had outlived her family by seven years.

He recalled the young woman with her baby who had been visiting him here, wondered if this was her grave. However, the dates on the stone indicated a woman age twenty-seven years old when she died; the ghost woman appeared to be much younger, perhaps seventeen or eighteen. This answered his question.

A sudden cold breeze tickled the back of his neck. Alarmed, Quinn pivoted, saw the leaves in the trees and nearby bushes were still, as were the remaining sections of tall dry weeds. Yet, the air blew gently against his face. Its iciness lingered upon his skin. A high-frequency vibration accompanied by a high-pitched screaming noise shot into his chest like a spear and exited painfully out his back. He fell from his squatting position onto his rear as he protested the invasion with a few cuss words.

A deep male voice intoned, dragging out the word, "Boy…" and added with a sigh of relief, "Found you."

Quinn waited for the ghost to appear. He waited only a few moments, yet it seemed to him like a long time. The ghost didn't appear, although Quinn could still feel its stifling presence. His voice trembled as he inquired, "What do you want? Who are you?" There came no audible response, but only the sensation of the entity weakening and leaving. After a few more moments, the energy in the cemetery returned to its normal serenity. Quinn decided it must have been a spirit passing through in search of a loved one who had been buried here. Whoever it was had accomplished his purpose to reunite with someone and they were both now gone.

Quinn calmed himself and returned to his task.

★ ★ ★ ★ ★

Stephanie arrived toting a rake and a hoe as he was uncovering another grave. She happily waved to him as she approached, talking a mile a second as she neared him. "Wouldn't you know it that as I was unpacking I came across this rake and hoe that begged me, positively begged me, to bring them to you in case you needed them. I told them you had all the tools you need, but they absolutely insisted and so, here we are!"

Quinn glowered at her. "Are you a nutcase, or what?"

She turned the rake to her as a puppeteer manipulates a puppet. "What do you think, Mr. Rake? Am I a nutcase?"

"What part of *I don't need help* don't you understand?" Quinn pleaded.

"My mother already knows about this place."

He frowned. "I told you not to tell anybody."

"Well, it was just my mom, and she already knew about it. So, calm down. I won't tell anyone else. I promise"

"How can I trust you when you can't keep your mouth shut?" Continuing his work, he asked over his shoulder, "She's not gonna tell anybody, is she?"

"Of course not."

"You can't tell anybody! Got that?"

"I'm sorry."

"I hope your mother's better at keeping promises than you are."

"She's solid."

"Good! Now, go home."

"Why are you such a dick?"

"Because I didn't invite you."

"It's kind of dangerous for you to be working out here all by yourself, don't you think?"

"Nope."

"What if you stepped in a hole or something and broke your leg? How would you get help? I don't see any phone on you."

"I'm perfectly capable of taking care of myself."

She flashed her cell phone at him, "Unlike you, I can call for help."

"Good for you."

"And, by the way… this place was a hangout, a real party place, back in the nineteen-fifties. Cops were out here all the time. My mom can tell you stories!"

"And now it has fallen into obscurity," Quinn said evenly, "And I'd like to keep it that way."

"So, let me help. This place may turn out to be part of my family history, too." She laid the tools on the weedy ground and settled on a rock from which she gazed at him sincerely. "Come on, Quinn. I'm going nuts for something to do. You can be boss if that's what you're worried about."

"You're really something."

"So I've been told."

The wispy ghost woman with her baby strolled soundlessly from the trail, her curious eyes on Stephanie. She stopped at Stephanie's side and observed her. Something in her expression told Quinn there was something about Stephanie she recognized but couldn't recall why or where.

Although Quinn was confident the woman posed no threat, he saw her presence as a tool to scare Stephanie off his turf forever. "There are ghosts here," he blurted.

She gave him a nonchalant smile and said, "Is that supposed to scare me?"

Oh, shit... he muttered under his breath. At that, he stopped what he was doing and faced her seriously. "I'm not kidding."

"And they're probably happy we're here doing something constructive instead of vandalizing the place. You've gotta chill out, man."

"You've sure got nerve..."

"And you've got some serious lack of people skills."

He laughed. He couldn't help it.

The wispy woman covered her lips; her shoulders trembled with her silent laughter. She slowly faded away, still laughing.

"My mom grew up here," Stephanie said. "She and my dad went to school with your dad. She told me she once had a crush on your dad when she was in high school."

Quinn groaned amusedly. "All the girls had a crush on him!"

"Is he still a hunk?"

"If you consider an aging, balding, overworked stress case, with a fat belly a hunk."

"Well, anyway, she wants to invite you and your parents over for dinner next weekend."

Quinn's eyes revealed his pain, although he was unaware of it. "My mom died two years ago."

"Oh." Stephanie slumped, tapped her fingertips to her forehead. "I'm sorry."

He gave her a forgiving glance. "How were you supposed to know? Anyway, I doubt my dad would want to go; the weekends are his busiest days at the store. He usually works late then."

"Well... okay. But, *you're* welcome to come for dinner."

He thought about school and the almost guaranteed prospect he would come home with bruises before the end of the term on Friday. Maybe it wasn't a good idea to commit to anything just yet.

"Let's see how the week goes," he finally told her.

She looked puzzled, her feelings mildly hurt.

"This is the last week of school," he explained. "Finals, you know, and other stuff."

"Well," Stephanie said, retrieving the rake, "Maybe some other time." She swept a glance through the cemetery, "Where do you want me to start?"

"Are you sure you want to do this?"

"Yeah. It'll be interesting, and I agree with you that someone should tend to this place. The people here deserve it. I'd feel horrible if my dad was forgotten like these poor people. It isn't right. It just isn't right."

Quinn rat-a-tat-tatted his index finger on his chest, "And I'm boss."

"Okay."

"And you'll keep your mouth shut about this!"

"Absolutely."

"Alright, then. Get off your butt and put Mr. Rake to work."

She giggled, saluting him, "Yes, sir."

Quinn showed her all the hazards, beginning with the exposed pins on the headstone bases he had uncovered, warned her there were plenty of them underneath the riot of tall weeds and tangled grasses. She paid close attention and proceeded cautiously.

Quinn squatted in front of one of the exposed pins and pulled clumps of weeds out by their roots. He made small talk, "Are you still unpacking?"

"We finished most of it last night." She paused briefly and added, "There's a lot of stuff in the house from Mom's family. Last night I got a look in the attic—just out of curiosity. You ought to see all the old antiques up there, and boxes and boxes of stuff. I haven't opened any of the boxes yet."

That piqued his interest. "Antiques?"

The tone of his voice told her everything, and she mirrored his sudden enthusiasm. "You like antiques, huh?"

"I like stuff about the past."

"So do I. Whenever you come over you can look at it all with me."

He smiled enthusiastically. "That'd be fun."

"But we can't go through any of my grandparents' stuff. Mom wouldn't like it. We can only go through the really old stuff. Mom said it all goes back four or five generations from when the Tarantinos first settled in America from Italy."

"Tarantino, huh? I saw that name in my dad's high school yearbook."

"Mom was a cheerleader. My dad, Ned Norris, was on the football team."

Quinn cocked his head to one side in thought. "I don't remember that name. I'll have to look again, I guess." He returned his attention to pulling the weeds.

She brushed and scratched at her shoulder. "Damned bugs."

"What?"

"Bugs."

He thought it silly of her not to expect encountering bugs. Her complaint was not worth dividing his attention between pulling the weeds and attending to her trivial frustration. Still, he repeated, "What?" out of politeness.

"Nothing. I thought I felt something land on my shoulder. Will you look?"

Through his peripheral vision, he glimpsed the ghost woman with her baby behind Stephanie. The woman giggled silently, her hand over her mouth. Quinn unconcernedly strolled over to Stephanie, looked at her shoulder that was bare because she was wearing a halter-top. "There's nothing there. It was probably just a fly."

"Well, never mind. Thanks for looking."

Without replying, he returned to the spot where he was working, uprooted another cluster of weeds and tossed them aside. He stole another glance at the ghost woman. She was circling Stephanie, her eyes curious. After a few moments, she evaporated. Quinn wondered if it was more than curiosity that drew her to Stephanie. Perhaps she was a prankster when she was alive. He had encountered many mischievous dead who did silly things simply out of boredom.

That thought brought memories of his mother. She told him that when she was in high school she liked playing harmless jokes on her fellow students, especially the boy she eventually married. The recollection reminded him of his twelfth birthday when she gave him a heavy gift-wrapped box that contained a solitary brick from the front yard. He didn't understand and was disappointed. She chuckled and made a gesture indicating he should remove the brick from the box. Under the brick was an envelope containing two tickets to a jazz concert. She included a note: *Some just you and me time. Happy Birthday*. Now all that remained was his memories of her. It angered him that he could see and converse with the dead, yet she had never made the effort to contact him. Why hadn't she come to visit him? Didn't she miss him as much as he missed her? How he wished he could talk with her!

Stephanie inquired, "Where's your mom buried?"

Her question startled him. Was she psychic? He kept his eyes pinned to his hands gripping and pulling the current clump of weeds. "She's at Oakview. Where else would she be?"

"So's my dad. Do you ever go visit her?"

He paused before answering, for the visits had only increased his pain, and he had stopped going there. "I visited a few times."

"How'd she die?"

"She was sick. I don't want to talk about it."

"Okay."

"You know, there are some things you shouldn't ask people about."

She stopped what she was doing and regretfully shook her head. "Okay. Sorry."

He tossed the weeds, sat on the dirt, and took a crooked cigarette out of his shirt pocket along with a book of matches. He lit the cigarette and eyed her, his expression a mixture of anger and defeat. "I suppose you hate me now."

"No. I was wrong to ask about your mom. I don't know why I asked."

"I was thinking about her."

As if that made perfect sense to her, she said, "Oh."

"Do you always read people's thoughts?"

"It happens sometimes."

Quinn became silent, smoked his cigarette.

Stephanie gazed at him dolefully. "We're still cool, right?"

He nodded without looking at her. After a while, her lengthy silence bothered him. He felt he had cast over her a cloud darker than the storm clouds over the mountains. Finally, he snuck a glance at her; saw the troubled expression on her face as she resumed raking all the weeds into a pile. Softly, he began to sing, *Puttin' On The Ritz*, and she smiled. He sang a little louder until he had her undivided attention and her lips spread into a grin.

"Do you know this song?" he inquired.

"I've heard it, but I don't know it. You've got a nice voice. Keep singing."

He continued, his voice strong and beautiful, at once joyful and encouraging. While Stephanie listened as she resumed raking the weeds, he sang the entire song.

He sang, not only for Stephanie but also for the petite young woman who listened from the trunk of an ancient oak. Out of the corner of his eye, Quinn silently acknowledged her, while she reclined there and rocked her baby in her arms. Smiling contentedly, she silently bobbed her head and tapped her outstretched bare feet to the rhythm. And Quinn knew it would be all right. It would be all right that he was there and Stephanie was there, and everything was right because he felt happy for the first time in a long time, and the woman felt happy for the first time in a long time as well.

* * * * *

Ida Norris unpacked the remaining box of small items for her office. She had already filled the drawers of her computer desk with her stationary, rolls of postage stamps, her stapler, tape dispenser, and other necessary items. Mailing supplies, folders, printer paper, printer toner, and carefully organized client files filled the cabinets. A tall oak four-drawer filing cabinet claimed a far corner of the room beside the bay window that looked out over the flower garden. From that window, she could enjoy the view of the garden, the fountain and birdbath, the two lilac bushes, the rose bush, and the ancient walnut tree from which she had hung two bird feeders, and the manicured boxwood hedges that framed the space on three sides. It was a beautiful place, once lovingly tended by her mother and father, Grace and Rudy Tarantino. The fragrance of roses, snapdragons, and jasmine drifted through the small open window beside her desk, and the fragrance brought memories of her childhood, memories of helping her mother cut the flowers to bring inside to fill vases all over the house. Her father had built a simple wood and rope swing he hung from a fat branch of the walnut tree. She had spent many a lazy summer day upon that swing in blissful daydreams. The swing was gone now, a victim of weather and old age.

She removed the bubble wrap from the framed photographs she had unpacked earlier and carefully set them on the worktable with the hammer and nails. One photo was of her at age ten with her mother and father, the second her parents' wedding photo, the third her own wedding photo. She gazed at it for a long time, studied the face of her late husband, Ned Norris. They were both twenty-four years old when they married, when she was still a natural brunette, and when Ned still had a full head of thick black hair. He had just landed his first job with a firehouse in Los Angeles, and she was still trying to figure out what she could do with her Liberal Arts degree. The move from rural Northern California down south to the congested Los Angeles Basin had been a culture shock for them, but they made the best of it, settling in the suburbs where their only child, Stephanie, was born.

Ida wiped a bit of dust off the fourth photograph, a studio master of her, Ned, and Stephanie in their "best duds," as Ned drolly remarked. Ned had never been one to enjoy dressing up, and he had purchased his one and only dark blue suit just for this occasion. The occasion had been Ida's thirty-seventh birthday, and Stephanie was twelve years old. Stephanie was at the forefront of the picture, her father's broad hand resting lightly upon her right shoulder.

"God, I miss you, Ned." She caressed the image of his face with her fingertips.

Their daughter was an attractive child who had inherited her mother's Italian complexion and dark eyes, and her father's oval face and strong chin. The girl was a talker from the get-go, friendly as a puppy and curious about everything. At school, she carried a B average but excelled in English. Ida and Ned were proud of her, and they encouraged her to follow her natural leaning toward literature, history, and the social sciences. As an athlete, she was mediocre. As a dancer, she was graceful and inventive and even started her own dance group at the age of eight with the neighborhood girls. They put on a show each summer at the annual neighborhood barbecue, and of course, Stephanie acted as both emcee and lead dancer.

Out in the flower garden, Stephanie replaced the rake and shovel into the shed. She wiped sweat from her forehead and went over to sniff the roses on one of the bushes. Ida watched her through the bay window. The woman thought she saw one of the snapdragon stalks bend and then spring back into position. There was no wind today, and her daughter was not near the snapdragon bed. How strange… maybe a cricket had landed on it and quickly jumped off, or perhaps it was nothing but a momentary hallucination. Ida had not had a full night's sleep in over a year, and sometimes she saw things that weren't there, like the time she saw Ned at the grocery store just the other day, and in the next instant, he wasn't there at all.

She left the window and took up the hammer and nails to group the treasured photographs on the opposite wall.

Stephanie retrieved pruning shears from the picnic table on the veranda and cut a small bouquet of daisies and snapdragons. She hummed the song Quinn had sung while she did this. Stephanie, after a few moments and with the bouquet in one hand, attempted a tap dance while she hummed the song, the lyrics of which she couldn't recall.

Ida caught the movement out of the corner of her eye. She looked out the window and chuckled at her delightfully silly daughter.

Ida called to her through the screen, "By the way, there's a dance studio in town."

Stephanie stopped and replied with a dismissive sneer, "Oh, hell no!"

"Suit yourself, potty mouth."

"You're not gonna beat me with that hammer, are you?"

"I'm hanging pictures."

She presented the flowers at the window, "I picked these for you."

"Thank you, sweetheart. Use the crystal vase from the china cabinet."

Stephanie brought the vase of flowers into her mother's office and set them on the sill of the bay window. Delicious fragrance immediately permeated the air. They talked as they hung the photos on the wall, talked initially about family and memories, and then the conversation segued to Stephanie's day with Quinn at the old cemetery, Quinn's apparent moodiness, and his revelation his mother had died. Ida was both shocked and saddened by this news. Bernice Talmadge Vanderfield had been a friend of hers since grade school, and they had both been on the cheerleading team in high school. She told Stephanie she would send a sympathy card and note to John Vanderfield, and commented she had neglected to send notice of Ned's death to him.

"They were both on the football team, weren't they?" Stephanie inquired.

"Yes, they were. Ned was the best player, though, and John was a little jealous of him. They used to joke about that."

"Quinn said his dad won't be able to come over for dinner on the weekend because he works late on the weekends."

"That doesn't surprise me. John was always a workaholic. Quinn can come over if he wants to. I'd sure like to see him again."

"Well, Mom... I guess that'll depend on his mood. He doesn't seem to like being around people very much."

"Why do you say that?"

"It's just a feeling."

"Maybe it's because he's still mourning his mother."

"Maybe."

4

Quinn aced all his final exams except trigonometry, which he hated. However, garnering a D in trig was not the worst thing that happened to him as the school week and the school year ended Friday. Just as he expected, Marcus Stanley and his buddies, Harry Richter, Bruno Ruiz, and bug-eyed Farley Larson, cornered him in the school parking lot and beat the snot out of him behind the cover of Marcus's giant red SUV truck. The reason for this thrashing was partly in retaliation for Quinn calling Harry Richter "Hairy Rectum," but mostly in retaliation for getting Marcus and Bruno in trouble over an incident that morning of which they maintained their innocence. However, the shouts of the observant principal interrupted this afternoon's beating. As Bruno and Farley scrambled into Bruno's truck, Bruno promised Quinn they would "finish the job" later.

Of course, this meant Quinn missed his bus home and, after washing away his blood in the restroom by the wood shop building, had to walk the five miles home in the afternoon heat, his sore body protesting. He entered the heart of downtown Providence slowly, as much from his pain as from the fact he did not want to face his father later that evening.

He walked onward at a slow pace, took connecting streets that eventually led to Main and Hawthorne where there were a few businesses, including a multiplex movie theater. The parking lot was filling up with cars of students taking advantage of their half-day of school to view the latest new films. Quinn seldom went to the multiplex, chiefly for the one reason that Marcus's crowd hung out there and, in the past, they had harassed him there as they did at school. There were few places in town where Quinn felt safe, particularly today after Bruno's ominous threat. However, Hawthorne Avenue was safe enough with its heavy traffic, both vehicle and pedestrian.

After a few blocks, he turned on Providence Road, the main artery into downtown. He sat and rested on the low stone retaining wall that encircled Oakview

Cemetery. A funeral was in progress. The mourners were few. He recalled his mother's funeral. The mourners had taken up a quarter of an acre at her graveside; that was how it seemed to him then.

He missed her, would miss her for the rest of his life. She understood him. Like her, he had the heart, soul, and mind of an artist. She tolerated his eccentricity, even came to appreciate it as one of his strengths.

If he tried, he could still smell her perfume, could feel the smoothness of her delicate fingers upon his cheek, her lips upon his brow. He could hear her voice, her beautiful voice, gentle and lilting as lake water stirred by a languid summer breeze, could hear her footsteps quick and light on the upstairs wooden floors at nighttime. He could see her as if she had never left him, her tall, elegant figure, her pale blonde hair, and her amber eyes, like amber resin.

He concentrated, imagined he brought her to his side, although he convinced himself she was actually there. She vanished quickly before he could tell her how much he loved and missed her. He reasoned the droning noise of traffic scared her away. Perhaps the cemetery scared her away. She once told him she hated graveyards and she could never bring herself to visit her parents' graves. She told Quinn it's only the body there and the spirit is in a much better world. She told Quinn not to look for her there when the time came. Therefore, Quinn seldom visited her grave, and would not today, even though the spot was in Section D far beyond the wall, on a little slope that rose ten feet closer to the heavens.

The mourners from the funeral sauntered despondently away from the gaping mouth of the place of sleep. They did not notice Quinn sitting on the wall watching them. To him, they appeared as walking death, empty, morosely glad to be done with it. At moonrise, they would snuggle into their beds, but they would not sleep. They would wonder about their own final moments upon the earth and wonder who would come to see them off to that mysterious yawning plot of ground. They would wonder if restful sleep will ever find them again, and if they will ever again awaken refreshed in the dawn, eager to experience another day, a day without sorrow, a day with promise. Quinn watched them leave, watched their cars turn onto Main Street at the south.

Inspired by the solemnity, Quinn began to softly sing to himself. He chose a song from a time before the world went mad, a time before the biggest war of the twentieth century, a time before Hiroshima and Nagasaki felt the wrath of American scientific know-how; a time before technology both united and isolated people. Quinn's song was a song from a very old movie musical that starred his favorite song and dance man, Fred Astaire. Quinn sang, *Let's Face the Music and Dance*.

Quinn felt better after resting there a while. He continued up Providence toward Cherry Street, humming to himself, feeling isolated, the usual scenario for him whenever he was away from home. He found a quarter on the sidewalk in front of Scrubs & Suds Laundromat and he tucked it in his pocket. If Quinn had saved every quarter he had found in his life, he'd have two hundred dollars by now.

He heard faint sirens from far away, presumed it was an ambulance taking someone to the hospital. He had not heard sirens since that morning when he covertly dropped a lit book of matches in the weedy vacant lot across from the high school where Bruno and Marcus routinely snuck their cigarettes between classes. As his process of getting even erupted into welcome flames, Quinn reported the fire and told the principal the truth that he witnessed Bruno and Marcus hightailing it to the campus from there just after the fire started. The fire department extinguished the fire in fifteen minutes, and classes were not disrupted by the incident. This time, though, an orchestra of sirens, both ambulance and police, sounded and built like the overture to a Broadway show, and then additional sirens and the rumbling, drumming, noise of heavy vehicles, which he assumed were fire engines, joined in.

Quinn said aloud to himself, "It's the new hit show, The Shit's Hittin' the Fan!" In a deep, mocking, voice, he sang out softly, bobbing his head to the beat, "The shit's hittin' the fan, the shit's hittin' the fan, the fan's splatterin' shit, a whole lotta shit, oh the shit, shit, shit's hittin' the fan!"

His amusement transformed into dire concern as the rumble came up behind him, far closer to him than the sirens and vehicle sounds going away toward the west. He stopped and turned, gasped as he saw Bruno Ruiz's familiar giant gray truck barreling toward him. Bruno was big and buff, his body heavily tatted, his head shaved. He was the star linebacker on the high school football team and a notorious ass kicker. Last year, Bruno broke Quinn's arm for flipping him off, broke his arm in two places.

Quinn spat a string of cuss words and started running. He dove for cover behind the Scrubs & Suds, where he hid beside a dumpster and listened for the rumble drawing near... and nearer... and nearer... and, *oh, shit...*

A huge streak of storm gray fishtailed around the corner of the building and came to a bucking halt in front of him, engine puttering like the growl of a predatory monster. Bruno was not alone. His sidekick, bug-eyed Farley Larson, who was as equally buff as Bruno, sat laughing in the passenger seat. Quinn froze. Bruno and Farley opened their doors at the same time, and their boots alighted with nary a sound upon the pavement.

* * * * *

Ida Norris had been working since ten that morning studying the proofs of her newest children's book, "Ollie Opossum's Holiday," which included her color pencil illustrations of Ollie and his new friends. She found no mistakes, deemed the proof ready for publication, and emailed the publisher her approval. Ollie was her fourth book for Little Feet Publishing, who gave her a larger advance for Ollie since her first three were still selling very well.

She logged off the Internet page and opened a music program, chose a list of favorites and clicked on it. She turned on the speakers, reclined in her chair, and closed her eyes as William Grant Still's *Summerland* filled the room with stunningly beautiful music she could only describe as inspired by the very soul of God Himself.

Memories of long-ago summers flitted through her mind, memories of swimming in the creek and laying half-naked along the bank, the feel of cool shaded earth under her body; the scent of catfish, willows, and wildflowers; the breeze playing through her hair, and birdsong in rhythm with the tiny islands of sunlight dancing upon the brown water. Then came a memory so mysterious and yet jolting in its clarity: the sensation of a calloused hand caressing her cheek. Her heart fluttered as she recalled her first pangs of love for the boy. It was there along the creek behind this very same house they shared their first kiss, a kiss followed by embarrassed and nervous chuckling, followed by a glance in all directions to be certain no one saw them. They grew silent as she rested her head against his shoulder, and he brushed his fingertips along her cheekbone. Memory and present time melded into one. She felt his warm loving hand caressing her heated cheek.

She responded by sighing, and then her voice came with a dreamy intonation. "Oh, Ned. How I miss you. How I love you."

Her own voice drew her out of her memories and fully into the present. She opened her eyes and glanced out the window to where Stephanie was pruning the rose bush at the left side of the garden. She had filled a small white bucket with spent roses and spindly stems and, holding the bucket by its metal handle, she approached the window and said through the screen, "I'm gonna dump this and go get the mail."

"Thanks, honey, but he hasn't come yet. I think we'll be last on the route again."

Ida patiently endured the girl's frustrated sigh of boredom. She wanted Stephanie to get out of the house and make new friends. Last night they had quarreled over her refusal to enroll in a dance class in town. The girl insisted she was not ready and added she didn't need a dance class because she already knew how to dance. Ida's suggestion that she instead take an art course at Parks and Rec drew the same hot refusal. After a short battle of wills, Stephanie retreated to her bedroom, slammed the door behind her, and Ida gave up.

Today Stephanie was in a better mood, although she seemed bored and preoccupied with her thoughts of Quinn. She missed him and was angry with him because he had not stopped by to visit. She considered going to his house to see him but decided against it. If he did not care enough to pursue their friendship, why should she? Maybe they weren't really friends, after all. .

* * * * *

Brought to a state of semi-consciousness by the roar of the truck's engine, Quinn rolled onto his side and covered his face with his arms to protect himself from the pelting of dust and gravel from the big tires. He stayed in that position until the engine noise became softer with distance and he was certain they would not return. A small puddle of blood on the broken concrete greeted him when he opened his eyes. His lips hurt. He brought his fingers to them and found the source of the blood. Every muscle in his face and body felt stiff and throbbed with pain. He groaned softly, mostly because of the pain but partly because he regretted his actions that had roused the two bastards to vengeance. Still, he had not expected them to deliver such severe payback.

His body was in such a compromised state that he did not sense the specter enclosed by a black aura that leaned over him and startled him by saying in a harsh venomous voice, "*You're weak like him!*" That was all it said. Quinn rolled over and sat up with much difficulty expecting to see the owner of the voice. There was no one. He decided it was a hallucination brought on by shock.

* * * * *

Stephanie spied Quinn limping up the road as she stood by the mailbox with the late afternoon delivery in her hand. Her mouth fell open as he slowly inched toward her. His face was hideously bruised; his nose and mouth dripping blood (which he kept wiping away), and his clothes were torn and soiled with both blood and dirt. As she sprinted to him and intercepted him, she saw the shock in his one uninjured and very glassy eye.

"My gosh, Quinn! What happened?"

He looked away from her into the dirt as silent tears rolled down his cheeks.

Gingerly, she took his hand and turned him with her toward the driveway. "You're coming inside with me. Mom and I will take care of you. Don't worry."

He jerked his hand away, "No! I'm going home."

"You're limping. Let us give you a ride."

"Aw, fuck you. Fuck everybody..." He resumed his painful journey, his shoulders sagging forward, his nose pointing at the hot pavement.

She landed her hand on his shoulder. "Let me help you, Quinn!"

Without turning to look at her, he swung his arm backward and struck her face. She reeled away and almost fell. The day's mail erupted from her grip, flew up into the air, and landed like scattered raindrops into the ditch. Unconcerned for her, and absorbed with his rage, Quinn continued to limp forward.

Stephanie watched him until he reached his house across the road and disappeared from view up his driveway. She gently rubbed her stinging cheekbone, at the same time forgiving him, for she believed he had struck her accidentally. Finally, she remembered the mail and retrieved it from the ditch.

The feeling she was being followed niggled at her as she headed toward her house, and she kept looking behind her suspiciously. There was nothing across the road except an orchard of oaks and walnut trees. She reasoned perhaps an animal had been drawn to the edge of the orchard by the noise of her confrontation with Quinn. Yet, there were only a few darting quail pecking the dirt alongside the blacktop, and they were oblivious to everything but their search for food.

* * * * *

After seeing the x-rays, the emergency room doctor diagnosed Quinn had suffered nothing worse than a cracked incisor, soft tissue damage, a strained ligament in his left knee, and generalized contusions that would heal in their own time. Neither the doctor nor John Vanderfield, nor Maria was able to persuade Quinn to reveal his assailants. All Quinn wanted was to go home to the comfort of his bed where he planned to stay for the rest of the summer, provided the doctor had not missed a serious complication that would end his life during the night. Secretly, Quinn hoped for that, hoped he would fall asleep and never wake up.

The hubbub ceased sometime after midnight once Quinn was safe in his bed and his father and Maria had retired to their beds. The house became quiet, adopted a strange stillness that, along with his pain, kept him awake. After a few hours of lying under the lightweight bedspread, miserable both physically and emotionally, a barely perceptible knock at his bedroom door startled him into full consciousness. He croaked "yeah?" through his tight and parched throat, and Maria slowly and quietly opened the door and peeked in.

"Are you okay, Quinn?"

"I feel like shit."

She flipped up the light switch, closed the door softly, and stepped lightly to his bedside. "Can I bring you anything?"

As if she was magical in some way, her presence made him feel better. He patted the space beside him on the bed, and she sat and kissed his cheek. Her long hair, smelling of flowers, tickled his neck. Her dark red cotton robe felt wonderfully soft against his naked chest. He rested his arm over her shoulders and whispered, "Don't be worried about me."

The light revealed the bruises and swelling had worsened since they left the emergency room. She sighed sadly and told him, "I can't help worrying about you."

"I'm sorry."

"And your father…" She sat up straight and continued forlornly, "He wishes you would talk with him, tell him who did this to you. They should be in jail."

"No," Quinn whispered wearily, "It was just a fight. No big deal. Dad got into lots of fights when he was my age. He likes to come off like he's perfect, but he's not. You know he's not. So, screw it. I ain't talking to him."

Her age-wrinkled eyes narrowed with consternation. "Then talk to me."

"It was just a fight." He then added a complete lie more to puff himself up than to assuage her concern for him, "The other guy looks just as bad as I do, so we're even. It's all done. Quit worrying."

Her eyes promptly glimmered with tears. "That's what my son said the night before he was murdered."

Quinn knew it was something she would never get over as long as she lived. There were many days he wished Maria's son would visit him. Then, and only then, would he break his silence and tell her what the man had to say about it—and about her, about her resolving her grief and moving forward with her life. He had been dead for over ten years. Quinn figured if he hadn't shown up by now that meant he was at peace in Heaven or wherever it was the dead went. He couldn't even begin to explain that to Maria without revealing his secret.

"Don't cry, Maria. Your son wouldn't want you to keep hurting over him."

"His name was Carlos."

"Yeah… Carlos. I forgot. I'm sorry."

"You fight the world just like he fought it. I don't want you to end up like him."

"I won't. I promise."

She stroked his hair comfortingly. "I can tell you hurt bad." She produced two Motrin from the pocket of her robe and set them in his hand. "These should help you. I can make you some herbal tea to help you sleep. Would you like that?"

He popped the pills into his mouth and swallowed them dry, shook his head in refusal of her offer. He had half a joint in his nightstand, and he intended to smoke it out in the driveway far from his father's side of the house as soon as Maria went to bed. Ironically, he had stolen the joint from his father's stash, and he found it amusing how easy it was to get weed from "the old man," since the guy was so toasted on booze and pot every night he couldn't keep track of his stash.

That's my dad… a pillar of the community.

Maria inquired humorously, "What are you smiling about?"

"You. You're such a mom." He squeezed her hand, knowing exactly what worked with her. "I love ya for it. Now, I'm gonna get some sleep, and you should do the same."

5

Stephanie could not explain why she felt compelled to take over the cleanup work at the graveyard while Quinn recovered at home. Her mother did not want her to go there alone. After a day of discussion and debate on the subject, Stephanie won her way with the assurance she would have her cell phone with her at all times. Therefore, Stephanie took up her yard tools early each morning and resumed the task of restoring the old cemetery to a place of respect, restfulness, and remembrance.

She uncovered a flat granite headstone the third day, very early in the morning when the light was bright and the air cool. She used her leather-gloved hands to brush away the dirt and broken remnants of weeds until the stone was clean enough to read the name and dates.

"Isaac Iversen, June third, nineteen-thirteen, seventeen years, three months, six days." She lowered from her kneeling position onto her rump and stared at the very plain stone. "Gosh, Isaac! Only seventeen. What happened? Sickness? An accident? You poor thing." Then she spotted additional letters at the base of the stone. She used a stick to clear the dirt out of the grooves. "Beloved." She sighed at the word, at the sentiment. "Gosh. You must have been something special." Stephanie leaned up on her knees over the stone and brushed her hand over Isaac's name. "Iversen. Don't we have that name in our family tree? Which means there must be some Tarantinos here, too? Oh, my gosh—I'm talking to myself!"

Stephanie did not possess Quinn's ability to see the dead, but if she had, she would have been awestruck by the pale hands that slowly and tenderly swept over Isaac Iversen's headstone. She would have gazed in astonishment mixed with compassion as the young woman—sans her baby this time—mournfully draped her vaporous spirit body upon the stone and rested her cheek upon Isaac's name. It was a blessing Stephanie could not see her or witness what followed.

The woman's mouth gaped open in a silent scream of torturous misery. She pounded her palms upon the stone. She rose and with tearful eyes accusingly searched the sky for the source of her endless torment, her mouth twisting with her effort to release the anguish locked inside her throat. Her energy caused a brief hot wind that assaulted the trees and blew Stephanie's hair in all directions as she raised her fist to the sky and attempted one last time to scream before her energy gave out and her wispy body with it.

Stephanie fell back upon her rear with the sudden wind and brushed her hair out of her face. "Jesus! What was that?" She looked again at the word *beloved* as the wind died. "Are you trying to tell me something, Isaac?" She expected no answer and received none. A brief tremor ran up her spine. "Well… that was…" A long stream of wavering breath exited her pursed lips, and she whispered, "Holy shit…" Slightly unnerved and deeply curious, she took her cell phone out of her pocket and pressed the one-touch button to her mother's number. Her mother's voice came after the second ring. "What's up, Steph?"

Stephanie said, "Do we have the surname 'Iversen' in our lineage?"

"My second great grand aunt on my father's side married a man with the last name of Iversen."

"Was it Isaac Iversen?"

"Um, let me think for a minute." There came a long pause accompanied by the sound of fingers typing upon the computer keyboard. Finally, Ida replied, "Isaac was her son. The father's name was William Iversen."

"Oh, my gosh, Mom. Well, guess what? I just found Isaac. He was only seventeen when he died. Why did he die so young?"

More sounds of typing on the keyboard. Ida answered, "I haven't found that information yet. I did find his death date, though."

Stephanie volunteered it, "June third, nineteen-thirteen."

"Yeah, that's it. What kind of headstone does he have?"

"Very plain. I think it's concrete or something like it. There's a word in capital letters at the base of it, though: *beloved*."

Her smile came through in her voice, "Aw, isn't that sweet. Have you found Lottie Tarantino? She was Isaac's aunt, born an Iversen."

"I haven't found any Tarantinos yet."

"Well, they're there. Carlotta and Frank Tarantino. They're most likely in the same plot as Isaac. He lived with them after his parents died."

"How'd his parents die?"

"A tornado. I found that through an old newspaper clipping. It leveled most of the homes on the outskirts of town, a little place in Kansas. It missed the town, though."

"So, his parents are buried in Kansas?"

"Yeah."

"And, Isaac came all the way out here to California to live with Lottie and Frank?"

"That's right."

"There must be photographs."

"I haven't had the time, Steph. You can look through the boxes in the attic if you want."

"I'll be home soon, Mom."

"Did Quinn show up today?"

"No. I don't know when he'll be back. I hope it's soon, though. It's kind of creepy here without him. Do you believe in ghosts, Mom?"

"Come home, Steph. Don't forget the tools."

* * * * *

After lunch, Ida returned to her work and, Stephanie, obsessed now with her new mission, explored the hot, musty smelling, attic. The afternoon sunlight poured through the two small windows and made the floating dust in the air shimmer like millions of microscopic fairies hovering about the large space. Stephanie forced open the windows after a short struggle; they had not been opened in years, perhaps decades. The buildup of dust and dilapidated spider webs on the glass soiled her hands, and she wiped them on her pants without giving it much thought other than the entire attic needed a good cleaning and proper organization.

There were two fat matching upholstered chairs, pink with a decorative spray of blue poppies, and an old pink sofa (or was it what they once called a "fainting couch") against one of the walls. Someone had piled a bunch of boxes on the sofa, and two stacks of binders containing old shellac 78rpm records on the chairs. Stephanie was curious about the records but decided to look through them later. Next to one of the chairs sat a very old windup record player that had a lily-shaped horn for a speaker. There was no cover over it, and the turntable was very dusty; nothing a vacuuming couldn't remedy. Extra needles sat in a little round box built in to a nook in the right-hand corner of the faded wooden base below the turntable. A sturdy pine rocking chair sporting a high, hand-engraved, backrest sat in a corner beside a small tea table. She ran her fingertips over the engraving, two geese in flight above marshy grassland, and wondered who had done such beautiful work. The artist had created a circle behind the geese. Stephanie couldn't decide if the circle was meant to be the sun or the moon. Perhaps that was the artist's intention. The piece was in remarkable shape, its varnish still glossy under the light layer of dust. The old rocker impressed her as being lonely as if it was waiting for someone. The tea table beside it impressed her as also handmade, for the center stem with its three curvy feet was perfect in its imperfection, the vertical lines slightly crooked as they curved down the feet. An ancient oil lamp sporting a red glass globe with a short soot-stained chimney sat upon this perfectly imperfect table as if it was meant to be there. She twisted the little brass knob that controlled the height of the wick. The wick, brown with age, rolled up and down as she turned the knob right and then left. The bowl was dry, the oil spent ages ago, but enough of it left at the bottom to leave a dark rust-colored residue.

"You'll be beautiful again," Stephanie assured it.

There were small bookcases and tables haphazardly piled upon each other. Some of the tables were bedside tables that matched a nineteen-twenties era Art Deco wardrobe cabinet, ladies' vanity table with a huge round mirror and matching bench, a headboard and footboard, all in fine shape, although slightly scratched from use. A little polish and the scratches would be barely noticeable.

I could turn this all into another room, Stephanie told herself, *I could turn this into the Stephanie Cave, my very own space.*

She returned her attention to the boxes upon the sofa, and she opened them carefully and searched them for photographs. There were no photographs, just old clothing, some sewing supplies, an old checkbook ledger, and miscellaneous paperwork. Disappointed, she looked about the room wondering where a person would store old photographs in this weather vulnerable environment. The Art Deco wardrobe cabinet, with a closet and built-in drawers, caught her eye. Stephanie went immediately to the cabinet and opened the drawers. The bottom drawer, which was the widest and deepest, held what she was looking for: neatly organized stacks of photo albums that ranged in age from the turn of the twentieth century through the 1950s. She removed the albums one at a time and set them gently on the floor after unrolling a stained old quilt to use as a rug to sit upon. The albums were older at the bottom of the drawer where she found a fat leather-bound tome that held stiff cardboard pages with pockets holding sienna-tone stills of her mother's ancestors. Stephanie could hardly keep her hands from trembling as she enthusiastically but carefully examined the pictures. They were studio portraits, some of groups of people posing uneasily for the camera, others of individuals. She removed each from their sleeves one at a time and looked for writing on the reverse. They were of the Tarantino family: Frank, Lottie, Rufus and Betty, all at different periods of their life together. There was not a single picture with the name "Isaac" written on it.

Frustrated, she muttered, "Damn it."

The rocking chair popped out a sudden cracking sound, which made her jump in her skin, and she thought she saw it move in her peripheral vision.

Once her heart stopped pounding, Stephanie set the album aside and took one of the three remaining oldest ones, and of course, the first one she opened would prove to be another dead end. The next one, with a black leather cover frayed and cracked at the edges, revealed photographs from the 1920s. She took up the last remaining album, a fat and heavy square-shaped relic. Its red leather cover was brittle, and flakes of it broke off easily upon her fingertips. When she opened it, the spine protested with a loud snap and the dry leather crumbled, exposing the thin wood that held it all together. The smell was awful, like wet mildew and dirt. She wiped her nose with the back of her hand, sniffled and coughed as microscopic particles of leather and dust rose and floated in the air as she exposed the first cardboard page. It contained a grouping of four small, yellowed, photographs. Two were wedding photos, one of Frank and Lottie Tarantino, and the second noted on the reverse as Mr. and Mrs. Serena and William Iversen. William Iversen's pale eyes were a contrast to Serena's dark eyes. The same people were in the two photos below, this time dressed in formal attire. The handwriting on the reverse of each noted they were first wedding anniversary photos and were stamped with the photographers' names and business addresses.

The following pages contained many slightly faded black and white photos of teenagers; two were boys and one was a girl. Stephanie focused her attention on a particular photograph of the three together in front of a background of leafy trees. They were dressed in their Sunday best. The eldest boy had his arm draped over the younger boy's shoulders, and the girl embraced his slim waist. Their happiness reminded her of the joy a child feels upon receiving a new puppy. The younger boy between them, the object of this affection, seemed flattered by their attention yet a tad uncomfortable, as if he was unsure of himself. Stephanie recognized Rufus and Betty from the marked photographs in the first albums. The second of the two boys she guessed to be between ten and twelve years old, shorter and slightly built. His hair was dark, his face oval. He had fuller lips than Rufus and Betty had. His striking pale color eyes enhanced his sun-darkened complexion. Stephanie was drawn to his eyes, to the uncertainty there, although a trace of hope mingled within the uncertainty.

She removed the photo and read the reverse. Someone had written in pencil, "Rufus, Isaac, and Betty. Isaac's first Sunday at church with us."

Stephanie smiled appreciatively. "Oh, my gosh, Isaac. Look at you. So, so handsome." In the next instant, she whispered, "But so sad."

She turned the pages and found many more images of him and his cousins, plus him with his aunt and uncle, Lottie and Frank Tarantino. They appeared to be happy together, playful and easygoing. Truly, Isaac had found happiness in the Tarantino home.

The pictures farther into the album showed Isaac and his cousins as the years progressed: Rufus in his sailor uniform posing alone in one, with Isaac in another; this time, Isaac's arm was draped over Rufus's shoulders. There were many of Betty's formal wedding, a group portrait of the Tarantinos with the in-laws and the bride and groom, the groom a young man identified on the reverse as Wilfred "Will" Loomis; Isaac was in that one also as a member of the wedding party, a stunning young gentleman in his three-piece suit and striped tie.

"Well, you sure did that suit justice." Stephanie gathered all the albums and piled them on her lap. "I've got to show these to Mom."

She spent the remainder of the evening scanning the photographs into her mother's online family tree. Later, after dinner and after discussing her findings with her mother, she searched the Internet for information about Isaac's death. Disappointingly, there were no digitized copies of the local newspaper from the early 1900s available there. Her next stop would be the town library, and she needed Quinn's help to wade through whatever information they might have.

6

The sun had not crested the horizon yet, but its gradually emerging light cast an almost vaporous apricot toned illumination below the surrendering night sky. A whisper of ash rose from the apricot light as if being born of that light, and pale lavender slowly ascended above the ash. The lavender, like a gently expanding flood of irrepressible determination, slowly developed into the lightest of blues. Beyond, the starry remnants of night gradually, almost imperceptibly, rolled westerly. One elongated sinuous cloud rode leisurely in front of the crescent moon, shortly obscuring a bright twinkling star at its fingernail curve.

Quinn watched the evolution above and behind the silhouetted trees surrounding the clearing, not with the optimism inherent in each new dawn, but with empathy for the remaining vestiges of nighttime. In his perception, the night seemed to be trying to retain its place in the heavens. This is how he felt with each new day: trying to hold on, to hold on, and not give up. Yet, the challenges and despair of each new day consumed him as the sun consumed the peaceful deep blue of the night.

Once he had written in his diary, "I hate every day." Since that entry, his feelings hadn't changed.

His body still ached, his lips were still swollen and bruised, and his left cheekbone was as purple as the bloated skin beneath his left eye. Yes, they were minor injuries as the doctor said. Yet, Quinn did not consider his suffering as minor. The Ibuprophen would soon take effect and alleviate some of the soreness, and the additional therapy of moving his body and concentrating upon his current project would relieve his spiritual torment.

He took a swig of extra-strong black coffee from his thermos and, leaving the transitioning sky to itself, surveyed the graveyard that was damp with dew from the previous night's light rain shower. Everything there was still dark, not completely dark, but brown and lacking the definition the dawning light would soon bestow upon it. Yet, there was just enough definition for him to discern someone had cleared more of the graves.

Quinn assumed Stephanie had done it. The thought of her working there on her own time without him asking her brought a half-smile to his stiff and sore lips. It was nice of her to carry on while he was recuperating, and he had to admit to himself he was beginning to like her. He expected she would arrive in a few hours with her yard tools and her big smile.

For now, he had the place to himself—well, almost to himself; the birds were starting to sing and soar off in search of their breakfast. He liked the sounds the birds made: liked their songs and chirps, the whir of their wings as they raced by him, the chit-chit scuffing of their little feet kicking away the leaves and dirt as they searched for worms and grubs in the dewy soil. This was his solitude, what had become his five-thirty in the morning meditation ritual. His work could wait. The next hour he reserved as an interlude: coffee, birdsong, the languid breeze soft and refreshing, singing its own melody; the soil, grasses, trees and bushes releasing their fragrances upon the cool air, and the peaceful sensation of being one with the heart of the universe.

He sat on a toppled tree trunk, sipped his coffee, and smoked a cigarette as the pale morning light revealed the true colors of the trees and flora as it progressed upon the clearing. A lizard brushed by his shoe and stopped, cautiously sniffed the air for predators, and then it ducked under the log from where it had emerged. Quinn watched a monarch butterfly flitter off, dipping sideways and soaring up again toward the trail that led to the road. He hoped the birds wouldn't spot it.

Quinn smoked and watched the sky become brighter and bluer, watched the first rays of pale orange crest the treetops. He absently swatted at a fly that landed on his arm, grimaced at nothing in particular—just life itself, his crappy life.

As the cigarette burned to the filter, he sucked in one last puff, inhaling some of the burnt filter with the remaining tobacco. He wondered what was more cancer causing, the filter or the tobacco. Perhaps both were equally malicious, and he considered that a good thing. Maybe if he added some kind of powdered chemical, such as rat poison, to his cigarettes, his lungs would explode and end his miserable life in a millisecond. Quinn seriously considered trying it.

The night he returned home from the hospital, his father had ranted bitterly about the assault and Quinn's refusal to identify the culprits. At the same time, he blamed Quinn for consistently making himself a target. He cautioned the boy, for the umpteenth time, to simply keep his wise-ass attitude in check so the bullies would leave him alone. Quinn could not explain the whole truth of the matter, and did not want to explain, for he secretly deemed himself culpable—willingly culpable, and he could not control his compulsion to berate them to their faces. Now it was at the point of ongoing war. It was Quinn's war, and damned if he would let his father fight it for him.

Beyond the graveyard in the dirt trail came the clink of metal against metal, the shuffling of footsteps upon the dead leaves. Stephanie pushed a low branch clumped with oak leafs away from her face as she emerged into the clearing. She grinned upon seeing Quinn, and her voice was cheerful as she called to him, "Hey, Quinn! How's it going?"

He looked up at her and smiled in response, although it hurt. "I didn't expect you this early."

"This is the coolest part of the day, silly." She dropped her tools at the base of a tree and approached him, looked intently into his bruised face. "I thought you'd be gone at least one more day. How are you feeling?"

"Like hell."

"Are you up to this?"

"I *need* this."

She settled beside him on the fallen tree trunk. Forgetting about the low-cut top she was wearing, she leaned forward and rested her forearms on her knees, intertwined her fingers in a contemplative gesture. As she twisted sideways to look at him, Quinn caught an eyeful of her cleavage and the rotund swell of her breasts. Embarrassed as much for her as for himself, he averted his glance to a lone digger pine sapling across from him.

She inquired concernedly, "Who did this to you?"

"The same ones who always do this to me. It doesn't matter. Don't ask me any more about it."

"Okay."

He sensed she was silently reprimanding herself. "I'm not mad at you for asking, or anything."

"Okay." She gave him a forced yet forgiving smile, her eyes full of self-reproach.

She hadn't changed her position, and he couldn't help taking another quick glance at her breasts. This time, he felt the urge to trace his fingertips gently upon her nearest lifted mound. A brief fantasy accompanied his urge. He imagined the smoothness and warmth of her skin beneath his fingertips. He snapped himself out of it and scolded himself. After silently blaming her for dressing so provocatively, he reconsidered. He couldn't be cross with her because she apparently had no idea. After a few moments of silent deliberation, he asked her in his gentlest voice, "Can I be blunt with you about something?"

"I guess."

"Don't take this wrong. I'm just looking out for you, okay?"

Impatiently, she demanded, "What, Quinn?"

"If you're going to wear something that low cut—"

That was all it took. She looked down at herself and saw what he was talking about. She sat up straight and covered herself with her hands, her face reddening. "Oh, my God!"

"Look, don't get upset. I'm just telling you because some guys... well, you know. I'm just telling you as a friend. Okay?"

Flustered, she stammered, "Yeah. Okay. Okay. But, I'm wearing a bra."

"I didn't see enough to tell. Listen, Steph... I think you're nice, and I'm just looking out for you."

The sincerity in his eyes won her over. "Okay. Thanks."

"Friends?"

"You bet."

He opened his thermos and took a swig of coffee, offered it to her. "Made fresh two hours ago."

She accepted it and took a sip. It was still hot, and it tasted good, although she preferred cream and sugar with her coffee. "I can't believe you've been up since five."

"I couldn't sleep."

She pointed in the direction of Isaac's grave. "I uncovered a distant relative yesterday."

"Looks to me like you uncovered a bunch of people. Thanks for doing that."

"It was fun. It's kind of like a treasure hunt."

Quinn frowned at her. "That's not why I do this."

She ignored his frown at her insensitive comment. "I'm surprised the City ignores this place."

"The City doesn't own it. The land belongs to my family."

"No kidding?"

"The Vanderfields donated the land to their neighbors way back in the day when there were a bunch of deaths from scarlet fever. Some people, though, preferred to bury their people on their own property. There are probably a bunch of graves on your land, for all I know."

"I hope not. My mom wants to plant some fruit trees."

"Instant fertilizer." His mouth drew up into a mischievous grin.

"You have a sick sense of humor." Yet, she couldn't help laughing.

"It gets me through the day." He stood stiffly, "Let's get to work."

They worked a while longer without talking. Stephanie focused on the area adjacent to Isaac's grave and, to the left of it, uncovered the headstones of Frank and Lottie Tarantino. She promptly took out her cell phone and informed her mother, and then she returned to task. Over her shoulder, she asked Quinn if he had a plot map of the cemetery.

"I'm still looking for one," he replied. "Why?"

"My mom thought it'd be interesting."

"Well, when I find it."

"Have you found any of your family yet?"

He pointed across at a shaded area at the base of the hill, "I think they're over there, closer to my house."

"Why didn't you start there?"

"Because I had no idea when I started how big this place is or where the boundaries are. The more we uncover, the more it'll tell us. If I could find a map, it'd make things easier."

"Well, who would have one?"

"I thought the library would have it in their local history section, but they didn't. The City had no record of it, either. This started out as a private family cemetery. I figure the only map has got to be in my house somewhere, but damned if I can find it."

Changing the subject entirely she blurted, "I could use your expertise with something."

He gazed at her suspiciously. "With what?"

"Research at the library. Old newspapers. I'd like to go today."

"No can do."

"Why not?"

"If you were all beat to shit like me, would you want to go out in public?"

She hadn't considered that. "Well, how about in a week or so when you're healed up?"

"I guess." He propped his rake under his armpit and lit a cigarette. "What are you looking up?"

"I want to know how Isaac died."

"Who's Isaac?"

She pointed at his grave. "He's one of my ancestors. He died very young."

"It was probably scarlet fever, diphtheria or something. Tuberculosis; that was rampant in those days."

"Well, I want to know for sure. Don't ask me to explain."

"Don't tell me; he visited you in the middle of the night and shook your bed."

"Don't make fun of me."

"I don't mean to. I swear there are days here when I feel like the dead are watching me." *She'd run away screaming if she knew the truth*, he thought playfully.

"I felt that, too."

"Glad to know I'm not the only one."

"I found pictures of him up in the attic. Would you like to come over and see them when we're done here today?"

He offered no reply, although his eyes revealed his curiosity.

Stephanie pressed on, "You ought to see all the old furniture and stuff I found. There's an old record player, a wind-up kind, and a whole big collection of seventy-eights."

His eyes lit up, "Are you kidding me?"

"Lots of them. I want to play them, but I have to clean up the player first; it's all dusty."

"Is the needle still attached?"

"Yeah, and there's a little container full of extra needles."

"Oh, my God! That is so cool!"

"I take that as a yes."

He giggled. His face lit up with enthusiasm and joy. "You have no idea!"

* * * * *

Quinn felt very self-conscious about his bruised face. Ida Norris made him relax about it by telling him about the time her late husband Ned had gotten into a fight in high school and came out looking just the same. Her opinion regarding fistfights between boys was that it was a necessary rite of passage—preparation for the battles ahead of them in life, which would be fought by wit and not fists. She had no idea Quinn's enemies thrashed him, not in the midst of battle, but out of revenge for insinuating they started the fire he had started across from the school. He was too ashamed to tell her this truth.

Thankfully, she didn't inquire about his home life or school. Instead, she asked him about his interests as she enlisted his assistance planting daisies in a corner of the garden behind her office. Quinn told her about his interest in antiques and how everything old and obsolete inexplicably appealed to him. He readily admitted Stephanie's revelation about the records up in their attic brought him to their house. He was anxious to see and hear what was up there.

"Well," Ida said, "Stephanie has been going on and on about all the treasures up there. She was up half the night cleaning and exploring the space. Looks like you've found a kindred spirit."

"Don't you care about any of it?" Quinn asked curiously.

"I do, but I don't have the time right now. I'm right in the middle of a project, and I've got a deadline." She pressed her spade into the soil and began to dig a new hole for the next cluster of daisies. With a sigh, she lamented, "I forgot how much work this place is—all this land. Did you get a look at the rear of this property?" After Quinn nodded, she continued, "The weeds are getting high. It's a fire hazard, and I don't have the time or the energy to tackle it. I just don't know how Mom kept this up all by herself."

"Caleb used to help her."

"Who's Caleb?"

"He used to go to my school. He graduated early, a couple of years ago, I think. I didn't know him; no one did, really. He kept to himself. Before your Mom died, he lived in the cottage out there." He pointed to a copse of pines beyond the boxwood hedge and beyond the field of waist-high weeds in the distance, "Back there along the creek."

"You mean that old laborer's cottage is still standing?"

"Yeah. Caleb and this old guy named Gene fixed it up. Caleb works for Gene doing construction."

A fleeting memory came to Ida of a few phone conversations where her mother mentioned someone named Caleb who helped her around the house. Ida had not paid close attention then, for her mother had employed many workmen over the years for various projects.

Oblivious to her thoughts, Quinn continued his comments; "I was watching them from my roof."

"Your roof?"

"I like to go sit up there sometimes. It's got a great view. I can see the lake from there, too."

She tilted her head to one side as if considering the perils of roof perching. "Well… how about that."

"It's perfectly safe."

"So, I suppose you watched us when we were moving in."

"Yes, I did. You can't blame me for being curious, can you?"

"No, I guess not."

"I was the one who called the ambulance when your mom collapsed by the mailbox. Oh. Shit… I'm sorry. I shouldn't have brought that up."

"You saw it happen?"

"Yeah. I'm sorry."

"No need to be sorry. Thanks for calling the ambulance."

"It was too late, wasn't it?"

"Yes. She was dead before she hit the pavement. There's nothing anyone could have done. I'm glad you saw it. No telling how long she would have laid there before someone found her." Despite Ida's stoic expression, her voice and subsequent silence revealed her grief for her mother had not ebbed. Quinn respected her need to reflect upon the lonely circumstance of Grace Tarantino's sudden death. He offered no reply or comment on the matter, gave her time to experience her loss before she moved on to her present dilemma. She resumed her planting, dug a new hole with the spade. "So, where do I find this Caleb guy?"

"I think he still works for Blackwell Construction. That's it—Gene Blackwell— that's the old guy's name."

"I'll look him up, then."

"Don't bother with the Internet, though. Blackwell doesn't have a website. You gotta do it the old-fashioned way with the telephone." At this, Quinn chuckled to himself. "Dinosaur…"

Ida laughed softly.

He removed the next clump of daisies from the pot and gently loosened the roots for planting. "Stephanie told me you write children's books. Do you make a lot of money with that?"

"Not really. However, it's always been something I enjoy. The money doesn't matter. We're doing okay. If anyone thinks they can make a substantial amount of money writing novels or children's books, they're in for a rude awakening. Did your mother ever tell you she wrote a novel when she was in school?"

"No."

"It was one of those bodice-ripper romances set in the eighteenth century – something about a pirate ship and pirates. She was only fifteen then, Stephanie's age, and she let me read it when she was done. Oh, my gosh! She had them all talking like teenagers, and she had this one part where the captain ordered the heroine to wash his dinner dishes for him, and she described how the woman angrily went over to the sink and turned on the tap and threw water on the guy to get even with him. They didn't have running water in those days! They didn't have sinks or taps, or plumbing, or even clean water! Oh, my goodness! We laughed for days and days over that. She never wrote another novel; she decided it was simply too much trouble with all the research she'd have to do."

"That's funny," Quinn said. "No wonder she never told me about it."

"The folly of youth. She was really something, though. Everyone loved her. I'm sorry she's gone."

Quinn ducked his chin, fell into silence.

"Are you doing okay?"

"Yeah, I guess."

"It takes time for the grief, the hurt, to lessen. Be patient."

"We got the card you sent. Thanks for thinking of us."

"How's your dad doing?"

This elicited a thoughtful, yet troubled, pause from him, and he mumbled, "Rolling along as usual."

"Rolling along?"

"Work. I don't see him much."

"Stephanie told me you said he works long hours."

"Yeah."

"He's always been like that."

"I guess."

"Can you stay for dinner?"

"I – I suppose."

"I promise I won't dig into your life anymore."

He smiled at her, a vague shyness overcoming him.

Stephanie appeared at the screen door in fresh and less revealing clothing, and she leaned out and said to Quinn, "I'm ready if you're ready."

He rose stiffly and said to Ida, "Thank you, Mrs. Norris."

"Call me *Ida*."

* * * * *

Leaving the windows open all night did wonders eliminating the stuffiness in the long neglected space. Stephanie had swept much of the floor the night before after she had picked up the loose items. She had rearranged some of the light furniture, had dusted and polished the table and the wooden rocker to where they gleamed in the sunlight streaming through the screens. There were fewer dust fairies dancing in the air, and the room was much cooler. Now manning a handheld portable vacuum, she set to work vacuuming the dust off the record player's turntable while Quinn eagerly searched through the boxes of 78's. Some of it was Opera, and some was Classical. The majority of it was Jazz and Big Band Swing.

Quinn, happily in his element, extracted disk after disk from the boxes, delighted with each new discovery: Duke Ellington, Fletcher Henderson, Paul Whiteman and His Orchestra, Bunny Berigan, Red Nichols and His Five Pennies, Bix and His Gang, The Glenn Miller Orchestra, and—how Quinn gasped at this: Benny Goodman and His Orchestra's *Sing, Sing, Sing*, in pristine condition!

"Ommagod, ommagod, ommagod!" He jumped up and down like a child receiving his first ice-cream cone.

Stephanie flipped off the vacuum, "What?"

"It's gold, it's gold, it's gold!"

She gazed at him, at the record in his trembling fingers. "What?"

"Do you have any idea what you've got here?"

"Old records?"

"Stephanie, Stephanie! Ommagod! This is a first issue mint condition copy of *Sing, Sing, Sing!*" He kissed it and held it to his chest. "This is *gold*!"

"What do you mean *gold*? There's no market for these things."

"Screw the market. That isn't the point. Don't you see? This is *history* in mint condition, the way our ancestors heard it."

"How do you know it's a first edition?"

"It's an RCA Victor, and it lists all the musicians on it."

She reached to take it from him, "Well, let's play it."

He pressed it to his chest protectively. "Oh, no you don't." He pointed an accusatory and derisive finger at the old wind-up player she had just vacuumed. "Not on that!"

"Why not?"

"That needle's way too heavy for it. It'll ruin the record."

"Well, how are we gonna hear it? This is the only record player in the house!"

"It can't be the only one. Most of these records are from the nineteen-thirties, forties, and fifties. People played them on better equipment made for these kind of records." He paused and searched with his eyes over the furniture and cabinets piled with boxes of God only knew what. "There's got to be a stand-up console combination radio and record player up here somewhere."

"A what?"

"Don't you know anything?"

"Not about this kind of thing."

"Well, then, let me educate you. The first thing we've gotta do is find that console."

"What's it look like?"

"It's about as tall as you, and it's made of wood, and it's got knobs on it—brown knobs, most likely, and it'll have an electrical cord wrapped up with cloth."

She gave him a confused expression.

"Oh," he shook his head, "Keep cleaning up. I'll look for it."

"Be careful where you step."

"Of course."

"And, put the record down on this table. I promise I won't touch it."

Quinn had to consider it for a minute before he decided to trust her.

"I tell you what," Stephanie offered, "There are some photo albums up here from that era. I'll look through them. If that console thing exists, it'll be in one of the pictures."

"Good idea."

"In the meantime..." She patted the empty space on the big round table with the perfectly imperfectly carved feet, "Set that baby over here, Quinn. I don't want to see you cry if you drop it and break it."

A silly embarrassed smile lifted his cheeks and brightened the gleam in his eyes. "I'm hopeless. I guess you've figured that out."

"You're not hopeless. As a matter of fact, seeing you so happy is making me happy."

He gingerly set the record on the table. "There. Okay. I'll look for the console now."

She pointed, "There's some tall stuff in that corner I haven't gotten to yet. Look behind that old dressing curtain."

They took ten minutes moving things out of their path until at last the way was clear, and Quinn moved the curtain. They both contemplated the tall *something* covered with an old sheet.

Quinn breathed the words, "Oh, I hope..."

He carefully lifted the sheet from the bottom up. The built-in speaker came into view. He up-rolled the sheet as if he was uncovering the Holy Grail itself. The four brown plastic knobs appeared, one of which referred to the phonograph.

"Ommagod, ommagod..." He uncovered the whole thing, a Philco with the radio at top and the turntable in the center behind a tilt-back opening. The wood veneer, resembling mahogany, had not a scratch on it. It gleamed in the light from the windows and the bare bulb overhead. He stood admiring it, his hands poised against his mouth, his fingers pointed up as if in prayer. "This is it. This is it. We found it. Ommagod."

"Can we move it out?" Stephanie asked.

"I'm not sure yet. Let me look at it. I hope the cord's still good. Is there an outlet anywhere?"

"Uh... I don't know."

He went up on tiptoe and looked first at the wall behind the device, then checked the other wall beside it. He found the outlet. He slowly went to his hands and knees, reached behind the console, and found the dusty chord wrapped in brown fabric just as he described. He unrolled it and wiped the dust off, checked the plug and decided it was good.

Stephanie, peering over his shoulder said, "There's no ground on that outlet or that plug. Are you sure it's safe?"

"The worst that'll happen is we'll short out the house. Is your mom still in the garden?"

Stephanie checked out the window. "Yeah."

"Is her computer on?"

"She never leaves it on when she's not working."

"This is as good a time as any." He plugged in the cord. No sparks, no strange smelling smoke from loose wiring, no house demons howling in protest. "So far, so good." With trepidation accompanied by anticipation, he stood and turned the power knob. The radio-tuning window lit up in yellow, and the letters and numbers glowed. There came a soft humming sound.

Stephanie looked at him worriedly. "Why is it…?"

"It's warming up. The tubes need a minute or so to warm up."

"Tubes?"

"That's what they used before transistors were invented."

"Transistors?"

"They came before computers and digital." He pointed with his thumb at the early 1900's player. "That old wind-up came long before this."

"Wow, Quinn. How do you know all this stuff?"

"I just picked it up along the way."

"Do you have one of these at your house?"

"A long time ago. My dad got rid of it, sold it cheap to some collector. I could've killed him for that. Dumb ass. Did he ever think to ask me? Hell, no."

"Never mind. Forget I asked."

"Just thinking about it still pisses me off."

"I notice."

"Sorry." He gave her a half-smile; the best he could do while his ire receded. "So, let's hear that record. You're gonna love it."

At once, the radio blared and startled them; Garth Brooks singing, *I've Got Friends in Low Places*. Quinn lowered the volume. "I hate Country music!" He flipped the control knob to PHONO, and said, "Now we're ready to hear Benny. Bring it over. *Carefully*."

She gave him a playful smirk. "Gee… Duh…"

He responded, laughing more at himself than at her, "Okay, okay." While she retrieved the disk, he checked the stylus to be certain it was good, and he found it good, then he picked a few pieces of lint off the turntable and set the rotation speed. "Someone took excellent care of this," he remarked as she handed the record to him.

She watched silently as he removed the record from its sepia paper jacket and placed it precisely on the spindle and then lowered it cautiously, as if it was made of nitroglycerin, onto the turntable. He switched the turntable on, and it slowly began to rotate, caught up to speed as it circled a few times. Lifting the tone arm, he told Stephanie, "By the way, this is in two parts, one on each side. Here goes the first side," and he delicately set the stylus at the first groove.

The record initially made some crackling and popping sounds, and then the music started with drums followed by brass. The recording came out clearly, no pops, no hissing, just Benny and his fabulous orchestra. Quinn raised the volume, ecstatically closed his eyes, rolled his head, and swayed his body to the tempo. He was as close to Nirvana as he would ever get in this lifetime. "Yes!" His face lit up as he turned to Stephanie. "This is a classic. A masterpiece!"

Stephanie listened from where she stood at the window. After a minute or so, she decided she liked what she was hearing, and she tapped her toes to the rhythm, and eventually her toe tapping became dancing. Out of the corner of her eye, she saw Quinn watching critically.

"What?"

"You do that modern dance crap that looks like cheerleading." He approached her and offered his hand to her. "Let me show you some real dancing."

"Huh?"

He grabbed her hand and began to lead her in a Swing dance. After a couple of missteps, she caught on, and they fell into sync. It went unsaid how impressed they were with each other. Quinn failed to warn her the song was a long one. She was having too much fun to notice. He was having so much fun he disregarded his soreness. When Side A finally ended they slowly collapsed together on the floor, laughing, panting, and glistening with sweat.

From the open doorway at the top of the stairs came applause.

Stephanie lifted her head, "Hey, Mom!"

"I haven't heard that since I was a kid."

"We found the old Philco." Quinn said.

"I can't believe it still works."

Quinn sat up with some difficulty, feeling the strain in his muscles and lungs. "The inside could use some cleaning if you'd let me. If the tubes get too hot with all that dust on them, they'll blow."

"My goodness, Quinn. You sure surprise me."

"Me, too." Stephanie added. "Where'd you learn to dance like that?"

"Watching old movies. I could teach you the Jitterbug. That is, after I heal up." In the meantime, the needle was at the blank space at the end of the record where all it played was an endless whoosh-pop-whoosh sound. Quinn attended to it and carefully replaced the record in its jacket. He closed the player, shut off the power, and afterward affectionately ran his hand over the sleek wood laminate, "This sure is a dandy. When you used the word 'treasure' to describe what Stephanie found up here, Ida, you weren't kidding. Do you have any idea how cool this stuff is?"

"I never gave it a thought. It was my great-grandparents' old furniture, already handed down to them through generations. My grandmother had it moved up here decades ago when she had the house remodeled. I forgot all about it until I moved back in here."

"You're not gonna sell this stuff, are you, Mom?"

"Oh, Stephanie. If you want to keep it, it's yours."

Stephanie and Quinn high-fived each other.

* * * * *

After dinner, they sat on the sofa in what in the old days was called the parlor. The room retained the original architectural features of white wainscoting along the walls, and sliding pocket doors between that room and the foyer. A teardrop shaped overhead light fixture flush-mounted to a lovely white plaster medallion with a circular scroll pattern adorned the ceiling. When Quinn observed all this and voiced his appreciation, Ida informed him her grandmother had lovingly restored all these features in the 1950's. The two carried on a conversation about old houses for the next fifteen minutes while Stephanie listened patiently and curiously, for she had not seen these things before Quinn brought them up. What dominated her interest was the old photo album containing the pictures of Isaac. Finally, when her mother retreated to the kitchen to clean up after dinner, Stephanie invited Quinn to join her on the sofa where she had the album open on her lap. She pointed to one of the photographs of Isaac and said to Quinn, who was sitting with her, "This is him."

"How about that," Quinn said, looking closely at Isaac in his suit.

"I think he's very handsome."

Quinn thought so, too, but he didn't say anything.

Stephanie said, "Look at those eyes. I've never seen eyes like that on anybody."

"Yeah," Quinn replied, "Unusual, like he could see right into your soul. I bet you'd go out with him if he was still alive and he asked you."

"If he was still alive he'd be, like, a hundred and fifty years old." It was a slight exaggeration; she wasn't about to sit and do the math.

"No. I mean if he was alive," he tapped the photo, "…at this age, now, and not dead."

"You can't date your relatives, no matter how far removed. The idea of that is just plain icky."

"He had no trouble getting dates, I bet you."

Her voice came wistfully, "Probably not."

Quinn grew silent for a few moments as he realized Isaac could pass for a twin of someone else connected with this house. He decided not to mention it to Stephanie and Ida; they would discover it on their own soon enough.

7

As they worked in the cemetery, Quinn became much more talkative as the days progressed. He impressed Stephanie with his knowledge about old music, old dances, old movies, and everything old. And, finally, finally, he invited her into his home where they watched Quinn's collection of movie musicals, from which she learned the names of his favorite actors and dancers and the names of some of the archaic dances they performed.

He taught Stephanie how to twist on the balls of her feet to dance the Savoy Swing, and once she mastered that, taught her the basics of The Jitterbug. In short, the terrace of the Vanderfield home served as dance studio and Ballroom Central.

Maria Rodriguez observed their teenage energy and enthusiasm from the kitchen window. Employed by John Vanderfield for just over a year and a half, she had only seen Quinn happy when he was listening to his music. Now, he was consistently cheerful, which she could only attribute to his new friendship with Stephanie.

However, once John Vanderfield returned home to his television and his customary three tumblers of whiskey, the atmosphere in the house grew heavy again, and Quinn escaped to the Norris house. Maria accepted this would be the routine for as long as Quinn remained friends with Stephanie, and she was glad for Quinn. Yet, there came many evenings when she missed Quinn, missed their banter as well as their serious talks, which had been many in the past.

The days were much warmer, the nights taking longer to cool. A portable room fan made the attic tolerable as he and Stephanie cleaned and rearranged the discarded furniture. At last, Stephanie had her "Stephanie Cave" just the way she wanted. Quinn cleaned the innards of the Philco, and they left it in the same corner of the attic near the only electrical outlet where it had sat for years. They arranged the 78's alphabetically by genre and then artist on one of the bookcases beside the Philco. With music playing, they explored the many boxes and beaten old trunks from which they extracted many interesting articles of antique clothing, which they tried on just for fun.

At last, came the day Quinn's face had healed and he felt confident enough to accompany Stephanie to the library. They mounted their bicycles very early one warm overcast morning and pedaled the five miles into town. Excitement turned to disappointment when the archives expert informed them the library's collection of 1913 through 1914 local newspapers had been lost in a fire decades ago before they could be transferred to microfiche film. Disheartened, Stephanie more than Quinn, they began the long return trek toward their rural neighborhood.

The temperature had risen higher, as did the humidity. Quinn predicted rain. No sooner had he voiced this than a rumble of thunder and flash of lightning came over the distant mountains. Quinn gave her a smug smile.

"Is there anything you don't know?" Stephanie's tone was more statement than question.

"Much more than I know," he quipped.

They passed a few spacious ranches, mooed at some cows along a fence, petted some horses, and continued homeward as the thunder and lightning graced the northern ridges. She labored to pedal up the gradual incline on the lightly traveled two-lane road. They would not reach the junction to the route that led to their homes and the lake for another mile. Stephanie gave in and finally stopped her bicycle.

"I need to walk it for a while."

Although Quinn was way ahead of her, he heard her and stopped. "You haven't been on your bike in a long time, have you?"

"I guess it's obvious."

"I don't mind walking it."

"You're a swell hep cat," she joked.

"Hep cat is right; I don't know about the swell part." When she caught up to him, he said, "The Clayfields' fruit stand should be open by now. Wanna stop for lunch there?"

"That sounds good."

"My treat." He had twenty dollars in cash he had stolen from his father's wallet that morning. He felt not the slightest remorse about it. "If I'd been thinking about it earlier, we could have stopped at the coffee shop downtown and had a real lunch."

"That's okay. Fruit's good for us."

"Next time, we'll go to the coffee shop. They have avocado sandwiches. I

Hell Is In Me

love avocado sandwiches. They also have—" The familiar roar of a familiar truck interrupted him. His face went white as Bruno Ruiz's giant gray monster barreled toward them. "Oh, shit..."

"Who's that?"

"Bruno. Aw, shit. Shit, shit, shit!"

The terror on his face revealed the answer regarding who beat him. Stephanie stood frozen. "Now what? What do we do?"

There was no place to hide, and Bruno had already spotted them anyway. Bruno slowed and hit the brakes, resting the truck beside the two gripping their bikes. Farley Larson popped his head out the open passenger window and grinned at Quinn.

"Hey, fag! What's up?"

"None of your business." Quinn suppressed his urge to tag "*Fartly*" onto the end of his reply.

Farley gave Stephanie a once-over, then an impressed second once-over. "I haven't seen you before."

Although he was slightly bug-eyed, his face was handsome. She liked the way his thick brown hair curled slightly at his eyebrows; it gave him a boyish look. For some reason, she could not picture this guy having a mean bone in his body. She debated within herself the best way to handle this situation. Finally deciding kindness and diplomacy was her best option she set her bike on the kickstand and offered her hand to him in friendly greeting. "My name's Stephanie."

Surprised by her affability, Farley gently shook her hand. "I'm Farley." Still gazing warmly at her, he pointed backwards with his thumb, "And this is Bruno."

Stephanie peered past Farley to Bruno in the driver's seat. At first intimidated by his tattoos, shaved head, and pockmarked bulldog face, she steeled her courage and addressed him politely and confidently, "Hi."

Bruno narrowed his eyes at her and then gestured derisively at Quinn, as he demanded, "How do you know this piece of shit?"

"Quinn's been my best friend since we were kids."

Bruno fell into a fit of laughter. "Jesus Christ, girlie!"

Farley said, "So, you've been friends since you were kids, huh?"

"Yeah," Stephanie replied with feigned sentimental warmth in reference to Quinn.

Farley questioned her suspiciously, "So how come we haven't seen you around before?"

"I just moved back into town."

"From where?"

"L.A. area."

"Why?"

"Lots of reasons. I don't want to go into it. I sure am glad to see Quinn again, though."

Brushing her fingertips with his, Quinn said in a low voice to Stephanie, "Don't bait them, Steph."

She ignored him and focused on Farley who was staring at her with his slightly bulging blue eyes. "What'cha guys up to?"

Farley said after a momentary stammer, "We're heading out to the lake. Wanna go?"

"No, thanks."

"Why?"

All of her mother's precautionary tales prompted Stephanie's polite response. "Do you have a sister, Farley?"

"Yeah."

"Would you want her to get in a truck with two guys she doesn't know?"

Farley cocked his head to one side, then subtly and confidentially whispered "no" to her. It was clear to Stephanie and Quinn he was hiding his response from Bruno.

Bruno hollered over the truck's engine noise, "You can get to know us."

Farley backhanded Bruno's shoulder, "Cut it out, Bruno."

Bruno cussed and lit up a joint, contemplated the road ahead as if it was just another journey to Boredomville.

Quinn gently took Stephanie's hand and nudged her away from the truck. His hand was cold and wet in hers. She stole a glance at him and saw his still slightly bruised jaw was set firmly with his simmering anger. It was clear to her he didn't understand she was trying to diffuse the situation before Quinn lost it and invited the boys' confrontation. It was also clear to her this most recent beating they had given him had left him traumatized; he was trembling and his eyes subtly revealed his fear. She squeezed his hand.

Farley leaned out the window again and told Stephanie, "Don't mind Bruno. He's harmless."

She silently begged to differ.

Quinn tugged Stephanie's hand, "We're gonna be late, Steph."

Bruno leaned over Farley and smirked at Quinn, "Late for your period, *Queen Quinn*?"

Quinn gritted his teeth and cursed under his breath. His skin flamed red.

The pot smoke escaped Bruno's plump snarling lips as he leaned fully across Farley and poked his scarred face through the passenger window and berated Quinn, "Quit shaking. Such a coward, man."

Quinn squared his shoulders and glared at Bruno. "I'm not scared of you." He immediately regretted saying that in case the bulldog decided to test him.

Farley blanched and quickly shoved Bruno to his place behind the wheel. He admonished him fearlessly, "Jeez, Bruno, let it go, man. It's too damn hot for this. I wanna get to the lake."

"Aw, fuck you, Farley. You just wanna get into her pants."

At this point, Quinn stepped up and wrapped a protective arm around Stephanie's shoulders. He gave Farley a beseeching expression that caused Farley to soften.

Farley nodded his boyish head. He then turned to Bruno, "Let's fly, man. They're waiting for us."

Bruno moved the gearshift and shouted to Quinn, "You're lucky today."

Still trembling, and ashamed he was trembling, Quinn sighed silently and looked away from him. Relief washed through him as Bruno hit the gas and raced up the road. Once they were far enough away, he turned hotly to Stephanie, one fist on his hip. "God! Are you trying to get me killed?"

"I was trying to distract them, and it worked. Besides, they weren't going to do anything with me here."

"I can fight my own battles."

"There doesn't always have to be a battle."

Quinn continued, her reply flying over his head, "Friends since we were kids, huh? I don't even remember us meeting as kids."

"My mom said we played together when we came up to visit."

"I don't remember that."

She laughed, "Well, neither do I."

They took up their bikes and resumed walking. Heavy raindrops fell sparsely and slowly, and the coolness of it refreshed them as they reached the crest of the hill.

With little warning, the telltale vibration rose from his toes to the crown of his head indicating the presence of a spirit. He expected it to be one of the victims of a recent fatal auto accident at the junction. Seeing nothing ahead of him, he looked behind him and spotted the entity. What he observed threw his accident theory all to hell, and he had to quickly reign in his shock.

Stephanie's eyebrows met as she gazed at him concernedly. "What is it?"

He didn't hear her. The sight of the wandering black shadow nearing the bottom of the hill along the road consumed his attention. Its form vaguely resembled a man, but the features were muted and distorted by colorful shards of light that shot into the air and then returned swirling to its source. Its slow gait indicated it was lost or confused, or searching for someone. Then the thing spotted him and came to an abrupt stop. Quinn felt it staring at him, analyzing him. It was too full of strange oppressive energy to be anything benign. His gut twisted and jumped, making him nauseous. This was bad; this was very bad.

Stephanie inquired louder, "Quinn?"

This time Quinn heard her, and he felt a strong need to protect her. He forced a smile and told her, "Thought I heard something. It's nothing. Race you to the junction! Let's go."

Stephanie hopped on her bike seat and fiercely pedaled. He let her get far ahead of him while he glanced over his shoulder now and then.

He couldn't see the entity anymore, but the ominous foreboding Quinn felt remained.

8

Quinn told his father. "You don't need me there."

John set his drink on the glass surface of the cast iron table beside him. He stretched his long legs out fully on the lounge chair and gazed out at the red brick terrace beyond the veranda; noted one of the path lights along the flowerbeds was dark. He made a mental note to change the bulb before he went to bed. Other than the dead bulb in the path light, it was a perfect night, warm and slightly humid. The day's rain had become a light mist of tiny drops almost imperceptible to the eye. The evidence lay glistening upon the bricks and lent a shine to the black metal crowns of the path lights. The clouds blurred the white of the moon, and the sight made him think of autumn and winter nights past, nights spent here with a glass of Merlot, and Bernice at his side. They were happy, peaceful times.

Those days were gone. Bernice was gone. All that remained of their life together stood stoically at the white railing of the veranda, this lanky kid who had inherited her eyes, her face, and her stubbornness.

"No," John remarked to Quinn, "I don't *need* you there, but I would *like* you to be there."

"I've already got plans."

"What plans?"

"Projects."

"Elaborate."

Quinn replied with stubborn silence. He didn't want to tell his father about the cemetery, and he was tired of this boating on the lake business.

John persisted patiently. "You can bring Stephanie along, if that's what you want."

"I don't like being on the boat, Dad. That's all there is to it."

"You don't like being with *me*; that's all there is to it."

Quinn rolled his eyes and turned away, a habit he had acquired from his mother, looked out at the obscured moonlight behind the cloud cover. "It has nothing to do with you. I just don't want to go to the lake."

The Fermented Four would be there. They spent most of their summer vacations there. They would spot him with his father and they would make fun of him like they always did. And then his father would get mad like he always did, and the whole day would be ruined like it always had been in the past. And later that night would come the lecture about how to be a man, his father encouraging him to get into sports and be like "normal" boys his age. The same old thing on an endless loop, like a TV show episode on eternal rerun mode.

John came up beside him and leaned his arms on the railing. "If it's got nothing to do with me, then what does it have to do with?"

"I told you; there are other things I have to do."

"*Have* to do? What? You don't have a job."

"I suppose that pisses you off like everything else about me."

"No, Quinn. I want you to enjoy your summer. You have the rest of your life to work. I've never pressured you about that. What pisses me off is your attitude. Ever since your mother died, you treat me like you wish I had died instead."

"I never wished that."

"You had a bond with her you never had with me."

"She never tried to make me into something I'm not."

"Have I done that?"

"Yeah. I'm sorry I'm not the jock you wanted for a son. Maybe you should get married again and try for a *real* boy."

John glared at him. "I have every right to slug you for that, you little shit."

Quinn cast him a challenging expression, his eyes blazing with hostility.

John had only seen that look once in Bernice's eyes; it was when her doctor told them her cancer was inoperable and untreatable.

She went into a rage that night, trashed their immaculate master bedroom, and then she drank herself into a stupor. Powerless in the face of this looming monster called terminal cancer, all John could do was drink with her until he passed out in her arms. They awoke with hideous hangovers, awoke to their son's eyes boring into them confusedly and accusingly from the foot of their bed.

Bernice told the boy, "It's all right, Quinn. Don't look at us like that."

"Why are you fighting?"

A weak smile. "We're not fighting."

"You yelled and broke stuff, Mom. Don't tell me it's all right."

"It *is* all right. It's all right now. Do us both a favor and start breakfast." After Quinn reluctantly left them, she made a stern request to John. "When the time comes, I want to die in my own bed."

John honored her request. Afterward, he never spent another night in their big bedroom. He got rid of all the furniture and took up residence in one of the two guest bedrooms. The master bedroom remained empty until he hired Maria Rodriguez to run the house and keep an eye on his increasingly rebellious son. The room with its two separate closets and luxurious ensuite bathroom served as a private and comfortable refuge for her.

Maria and Quinn bonded almost instantly, Maria as a combination mother substitute and friend.

Yet, Quinn's anger lay below the surface, simmering, sometimes ebbing, but inevitably simmering again. John had learned to give the boy plenty of space and plenty of time to work through his grief; he didn't know what else to do. Maybe someday Quinn's wrath would leave those beautiful eyes he had inherited from his mother. John sensed that day was still far away, and tonight those eyes burned into him. They burned into him not only with anger, but also with resentment and hurt.

The boy's voice was deep with defiance. "Go ahead and slug me."

"What good would that do?"

"It's your choice."

"I choose not to."

"Why? Because I'm too fay to fight back?"

"God, Quinn..." John had to admit to himself Quinn's questionable sexuality had been a long-time issue. "You're right; I haven't been fair to you. I haven't been... it was easier for your mother to accept..."

"Look, Dad, I don't know if I'm a homo. I don't know anything yet. That's what you're getting at, right?"

John was glad to finally have this out in the open. "Are you attracted to Stephanie?"

"I like her. As far as attracted to her, I don't know."

"Bring her to the lake with us."

"I'm not going to the lake. You go ahead without me. I'm done talking about it."

John retrieved his drink and sullenly retreated into the house. Bernice had told him to have patience with Quinn, but his patience was near exhausted.

* * * * *

Quinn discovered he had fallen asleep on the lounge chair when birdsong awoke him in the twilight of dawn. There was still a mist of rain falling languidly beyond the overhang of the veranda, and the air was cool. Tiny raindrops dripped off the tips of the shimmering low foliage of his mother's gardenia plants along the chain-link fence separating the Vanderfield property from the weedy roadside below. Quinn appreciated their beauty and the accompanying memory of his mother who loved gardenias more than any other flower. At one time, the gardenia bushes had grown tall enough to block the view of the roadside below, but his father had pruned them last winter to reinvigorate them. Now the view was not so pretty. Ugly, neglected scrub and unruly weeds followed the gradual descent of the hill from the fence to the flat section along the road. It was mostly low-growing stuff that afforded an unimpeded view of the two-lane thoroughfare.

This morning, the road to and from the lake was unusually vacant, save for one older model GMC pickup towing a small motorboat. The pickup puffed white exhaust as the driver pressed the accelerator to crest the hill. The driver slowed his vehicle at the curve where the road continued around from the front corner of Quinn's house to the rear in a crescent shape. Farther on, he would have to slow again for the notorious "S Curve" also known as, "Coroner's Curve." Beyond that, the road became straight again. After the truck towing the boat passed, there came no others. Quinn guessed it was because of the rain and the early hour. He expected things would pick up later once the clouds moved on.

Lethargic and vacillating between another hour's sleep or staying up to start the day, Quinn reclined and passively observed his surroundings, delighted in the fragrance of rain, gardenias, and wet soil, and felt lulled into a state of near hypnosis by the rhythmic patter of raindrops. He seldom felt this relaxed and, although a part of him wished to surrender to sleep, another part of him felt compelled to take in the beauty of this rare early summer rain. So he watched the world awaken, watched the birds begin their morning rituals, watched the first rays of light emerge at the horizon.

Something moved among the scrub beyond the fence, something tall and shadow-like. Quinn at first thought it was an animal, perhaps a big raccoon or coyote standing up on its hind legs. Quinn dismissed that thought when it drew closer to the fence, and then he didn't know what to think.

Concurrently, the vibration commenced in his body, rolled up from his toes to the top of his head where it exploded into a million screaming stars in his brain. His skin tingled as if electrified.

Another one.

A dark form, human in shape but almost translucent, emerged through the thick scrub and began to ascend the hill toward the terrace. Initially thinking his eyes and the dim gray light of morn was playing tricks on him, Quinn sat up and watched the slowly ambling figure as it approached the chain-link fence at the property line. The longer he observed it, the more he concluded it was a man, but not an ordinary man. The blackness surrounding the man's form shimmered, contracted, expanded, shimmered again, contracted again, expanded again. The process continued in an endless pattern of shimmer, contraction, and expansion as he trudged up the rise of the hill toward the chain-link fence at the Vanderfield yard.

Quinn could feel the visitor's innermost emotions; it made him nauseous.

Confused, lost, burdened, and broken, this strange entity wandered along the chain-link fence until the fence caught his attention. He stopped and stared at it, placed his soiled fingers through the links and tugged on them. It seemed to Quinn the barrier made no sense to him. The ghostly man's aura shimmered again and then expanded in front of him like a parasite tasting its environment. The aura passed through the chain-link fence and quickly projected itself into the yard in Quinn's direction. Quinn ducked as the aura, still attached to its host, shot over his head and landed on the wall behind him. Eight tentacles sprung out of its mass. It wandered upon the surface like a giant shimmering black spider on a long fat leash. Quinn watched it, curious and repulsed, his breath coming in short spurts. Never had he seen anything like this. Abruptly, it retracted its tentacles and propelled itself onto Quinn's chest. It immersed itself into his body in one sinking movement. Quinn had no time to react and brush it off. Now helpless, he felt tingling and heat spread through his body as the thing's energy scanned his core. His heart suddenly raced as his terror grew with the realization the aura discovered the gift he had hidden and had transmitted the knowledge to its host. Quinn folded into himself in reaction to the sudden chill in his body as the spectral man rapidly sucked the aura energy back. It made Quinn picture a tape measure rolling back to its source. It entirely enveloped its host upon reunion.

The dark shimmering man stepped through the fence and, satisfied, gazed at Quinn with a slow and triumphant smile at their sudden connection. Their eyes locked. Quinn's breathing and heartbeat increased. His mouth went dry. This *thing, man, demon*, whatever it was, was unlike any of the roving dead he had ever encountered. Frozen in place, he could only gape wide-eyed at it. Slowly, the man faded away. Somehow, Quinn understood he would return.

Quinn felt his ribcage release its vice grip around his heart and lungs. He inhaled deeply, pursed his lips and released his breath. He closed his eyes, panted slowly and gently, inhaled and exhaled, each breath decreasing the speed and power of the blood surging through his arteries. He could hear his heart beating in his ears, could feel the percussion in his chest slowing, slowing.

He opened his eyes. He wished he hadn't.

The dead man was bent nose to nose in front of him, and their eyes locked again. Dead eyes. Eyes veiled behind a thin viscose white crowned by thick black eyebrows. As if that wasn't frightening enough, he reeked of pungent chemicals and regurgitated cheap whisky.

"D—don't…" Quinn whispered, recoiling.

The voice was raspy, playfully taunting, "Don't what?"

He couldn't control the trembling of his body or the tremor in his voice. "I can't help you."

Man, creature, demon, thing… it didn't seem to breathe. It mouthed words, but the sound of the words transmitted from its mind as it replied gently, "You can, and you will."

Its only clothing was the shimmering black aura that continued to expand and contract. Yet, everything else about it impressed Quinn as intrinsically human. Suddenly, its aura spit colorful pinpoint fragments of energy that died within seconds of meeting the air. The colorful emissions triggered a recent memory in Quinn's mind of seeing this thing along the road when he and Stephanie were returning from the library – that same day Bruno and Farley pulled over to hassle him just for fun. How long had this entity been stalking him? And what in hell was it?

"What… what are you?"

"The sum of my errors."

"God forgives."

"God forsakes."

Quinn's voice came as a plea. "Go away."

It leaned its face closer to Quinn's. "I've come a long way for this."

Quinn could barely speak. "…can't help you."

The man smiled ever so slightly, enough to exude an underlying gentleness. His voice was full of patience and encouragement as he told Quinn, "You can, and you will." He broke into a grin that deepened the cavernous lines upon his decaying face. He giggled softly and said in a singsong manner, "Scaredy cat. You pissed your pants."

I sure did, Quinn realized ashamedly.

The man gradually faded away.

For many minutes, Quinn sat still, a vague almost hypnotic sensation of shock rooting him to the lounge chair. His body felt drained of energy. Nausea filled his gut like a giant rock that refused to be dislodged. This was all something new, and it worried him.

The click of the lock on the French doors leading out to the terrace jolted him out of his stupor. His father pulled one door open and leaned out, mug of coffee in hand. "Changed your mind, son?"

Heat and a sudden rush of perspiration rose in Quinn's face. "I don't feel so good."

Quinn easily sensed his father thought he was giving him another lame excuse. He felt relieved when the man's expression changed to one of concern as he stepped onto the veranda and saw Quinn's pale wet face and lifeless eyes. "When did this—? You really are sick, aren't you?"

"Woke up like this."

John noticed the large wet spot at the crotch of the boy's jeans. His brow wrinkled with sudden revulsion. "Did you piss yourself?"

Embarrassed, Quinn folded his hands over his crotch. "Yeah. I guess I slept real hard."

"You haven't pissed yourself since you were three years old."

He was surprised his father remembered. "Yep."

"Did you get into my liquor last night?"

"No, sir. I did not!"

"I'll stay home today."

"No. Go fishing like you planned. I'm okay."

"Clean yourself up and go to bed."

He sat up and viewed his father sincerely, "I really didn't get into your booze. I didn't. I'm just sick. That's all."

"Go to bed. I'll tell Maria."

"Don't. You know how she gets." He stood slowly, slightly dizzy, very weak. His father's alarmed expression told Quinn he planned to stay home anyway. Quinn didn't want that. His nerves were frayed. He wanted his privacy and peace and quiet. "It's nothing to worry about, Dad." He forced an encouraging grin. "Go catch us some fish for dinner. Catch some big ones, too, because I'm gonna be hungry by then."

John tried unsuccessfully to sound casual. "Is that a promise, son?"

"That's a promise." Then, as he weaved past his father in the doorway, "I didn't mean to be such a shit last night. I think I was coming down with this then."

* * * * *

Quinn slept a few hours until he awakened to the engine noise of Maria's Escort as she pulled out of the driveway. Quinn lifted the curtain and peered out the window behind the head of his bed, watched Maria point the car down the hill toward town. He assumed she was going shopping, and her shopping would include some over-the-counter flu remedies. It was Maria's job to watch over him, more than anything else. He drifted again to sleep, and the sunlight gradually shifted its play of shadows upon his bedding and the walls.

Television. Loud. Partial dialogue, canned laughter, fragments of commercials, finally the obvious buzz and hum and commentating of a NASCAR race.

Gordon'll probably win again... Dad must be home early. Thirsty. Damn, I'm thirsty.

He felt better. Whatever it was had passed. He drank two glasses of water in the bathroom then trudged down the stairs to join the "old man" in the den.

However, the unruly black hair on the shimmering head of the intruder on the sofa was not that of his father.

It was... *him.*

Quinn's first reaction was to turn and sneak up the stairs, but it was too late.

The entity spread out on the sofa had heard him and turned to him with a sneering grin. "When I died, television was still in black and white."

Quinn replied with forced bravado from the bottom step, "Go haunt somebody else."

"I need you, boy." His shimmering black aura swirled around his form, then darted like a bullet through Quinn's body.

Quinn felt the burning as it investigated his soul. "Stop it!"

The entity gestured to John's recliner. "Have a seat, kid." He pointed his finger at the television, and the set shut off. "I never could understand what people found entertaining about a bunch of hicks speeding around in a circle. Obviously, the human race hasn't progressed one inch since my time."

"It's only gotten worse," Quinn replied.

Again, he pointed to John's recliner. "Take the old man's throne."

How does he know about that?

"I have been reading you," he explained matter-of-factly.

Quinn reluctantly took the recliner, perched at the edge of the seat in case he needed a quick escape. "Why me? There must be somebody—"

"Not around here. Tag! You're it!"

"Shit…"

"I'm a dead man on a very long mission."

"What mission?"

"Unfinished business."

"I can't help you. I told you I can't help you."

"Let's not go through that again."

The air in the room quickly grew frigid. Quinn shivered, bent forward, crossed his arms in front of his chest and rubbed his upper arms. He knew from experience the colder the air, the more troubled and possibly dangerous the ghost.

A heavy odor of alcohol emanated from the dark aura enveloping his form. The stench grew stronger with the aura's increasing energy as it sent fragmented shards about the room. Quinn felt paralyzed as he watched the shards penetrate the furnishings and electronics; boundless insatiable energy investigating this, investigating that.

Finally, Quinn summoned the courage to inquire, "What is all that blackness around you?"

"It's heavy. It won't leave me." He gazed at Quinn, a tormented expression in his gray eyes. At once, the aura subsided enough for Quinn to see the details of this dead man's appearance. His face was lined, prematurely lined, as if he had spent his life in despair. His hair was black with tiny streaks of silver that glistened in the pale sunlight spilling through the window. He had a crooked, bumpy nose. Quinn thought the man's nose might have been broken at one time, for the nose was small and all the bumps just didn't seem natural for what was otherwise a very handsome face. One of his front teeth was broken, and two on one side were missing. The man understood Quinn was studying his face, and he allowed this, for Quinn was the only one in countless years who could see him.

Quinn didn't understand why, but he felt compassion for this tortured soul. "I've never seen it around the others. What is it?"

"My burden. My punishment, I guess."

"For what?"

"My stupidity. My ego. My arrogant youth."

Quinn considered him sympathetically, and he sensed a disturbing schizophrenic duality in the man that warned him this one was beyond his expertise. Quinn's gut twisted inside him, a warning of danger ahead. He learned from his research into the paranormal the worst thing he could do was reveal his fear to this entity; they fed on fear, which increased their power and strengthened their connection to the earth. Quinn subtly inhaled deeply and willed his body to relax. Once his tension subsided, he took control of the situation and spoke gently, apologetically, to his unwelcome guest, "If you think I can help release you from it, I can't."

"I need to find him."

"Find who?"

"Isaac."

"Isaac? The only Isaac I've heard of is that Iversen guy down in the cemetery. He's been dead for almost a hundred years."

"I need to find him."

"He's dead. He's passed over."

"No. A part of him is still here. I've searched coast to coast for decades, and I finally traced him to this place."

"This house?"

"This *town*, asshole!"

"That's impossible. I know from all my encounters with the dead once they pass over, they're gone for good. Not a single minutest fragment of them can remain in this dimension once they've moved on. I'm telling you the truth. Now you, whoever you are, have to do the same."

He took offence at Quinn referring to him as, *Whoever You Are*. He made it clear to the boy as he stated, seething, "My *name* is *Jake*."

"Jake?"

"*Jacob*, but everyone called me Jake. *Duh*, kid. That's simple enough, ain't it?"

Quinn's eyes narrowed. "I'm not a moron, so don't get snippy."

He raised his hands to his temples, cradled his head, and grimaced. His spirit body began to grow fainter, as did the darkness surrounding him. "Oh, God... So tired. So tired. Tell Isaac I need to talk to him. Tell him..." Jake was slowly fading away. He trembled and hugged his torso. His aura gradually evaporated into a thin veil of static gray mist. "Help me, boy. Oh, what they did to me! I paid and paid and it wasn't enough!"

Quinn could not move, could hardly breathe as he watched Jake slowly disintegrate into nothing. The room temperature returned to its normal warmth, and with the warmth Quinn's sensibilities returned. His body rebelled from the physical and psychic trauma. He reached the main floor toilet just in time to fill it with his bitter vomit.

* * * * *

Stephanie phoned him from the cemetery an hour later. He begged off working there, citing illness, and advised her to take the day off. The events of the day unnerved him to the point he feared not only for his own safety but Stephanie's as well. What if Jake was wandering the grounds, watching the girl as she worked? What if Jake was this very moment scanning her soul in search of her cousin Isaac? Could Jake truly detect the presence of the dead boy's lingering spirit within Stephanie's genetic make-up? Quinn considered Stephanie's obsession with learning everything she could about Isaac. Was it possible Isaac was attempting to violate the natural laws of time, space, and death and whatever came beyond death by using their shared DNA as a sort of cosmic communication system?

Outlandish ideas, certainly; yet, Quinn had learned enough from his encounters with the dead—especially at the hospital during his mother's illness—to believe anything was possible. There was that bedside visit from a doctor one night while his mother lay oblivious in a drug-induced sleep. He was a specialist in genetics research, a groundbreaker in his field, and he hovered over Quinn's mother that night and told Quinn his theory that we contain not only our ancestors' DNA in various quantities, but also a smidgen of some of our ancestors' souls, as well. The doctor, a man dead for over five years, refused to pass over to "*that good shore*," as he put it, in order to confirm his theory. Quinn, enraptured, listened. When the doctor encouraged Quinn to explore the field for himself in the future, Quinn seriously considered it. The doctor's late night visits ended when Quinn's mother came home to die. Quinn understood then the doctor had tethered himself to the hospital and would conceivably never leave the place, so great his determination to learn the truth of what makes us who we are and what laws of science—or God—determined the specific traits and diseases all humans inherit through their ancestors over the centuries.

It was enough to drive the sanest person certifiably insane, and Quinn felt at this moment he would indeed go insane if he continued to dwell on it.

Oh, Steph... is it you? If such a thing is possible, are you the one unknowingly hosting a fragment of Isaac Iversen's soul? Does Jake know?

And, what, in the name of God, is the unfinished business Jake has with Isaac?

"Go home today," Quinn told her over the phone. "I'll let you know when I feel better and we can go back to it. Promise me you're going home, Steph."

She protested, "But I can get a lot done here"

"I know you can. Let's wait until I'm better so we can work together. Take a day off, for crying out loud."

"You sound stressed, Quinn, scared, even. What the hell is going on?"

He thought quickly and replied, "That cemetery is my project. I'm boss; remember? I don't want anyone messing around in there without me there. And, besides that, what if someone sees you go in there and knows you're alone? What if Bruno and those guys spot you on their way to the lake? I'd die if something happened to you, Steph. Don't go there alone anymore. Promise me, damn it, promise me."

"Jeez, Quinn... Don't be a such a drama queen."

"Don't piss me off."

"I'm not trying to."

"And don't make me go down there all sick like this. I'll do it if I have to. And, by the way, I have a clear view of the place from my bedroom window. I'll know if you're there. Go home. We'll talk tomorrow."

She finally acquiesced, and Quinn watched from his bedroom window to be certain she obeyed him. While he watched her, he recalled his conversation with his father the previous night, and the fact he had hidden his true reasons for avoiding the lake. It seemed laughable now, his fear of Bruno's gang.

They were insignificant compared to the danger posed by this dead man named Jake.

9

"I'm concerned about you spending so much time up in the attic," Ida said.

"I'm still organizing it." Stephanie spooned whipped cream onto her peach pie, avoided her mother's eyes. "Do you want whipped cream?"

Ida, now sporting her natural hair color, joined her daughter at the picnic table out on the rear veranda. She was wearing a light robe over her summer nightgown, and she welcomed the cool of the night after such a warm day. The heat of summer never bothered her when she was young and growing up in this house. The beginnings of menopause changed that. Although she didn't answer Stephanie's question, the girl dropped a spoonful of whipped cream on top of the sliver of pie on her plate. Just what she needed, more calories to add to her menopausal weight gain. She sighed and decided it didn't matter; pie was yummy and whipped cream made it even yummier.

"I thought I heard opera when you were up there."

Stephanie laughed self-consciously. "I was curious. Man! I don't know how people can like that stuff. Did Grandma and Grandpa listen to it?"

"God, no."

"Well, someone liked it. There's a whole bunch of them up there. I had thought of tossing them out, but Quinn said not to. He said they should stay there because they were important to someone in our family. He said it would be like disrespecting that person to throw their favorite music away. I thought that was kind of weird, don't you?"

This didn't surprise Ida. Upon their first acquaintance, she sensed he had a sentimental side. "No. Quinn sees things differently than most people. Are you two going back to the cemetery tomorrow?"

"First thing in the morning, now that he's feeling better. We've got most of it uncovered. We don't know what to do about the toppled headstones. They're too heavy for us."

"Quinn should ask his father."

"His dad doesn't know about it. Quinn's been doing this on his own. He hasn't told anyone about it."

"Why won't he tell his father?"

"I don't know. Quinn keeps a lot to himself."

"John would be glad to help him with it. He knows all kinds of resources in this town."

"John?"

"Quinn's father."

"He doesn't trust anyone except you and me."

Ida scoffed, "Quinn has a skewed impression of people."

"That's because most people have been rotten to him."

"I don't believe that."

"Jeez, Mom. You saw what they did to his face."

"John said he brought it on himself."

"When was that?"

"I stopped in at his store this morning."

"You didn't tell him about the cemetery, did you?"

"Of course not."

"Thanks, Mom."

"John told me Quinn's been having trouble ever since his mother died." Ida paused and considered whether she should tell Stephanie the rest of what John Vanderfield told her. She decided it might be in the girl's best interest, in case she was developing a crush on the boy. "There's also the fact Quinn has a habit of blurting out insults to the jocks at school, spreading rumors about them, and falsely accusing them of vandalism he himself has done. He was suspended a few times last year for all of it. In a rural, good ol' boy town like this full of rednecks and yahoos, a boy like him with a combative attitude and eccentric ways can attract a lot of trouble to himself."

"I already figured that out. He's just going through a rough time. That doesn't make him a bad guy."

"It makes him a target. It isn't right, but that's how it is. I don't want you to get hurt, Steph."

"By who? The good ol' boys or Quinn?"

Ida sighed and stared at the pie and ice cream on her plate.

Stephanie said, "He's my friend. I don't care what anyone thinks. Please, be his friend, too."

"You know I'd never turn him away because of that."

"Then, it's a non-issue. You're concerned about nothing, really, Mom."

"Nothing? My concerns are *not* about *nothing*! What if he picks a fight while you're with him? That's what worries me."

"Actually, Mom... He's kind of scared of those guys. I don't think his dad has the full story."

"And you do?"

Stephanie did not reply immediately, which drew Ida's suspicion. She noted the sadness in her daughter's eyes and voice when the girl finally explained compassionately, "Quinn told me those guys have picked on him since elementary school. This last school year he just finally had enough of it. And then they chose the last day of school to pay him back. That's what happened. His dad doesn't know everything."

"Well, he needs to talk with his dad and tell him everything. Honestly, Steph, I like Quinn. However, I'm very concerned about him."

"He'll be okay. He's slowly starting to talk more about it with me. He's sick of it all. He doesn't want any more problems with those guys. He just wants them to leave him alone."

"Well, I trust you, Steph. Just be careful. If he begins to show any signs of... bursts of anger, or depression, or..." She paused and shook her head mournfully. "I suggested John get him into counseling over the summer. Whether he takes my advice is up to him."

* * * * *

Curious about her daughter's obsession with the attic, Ida took the opportunity the next morning to go explore the space while Stephanie was out working in the cemetery with Quinn. The heat of the day increased as she ascended the hard oak stairs, and she had begun to sweat by the time she entered the room. Today was the Summer Solstice, and so far, it was the hottest day of the year in northern California, predicted to hit one hundred and five degrees by five o'clock that afternoon. She flipped the light switch at the entrance and, from there, observed the many changes Stephanie and Quinn had made over the past two weeks.

It looked like an old Victorian parlor with its cast-off early twentieth-century furniture and knickknacks. Everything was clean. Stephanie had vacuumed the furniture and faded pillows, she had polished the old wooden tables, had cleaned to a shimmer the gaudy glass-shaded lamps and had even restored the only oil lamp until it appeared as new as the day her ancestors purchased it. A small bookcase against one wall held obscure books organized according to size. They were mostly novels with ragged fabric covers and a few textbooks about woodworking and electricity. The bottom shelf held a few early versions of *Better Homes and Gardens* magazines from the 1910s. Among this small collection was one thin magazine from a defunct local department store entitled, *Harper's Fashion Collection 1921*. Ida thumbed through it, noticing many dog-eared pages, mostly women's fashions, except one page containing men's clothing styles. The thought crossed her mind she no longer had the figure to get away with wearing the flapper dresses and ornate evening wear of that day, even if she was living in that time. Yet, she recalled then a photograph of her pudgy great-grandmother posing proudly in a flapper dress, and she looked okay in the style.

Hat boxes, some covered in floral fabric, and others in brittle cracking leather, lined the top shelf of the bookcase. Ida opened one of the floral fabric boxes and saw it contained a cloche style hat, bright red, with a red netted material for draping over the face, and a small cluster of red, orange, and black feathers attached to one side. The feathers were falling apart from age. The other boxes held similar fancy hats and some men's hats that were in very good condition. The hats were all different styles representing many different periods of twentieth-century fashion. On closer inspection of one of the men's hats, she discovered a strand of blond hair, hair so blond it was almost white. None of her family had blond hair. Ida immediately surmised Quinn had tried on the hat. She smiled at the thought.

She moved on to the wardrobe cabinet that was still in very good condition although scuffed and scratched at the base. Stephanie had carefully hung dresses and two men's suits inside. The clothing was very old, some from the days of Teddy Roosevelt, and the rest were from the 1920s through 1950s. Women's shoes, still in boxes, sat below the hung clothing. The shoes were in good condition, although obviously worn.

The heat was becoming unbearable, but Ida's fascination and curiosity with her daughter's obsession with this project overrode her desire to return to the cooler downstairs. She continued her tour, noting the bigger shelving unit that held the shellac '78 records all organized according to musical genre, a task no doubt completed with Quinn's assistance. The Philco sat across from the shelving unit, thin rays of dappled sunlight gleaming upon its oiled and polished wood laminate. Someone, almost certainly Stephanie, had cleaned the dial window to spotless perfection.

An old wool throw rug with a predominately pink, blue and green floral pattern sat on the floor in front of a shining wood rocking chair beside a beautiful wooden table. A curiosity sitting on a doily on the table drew her attention. Stephanie had photocopied the photograph of Isaac, the photo of him in his suit, a handsome, hopeful, teenage boy, and had mounted it in an old copper frame. Ida took it and gazed at the boy, a boy whose blood and DNA they shared. Stephanie was still on a mission to discover how he died so young. Ida was certain illness had taken him, but Stephanie would not rest until she knew everything there was to know about him. Ida carefully replaced the photo onto the table. She delicately ran her fingers over the flying geese artfully carved into the backrest of the rocking chair. The quality of the work was impressive, and she wondered about the artist. She gently lowered herself into the chair, and it made a soft cracking sound with her weight. The chair was comfortable to sit in, and Ida imagined it was somebody's favorite at one time. Why it ended up here in the attic she couldn't fathom. The thought of bringing it down to the living room crossed her mind. She quickly changed her mind when she recalled Stephanie had claimed the chair as her own. And, the longer Ida sat there, the stronger she sensed this chair was sacred in some way, and it was right where it should be beside the table built with the same wood; they were companion pieces, never meant to be separated, once cherished, once forgotten, now cherished again. She surveyed the space from there.

Her child had been very busy creating another world up here. Ida couldn't decide if that was a good or a bad thing, yet something about it caused her to wonder if Stephanie subconsciously wanted to recede from the present day and live in a time she perceived as less complicated, less demanding, and less tragic. If only Stephanie had been a better student of history she would have known those times long gone were hard times, full of complications, full of unreasonable demands on girls, and full of heartbreaking tragedy – tragedy mostly prevented by the science of the present. And then Ida thought about Quinn, another who disdained the world of the twenty-first century and preferred to live with the remnants of the past – a past he had never experienced first-hand. Was he inadvertently encouraging Stephanie into his dream world of a better day that never really existed? And, why? Why were they like this? What was so bad about their present lives that would make them want to escape into this backward time travel?

The sunlight was moving away from the window. Stephanie had washed the window and installed a lace curtain there. The room smelled like lemon polish and window cleaner, the fragrances strengthened by the oppressive heat.

Ida turned on the portable fan Stephanie had set on the floor beside the chair. The girl had attached it to an extension cord plugged into the outlet by the Philco. The fan blades turned, sped up, and then died. Ida shut it off. The central air conditioning did not include this attic space, and something had to be done if the kids were going to continue to spend their time here, which they would do whether she approved or not. She would add a portable window-mounted air conditioner plus electrical upgrades for this space to the list of work needed. Ida hoped Gene Blackwell would have time to perform this work, and she intended to ask Caleb about it when she interviewed him tomorrow morning.

For today, she had other things to do, and she went downstairs to her mother's room. It was just as the old woman left it the day she died. The bed was still unmade. The pillow still had a dent in it from her last sleep on this earth. Her pink slippers, ragged from years of use, still sat on the floor at the side of the bed that faced the door. The curtains were still open, as was her mother's habit to open them first thing each morning.

Ida paused in the doorway. The task would be difficult, but it had to be done. She gathered the boxes from the garage and returned to the room with them, decided to begin with the easiest task, the clothing in the closet. On Thursday, the Salvation Army would arrive with their biggest truck for everything, including the furniture, which Ida was glad to donate. She had been sleeping in the guest bedroom since she had moved in with Stephanie, and it was now time to claim this room and this house as her own. Once it was emptied, Stephanie would help her clean it. They would polish the wood floors once the painting was finished, something she intended to ask Caleb about provided she decided to hire him.

Ida found it curious she did not recall until recently the woman's casual comments about her "groundskeeper" who kept the yards neat and tidy and helped her with things around the house. A year ago, or thereabouts, Ida had pictured the groundskeeper as an old man, not a teenage boy. Her mother had gone on about him, what a strong man he was, honest as sunrise and, *"Oh! Dear Caleb! Such a help to me in so many ways!*" The comments had lingered only a few moments in Ida's brain before they were off on other subjects, mundane things she only half listened to.

As she packed the clothing into the boxes, Ida silently berated herself for not paying more attention. Her mother had a frustrating habit of going off on tangents during conversation. Sometimes she was so hard to follow Ida simply muttered "uh-huh" as the woman chatted on and on—usually about her health problems and how difficult it was becoming to drive, and about people Ida had never met, like the groundskeeper, and local gossip about people long forgotten and insignificant. It was all chatter Ida suffered through as a good daughter.

"I'm sorry, Mom," she said softly to the air.

The clothing took little time to sort and pack; there wasn't much. Her mother didn't go out as often as she used to. There were three purses, one still sporting the sales tag. Ida went through them all, found the requisite items in only the black one: car keys, her wallet with her driver's license, Medicare card, library card, one hundred and fifteen dollars in cash, and thirty-three cents in change. No credit cards. Ida thought that over and remembered her mother mentioned she had canceled all her credit cards and paid them off; she was convinced the new "chipped" cards planned to replace them were the Biblical Mark of the Beast. Ida tossed the spent tube of ruby red lipstick into the trashcan beside the bed, tossed the comb with one broken tooth there, too. Sadness enveloped her from the inside out.

The worn black purse joined its companions in the box. Ida kneeled on the floor to gather the three pairs of dress shoes that were twenty years out of style and too well-worn to donate. She tossed those into a large plastic trash bag and gathered more of her mother's discarded and forgotten items from the closet.

A large and very fat manila envelope propped sideways against the wall in the rear corner of the closet caught her eye. She took it and jumped off to the side as a spider rushed out from under it. The spider sought refuge under the bed. Ida let it go, waited for her heart to stop pounding. Finally, she looked at her name written on the envelope in her mother's writing:

"*Ida. Important.*"

Ida exclaimed, "Important, and you stuff it in the back of your closet? What were you thinking, Mom?"

She spilled the contents onto the floor. A very fat brown envelope landed face down, a second thinner white envelope with her name on it landed face-up, and two keys held together with a safety pin tumbled out and bounced on the wood, finally coming to rest. She opened the envelope addressed to her, found a letter and five thousand dollars cash in one hundred dollar bills. After gasping at the money, she set it beside her and read the letter:

"*Ida, I hope this $ will help with Stephanie's college education. Silly me, I forgot to tell my lawyer about my safety deposit box at the bank. My good jewelry and some more cash are there for you attested by this letter and my signature below. One key is for that. The other key is a spare that goes to your father's truck that I gave to Caleb. Please see to it he gets this extra key, and please give him the envelope I addressed to him, the contents of which are his, attested by my signature in the letter I wrote to him.*

"*I love you and Stephanie so much. Please be happy and treat others with the same kindness and respect you desire from them. I will tell your dad and Ned you say hello.*

"*With eternal love and hugs, your mom, Grace Meylor Tarantino.*

"*P.S. I made an oral agreement with Caleb that he lives in the caretaker's cottage as long as he wants. I hope you will honor that agreement.*

"*P.P.S. I really did meet Janis Joplin!*"

Grace had drawn a smiley-face next to Janis Joplin's name.

There was a notary's stamp and signature at the bottom of the page. "Thank you for thinking of that, Mom." She folded the letter and replaced it in its envelope.

Ida lifted the envelope on which her mother had written, "*For Charles Caleb Anders.*" It was very thick, heavy, yet pliable as if full of papers. The sneaky desire to steam it open teased her conscience, and she reprimanded herself for considering it, even though it was just for a second. She would present it to the young man in the morning, provided he showed up at all, as he promised over the telephone. However, he did sound anxious to meet her, and he expressed his condolences for the loss of her mother, his voice breaking a little in the process. The memory of their brief conversation brought her reassurance he would indeed arrive, and she was looking forward to meeting him.

* * * * *

The doorbell rang at seven a.m. before the coffee was done brewing. Ida hurried to answer before the bell would ring a second time and awaken Stephanie, who was sleeping in after a long night researching her family history on the Internet. The girl had spent hours looking up old newspaper accounts from the local area, all in search of information about her long-deceased cousin. Ida was beginning to find her daughter's newest obsession disturbing, and she finally forced her to log off and shut down the computer. The recollection settled into her subconscious as she opened the door and peered at the tanned timidly smiling young man on the doorstep. Her heart felt as if it did a back flip in her chest.

The young man with the penetrating pale blue eyes immediately understood something about him shocked her. His smile faded quickly with concern.

"Ma'am…?"

She regained her composure; her smile took no effort at all. "You must be Caleb."

"You said seven. If this is a bad time—"

"Not at all." She unlocked and pushed open the screen door, stepped aside for him to enter. "Please come in. I'm Ida, Grace's daughter."

He shifted from foot-to-foot before he moved forward into the foyer where he offered her his hand in polite greeting. "Pleased to finally meet you, ma'am." As she placed her hand in his, he said solemnly, "I'm very sorry what happened to Mrs. Tarantino. She was a fine woman. I miss her every day."

The depth of sincerity in his eyes drew her in and for a moment, they were united in mutual mourning. It was not until he released her hand the spell was broken and she responded, her voice tight in her throat, "I miss her, too." Ida motioned him to follow her, "Let's go to the kitchen,"

She had pre-set coffee mugs and spoons, plus the fine china sugar and creamer servers from her mother's collection. They were treasured items Grace Tarantino used only on special occasions due to their fragility. Ida did not share her mother's opinion; the way she looked at it, why have nice things if you were only going to use them once or twice a year?

The sight of the light blue floral patterned china evoked a sentimental smile from Caleb. "I remember these. She took them out once every four months to wash them. We used to stand together at the sink there and I would dry them and set them right here on this table. She told me the set was a wedding present from her parents."

"Yes, it was." Ida poured their coffee. "Please sit down, Caleb. Make yourself at home. How long did you know my mother?"

"A little over four years."

"And, how did you meet?"

"We met at the library."

"The library… really…"

"She was a volunteer there."

"Oh. Now I remember. She mentioned that. It didn't last long because of her stroke."

"Yes, ma'am. But it wasn't that serious – the stroke, I mean. She was back at the library a month later. It was being on her feet that got to her. That's why she quit. This is good coffee, ma'am."

"You're from the South… Louisiana?"

"Yes."

"Chased out here to California by Hurricane Andrew?"

"No. We moved here when I was eleven. I've been trying to get rid of my accent ever since."

"I like it."

He met her eyes with a serious, determined, expression. "I don't."

She moved on. "I understand you lived in the caretaker's cottage out back. How did that come about?"

He stared into his coffee mug for a few long moments, conflicted as to how he should reply. "She decided that would be easier for both of us."

"Pardon…?"

"I was working weekends for her by then. Taking care of the weeds, cutting the grass, cleaning the gutters—you know, that kind of thing. Sometimes I would miss the bus out this way and have to walk."

"So, she had you come live here?"

"Yes, ma'am."

"My name is Ida. You can call me Ida."

He nodded.

"How old are you, Caleb?"

"I turned nineteen in March."

"How long have you been living in the cottage?"

"About three years."

"So you were fifteen, sixteen, when you came to live here."

He nodded again, "Uh-huh."

Ida continued, curious to get the whole story. "And, your parents were fine with that?"

"Yes, ma'am—Ida."

It was obvious there was a lot missing from his story. She fell into silence, observing him, he observing her. "Tell me the rest, Caleb. I find it strange your parents would agree to such an arrangement. Was there trouble at home?"

He sighed and looked away from her. His cheeks reddened perceptibly, although his expression was impassive. "Your mother was a very wise woman, and very compassionate. I'd rather not talk about my home life."

"Do you have brothers and sisters?"

"It's just me, ma'am." He paused long enough to take a sip of coffee; aware she was hesitant about the idea of him working for her. Compelled to redeem himself, he contemplated what he would say next. "I'm a good worker. I don't steal. I don't take advantage of people, and I don't do drugs or drink. I do smoke, but I'm careful with my cigarettes, and I never smoke in the house. You can talk to Gene, my boss. He'll tell you. Your mom introduced me to him. She saw how good I was with construction type stuff—I used to fix everything here for her. She thought Gene would be a good mentor for me, and she was right."

"Where are you living now?"

"Mostly at Gene's place."

"Mostly?"

"Sometimes I get a motel room to have some time to myself. Gene's a man of routine, and he sleeps with his TV full blast. It's hard for me to sleep there because of that."

"I understand." She arose then and took the brown envelope and the spare key to the truck from the counter, returned to the table and sat, handed first the key and then the envelope to him. "This is the spare key to your truck." She tapped the envelope, "Perhaps this will help you. It's for you from my mother."

He silently pondered the envelope, read Grace Tarantino's familiar handwriting, touched by the fact she had written his full name on it as if to make it official and legal for some reason. Uncertain whether he should open it right away or wait until he was alone, he glanced at Ida inquiringly.

Ida remarked, "She obviously thought the world of you, Caleb." She left the table and headed to the counter and cooking area. "I'm going to make toast. I like it with butter and cinnamon sugar. How about you?"

"Thank you. That sounds good."

As she opened the bread, she said over her shoulder, "My mother told me in a letter she gave you permission to live in the caretaker's cottage as long as you wish. Do you want to return there?"

"I would, very much. But I understand if you don't want that."

She turned to him, her expression thoughtful. "I don't know you, Caleb. However, my mother seemed to have one hundred percent trust in you. It was her wish you continue living there as long as you want." She stopped talking, searched the room with her eyes, and finally said, "I have mixed feelings about this."

"If you're worried about your daughter—"

"You know I have a daughter?"

"Your mother showed me her pictures. She showed me lots of her family pictures. I understand your concern. I would question your qualities as a parent if you were not concerned."

"Well, this is a dilemma, isn't it?"

"I don't have to move back in there. How about this: You told Gene you needed work done around here. I'm available when Gene's doing big jobs I can't help him with because I'm not licensed yet. How about I don't return to the cottage, but continue working here when needed? The rear of this property has grown into a fire hazard, your gutters are full of debris, and I noticed the front steps are getting spongy. It's all work I can do, and through my working here, you and I can get acquainted and you can decide if you trust me. How does that sound?"

"That sounds good to me. I have a list of things I need done. Have you had experience painting?"

"Of course."

"Electrical?"

"I'd prefer Gene be on site for that."

"Minor carpentry?"

"My specialty." This statement was accompanied by a confident grin.

"This week I'm getting rid of the old furniture in some of the rooms. Are there any pieces, in particular, you would like to keep for when you get your own place?"

"No thank you, ma'am."

"*Ida.*"

"Sorry... a habit of mine. The way I was taught."

"As soon as I clear the furniture out, I want to repaint the rooms. Are you available on Friday to start that job?"

"I'll check with Gene."

"Are you available today to cut down the weeds and do some trimming out back?"

"I am."

"Then we'll have breakfast, and you can start. Look it over and name your price."

Caleb went out the kitchen door to the rear veranda where he delicately placed the large envelope from Ms. Grace upon the picnic table. From there, he walked the property. Ida watched him through the window over the sink, a bit amused by his slightly loping gait as he made a path through the tall dry weeds. He apparently knew every inch of the property, for he anticipated every spot where there were rocks or other hidden hazards. He stopped at every tree and examined their condition. Once far enough away and upslope from the house, he turned and surveyed the house itself, his pale eyes carefully scanning first the roofline, and then the tree branches that had grown over the roof. He shook his head as one scolding a child, produced a pen and a small wire-bound notepad from his shirt pocket. He diligently recorded his notes. Afterward, he circled the perimeter, and Ida went from window to window watching him examine and notate the sprinkler system, the downspouts, the vent screens both above and below until he returned to his original starting point on the veranda off the kitchen. He sat at the picnic table there and completed his list of findings. Once finished, and with an air of intention, he replaced the notebook and pen into his pocket. For a few minutes, he took in the wild beauty of the neglected surroundings, the expression on his face too sentimental for the reality before him. Ida, still discreetly observing him, supposed he was seeing a vision of what once was and what could be again.

As if awakening from a dream, Caleb became aware of the envelope from "Ms. Grace," as he called her. He read the two-page letter twice. When he finished the second reading, he wiped tears from his cheeks. The tears kept coming as he carefully folded the letter and placed it in his shirt pocket. Ida felt her heart break for him. Then, manning-up and taking charge of the situation, he emptied the remaining contents of the envelope onto the table: three fat stacks of bound cash. He slowly shook his head in both amazement and consternation, counted off a few bills from one stack and set it aside. The rest he returned to the envelope and loped slowly to the house, where he knocked softly on the kitchen door before he opened it and popped his head in.

"Ms. Ida?"

"Come in. You don't have to knock."

He pushed the envelope full of money at her, "I don't feel right taking this. I'm only keeping the three hundred dollars I earned that month before she passed."

She rested against the counter, crossed her arms in front of her chest. "I don't know how much is in there, Caleb, but whatever the amount, she wanted you to have it. Just take it and shut up."

"I didn't earn it."

"It's her gift to you. Just shut up and take it."

"Give it to a charity."

"*You* give it to a charity."

"I don't know why she..."

"Obviously, she wanted to give you a head start in life. She must have loved you very much or she wouldn't have done that. My mother never did anything without thinking it over first. Follow her example and put the money aside for when you need it. The best thing to do is put that money in a safety deposit box at the bank and let some time go by as you decide what you want to do with it. Whatever you do, don't give it away. Let it sit for a while, and perhaps consult a financial advisor when you feel up to it."

"A financial advisor? What's that?"

"They give you ideas on what to do with your money to help it grow. Think about your future, Caleb. Don't you want to be financially secure?"

He chuckled, "I couldn't tell you what that is. I've never had much money."

"Well, now you have some money. A substantial amount, knowing my mother's generous nature."

"Yes, ma'am."

"Take it to the bank today and get that safety deposit box. It's private. The bank will never question you about what you put into that box."

"Okay. I'll do that. In the meantime, I'd like to clear that yard for you."

Stephanie's voice came sleepily from the stairs, "Mom? Who are you talking to?"

"I'd like you to meet someone, Steph. Come in here."

The girl made it as far as the kitchen entrance when she stopped and gaped at Caleb who had turned and offered his hand in greeting. Her face went white. Caleb bounded to her and caught her as she fainted.

"Oh, my gosh!" Ida blurted. "Take her to the sofa."

As he set her very gently there, he amusedly inquired to Ida, "Does your daughter always faint when she meets new people?"

Ida stifled a giggle. "It's a strange thing. You look exactly like a distant ancestor of ours, a young man who died very young about a hundred years ago. She's been obsessed with finding out how he died. I'll have her show you his picture once she wakes up and gets her bearings."

"Is that why you looked at me in the same way when you first opened the door?"

"Yes."

He smiled, thought a few moments. "Your mother used to think this house was haunted."

"Don't ever tell Stephanie that!"

"No siree…" he replied.

An hour later, as Ida and Stephanie observed him clearing the weeds from the yard, Stephanie said to her with a silly grin on her face, "Please, Mom, please, can we keep him?"

10

It was near five o'clock when Caleb arrived at Three Valleys Bank in the heart of Providence. He deposited the hundred-dollar check Ida gave him in payment for the day's work at Ms. Grace's old place, and then rented a safety deposit box and stowed the envelope containing twenty thousand dollars there. He had never seen that much money in his life, and the idea of just *having it* caused him some anxiety. It wasn't enough for a down payment on a small house but, as Ida advised him, he could build the money through smart investments.

Sitting behind the wheel of his truck in the parking lot, Caleb counted the cash in his wallet. He had one hundred and twelve dollars. It would pay for a decent motel room for the night. He reconsidered when he remembered he needed gas. One other possibility came to mind. Gene Blackwell still owed him thirty for their last job. Gene was good for the money and had promised him he'd have the cash for him by today. Caleb decided this was a good time to head out to Reyton to see him, not only for the money but to tell him what happened at Ida's and show him the list of work she needed done. As an added plus, Gene had a new washer and dryer, and Caleb had a duffle bag full of laundry. If all went well, he could wash his clothing there and bum a meal at the same time.

He filled the tank on his way out of town and took the back road into Reyton to avoid the commuter traffic. It was a quiet ride on the narrow two-lane road into the sparsely populated northern hills. There were no other vehicles behind or ahead. Caleb rested his foot lightly upon the accelerator, his spirit lulled into exquisite serenity by the stillness and isolation. The arid golden hills dotted with ancient oak trees rolled to the cloudless amethyst horizon leaving the sweet perfume of dry grass in its wake. Caleb inhaled it deeply as he rested his elbow upon the ledge of the open driver's side window. He delighted in the baking summer air that caressed his cheek and played havoc with his hair. It was in moments like this he felt free, and he wished he could feel this way all the time.

He crossed over the little bridge above the dry creek bed that would be raging water in wintertime. There was a story the bridge was haunted by a murder victim found dead in the creek during the eighteen-nineties. Caleb slept overnight there one time, just to see for himself. No ghost ever materialized, and he dozed like a baby until the mosquitoes rudely woke him. So much for small town rural legends, and damn the mosquitoes. Caleb mused for a few moments about becoming an exterminator.

Naw, I'll stick to construction.

He loved the physical workout that came with the job. He loved learning how things worked, loved learning how to build things and how to fix things. Once he mastered the craft, (and Gene was a good teacher) he could take those skills anywhere.

He turned the truck left at the sign on the main road that read, "Blackwell Construction" that had a big faded red arrow pointing to a gated dirt road. Gene left the gate open unless he was gone for the day. His turquoise Chevy pickup bounced and kicked up yellow dust on the long gravel drive that led to Gene's property. He parked in front of the wide metal shop that sat diagonal from the small white house with its immaculate screened-in porch. Caleb shut off the engine and let the dust settle before he exited the vehicle. He saw Gene's big white truck in the open garage.

Heavy silence lay upon the landscape like a warm flannel blanket. In an hour or so, the songs of insects and critters would fill the air, a symphony Caleb found comforting. If he had his choice of places to spend the rest of his life, this would be it.

He felt something weave around his leg. He bent and lifted the skinny black and white cat and brought her to his chest. "Hello, Petunia. How is my pretty little girl?"

She squinted at him and purred, rubbed the top of her head against his chin. He gave her a kiss, and cuddled her, stroked her soft fur. She was an old lady, as far as cats go, and he was careful to be extra gentle with her. "Where's the old man, huh?"

Gene poked his head out the door that led from the garage into the kitchen. "I thought that was you. I got your money for ya."

"I'll take twenty-five if you let me use your washer and dryer."

"What the hell. I'll throw that in for free. Come on in." He held the door open as Caleb grabbed his duffle bag out of the truck bed and entered the house still holding Petunia to his chest. Gene chuckled at him. "I do believe that girl's in love with you."

Caleb snuggled her, "Are you in love with me, Toonie?"

"Aw, get your ass in here before the neighbors see you."

"What neighbors?"

"Them ground squirrels out there. They're laughin' at you. Can't you hear it?"

"Why, Mr. Blackwell, I believe you're startin' to go a little bit loony out here in the sticks."

Gene guffawed and amicably slapped his shoulder blade. "Damn good to see ya, boy. Want a beer?"

"I'd better not. I made a promise."

"To who?"

"To me."

Gene grabbed a beer and a Shasta Cola out of his fridge. He tossed the soda to Caleb. "Teetotaler." Then, with a point of his thumb toward the metal shop outside, "How's the truck runnin'?"

"Great. No problems. I sure appreciate your fixing it, Gene."

"Well, you need it if you're gonna keep workin' for me."

"I'm glad you still want me."

"Just don't fall through any more roofs, dammit."

"Well, at least I found the rotten spot for you."

"Smartass." Gene plopped his ample weight into the solid oak chair that matched the round solid oak table off his kitchen. He motioned Caleb to take his choice of the other three chairs. Caleb took the one that faced away from the wall and gave a view of the dry foothills out the sliding glass door. The sunlight cast shadows within the crevices between the mounds, shimmered upon the dark brown trunks and branches of the scattered oak trees. A parade of cows trod in a line toward the crest of one of the hills to the feeding trough at a neighboring ranch below on the other side. Gene paid no attention to the view. He took a roll of bills from his pocket and removed a twenty and a ten, and gave them to the boy. "You've been doing damned good work." He then removed an extra ten as an afterthought and slid it to Caleb. When Caleb protested, Gene said, "Just shut up and take it, you skinny bastard."

"What's on the schedule for this week?"

"Got a deck that needs waterproofing over on Thornwood in Cedars tomorrow morning. Let's see, there's an electrical upgrade up in Valley View Ridge, but you're not trained for that yet. How about you take the deck job? You can't screw that up. I'll be with you for some of it, till you get your waterproofing wings. How's that?"

"Well, I just finished some weed whacking over at Grace Tarantino's place. Her daughter Ida has a list of jobs for us—well mostly for me, but a lot only you can do. What day would that deck job be?"

"Tomorrow."

"Perfect! Grace—I mean Ida—wants me to repaint a couple of rooms there on Friday. She also wants to show you some stuff she needs done that I can't do."

"That's on Friday? I got a foundation job a couple miles out that way on Friday."

"Well, can you—"

Gene had opened his schedule planner and his attention was dedicated there. "I also got a toilet and bathroom floor to replace in that same neighborhood on Tuesday. If you can get there between your jobs at Grace's place, you can help me with the toilet. My back ain't what it used to be."

"Got it."

Gene stretched his meaty arm across the table. "Lemme see that list you got. Where's your schedule book I gave you?"

"In my binder out in the truck."

"Won't do you no good in there."

"Can I start my laundry first?"

"And I suppose you want dinner."

"We can order pizza. I'll pay."

"That's like the church mouse telling the pastor, 'I got a donation for the basket.'"

Caleb rolled his eyes.

Gene said, "Lucky for you I just went shoppin'. How about ribs off the barbecue?"

"Now you're talking!"

"You need to flop here?"

"No. It's warm enough tonight. I'll be fine."

"Never saw anything like it… you always sleepin' in the bed of that damned truck."

"I like the stars over me."

"It wasn't that way when you had that little cottage at Grace's. Goddamn… I miss that woman. Well, go get your laundry while I look over this list here. What'd you say her name was—that daughter?"

"Ida"

"Well, if she looks anything like Grace did when she was younger…" He slowly shook his head, grinned and whistled. "Man, oh, man! Grace was a looker!"

"Yeah. She showed me her old photos."

"A *dish*, man!"

"Oh, yeah."

"God, I miss that woman! Is her daughter gonna let you have that cottage back?"

"She hasn't decided. She's got a daughter of her own she wouldn't want the likes of me to be around."

"The likes of you? Shit! She'll change her mind."

"I don't know. We made a deal that I'll work for her while she decides if I'm a threat or not."

"Ain't her husband got a word to say about that?"

"She's a widow."

"And I'm probably too damned old for her."

"I don't think she's looking for anyone."

"They never are. How long's she been widowed?"

"I don't know."

"How old's her daughter?"

"I don't know. Fourteen or fifteen, I'd guess."

"Good lookin'?"

"She's okay. Kinda scrawny and wiry. Future jail bait, for sure."

"Smart boy, Caleb. You keep it tucked away and stay outa trouble."

"That's the last thing on my mind these days, Gene."

* * * * *

Caleb smelled food cooking as he applied the paint roller with careful light strokes on the east wall of Ms. Grace's former bedroom. He stepped back and checked his work. The coats of light peach colored paint were even, and he had managed to get very little on the blue painter's tape covering the window frame and the crown molding.

One wall to go… He moved the paint tray and two-gallon bucket to the wall that included the closet. Ida wanted the inside walls of the closet painted, too. He removed the hanger bars and set it in a corner of the hallway with the shelves he had already painted, and then he stepped into the closet, his heavy work shoes making indentations upon the brown paper he had pre-set on the floor there. It was a walk-in closet, easier to move in than the elongated versions found in modern homes. However, it reeked of stale lilac from the fragrance packets Grace had generously thumb tacked to the interior walls, and he found the odor revolting. He was looking forward to applying the first coats of paint there that would eliminate the scent.

The rib roast baking in the oven downstairs sent a reminder to his gurgling stomach that he had skipped breakfast with Gene to arrive early for this job. Voices drifted up, Ida's and Stephanie's, plus a deep masculine voice. Laughter.

Stephanie exclaimed loudly, "I'm serious, Quinn! Tell him, Mom!"

Conversation. Caleb could not discern all the words, yet the joyousness in their tone reminded him of all the times he and Ms. Grace talked and laughed. She was a real character sometimes, occasionally smoked pot out on the veranda off the kitchen; said it helped relieve her arthritis. The higher she got the more she talked about the past: thumbing her way across the country to California to escape her wealthy suffocating parents, her short stay at a cattle ranch in Nevada, her short stint at U.C. Berkeley (which she dropped out of), and how she met Rudy Tarantino there. Rudy brought her home with him to meet his folks at this very house. She was pregnant then with Ida and they married just before Ida made her debut into the world. She said she met Janis Joplin once. Caleb never believed that story; Grace had smoked a full joint by then and had drunk half a glass of wine. He knew from experience that people tended to come up with all kinds of stories when they were high, stories that were nothing but wishes that never happened. Ms. Grace was full of stories. Whether they were real or fiction didn't matter to Caleb. He recognized her true happiness lay in days past, and it distressed him to see her falling further into self-medication to numb her grief.

One night, a night that happened to be her wedding anniversary, he found her on the veranda as high as the moon, having a conversation with her dead husband Rudy who, at that moment, was the walnut tree in the yard. She was talking away to that tree, "Oh, Rudy! We just gotta take Ida to see the Grand Canyon before school starts up. I want us to go see it again. You work too hard, you really do." At that point, Caleb relieved her of the drink in her hand, and poured it in the dirt, at which point she giggled and asked him, "Now, Caleb... why'd you go and do that?"

"Because I love you, Ms. Grace, and I can't let you do this to yourself."

She followed him as he gathered every alcoholic beverage and every joint she had stashed, and then she followed him into the kitchen and watched, laughing gleefully, as he put it all down the garbage disposal. And then, when he thought he had gathered everything, she pulled a joint out of the pocket of her robe and ceremoniously dropped it into the garbage disposal. As the machine ground it up, she laughed triumphantly. Ms. Grace Tarantino never touched the stuff again.

At least Grace was happy when she imbibed, not like his mother and Richard who stayed high all the time and were hostile toward the world, each other, and him. His life with them would have been tolerable despite that until they discovered meth.

Caleb had to remind himself that was all in the past. He had to keep moving forward, as far away from the wreckage as possible. It was better now. It was all better and would keep getting better so long as he kept his head straight and his body strong.

He finished the closet "lickety-split," as Ms. Grace used to say, wrapped the paint roller in a wet paper towel, then stowed it in a plastic bag and set it crosswise upon the sealed paint can. The closet door was outside on two sawhorses waiting for him to apply the pale blue paint to it, the same color Ida chose for the wainscoting. He at first thought the colors would clash, but once he saw the combined effect with the peach, it wasn't so bad after all. As he went out the kitchen door, he saw Stephanie painting the door with a fat boar bristle paintbrush. His blood immediately boiled over and he ran to her and swept the brush out of her hand.

"What do you think you're doing?"

She looked at him confusedly. "I'm painting the door."

"Not with this brush! And this is not your job! Who told you to do this?"

"No one. I thought I'd help."

"You're not helping."

At once, Ida appeared in the doorway, her arms crossed in front of her chest. "Stephanie, please come inside."

"I was just helping!"

"That was thoughtful, honey. But I'm paying Caleb to do this work. Come inside now and set the table for lunch."

Stephanie said in a low spiteful voice to Caleb, "You won't last long here with a temper like that."

Ever patient, Ida repeated, "Come inside, Steph." She waited until Stephanie was out of earshot, and then she casually approached Caleb, whispered to him, "Don't ever yell at my daughter. That is *my* job. If you have a problem with her, come to me about it."

"Yes, ma'am. I'm sorry."

Ida examined the door, "I'm sorry too. She sure made a mess of this. Can you fix it?"

"I have a special roller I use just for doors and other smooth surfaces. I can fix it, but it'll take three coats of paint to cover it. I'll try to rub some of it out before I start. Again, Ms. Ida, I'm sorry. I just want to do a good job for you."

She smiled warmly at him, "I understand. Don't stress over it."

"Thank you."

Quinn stepped out onto the veranda, a worried expression on his face. "Stephanie's really mad. What happened?"

Caleb answered, "I yelled at her for messing up this door by trying to paint it herself."

Quinn looked at Stephanie's disastrous attempt at painting. He laughed and told Caleb, "Man, that looks like a toddler painted it. I would've yelled at her, too."

Caleb smiled at Quinn, appreciating his honesty and compassion. Although Caleb regretted his behavior had hurt the girl's feelings, he felt some people had to learn the hard way not to infringe on someone else's territory. He busied himself trying to smooth out the sloppy, half-hardened ridges of paint with a damp rag.

Ida gently placed her hand on his shoulder. The warm sensation of her delicate touch caused him to quiver inwardly. "Caleb, I'd like you to meet Quinn. He lives up the road."

Caleb stopped long enough to extend his paint-stained hand to the tall, pale-haired boy. He then remembered the paint on his fingers and withdrew his hand. "Sorry. I'd shake hands with you, but…"

Quinn's heart sped up, and his mouth went dry. Grinning, he extended his hand, "No big deal." As Caleb accepted his gesture, Quinn said to Ida, "I was going to mention it to you. I decided instead it'd be more fun for you to find out for yourselves."

Caleb's eyebrows plunged. "What?"

Quinn replied, "You look just like Isaac. You could be twins."

"Isaac?"

Ida explained, "Our ancestor I told you about. Steph showed you his picture."

"Oh," he said with a brief chuckle, "Him." He felt like he was on display at that moment.

"You went to our school," Quinn reminded him.

Caleb waited for Quinn to explain why that was important in any way.

Quinn inquired, "How'd you graduate earlier than the rest of your class?"

Caleb didn't consider it as impressive a feat as Quinn's tone of voice indicated. "I finished all my courses."

"College prep?"

"Those, too."

"Which college are you going to?"

"None." He tapped the one dry spot on the door, "This is what I like doing."

Quinn's shoulders slumped with his confusion. "Oh."

"You don't need a college degree to make a good living," Caleb said. "Ms. Grace told me to do what I love." He quoted her, "*A fulfilled spirit is more satisfying than a bulging wallet earned doing a job you hate.*"

Ida smiled. "That's my mom, all right."

Quinn saw the wisdom in that, and he respected Caleb's easygoing outlook. He wished to emulate him. "I'd like to learn how to paint."

Caleb sensed the boy's desire to connect, a need he knew intimately. "We'll see."

* * * * *

Quinn enjoyed the candied yams with raisins the best of all the food Ida cooked for lunch. It felt like Thanksgiving and Christmas rolled together, everyone gathered at the table sharing conversation and laughter along with their delicious meal. While he was enjoying his second helping of the yams and raisins, chewing while he listened to the conversation between Ida and Caleb, he felt the familiar wave of vibration begin in his chest and then emanate throughout his body.

Someone's here.

His intuition told him which direction to look. Jake, his form almost transparent, emerged through the glass panes of the china cabinet doors. He began to circle the dining room table, his black aura stretching and tasting each of them until he finally hesitated beside Caleb. Jake bent and put his face close to Caleb's, his aura stretching once more and then embracing the young man. Quinn could see the image of Jake's thoughts, a memory of a young man who looked like Caleb but was not Caleb. Jake hovered beside him, and then his aura entered Caleb's body. Jake felt confused; Caleb resembled who he was looking for, but the soul inside his body was not the soul Jake expected to find.

"*Not Isaac...*" Jake murmured. "*Yes... no... yes... a remnant... yes... Oh! So tired. So tired. Not now, not now, hang on...*"

Jake slowly evaporated away, his shimmering black aura delayed for a few moments before it followed him.

Stephanie noticed Quinn gazing off as if entranced, "What are you looking at?"

"Oh," he answered slowly, "I was just thinking."

"About what?"

Quinn thought quickly. "I want to learn how to make this yams and raisins dish. It's so good."

This compliment touched Ida to her core. "Well, Quinn, the next time I make it, I'll have you over to help me. Okay?"

"You're on!"

Caleb added, "This truly is delicious, Ms. Ida."

Quinn caught Stephanie's resentful expression. No doubt, she was sending mean thoughts at Caleb, probably silently mimicking the young man's accent. Quinn wondered if the girl would ever forgive Caleb's earlier faux pas.

However, Quinn felt there was a more pressing issue at that moment than Stephanie's boiling ire at Caleb. There was the issue of Jake and the fact he had discovered Caleb and sensed something in him worthy of further investigation. What had Jake discovered?

"*...a remnant... yes...*"

A remnant of what? A remnant of Isaac's energy? A remnant of his soul? If Isaac had ever been at the table with them, Quinn would have seen him. Isaac was not there, had not been there in any possible form at all. Yet, Jake seemed to have detected a trace of the long-dead young man somewhere inside Caleb's soul.

DNA, as the doctor said; a fragment that had traveled for centuries and found its way into Caleb.

"When you get right down to it," the doctor had told Quinn, "We are all distantly related, right down to Adam and Eve."

I have to find some way to protect him, Quinn determined. He would have to find some way even if it meant revealing his secret.

* * * * *

Caleb continued to work there through the weekend until Ms. Grace's former bedroom and the guest bedroom downstairs were ready for the new furniture that was delivered on Sunday. He helped Ida arrange things as she wanted, he doing the heavy lifting and shifting, she doing the pointing, changing her mind, and pointing elsewhere until it was all perfect. In return, he got the best food he'd ever eaten, three hundred dollars cash, Ida's trust, and Stephanie's unremitting surliness. Ida assured him the girl would eventually forgive him for yelling at her.

"Would a dozen yellow friendship roses help?" he joked to Ida.

"Give her time, " Ida answered, "She's a teenager; you know how it gets."

"No, I don't." They paused at his truck in the driveway while he checked his schedule. "I'm helping Gene on Tuesday morning, but I think we'll be able to stop by that evening for him to look over the rest of the work you need done here."

"That will be fine. Give me a call and let me know for sure." She caressed the hood, "My dad loved this truck. I'm glad you're taking good care of it."

"It was so nice of your mom to—"

"I'm glad she gave it to you. When Stephanie gets her license, I'll give her Mom's car. That won't be long now."

"Tell her I didn't mean to hurt her feelings." He got behind the wheel, lowered the driver's side window, and set the key in the ignition.

Ida followed him and replied through the open window, "I already did. No worries. She'll come around."

At once Quinn's voice rang out calling to Caleb, "Don't leave yet!" He ran up the drive and stopped at the driver's side window.

Caleb ducked his head out the window, "What's up, Quinn?"

Panting, he said, "Our housekeeper Maria wanted to give this to you."

"Why does your housekeeper want to give me something?"

"Because I told her about you and she wants to butter you up to fix her c.d. player." He thrust a small Ziploc bag of colorful cookies to him through the window cavity. "They're Mexican cookies. Not real sweet, but super, super, good. She bakes them herself. And, there's something else—"

"Whoa! Thanks!"

Before Caleb could ask about the *something else*, Quinn pulled it out of his jeans pocket and set it carefully in his hand. "Now, I don't know if you're religious or not, but Maria has this thing about Jesus. She said this is to protect you. Just hang on to it."

It was a small metal crucifix. Caleb stared at it, wondering why she would think he needed "protection," and from what?

"Well, thank you, Quinn. Tell her I said thank you."

"Uh, Caleb...." At this Quinn leaned through and whispered, "Whether or not you're a Christian, just keep it."

"Uh..." Caleb peered at him confusedly. "I never thought about it. This is weird, Quinn."

"Well, uh, she gave me one, too. It's just something she does ever since her son died." His statement was half-truth and half lie. He had to come up with some explanation to get the sacred object into Caleb's possession.

Caleb didn't know what to make of this. "Okay."

"Just... keep it, okay?"

Caleb glanced at Quinn inquiringly, then examined the crucifix and closed his fingers over it. "What am I supposed to do with it?"

"Just keep it with you. That's all."

Caleb saw then the concern in Quinn's eyes. He didn't understand what was behind it, but he sensed there was plenty more to the story than Quinn was revealing. Now was not the time to inquire further with Ida present.

"I tell you what, Quinn. Tell her I'm gonna go buy a chain to hang it on so I can wear it all the time. That way I'll always have it with me. How's that?"

Relief washed through his face. "We'll see you again soon, huh?"

"In a couple of days."

"Good."

"You'll see it when I come back." He started the engine, then extended his hand to Quinn, and they clasped hands. "See you soon, Quinn. In the meantime, wipe that scowl off Stephanie's face."

"I'll try, man!" he replied, laughing.

* * * * *

Caleb splurged on a secluded room at a hotel given three stars by AAA. He took a leisurely shower and then took a soak in the bathtub just because he could. While soaking in the hot water amidst a mountain of bubble bath suds, he began thinking about AAA's hotel rating program and the people who did nothing except stay at hotels to rate them. What a cushy job that must be! And he decided, should he ever get sick of doing construction, he would apply at AAA for the job of Hotel Rater, or whatever they called the people who did that.

The bedroom smelled like floral air freshener with a hint of stale cigarette smoke. He leaned at the edge of the bed and slid open the window just a crack, and then he lit a cigarette and examined the fancy clear glass ashtray with the hotel's name, address, phone, fax, and website address. The printing took up the entire bottom of the ashtray. Gene had a collection of hotel and casino ashtrays; Caleb toyed with the idea of taking one for him. He changed his mind when he considered it as stealing. He had never stolen anything in his life and he didn't want to start now. The promotional complimentary matchbooks were another story, and he tossed two into his duffle bag, along with the leftover hotel shampoo, unopened spare bar soap, and small tube of toothpaste. That was not stealing. These items the hotel provided with the price of the room. *Not stealing.*

His belly was too full for him to rest comfortably. He arose wearing only his underwear and went out on the balcony where he took in the view of the river. It was a still clear night with a bright full moon reflecting upon the water. He leaned his arms on the railing and watched the moon and starlight dance upon the leisurely current. It was so peaceful, almost otherworldly.

"*Isaac?*"

The soft male voice came from his right. Caleb glanced over to the next balcony, expecting to see another guest. There was no one. He listened but heard no more. He decided the voice had come from the riverbank, someone calling for someone. By the time he finished his cigarette, he had not heard anything more and returned inside.

His clothing strewn across the end of the bed begged to be folded. He set about it after removing the clean clothes for the next day from his duffle bag. As he lifted the shirt to fold it, the crucifix Quinn gave him fell out of the breast pocket. He set it on the nightstand and finished folding everything and put it all in the duffle, which he placed on the suitcase rack. Fatigue setting in, he went to bed and leaned to turn out the bedside lamp. The light enhanced the details on the crucifix. Drawn by its beauty and curious about the details, he held it in his palm and looked closely at the man attached to the cross.

Caleb had never been to church, had never read the Bible, and only had a vague idea about the story of the man who had suffered a hideous death upon this Roman contraption of execution. He understood this thing Quinn's housekeeper had given him as a venerated representation of the man's sacrifice to save mankind. He had no opinion either way about the validity of the story. The earnestness in Quinn's eyes told him he completely believed it.

He was still puzzled as to why the housekeeper had given him this to protect him. There was once a time in his life when he was in danger every day. Those days were behind him. What could have given the woman the idea he needed protection *now*? How could a piece of metal protect him? Did it have some kind of hidden power?

He concluded the housekeeper's gesture was simply an extension of her natural maternal instinct to protect those she cared for, and perhaps her religious beliefs had much to do with it too. He remembered something Quinn said about a son who had died and a c.d. player that needed repair. Caleb couldn't recall everything Quinn had said. The one thing he remembered clearly was the determined expression in Quinn's eyes when he insisted Caleb keep the crucifix with him at all times. Caleb decided he would buy a silver chain for it in the morning so he could wear the thing around his neck under his t-shirt, and he would show it to Maria when they finally met. Tonight it would rest beside the ashtray on the nightstand beside his bed where he was sure to see it in the morning.

11

"I don't care what Mom says. I don't like him."

Quinn continued bagging up the piles of dislodged weeds at the perimeter of the old cemetery. "Give him a chance."

"I did, and he blew it." She raked more weeds into the pile, her expression grim with both the work and her mood. "I hope Mom doesn't give him the cottage. He doesn't deserve it."

"You don't know anything," Quinn said over his shoulder.

"And you do?"

"I saw how hard he worked when that place belonged to your grandmother. He was always working out in the yards maintaining everything. I saw him take apart the irrigation system and put it back together. It took him half the day, but he did it, and he fixed everything right. Those yards went from brown to green in no time, and he kept everything mowed and even pruned her rose bushes and stuff. You don't know a damned thing."

She slammed the rake down, the butt of the handle denting the hard red clay soil. "How do you know? You weren't there."

"I saw it from my roof."

"Oh, your roof. I forgot."

"The fourth of July is coming up. I can see the fireworks from there. Wanna sit up there with me?"

"Up on that sloping roof? Hell, no."

"We stand inside the widow's walk and watch it from there." He pointed at his house that abutted the cemetery. "See that space up top that looks like a room, that part up there with the short walls and the openings above the walls where windows could be? See that?"

She shielded her eyes from the sun and looked where he was pointing. "I don't know what you're talking about."

"See that loopy cross-like thing where the roof meets in a point?"

"Yeah."

"That open room below it is the widow's walk."

"Oh. Why do they call it that?"

"Because in the old days the wives of sailors used them to watch the ocean for their husbands' return. Sometimes the men never returned."

"There's no ocean around here, Quinn."

"It's just the style of the house," he responded, irritated.

"So, you watch the fireworks from there. How do you get up there?"

"There's a door from the inside. Gotta climb lots of stairs, but it's worth it. It's a hell of a lot easier than putting up with the traffic and parking, plus the five-dollar fee to sit in the park with all the asshole people and their bawling kids."

"And, you do it this way every year?"

"Every year with my mom and dad. Well, it's just Maria with me now. Dad doesn't care about it anymore. We bring snacks up there and have a swell ol' time. You'd enjoy it."

"And my mom, too, of course."

"That's right."

"Okay. I'll tell her. But, Caleb can't come. Don't invite him."

"I'll invite whoever I want."

"If you invite him, I won't come."

"Then have fun sitting at home by yourself."

"You can be a real asshole, Quinn."

"Like you're the first person to ever tell me…" He turned and glanced at the toppled headstones. "I wonder if he'd know a way to put these back up."

"Aw, Quinn! Don't get him involved with this! This is *our* project."

✶ ✶ ✶ ✶ ✶

On the morning of July fourth, Quinn interrupted Caleb and Gene as they were installing the air conditioner in the Stephanie Cave. The two men met him at the old cemetery as soon as they were finished. Gene assured Quinn they could do the job and offered to do it for free. The only thing he required was an original plot map so he would be certain to put the tombstones and headstones in the correct locations.

Quinn set about searching his father's home office file cabinets for the plot map. He couldn't find it there, so he searched the basement and found it up in the rafters in a dusty cardboard box containing old family photos, miscellanies, and local news memorabilia. He and Stephanie anxiously went through the contents of the box: Quinn for additional information about the cemetery, while Stephanie scanned the piles of ancient newspaper articles someone had cut out and saved.

Stephanie blurted, "Oh, Jesus! I found him!"

Quinn glanced up at her. "You found Jesus? Nice find!"

"Isaac was murdered!" She was shaking, and her eyes were practically bulging.

"What?"

"It says here he drowned in Riddling Creek. That's the creek that runs behind my house and into town behind where the mall is now. Right?" She barely noticed Quinn's nod as she continued, "There was evidence he had been beaten first, and his spine was broken!"

Quinn sat back on his haunches, stupefied. "Oh… shit!"

"Yeah. *Oh, shit.*"

"Did they find who did it?"

She shuffled through the articles until she found it. "They had a suspect. Some guy named Jacob Sheers. Isaac was courting his sister. I guess courting is the same as dating, right?"

Quinn shivered inside at the mention of the name *Jacob Sheers*. He hid his reaction as he replied to her question about courting. "That's what they called it back then."

She flipped to the next article stapled behind the first. "It says here the jury found Jacob not guilty, as there was not enough evidence to convict him. Why would someone in your family keep these news articles?"

"They were friends with the Tarantinos. Isaac lived in your house. They probably spent a lot of time together and knew Isaac well." Quinn knew additional facts as to why Isaac's death was important to them, but he kept it to himself so as not to further upset her. "So, what happened to Jacob?"

"I don't know." Stephanie rummaged through the box. "There's a lot of stuff here. Is it okay with you if I take it home for just tonight so I can read it all?"

He hesitated before deciding he could trust her. "Yeah. Just for tonight. Tell me right away if you find anything else. Bring it all back tomorrow. Promise!" After she promised, he waved the large folded paper in his hand, "I got the plot map, and now we can set everything right for the people buried out there, including Isaac."

She managed a weak smile. "Yeah."

He rubbed her shoulder. "It really sucks that he was murdered. So… hey…"

"What?"

"You're still gonna be here to watch the fireworks tonight, right?"

"I suppose."

"Are you gonna be mad at Caleb forever?"

"I'm not mad at him anymore. You know why?"

"Why?"

"He was careful not to mess up my cave while him and Gene were installing the air conditioner. He even touched up the paint on the window frame when they were done, and he didn't get a single drop on the floor. And then he complimented me on what a good job I did up there fixing-up and rearranging all the furniture. He said it was like taking a trip back in time, and he thought it was cool." She managed another smile, this one lit by genuine happiness. "I guess he's not so bad, after all."

"Is your mom gonna rent him the cottage?"

"She hasn't decided yet."

* * * * *

Quinn realized at the last minute he had two worries which necessitated his performing damage prevention as his guests arrived for his Fourth of July fireworks viewing: The first that Maria would discover Quinn had given the crucifix she had originally gifted to him to Caleb. Quinn's heart just about stopped for fear of both Caleb and Maria discovering his well-intentioned lie when Maria saw the crucifix on a chain around Caleb's neck. Maria, assuming Caleb was a good Catholic boy who had worn the thing around his neck for years, was very disappointed to learn Caleb had never attended church. She then spent a good three minutes trying to convince him it would be to his advantage to attend. Caleb gracefully assured her he would consider it, but simply could not at present due to his work schedule. As compensation, Caleb offered to repair her c.d. player, the only thing Quinn had been truthful about, and Quinn managed to intervene and steer Caleb away from her just before Caleb thanked her for giving the crucifix to Quinn to give to him.

Quinn's second damage prevention challenge came when, to Quinn's complete surprise and bewilderment, his father joined him and his guests on the terrace before the evening's conclusion at the widow's walk to view the fireworks. He discovered Gene Blackwell had been a friend of his dad for years and when Gene introduced

Caleb to him, John Vanderfield instantly took to the young man. This produced Quinn's second worry, which was that Gene or Caleb would forget their promise to keep the cemetery project a secret from his dad. His concern abated when he took Caleb aside and reminded him about it, and reminded him to remind Gene about it. Caleb assured him their secret was safe.

As to his father's sudden affinity toward Caleb, Quinn hovered between jealousy and happiness. He couldn't understand why he would be jealous since he had never felt close to his father. Quinn's happiness, however, sprouted from observing Caleb's acceptance and trust of John Vanderfield's fatherly interest in him. Caleb simply glowed with happiness as John took him on a short tour of the house and property, seeking the young man's advice about landscaping and minor repair projects, as well as sharing their fond memories of Grace Tarantino.

Quinn suspected part of their private conversation was about him as well. His suspicion was verified when at one point Caleb took Quinn aside to tell him, "Your dad's really cool. He's a good man. He loves you more than you realize. I never had that in my life until Ms. Grace and Gene. Do you have any idea just how blessed you are?"

To which Quinn countered defensively, "My dad's a workaholic drunk who bullshits people into thinking he's a great guy."

"If that's all you've got against him, you're goddamned lucky. If you only knew the mess I barely survived. And, no—I'm not gonna talk about it. I just want you to take a second look at your life and see how good you've got it."

Quinn bristled at Caleb's straightforward manner. "I didn't invite you here to lecture me."

"I'm speaking plain to you because I like you." Caleb cast him a brief gentle smile that put him at ease. "Let's go for a walk while they're all chowin' down on that barbecue. The fireworks'll start soon. I don't want to miss it."

"Walk where?"

"How about we sit on the front steps while they all stay back here? I don't want them butting in. I want to ask you about some stuff privately." Taking the lead without waiting for Quinn's response, Caleb strode toward the front of the house with an air of purpose.

"What stuff?" Curious and wary, Quinn kept pace with him.

"First off," Caleb began compassionately, "I don't take lightly your dad's drinking problem, but I suppose he's got some kind of devil behind it that he doesn't have the strength to battle right now. Whatever it is, you are not the cause of it. Get that through your head. I've seen this all enough in my life to know what I'm talking about."

Quinn felt the tightness in his shoulders loosen; surprised Caleb detected his inner battles. "Okay."

"Second," Caleb continued considerately, "You've kind of put me and Gene in a bind keeping the cemetery project a secret from your dad. Why don't you want him to know what you're doing?"

Not prepared or willing to explain it, Quinn stammered, "I, uh, want it to be a surprise for him. He hasn't had the time and doesn't want to spend the money to clear it out. I decided I'd do it just so he'd see I could do something good on my own and do it right. That's all there is to it."

"Well, now," Caleb replied perplexedly, "Stephanie tells it differently. From what she said I gathered you're doing this more for those buried there than for your dad."

Quinn did not feel comfortable enough with Caleb to confirm that. Most people would see his efforts to tidy up for the dead as just plain weird. It was bad enough Stephanie had broken his trust by telling him. Yet, Stephanie's breach of confidence provided a good way to steer the conversation away from his eccentricity. "Goddamn Stephanie…! She's a ditz. She don't know what she's talking about."

That damned brief and oh-so gentle smile Quinn was beginning to mistrust accompanied Caleb's statement once more. "So you just want to show your dad you can do this on your own; this grand, great, exhausting project for *him*."

Bastard hangs on like a pit bull. "That's what I said. I guess Stephanie didn't understand that part."

"Does Maria know about it?"

"Maria can't keep a secret."

Caleb studied him, his lowered eyebrows and twitching jawline indicating his contradicting thoughts. His face and eyebrows subsequently relaxed, which told Quinn he had made a decision. The thought crossed Quinn's mind Caleb would make a very good cop, and with that thought, he tried his best to adopt a poker face. Caleb reacted to that with an intentionally disarming smile that did not disarm Quinn, and, with that smile, Caleb assured him, "I think it's a good thing you're doing, Quinn.

And, thanks for inviting us all here, by the way."

"I'm glad you came." *Actually, I wish I hadn't invited you.*

They rounded the corner of the house and settled upon the front steps. Caleb took a few moments to glance over the front of the property, and then he swiveled and looked at the house itself. "This sure is a nice house. Your dad said it's been in your family since they first settled this town."

Thank you for changing the subject. Quinn bit his tongue between his teeth. He had a choice to refer to his father disdainfully, as was his habit, or refer to him neutrally to discourage Caleb's further investigation into his life. He chose to adopt neutrality in his voice as he replied, "He didn't want it. But when my grandfather died, Dad found out he'd been on the deed since he was born. My mom was the one that wanted the house. She made Dad sell their house in town and move in here. Been here ever since."

"It's a lot of house."

His home was the one thing he was proud of. "It's been modernized over the years. Our garage used to be a carriage house back in the old days. My grandfather had walk-in closets installed upstairs 'cause the originals were too small. He discovered some hidden rooms in the process. Don't know what those were used for—storage, maybe." Quinn added with a chuckle, "Got one floor we've never used."

"It's nice to have a family home no one can take away. It'll be yours someday, huh?"

"I hope so." He couldn't help but feel sorry for Caleb that he had no permanent place to live. Now he understood what Caleb meant by how good he had it. Was Caleb hinting around to rent a room? If so, he was shit out of luck. Quinn liked his privacy and had no intention to give it up for anyone.

Caleb lit a cigarette. Quinn gestured for one, and Caleb gave him one and lit it for him. They sat there smoking and appreciating the beauty of the evening and warmth of the weather. Quinn expected Caleb would have more questions he didn't want to answer, and the young man proved him correct. He felt a sinking feeling in his chest as Caleb produced the crucifix from under his t-shirt and held it up for him to see. "I couldn't help but notice you were hell-bent on getting me away from Maria. What's the real story on this?"

Quinn tried to sound casual about it, "Well, it's just that once she gets going on religion she can be kind of overbearing. I wanted to save you from that."

A perceptive smile lifted one corner of his mouth. "I can smell bullshit ten miles away, Quinn."

Quinn glowered at him and finally surrendered. "She originally gave it to me as a gift. I didn't want her to know I gave it to you. I thought it'd hurt her feelings that I gave it away."

"Why'd you give it to me?"

Quinn shrugged, tried to think up a good lie, couldn't come up with anything.

Caleb pressed, "You seemed determined about me keeping it… for my protection. Protection from what? I'm curious."

"I… I don't know. Why are you giving me the third degree? What the hell! What'd I do?"

Caleb scooted closer to him, looked straight into Quinn's eyes with pure sincerity. His voice came gently, his Louisiana drawl more pronounced with his emotion. "I'm just trying to understand you. It's taken me a long time to learn to trust people. I wanna know I can trust you. I don't like games." When Quinn offered no reply except a frustrated sigh, Caleb continued. "Why is it so important to you that I keep this crucifix with me at all times?"

Quinn answered with a partial truth after some creative out and out lie-concealing planning. "Because I know you've had a rough time. I used to hear them talking at school behind your back. Stuff about how you looked and smelled, and how you were so quiet all the time. I figured your home life was pretty bad—didn't take a genius to figure that out. But, since you and I have got to know each other a little, I got to thinking about how the… darkness… yeah, the *darkness* of those… circumstances… can follow some people for the rest of their lives. I believe the blood of Christ protects us from that darkness. That's all. I think you deserve a good life, Caleb. I want you to have light in your life. I'm sorry if my good intentions rubbed you the wrong way." He thought he handled that very well, although his comments about Caleb's school days elicited a hurt frown from Caleb. To soften the blow, he grinned encouragingly and added humorously, "But the *cookies* really were a gift to you from Maria, if that's worth anything."

Caleb laughed, which caused Quinn to laugh with him.

"Do you still want to learn how to paint?" Caleb offered.

"Yeah." On second thought, he wanted to kick himself for agreeing so readily. Was Caleb's offer in friendship, or was it cast as bait to manipulate him as so many others had done in his past?

"I'm gonna make some birdhouses for Ms. Ida. How about you help me paint them?"

Yet, Quinn could not resist playing along just so he could prove himself right. "That'd be cool."

Caleb slapped his hand on the boy's shoulder, gave him an appreciative smile. "We'll do that soon, then. Now, let's get some of them ribs before they're all gone."

The spontaneous fond glint in Caleb's eyes convinced him Caleb was sincere. In his heart, he hoped it was true.

* * * * *

The party had gone better than Quinn expected. Stephanie had not objected when he briefly held her hand as they viewed the fireworks from the widow's walk. What surprised him more was Ida's unspoken consent when she saw him holding Stephanie's hand. He took that as a good sign the woman approved of him, and did not fear he would become a drunk like his father. Disheartening, though, was the fact she was very disappointed in John Vanderfield as she discovered just how serious his alcoholism had become over the years. Yet, she did her best to hide it, although it was apparent to Quinn. When he took her aside to apologize, she told him, "It's not your fault. Don't let it spoil this wonderful party. We all have our problems. His problem does not reflect upon you. I want you to know that."

At this moment, his father was comatose in the king's throne in front of a rerun of "*1776.*" Their guests, forbidden to help clean up after the party, had left. Maria was in the kitchen scouring pots and serving dishes. Quinn was cleaning the barbecue grill with a wire brush, the yard lights obscuring the starlight and sending shadows upon the property. His thoughts bounced from his conversation with Ida to the recollection of the warm and soft sensation of Stephanie's hand in his, to his very unsettling conversation with Caleb. He still wasn't sure if Caleb was his friend, or if he had blown it by trying to protect him with the crucifix and then lying about it. But if Caleb learned the truth, how would he react? There were too many possible scenarios, and they bounced around in his brain like tiny balloons in danger of popping among the flying electrons there.

Jesus... Balloons and flying electrons. Does anyone else's brain come up with visions like this?

His toes began to vibrate. The vibration traveled up his legs, spread like hot water through his torso and up into his brain. Colors. Humming.

Aw, shit...

Jake's voice from beyond the hedges at the side of the house, "Ollie ollie oxen free!"

Quinn abandoned the grill and followed the sound to Jake where he whispered to him, "Have you been lurking around here all this time?"

"This ain't the first party I wasn't invited to." He chuckled at his own remark and then became serious. "You haven't done shit to help me, Quinn. Keep this up, you're gonna find my patience is limited."

Quinn was too tired to deal with him. "I'm not a magician that can conjure up a dead guy for you. I need time to sort this out."

"Don't test my patience." He glared at Quinn and shot his sparking aura into Quinn's body.

Quinn doubled into himself in fear and reaction to the burning. "Give me time, damn it!"

Jake giggled snidely. "There's more where that came from. I'm giving you a month to bring me results. I've got a strong suspicion Caleb is the key. You know what to do. Don't disappoint me."

Quinn tried, but Caleb guarded his privacy like a mother bear guards her cubs.

12

July passed slowly, hot, dry, yet with perfect nights of bright starlight and shooting stars. Most nights Caleb enjoyed the celestial show from the bed of his pickup truck, content with the weather and the forward progress of his life. Between his jobs with Gene, he worked at Ms. Ida's home making small repairs and bringing new vitality to the gardens and yards that circled the property. One day he snuck behind the hedges to the cottage nestled in the center of the copse of pines, curious to get a closer look at it, for that one day he had brought the furniture there Ida had given him, he had not had time to check it out. His heart sunk at the sight. The roof and downspouts were loaded with pine needles, as was the small porch. Fat brown spiders had built webs in the corners of all the windows, and there was a hole at the corner of the foundation where a rat or something had made an entrance. He took time to assess the damage, decided it was nothing he couldn't fix—and he wanted to fix it, whether the cottage would be his or Ms. Ida would find another use for it. He wanted to discuss it with her, but was uncertain if it was too soon. He was sure she would interpret his intentions as trying to secure the place for himself. So, the cottage sat in its dilapidated condition for another week as July unhurriedly rolled on with higher temperatures and gusty winds.

* * * * *

On the third Monday of July, Ida met John Vanderfield in town for lunch at a small Mediterranean restaurant. Her reasons were simply to get his input and advice on matters she had been considering and putting off for the last weeks. After some reminiscing about their high school days, they moved on to discussing their family woes (as in Quinn and Stephanie), and when that was exhausted, Ida brought up what mattered to her most at the moment: her search for a competent financial advisor, and if she should allow Caleb to resume residency in the cottage. The financial advisor was a slam-dunk; John gave her the contact information of the man he trusted. The subject of Caleb required further discussion that took more time and a second glass of house Pinot Grigio.

"He's a very industrious young man," John began. "Gene told me he's never been any trouble. Very well-behaved, eager to learn, eager to work." John paused to down a generous sip of his wine. "He said the kid's kind of stodgy, like an old man, in the way he leads his life. Not one for going out chasing girls, never even caught him with a girlie magazine. Quiet most of the time, like he's thinking about something, you know, preoccupied with his thoughts."

"Do you have any idea why my mother set him up in the cottage?"

"Because he worked there, I guess."

"According to Caleb he was about fifteen or sixteen when he moved in there. Now, why would my mother trust a kid to live out there in that isolated cottage all by himself? It makes no sense to me. And, why did his parents allow it?"

"You should ask Gene."

"Why?"

"He and your mother were friends since childhood. I doubt there was anything she kept from him. If anyone knows the whole story, it's him."

"And, here's something else: I remember just about everyone who attended my mother's funeral, including you and Quinn, but I don't recall seeing Caleb there."

"Caleb was there."

"No. I would have remembered. I would never forget someone with eyes like his."

"He was away from the rest of the mourners. He and Gene stood away by the cemetery personnel behind you. I remember it because he was wearing a suit that made him look like he was one of them, only he was crying."

"Oh, my gosh… I really didn't notice—"

"You were mourning, Ida. When Bernice died I was in such a blur, I hardly remember the funeral at all. And, Ida… I'm sorry I didn't know about Ned and his funeral. I was gone all that month up north with Quinn. I wanted to get him away from the memories of his mother for a while." He looked away and gazed at the pavement beside his chair. "A lot of good that did."

"It's hard on kids, especially when it's a parent."

"I don't know what to do with him, and school's starting soon. If it's anything like last year…"

"Stephanie will be there, too. So, maybe things will be different. They've become so close."

"Quinn likes her very much. I've been wondering if they're getting... uh... serious."

Ida found that amusing. "As far as I can tell it's basically friendship."

John couldn't hide the disappointment in his voice, "Oh."

His tone puzzled her. "What is it, John?"

"I destroyed his laptop."

"Why?"

"I caught him watching gay porn."

"When?"

"Last year."

This took her by surprise. She stammered a bit before she could put her thoughts together. "Perhaps he'd been watching *straight* porn before you caught him. Really, John, boys are very curious at that age. You know that. I remember you and Ned thumbing through *Hustler*."

"*Hustler* wasn't men doing men." John then leaned very close to her and whispered, "Or people actually *doing it*. What kids have access to nowadays is absolutely appalling! And *that's* why I won't let him have a cell phone! Do you know they've come up with cell phones that have Internet access? Who knows what that damned kid would be into if he had one of those!"

Ida sat back in her chair and thought about it. "I sure don't want Steph getting one of those. A regular cell phone is fine—for her safety. But unsupervised Internet? No way! Well, surely they must be way too expensive for kids to have, anyway."

"One of the boys working for me has one. I had to take it away from him because he was paying more attention to that than his work."

"We can't stop technology," she said with a sigh.

"And, here we are talking about our kids again."

"Well..."

"But what you really wanted to know about was a financial planner and that boy, Caleb. Right?"

"Was I that obvious?"

"You jumped right into it after our initial small talk. It's okay, Ida. I'll be glad to help you with advice when you ask me."

"I just don't know what to do about Caleb. My mother wrote me a letter stating she wanted him to keep living there—an oral agreement she made with him that she wants me to honor. He seems okay, but I've heard horror stories about tenants from hell. I can't for the life of me figure out what made her *adopt* him in the first place."

"Like I said, see what Gene has to say. I bet he knows."

The next evening, Gene met her at the outdoor dining section of a burger place on the two-lane road leading from the rural outskirts into Providence. The restaurant was in the same old building Ida recalled from her childhood, the business still owned by the same family that had run it for generations. Little had changed about it; even the outdoor tables and benches with their multiple layers of red paint were still the same.

The sun hovered over the western horizon above the mountains. The wind had died down, and the air had warmed considerably with only an occasional wisp of a breeze. The scent of broiling hamburger lingered with the aromas of hay, alfalfa, pine, and vehicle exhaust. At this time of day, traffic was light, and there were few customers at the restaurant. Ida and Gene had the outdoor dining area to themselves.

Gene ordered the giant "Trucker Burger" with fries and green salad for himself. Ida ordered a coffee milkshake.

Gene mumbled through a mouthful of burger that dripped mayonnaise and meat juice down his chin, wiped the mess with a napkin, and swallowed before he spoke again. "Now, what brings you here to dine with this fat old bachelor?"

"My mother and Caleb."

A grin lit up Gene's ruddy face. "That woman just loved him. Just loved him. He loved her just as strong."

"Why?"

"He treated her with respect. He listened to her, learned from her, cared about her. She taught him how to function through life; taught him how to care for himself, how to shop, how to cook his own food, keep a clean and organized house, how to manage his money. And… damn… that boy soaked it all up like a thirsty sponge. He gave her a purpose, and she gave him the love and encouragement no one else had ever given him."

"How did they meet?"

"When she was volunteering at the library."

So, he didn't lie about that… She needed to understand what compelled her mother to take in this reticent young man. "Why him? What drew her to him?"

Gene took another bite of his Trucker Burger, thought while he chewed. The impatience on Ida's face almost made him laugh. Finally, he swallowed his curd and replied, "The boy was there every day after school until the place closed. When summer came, he spent entire days there. That kid read just about every book they had, mostly on how to fix things, how to build things, how to live out in the wilderness, things like that. That ain't normal. So, one day she started talkin' with him, tryin' to find out his story. He dodged that by sayin' he loved books, and this was the only place quiet enough for him to concentrate. Said that's why he spent all his time there after school, too, to get his homework done."

"So, where he lived was noisy."

"You could say that."

"A large family, a lot of kids there? What?"

"He wouldn't want me talkin' about it."

"I won't tell him you told me. I need to know."

Burger in hand, he drew a long gulp of root beer through the plastic straw, thought about Caleb's ire if he discovered he had exposed the shameful truth about his life before *Ms. Grace*. But Ida's need to understand her mother's reasons for taking in the boy overrode Caleb's desire to leave it all in the past. Besides that, Gene knew Caleb was not happy bunking at his house; he needed his privacy and solitude so much he preferred to sleep in the bed of his truck under the night sky. Gene wanted Caleb to have what he needed most: a place of his own where he would feel safe.

"There were drugs at the house. His mother and her boyfriend were gettin' deeper into drugs. The place was becomin' a flophouse for drug users. He couldn't stand bein' there."

"Was there violence?"

At this point, Gene set his burger into the plastic tray that held his fries. He wiped his hands on his pants, glanced to be certain no one was near enough to eavesdrop. The coast clear, he leaned a bit forward, his elbows on the red-painted wood table, his fingers entwined, and his eyes sad.

"Daily. And, no one cared a lick about him. One thing Grace noticed was the odor. The kid stunk. He was always wearin' the same clothes and the same worn-out shoes his toes were growin' out of. His hair was long and always a mess. And then one day, she noticed he was hurt, had a sprained wrist—all swollen up. He had handprint bruises around both his wrists. His left ear was all red and swollen up. Well, she set him down privately where no one could hear, and asked him to tell her the truth of what else was goin' on. Well, the truth was that boy had been livin' in hell, and he couldn't go back anymore. He'd spent the weekend sleepin' behind the pallets on the loadin' dock behind the library. Hadn't eaten, or nothin'. Said he was just fine livin' back there, and he wasn't goin' home no matter what. Well, Grace got real mad, not at the boy, but at the so-called adults who should've been takin' care of him. She took Caleb out in her car and said, 'You're gonna pick up your stuff you need from home, and you're comin' home with me.' And that's what she did. She drove him home and went in with him to protect him while he stepped over all these passed-out druggies to get to his room that was also full of passed-out druggies. She told me that house was a pigsty, full of cockroaches, garbage, used needles, piss an' puke all over the floor, and it smelled god-awful of piss and who knows what else. Said she could hardly breathe. And those junkies never moved, never woke up—hell, some of 'em might've been dead—as that boy stepped over 'em. He came outa that room with only one thing: his birth certificate. That's all that was important to him. Grace and him left that filthy hovel and never looked back. Nobody, not even his no-good mother, looked for him. That's the God-blessed truth, Ida. And if you let on even a little that you know about this, that boy will never forgive me."

* * * * *

Early the next morning while Stephanie and Quinn were out on a bike ride, she set about cleaning inside the cottage. It had one main room that included a kitchenette. Off the kitchenette was a little space with a washer and dryer. A broom sat bristles up in the corner next to the dryer. The room behind the wall adjoining the little laundry room was a bathroom containing a toilet, sink, and shower. There was still a roll of toilet paper on the holder. Beside the bathroom on the other side of the wall was a small walk-in closet. Caleb had neatly stowed the bed rails, chest of drawers and bedside tables she gave him from her guest bedroom in there. In the main room, a sunken mattress sat on a box spring foundation on the oak floor. The bed was covered in a simple white sheet and a beige blanket, neatly made, and with a thin pillow in a white pillowcase. There was a small white table with a metal desk lamp beside the bed.

She removed the old yellowed lace curtains and the brown roll-style shades from the two windows in the main room, wiped the spider webs from the corners of the windows and cleaned the sills, cleaned the small oven and range top, wiped down the surfaces of the washer and dryer. The bathroom needed no attention; it was spotless. She cleaned the wall-mounted air conditioner, vacuumed the dirty filter and reset it.

Tired now, Ida rested at the edge of the worn-out mattress and re-thought her reasons for considering his return to the cottage. Was it only out of sympathy? Initially. It also made sense to her that he should live there if he was going to continue taking care of the grounds and making minor repairs when needed. It also occurred to her winter would be at the door soon, and Caleb – needing his privacy and therapeutic quiet—still preferred to sleep in his truck rather than Gene's home. Yes, he had the money from her mother, but that money would disappear fast renting motel rooms or even a small studio apartment. He needed to build that money, not spend it; Ida was certain that's what her mother intended.

John and Gene had both stated Caleb was the quiet sort, not a partier, a boozer, a druggie, or—God forbid—nuts in any way. He had learned self-control and personal responsibility from Grace Tarantino, and would make a good tenant because of it. Yet, there was so much Ida still didn't know about him. She sensed he was all wound-up inside and put much of his energy into controlling that part of himself that needed, *needed*, to let go and rage at the world, his mother, and all those who failed to recognize he needed help. He needed to rage at the injustice and violence perpetrated upon him by the very people who had no control over their own rage. Would he unravel someday?

Am I a damned fool for doing this?

Yet, her heart was telling her it was the right thing to do. Right for Caleb, and right in the fact that she would be honoring her mother's wishes. Thinking of her mother, she recalled the woman never did anything without giving it much thought. The woman trusted Caleb and, as far as Ida knew, Caleb had never violated her trust.

Gene had told her Caleb fell apart when Grace Tarantino died, and the young man still grieved. Gene said the loss of the cottage mattered to Caleb; but not as much as the loss of the only true mother he had ever known, the loss of a caring soul who had brought light into his existence.

Ida then made a list of things to buy, and she set off for town.

Two days later, she summoned him to the house to pick up his paycheck for the work he'd done for her over the past two weeks. They sat in the kitchen and discussed her idea for a gazebo in an area at the west side of the property. Her father's carpentry tools and equipment had sat idle for too long, she told him, and it was time he put them to good use. After he assured her he could do the work, she suggested they tour the spot, and afterward, she led him to the cottage and unlocked the door.

"Welcome home, Caleb."

He gazed in awe at the revamped space, the new bed with new sheets, blanket, and serene light blue bedspread with pale green stripes, and the matching pale green insulated curtains over the windows. Ida had placed both of the nightstands on either side of the bed. Matching lamps sat on both, and there was a beige touchtone telephone on the stand near the far wall. A white plastic ashtray and combination black digital alarm clock and radio sat on the other stand.

"I put a matching winter comforter and an extra set of sheets in your closet," she told him. "There are extra towels, too, and a portable oil filled space heater in there. Come see the kitchen."

She had fully stocked the kitchenette with a new set of cookware, dishware, silverware, towels, dishcloths, and cleaning supplies. On the counter sat a new microwave oven, coffee maker, and her mother Grace's old but well-preserved aluminum coffee service beside it. A new pine table, small and round, with two chairs glimmered with sunlight against the wall. A glass vase full of snapdragons, lavenders, white daisies and yellow mums adorned the center of the table.

Caleb rubbed his eyes, rested his fingers against his cheeks. "You did all this for me, ma'am?"

"*Ida*," she reminded him, smiling.

His eyes moistened, and he looked away from her. "You even put rugs on the floor…"

"Winters are very cold here, you know." She stepped over to one of the windows. "You also have new shades for privacy." She pulled the thick white shade down and then rolled it up again. "Gene repaired and repainted the rear porch for you so you can sit out and enjoy the summer nights and the sound of the water in the creek out there. He also cleaned the roof and the gutters for you, and got rid of all the spiders and their webs. Our exterminator comes every two months to spray, and this cottage is now included with the service. I had a telephone installed for you—your own number, not our house phone. If you want TV, you know what to do. I'll give you the extra TV from my house."

"No, I don't want TV. I like quiet. Thanks, though."

"There's still an extra bookcase in my guest bedroom. You can have it if you want."

His two boxes of books were still in the space behind the seats of his pick-up. "I'd like that very much. How much rent do you want?"

"None. Just be happy, Caleb." She pressed the keys into his hand.

"May I hug you, Ida?"

"What the hell…" She hugged him, and he hugged her with genuine gratitude.

"Thank you," he said softly.

13

Stephanie had an idea that brought her and Quinn to the Hall of Records department at the City Hall building in the heart of Providence. With Quinn in tow, she boldly approached the obese young woman at the counter.

"How may I help you?" The woman's voice had a high-pitched, child-like, quality. She revealed a gap between her front teeth when she smiled warmly at them.

"I need a copy of a death certificate."

"Name, date of birth, and date of death?"

Stephanie knew the date of death, but not the precise date of birth. She stammered, "I've got to do the math…"

Quinn stepped forward and gave the woman all the necessary information.

She typed it up into the computer and waited for the record to show in the system. "Yes, we have it here. That will be ten dollars."

Stephanie shrieked, "Ten bucks? Your website says five!"

"Oh. They haven't updated it yet. Sorry. It's still ten dollars."

Stephanie found only eight dollars in her wallet. "Will you take eight?"

Again, Quinn came to the rescue. He pulled a twenty out of his pocket and set it on the counter. "We'd also like a copy of the coroner's report if you have that."

"I'm sorry. We can't release that without a court order."

Stephanie inquired, "Will any of that information be on the death certificate?"

"In a condensed form," she answered, "None of the details."

Stephanie grimaced with frustration. "I really need that."

Quinn added a ten-dollar bill on top of the twenty. The woman eyed him suspiciously at first until he gave her a pleading expression. Her eyes darted to the twenty. She took the ten and rang it up. While she did that, Quinn retrieved the twenty and folded it into a square. When she passed him the receipt, he slipped the folded twenty into her hand as he took the receipt from her. She slipped the cash into her trouser pocket.

Pointing to the rows of empty chairs across from the counter, the young woman said, "Please wait over there. It will take a while, so be patient."

Quinn gave her his best and most sincere smile, "Thank you very much."

Although he was at least five years younger than her, she blushed and returned his smile. Still beaming, she went through the open doorway with a sign over it that read, "RECORDS."

As they sat, Stephanie whispered to him, "You sure know how to charm the ladies."

"I learned it watching the old man." With a sly wink, he added, "A little extra green doesn't hurt, either."

"You're very handsome, Quinn. Don't you know that?"

"I look like a dork."

"No, you don't. I bet a lot of the girls at school give you second and third glances, and you don't even know it."

"They look at me, all right—while they're laughing their asses off. I'm Providence High's running joke."

"I think that's your perception, not theirs."

The wheels began turning in his brain, assessing the validity of her comments. No female except his mother had ever told him he was handsome and, before Stephanie, no female besides his mother had ever considered him pleasing and worthy of their friendship. His negative feelings about himself challenged and challenged by someone of whom he had come to care deeply left him adrift. A glance at her soft sincere eyes proved she meant every word, yet he could not fathom how to respond. Finally, he opted to respond with ambiguity, "I don't care either way." Then, doing his best Humphrey Bogart impression, he told her, "Don't go gettin' all soft on me, Doll Face."

And, Stephanie, in her best Lauren Bacall, replied, "You're getting soft in the brain, Lefty."

And so it went, them doing bad impersonations of long dead movie stars for the next fifteen minutes until the woman from the counter returned with a manila envelope and set it in Stephanie's eager hands.

Quinn was craving an avocado sandwich, so they stopped at Belle's Coffee Shop where Stephanie read the coroner's report about Isaac's death, while Quinn ordered their food.

"He had been in the water for three days before someone found him." Stephanie read aloud in a morose whisper, "*Extensive and diffuse purpura*" (which she pronounced after a stumble as per-PEW-ra) "*extending horizontally across C3, C4, C5, and C6; dislocation of the C5 and C6 disks and multiple fracturing of the vertebra C4, C5, and C6 with fragmentation and dislocation toward the subject's left side.*" She stopped reading and asked Quinn, "What the hell does that mean?"

"Something to do with the spinal column. Keep reading."

"How do you know this stuff?"

"I've spent a lot of time in hospitals."

She frowned at him. "Did you order my coffee?"

"Yes, I did."

"What's *per-PEW-ra* mean?"

He corrected her pronunciation, "*Pur*pura."

"Well, what does it mean?"

"Bruising."

"Why don't they just call it that?"

Quinn smiled and replied drolly, "Then we could all be doctors."

"What are all those numbered *C's*?"

"The cervical portion of the spine, from the base of your skull to just at your shoulders."

Her eyebrows dipped and fused together, "You really know all this stuff, don't you?"

"Despite what my dad thinks, I *do* pay attention in class."

She slid the paper to him. "You read it and tell me what it says in plain English."

He waited until the waitress poured their coffees before he scanned the heading on the report. His eyes lit up and he exclaimed in a confidential tone of voice, "This is my third-great-grandfather! He was the coroner that wrote this report. I'll be damned… And all this time I thought he was just the town doctor and mortician."

Stephanie lowered her eyebrows impatiently. "How about that? Now, read the report and explain it to me."

He commenced reading silently, his lips seriously down-turned, his eyebrows scrunched close together in concentration. Now and then, he tilted his head to one side and then the other, muttered something unintelligible to himself, tilted his head again, and sighed sadly. Finally, he looked at Stephanie, his expression grievous as if he felt the victim's suffering. "It's bad, Steph."

"What? Tell me."

"It looks like someone struck him on the back with something wide and heavy." Quinn stretched his arm behind his neck and tapped the vertebra there, "Right here. That broke his spine. Either he fell or was thrown into the water. He couldn't swim because his legs were paralyzed and his arms were paralyzed, too. There was nothing he could do to help himself. He drowned."

"So, that's why it was ruled a murder..."

"Yeah."

She sank against the backrest of the booth, at first stunned. Her eyes filled with tears, and her cheeks and nose reddened. Her voice, when it came, quivered with the realization of what Isaac suffered, and she saw the scene in her mind, felt his panic and helplessness. "That's horrible! What he must have gone through in his final moments! Oh, Quinn! Poor Isaac!"

He reached across the table and gripped her hand. "Jeez, Steph!" he whispered, "Don't start crying *here*. Just chill. You can cry later."

"But the newspaper said he'd been beaten. Is that what they meant, or was there more evidence?"

Quinn silently reviewed the report again. After scrutinizing the information regarding the condition of Isaac's body this second time, he delivered the news to Stephanie in a confidential volume. "There were bruises and scrapes on his hands, arms and legs, and also scrapes along his ribs, forehead, nose, and cheeks. My third-great-grandfather's opinion was that the bruises and scrapes were caused by Isaac's body hitting logs and rocks as he floated downstream; but he was positive the cervical injuries were caused by an assault. You gotta keep in mind, this happened way before modern forensics."

"It's a horrible death..." She wiped her eyes with her napkin and then gestured to him for the report. He handed it to her and she replaced it in the envelope. "I'll look over the death certificate later, I guess."

"Yeah," he remarked gently, "This kind of shit sure spoils your appetite, don't it."

"Well, we ordered, so let's stay and eat."

"No more bawling until we head out."

She sniffed and nodded.

* * * * *

They showed the documents to Ida when they returned home. Ida was shocked by the news and didn't fully believe it until she read the documents herself.

"Well, you two are quite the detectives," she finally said after a while.

"It's horrible, Mom!"

"Stephanie, this happened almost a hundred years ago. There's nothing anyone can do about it. Please stop crying."

"I can't help thinking about what he went through."

"And now he's at peace. Let him rest in peace."

Stephanie gaped at her. "That's all?"

"It's time you stopped this. Let him go, Steph."

"They never found his murderer."

"And you won't either. They're all dead. Let God deal with it."

"You don't understand."

"Do you?"

Stephanie had no reply.

* * * * *

Stephanie had examined every piece of paper in the box Quinn had found in his basement back on July fourth, but discovered only one additional article related to the suspect in Isaac's murder: Jacob Sheers's father was a high-falutin' lawyer in the town of Providence, and he sent Jacob back East to attend Dartmouth University to study law.

Hungry for more information and having a gut feeling the Vanderfields were very close friends with her Tarantino ancestors, Stephanie convinced Quinn to explore his basement further for more boxes of Vanderfield historical items related to the Tarantinos and the early town of Providence. Quinn hunted and delivered his most important find to her: an old cedar hope chest that had the name *Emily* carved on the lid.

She eagerly retired to her bedroom soon after dinner that same evening and began to explore the contents of the chest. The top layer consisted of various articles of clothing accessories: three pairs of lace gloves in white, black and beige, a red silk scarf, a black hairnet, three pairs of woolen stockings in white, black and beige, and a crushed white hat stained with age which still held a fabric red rose missing some of its petals. Stephanie carefully removed the items and set them on the floor where she sat at the foot of her bed. Their musty odor rose up from the wood, and she wrinkled her nose and muttered, "Stinks… I thought they all used potpourri in those days, but I guess not. The stuff is sure pretty, though. Now, what else we got here?"

She spotted a small wooden box with a hinged lid along the left side of the chest, delicately lifted it and set it on her lap. The box was obviously handmade, the pieces connected by tiny brass nails the heads of which were green with age. The hinges and the clasp were also brass and tarnished. A carved single rose adorned the lid, and the phrase, "To My Love," in cursive like a title. The sentiment touched her heart and made her smile. Miss Emily Vanderfield obviously had an ardent admirer in her time.

Her smile became a frown of confusion when she opened the lid and found the name "Sarah" carved inside the lid. Stephanie wondered aloud, "Why would Emily have a jewelry box belonging to someone named Sarah? Oh, maybe she had a sister named Sarah. Of course. I'll have to ask Quinn. And I'm talking to myself again." She giggled self consciously as she removed the only thing inside, a small purple felt pouch with a tasseled purple satin drawstring. She felt a couple of small hard objects inside it and loosened the drawstring, dumped the contents into her hand: a little pearl pendant on a delicate gold chain, and a ring – a band of fourteen-karat gold. "Hmmm…"

Sarah's? Had Sarah gotten married?

Stephanie replaced the items into the pouch with the intention to show them to Quinn. She returned the pouch into the jewelry box, resumed her exploration of the hope chest's contents that were mostly holiday cards, postcards, souvenirs and memorabilia of local events and county fairs. The one thing she noticed was the fact the name and title "Vernon Sheers, Atty. at Law" was printed prominently on some of the event notices as the financier and coordinator, along with the name of one of Quinn's ancestors, Dr. Wendell Vanderfield. Stephanie assumed the good doctor was Emily's father. Other than the names, nothing about the advertisements and notices meant anything to her.

A neatly folded floral patterned quilt lay beneath the papers and cheap souvenirs. It was clean but reeked of stale wood odor, and she removed it without unfolding it and set it beside her.

Oh, my gosh…!

Two autograph books, one decorated in pink felt, the other in blue, the word

"Autographs" in gilt lettering on each. Beside them, two small books bound in brown suede containing the words, "My Diary" in cursive gold lettering. Stephanie discovered upon opening the diaries they both belonged to Emily Vanderfield, and all the pages were full of her penciled handwriting.

Stephanie exclaimed in a whisper, "Mother lode!" Her impatient curiosity screamed at her to drop everything to begin reading the diaries. She calmed herself and simply sat there with the little books staring up at her from her lap. "I can't read these while I'm this excited. I've got to calm down, got to wait, got to wait until I can concentrate. Oh, Quinn, you're gonna shit when you see all this stuff. No, wait… he can't see it till I've seen it first. I've got to be the first. I bet there's stuff about Isaac here. That's what I'm looking for. Gotta stay focused. Oh, Jesus… I've gotta stop talking to myself like some kind of nutcase."

* * * * *

At the same time, Jake lifted Quinn off his feet and pinned him to his bedroom door.

Jake tightened his dry cold fingers around the boy's throat. "Get it back now! Get it back from her or I'll kill her! I'll tear her apart right in front of you! Tear her guts out and feed them to you!"

Quinn's eyes were practically popping out of their sockets. He couldn't breathe. He wanted to obey, but it was impossible.

"Do you hear me?"

Somehow, Quinn managed to nod, *barely* nod. It was enough for Jake to release him and allow him to slide to the floor. Jake slid down with him and pushed his face into Quinn's.

"You've got seven minutes. Seven minutes, or I'll kill her mother, too. Get moving."

* * * * *

There came fierce pounding on the front door, frantic ringing of the doorbell, more pounding, and Quinn's hysterical voice, "Open the door! Open the door! Open the door!"

Stephanie heard her mother downstairs shout, "Stop it! I'm here. I'm here. I'm on my way!" Footsteps running with heavy footfalls accompanied the replies, and then the pop of the bolt lock and the door opening. "Good God, Quinn! Don't knock me over! What on earth?"

Hell Is In Me

Stephanie had not yet reached the upstairs hallway when Quinn bounded up to the landing and sprinted for her bedroom doorway. In the process, he swiped her aside with one arm and dived for the hope chest on the floor, began throwing the items inside it.

Stephanie knelt beside him, tried to shield the hope chest with her body. "What are you doing? You can't take it! Stop it!"

Panting, he wrestled her off to one side. He didn't look at her. "I'm in deep shit right now. My dad is super pissed. I wasn't supposed to give this to you or anybody. Get out of my way!"

"Give me one more hour to look through it all," Stephanie shouted.

Quinn practically screamed, his face red, his eyes full of desperation. "I've got less than five minutes!" He gathered what remained on the floor, tossed it into the chest and slammed the lid, stood with it in his hands and raced for the hallway. In his haste, he almost collided with Ida who had wisely stepped aside.

Stephanie descended the stairs hurriedly as he cleared the porch. He rushed down the front steps and dashed to the road before she could reach the foyer and the open front door. From there, she called after him, implored him to return, and ultimately cussed him out for ignoring her.

Ida placed her hand on Stephanie's shoulder and firmly guided her away from the doorway. She gently shut the door and locked it, gazed concernedly and disappointedly at her incensed and trembling daughter.

"The answers were right there," Stephanie moaned. "Right there."

"You have to stop this."

"But there were diaries. She knew Isaac."

"Stop it."

"But, I could've—"

Ida gripped the girl's arms, gave her a gentle shake. "Stop chasing the dead. I've had enough of this. *Enough!*"

* * * * *

Quinn replaced the chest to its place in the rafters in his basement. He threw an old sleeping bag over it to conceal it. Jake amusedly watched the boy's actions, delighted he had terrorized him into submission.

"You're gonna burn it," Jake demanded flatly, "You're gonna burn it all."

"I can't burn it all," Quinn protested, still trying to catch his breath. "It's against the law to burn stuff here in summer. How the hell can I do it without getting caught?"

"You've got that barbecue grill out back. Burn the shit piece by piece."

Spent and trembling, Quinn sunk to the concrete floor. "Maria will see."

Jake joined him there on the concrete. He pushed his face close to Quinn's, his expression stern. The energy from his aura danced through Quinn's body. "Tell her it's your shit."

Quinn felt his stomach churn, felt his insides burn as Jake's energy invaded him. "Tomorrow, Jake. Okay? I can't do it tonight. My dad'll be home soon. How could I explain it to him? Let me do it tomorrow when he's at work and Maria's off shopping."

"And you'll help me wake up Isaac."

"How is that possible?"

"Through Caleb."

"Caleb?"

"He sleeps in Caleb."

This didn't surprise him. Caleb's stunning resemblance to Isaac had gotten him thinking there was a genetic link. "Not Caleb. Don't hurt Caleb."

Quinn felt his eyes moisten and sting. He didn't know until this moment how much he cared for Caleb.

Jake regarded Quinn with sudden compassion. "I know how you feel about him. I know a lot about you, Quinn. In my day boys like you had to hide."

"I don't feel *that way* about him!"

"If he was that way, you would go for him. Admit it."

"You're wrong."

Jake smirked at him. "Am I?"

"Yeah. You don't know everything. And stop scanning me. You're making me sick."

"You're so delicate."

"Fuck you."

"I could live in you if I wanted to."

"Fuck you."

* * * * *

As soon as his father and Maria were gone the next morning, Quinn fired up the barbecue and burned all the paper materials from Emily's hope chest, including both autograph books and the only diary he found. He was curious to read the diary, but he could sense Jake's energy hovering behind him, and he didn't want to test Jake's temper. As the last of the paper charred and curled into ashes, Quinn voiced his acknowledgment of Jake's presence, and he did so in a very sarcastic manner.

"Are you happy now, you bastard? Or do you want the blankets and gloves and crap burned too?"

Jake responded by sharply slapping the back of Quinn's head.

"I did what you ordered," Quinn hotly retorted, "Keep your rotten stinking hands to yourself."

Jake appeared and, just out of pure meanness shot his aura energy through Quinn's body.

"You mother...!" Quinn hissed through his clenched teeth and the burning in his bones.

"I like you, Quinn," Jake said. "I like that you don't take shit from me. Just don't push me too far."

"Are we done here?"

"Burn the rest of the crap."

"It'll raise too much smoke. Someone'll call the fire department."

"Red lights and sirens! Whoo-hoo!"

"Be reasonable, Jake." It was a demand, not a plea.

"I don't care what you do with the rest of it."

"You killed him, didn't you?"

"Killed who?"

"Isaac."

"They think I did, but I don't remember doing it."

"Selective memory," Quinn said.

Jake replied fiercely, "I don't select my memories, asshole. There's not much left of my brain, not after those bastards got done shocking it."

"Shocking it?"

"Electric shocks."

Quinn took a minute to think, recalled a couple of movies he'd seen about crazy people getting electric shock treatments in archaic asylums. Was that what Jake meant?

Jake read his mind. "Yeah... just like that."

The very idea of it sent chills through Quinn, and he found himself feeling very sorry for Jake.

"They did other things, too," Jake said, "Things you couldn't imagine."

"So your dad never really sent you to Dartmouth."

"My upstanding, civil-minded, perfect father sent me to the mouth of hell. Not that home with him was much better."

"Tell me more. Tell me what you can remember."

"Why?"

"So I can understand."

"Understand what?"

"You."

"Why?"

"No one is born bad."

"Devils and demons are born every day."

"I don't believe that."

"You ain't seen what I've seen."

Quinn closed the grill lid and took a seat on the chaise lounge. This time he was determined not to piss his pants. He looked across at Jake who was still standing beside the grill, his swirling, frenetic aura sending shards of neon colors and black lightning into the air. "Does it hurt?"

"Does what hurt?"

"The black and everything."

"Of course it hurts."

"You once told me you are the sum of your mistakes. Do you remember?"

"Yeah."

"And the black is your punishment."

"Yeah."

Quinn sat forward, gazed at him thoughtfully. "Do you really think awakening Isaac will help you get rid of it?"

"I never said that."

"How will awakening Isaac help you in any way?"

A pathetic expression of misery filled Jake's face. His eyes filled with tears. "He can tell me what happened."

"You really don't remember?"

"They burned up my brain. How many times do I have to tell you?"

"What did you have against Isaac?"

"It was my parents. Nobody was good enough for them. Sarah loved him. That's all I remember. Sarah loved him and she went away with him. I can't remember the rest."

"Sarah?"

"My sister."

"Is that why you wanted Emily's diary burned? Did Emily write about it?"

"They were best friends. Sarah spent more time in this house," He waved his arms to indicate Quinn's house, "than our own. Emily knew everything. She knew too much."

"And I guess she made it easier for Sarah to see Isaac since Isaac lived right across the road."

"Girls are like that. Conniving little bitches."

"What were your feelings towards Isaac?"

"Not in our league; too common for a girl as fine as our Sarah. Like our mother, she could speak fluent French. She had manners, breeding, and grace. Mother and Father had plans for her, great plans. She threw them all away for a common woodworker. Everything that happened was Isaac's fault. He wouldn't let her go. She didn't want him to let her go. He tried to take her from us." At this, Jake doubled over and wrapped his arms around his middle. "I'm so tired. So much pain. I used to think I was in hell. Now I know hell is in me. You're my last chance, Quinn. Help me."

"I'll help you, but only under certain conditions."

"What's that?"

"I want my life back. I want my health back. No more torturing me with your black energy and no more popping in on me anytime you feel like it. No more threatening Stephanie, her mother, or Caleb. None of this was their doing. As for Isaac, you've got to give me time to figure out how to… wake him or whatever without Caleb knowing about it or suffering for it in any way. If you can't or refuse to meet my conditions, I will kill myself and you'll never find anyone else to help you."

Jake laughed. "You'll kill yourself?"

"To protect the rest of them, yes."

"You're full of shit."

"I've already tried it twice. I'm already three-quarters crazy from all of this. It won't take much more to send me over the edge. Think I'm bluffing?"

14

The cottage was filled with the aroma of lavender from the vase of flowers Ida had placed on the little table off the kitchenette. Caleb heard the scent of lavender was conducive to deep sleep, and the thought of lavender as sleep inducing was the last thing that crossed his mind as he slipped between the crisp sheets and rested his head upon the pillow. He drifted quickly into a peaceful sleep for the first few hours.

A pleasant dream played in his mind. Geese were honking in a pond far away to his left, and the ducks that had joined them replied with raspy calls. Far in the distance, sheep bleated in the damp golden-brown meadow under a gentle rain. The cool air smelled of apples, wet leaves, sheep dung, saturated mud, and lavender. *It isn't time for lavender to be blooming*, he thought as the fragrances drifted through the open door of the woodshed in which he found himself. He saw his own hands carefully manipulating a slender metal tool with a razor sharp tip, carving the finishing touches on the wing of a flying goose onto the top of the wooden backrest that he was conscious he would later attach to a rocking chair. He had already carved the big round moon in the center. Now finished with the first of the geese, he stood at a distance and viewed his work, judged it satisfactory. Tomorrow he would carve the second goose he had carefully drawn on the wood in pencil, a goose in flight three-quarters of the way past the upper left arch of the moon. He wiped the tiny wood shavings off the chisel and set it down with the other tools on the bench, wiped his sore hands along his denim trouser legs.

The rain began to fall heavier in a steady rhythm upon the slanted metal roof, and a soft wind came up and sent a cold wet breeze through the doorway. He sauntered over and leaned against the doorframe, watched the rain nourish the paths and meadow, gazed over to the main house where the gutters were dispatching the overflow off the roof onto the barren front yard. The thought crossed his mind he would be scything the weeds again next spring.

The sound of wagon wheels nearing the yard grew louder under the pointed tapping of raindrops. Caleb leaned out the doorway and saw an approaching surrey led by a gray mare. Two girls jostled side to side on the fancy black leather seat below the dark blue canvas cover. The passenger was a blonde haired sprite wearing a small gray rain bonnet that barely covered her curly hair. He somehow knew her name was Emily and she was fourteen years old. She had enormous blue eyes and a pert little nose. She was the genteel kind of girl every boy in town sought to make his own. Caleb found her attractive, but not attractive in the way that made his heart pound and his mouth go dry. That honor went to sixteen-year-old Sarah (*How do I know her name?*), who was at the reins. Although she was no beauty, he found her blatant honesty and rebellious spirit irresistible. His heart thudded at a merciless pace and his mouth went dry as the Mohave Desert the moment her eyes met his as she pulled back on the reins and brought the mare to a halt in front of the woodshed doorway.

She adjusted her wide brimmed straw hat the wind had blown askew. The cloth band encircling the hat matched her dark red skirt and hip-length overcoat. The band was long, draped through small slits where the brim met the crown of the hat, and she retied it snuggly under her chin to keep her hat in place. The daintily buttoned high collar of her white shirtwaist peeked above her overcoat like a second set of eyes. Her overbite, which he found charming, showed when she grinned at him, and her eyes sparkled mischievously. "Good afternoon, Isaac! Hard at work as usual?"

Emily tagged on, her voice deeper than Sarah's, "You're always working."

He wanted to reply to both of them, *My name is Caleb*, but instead, as if he had no control over his own faculties, he heard himself tell them brightly, "There's always work to do. What brings you to Casa de Tarantino today?"

Sarah's big blue eyes widened in an exaggerated manner, "And, in all this rain, too!"

Caleb, again conscious he was not in control of his reactions or his voice, or even the rapid pounding of his heart, remarked with a smile, "Yes, ma'am."

"Oh, Isaac! Don't call me *ma'am*; you make me feel *old*!"

He wanted to shout at her, *My name is Caleb*! Instead, a playful tone accompanied the spontaneous words that spilled from his mouth, "God forbid you ever feel old, Miss Sarah."

Her appreciative smile indicated she knew he understood her better than anyone else did. At once her smile softened a little as she said, "My father is sponsoring the annual Halloween Festival in the square this year. You missed it last year.

I hope you'll come this year. Say yes, Isaac. Say yes. I came all this way out here to personally invite you."

The mare stamped her muddy front hooves. The action jostled the surrey and the two girls inside it. Sarah gripped the reins tighter and gently tugged them. The mare obeyed with abrupt stillness, like a soldier at attention.

Caleb saw the girl was wearing black leather gloves too large for her hands. That was the final image playing behind his closed eyes as the dream faded away and consciousness slowly surfaced in its place. He opened his eyes, stared first at the dark ceiling, and then he rolled over and looked at the red numbers illuminating from the digital clock on his nightstand.

4:32.

Sarah... I don't know any Sarah.

Dismissing the dream entirely, Caleb let his eyes close and drifted to sleep. He slept well for another hour or so – no one asleep is aware of time passing – an hour or so of drifting images that meant nothing dissolved into nothingness in the dream section storage place in his brain. However, the vague picture of Sarah's black leather gloves returned and, with it, the thought of her hands, the smallness of her hands, the softness of her smooth warm hands in the envelope of his large calloused hands. Pleasant, peaceful, familiar... His heart sped up again with joy. His mouth became dry with shame as forbidden sensations raced through his body, heated his body. His shame became sudden terror as his throat seemed to close, and he became aware of pressure upon his throat, became aware he was trapped.

He was in his room at his mother's tiny house on the outskirts of town. Although it was dark, he knew it was his room – what used to be his room but was no longer only his room. It was filled with people, sleeping people. No. Not sleeping. Not all of them. Most were snoring or gasping; half conscious as the drugs were wearing off and their bodies begged for more. Many were hallucinating, moaning or muttering to themselves, their arms and legs shaking, their dark forms spastic.

Hands squeezed his throat. A vice-like hand clutched his mouth, held it closed. He struggled vainly to breathe, tried with his fingers to desperately pry the hands from his throat.

A whisper, gruff, ragged. "Shhhh... don't make a sound, boy."

Muffled laughter. There were two of them. They smelled like cat piss.

Moonlight shone through the window to his right, the only light, yet the light was too weak to reveal anything except the dark mass of twisted bodies on his bed and on the floor. He was on the floor; this he knew. The carpet was filthy with scattered crud, spilled beer, and fresh cold piss and vomit. His shoulder and his arm lay pressed into it.

Hands groped and removed his underwear, exposing him.

The one released his throat, and then they both forced him down on his belly. The other kept his grip over his mouth.

Can't breathe!

Fingers played over his bare skin. Repulsed and horrified, he struggled to escape, wriggling and kicking. He flailed his arms behind him, attempted to strike them.

A third body in front of him came to life, sat up and kicked the side of his head. He felt his ear pop and burn.

The gruff voice ordered the third body, "Hold his arms!"

Can't breathe! Can't…!

Caleb awoke, gasping, gulping air.

At first, he lay paralyzed until oxygen filled him and brought him to full consciousness. His body, damp with sweat, trembled. Slowly, the familiar scent of lavender reminded him of his surroundings. Still, he did not feel safe, did not feel safe like he did when he slipped into this welcoming bed earlier that night. Now, everything about the bed and his body felt tainted.

He bolted from his bed in the darkness and crossed headlong into the shower where he turned on the hot water tap. It delivered cold water at first. He stayed under the needles of spray as it quickly warmed. When it became too hot, he turned the coldwater tap but didn't let it get too high. He needed the hot water, needed it to be as hot as he could stand it without burning himself. He lathered himself, scrubbed every inch of his body, rinsed off, lathered and scrubbed again, rinsed again. He did this six times.

It would never be enough.

His knees weakened and he let them guide him to the steaming tile floor. There, dry heaving as the water rained upon his back, he curled up into himself. He stayed in that position, miserable and defeated, while the dawn sent light into the cottage and spilled sharp glistening beams upon the shower surround and fixtures.

His dry heaving became sobbing, and his wretched tears followed.

When will this stop? Will it ever stop?

* * * * *

The mailman delivered the Providence High School application and schedule of classes offered that Saturday. Ida looked through it first and completed the application form, set aside the list of classes for Stephanie to choose. School would begin in one week. Stephanie procrastinated, which was her habit, and Ida did not want her to wait until the last minute only to discover her choice of classes were booked solid. So, while Ida prepared the morning coffee, Stephanie sat at the kitchen table reading the descriptions of the different class offerings.

"Start with the electives," Ida advised, "There's a lot there you'll like. Remember, you only get two this semester."

"They're offering something called, 'Big Band Blast' under Dance, which is listed under Physical Education." Stephanie screwed up her face with both curiosity and confusion, read the description aloud. *"Fun dances from the heyday of the Big Band Era of the 1930s and 1940s; the Jitterbug, Swing, and others that will leave you invigorated. Offered as an alternative to Physical Education for the first time in response to current interest in reviving these once obsolete styles. Boys are highly encouraged to join in order to balance out the class. Concludes with a show at semester's end. Participants in the show will receive extra credit towards fulfillment of Physical Education requirement."*

"Sounds like fun," Ida remarked. She added with a smirk and a bit of sarcasm, "And, I *know* how much you *love* Phys-Ed!"

"Yeah..." she moaned disconsolately, "And poor Quinn, too!"

"Well, that will get you both out of the locker room and out of the weather."

Stephanie filled-in the box with her pen, and then she circled the box and posted an exclamation point beside it. "I've got to tell Quinn. I hope he doesn't chicken out."

"Why would he chicken out?"

"Because the guys would tease him for it."

"What guys?"

"Bruno, for one."

"Who's Bruno?"

"Local football star. He's beaten the crap out of Quinn ever since elementary school. He and his gang think Quinn's a fag."

"Don't use that word, Steph."

"Well, that's what they call him."

"Tell Quinn to come over and bring his class schedule with him."

"Are you gonna talk to him about it?"

"Damned right I am. Dance is just as brutal a workout as football is, and Quinn shouldn't pass up this class because he's afraid of being bullied. I'd like to see that *Bruno* character try to do those dances!"

Stephanie regarded her mother with a grin and her eyes wide with admiration. "Jeez, Mom!"

"Don't say *Jeez*, either."

"I forgot."

Ida handed her the cordless phone off the counter. "Call him."

While Stephanie took the phone into the living room, Ida returned to measuring out the coffee and starting up the coffee maker. As she waited for the brew cycle to complete, she looked out the window at the rear garden. The flowers and hedges glistened with drops of water from that morning's irrigation.

Caleb was using hedge clippers on the boxwoods, leveling the stray branches that had over grown the tops of the neat row. Although the temperature outside was still cool, his face was shiny with sweat. Now and then, he stepped back to judge his work from different angles, found a spot he missed, snipped the errant branches, and began the ritual again. Ida had learned from watching him he was very detailed and precise when it came to the boxwoods, never satisfied until the tops were level enough to stand a glass of water on. She also learned he did not pay attention to the days of the week. He never took a day off. She wondered if it was some form of self-therapy that compelled him to always find something to do, no matter how mundane the activity.

Today something was different about him. He seemed… sad. Ida could not identify what made her think that, but, whatever it was, he was definitely sad.

She went out and met him there at the boxwoods while he stood surveying his work for the umpteenth time, his pale eyes searching every detail. He was unaware she had approached him until she spoke cheerily to him.

"Say, mister, it's Saturday. Take it easy."

He startled for a second and then awkwardly smiled at her. "These will get unruly in a hurry if I don't keep after them."

"Have you had breakfast?"

"Yes, ma'am. I mean—Ida."

Ida suggested, "Why don't you come inside for a bit where it's cooler. I just put on a pot of coffee."

He used the toe of his boot to gather into a pile the little leaves, branches and twigs littering the grass. "I should clean this up first."

She shook her head in a gentle, encouraging, manner. "It's not going anywhere, Caleb."

"But, it'll be windy later."

"The TV said tonight. Really… It can wait. Come inside for a while."

He let the hedge clippers dangle at his side, regarded the hedge as if thinking abandoning the job in progress would be like abandoning an injured person in need of his help. "Well…"

His eyes, enhanced by his tanned face, were even more beautiful in the sunlight. Ida couldn't help appreciating the penetrating quality as he allowed his conflicted gaze to rest on her for just a moment. It occurred to her he should be fighting off smitten young women instead of spending his Saturday snipping overgrown hedges. Why was this kid so introverted?

"Listen," she said apologetically, "It isn't requisite with your duties here that you should accept my invitation."

He wavered, stared at the grass, shifted his weight from foot-to-foot. A nervous habit he had tried to conquer for years with no success. It was something his mother did when she was unsure, something he inherited only by association.

His gaze did not leave the damp grass at his feet. "It isn't that."

"What is it, then?"

"Nothing. I'm just not used to—" Caleb could not think how to describe his hesitancy.

"You used to visit with my mother."

"Yeah, but she was kinda like… I don't know. After she took me in… Oh, I don't know. I never thought about it." He bounced the hedge clippers in his hand lightly against his leg. He didn't notice this, either; it was just another automatic nervous twitch he paid no attention to. After a long thoughtful pause, and with a sweep of his arm toward the hedge, he added, finally glancing at her, "I should finish this. It'll bug me if I don't do it now."

His reluctance puzzled her, and she stepped back to give him some space. "In that case, I'll leave you to it. I'm very pleased with your work here, Caleb."

"Thank you, ma'am."

"*Ida.*"

A slight self-conscious smile. "Ida."

When she returned inside, she found Stephanie at the counter near the window pouring a cup of coffee. The girl said nothing. Ida sensed the guilt emanating from her.

"You were watching us," Ida stated with a hint of amusement.

"I just wanted to see what you were doing."

"Satisfied?"

"He's weird."

"Oh? In what way?"

Stephanie leaned against the counter and sipped her coffee before she answered, "He hardly ever talks."

"Not everyone's a talker."

"He sure is good looking, though."

"And too old for you."

"I didn't mean it that way. I said the same thing about Isaac, and Isaac's been dead for years. It's so weird how they look alike. Do you think they're related?"

Ida laughed. "You've got to be kidding! Do you have any idea what the chances would be? Besides… Caleb's from Louisiana; Isaac was brought up here."

"But born in Kansas."

"Which is a long way from Louisiana."

"Is it possible for people who are not related to look like twins?"

"Yes. I knew a girl in college who had a doppelganger living across town. They were often mistaken for each other."

"A doppelganger?"

"An unrelated twin."

"Oh."

"Did you get hold of Quinn?"

"He'll be here soon."

Ida tapped her daughter's hip, "Move over. I want some coffee."

"Where do Caleb's parents live?"

Hell Is In Me

"I don't know."

"He never talks about them."

"It's not our business, Steph."

"Do you think they're dead?"

"It's not our business. It's time you finish choosing your classes."

* * * * *

The moment Quinn entered the house he rushed excitedly to Stephanie at the kitchen table, slid into the chair across from her.

"Guess what, guess what, guess what!"

Stephanie seldom saw Quinn this excited. "What?"

"Gene's on his way out here with equipment. He just called me. He and Caleb are gonna re-set the stones today. Cool, huh?"

"Well, where's the map?"

He lifted one ass-cheek and pulled a folded packet of papers from his back pocket. "Right here with my classes list. I wanna get through this crap," (referring to his classes list) "—so we can get to the important stuff."

Ida, at the counter with her second cup of coffee, inquired in her *Mom Voice*, "Your junior year classes are *crap*?"

He cast her an innocent, endearing grin. "I already chose most of what I need."

Ida lifted one brow. "What about the dance elective? It gets you out of P.E."

"I marked it already. Fuck Bruno and those guys!" Then, realizing the mother of all cuss words that fell out of his mouth, "Oh, sorry! I didn't mean to cuss!"

Ida chuckled and replied. "I'll let it go this time. How about some coffee?"

"Would love it, thank you!"

She poured Quinn his coffee and brought it to him at the table where she settled in the chair beside him. Hand extended expectantly, she told him, "Let me see what classes you're taking."

After a brief déjà vu moment of him and his mother playing this same scene many times in the past and, flattered by Ida's interest in him, Quinn passed the papers to her.

He then transferred his attention to Stephanie who was making her final selections. "Gene's got some kind of rig on his truck that'll lift those headstones and place them on their bases. I can't wait to see this!"

"Is Isaac's in the right place?"

147

"It is." He unfolded the map and showed her. "And so are the Tarantinos. They're right next to him."

Stephanie's hand went to her heart. "Oh, I'm so glad."

"I don't know how they're gonna fix the broken ones, though."

The girl replied mischievously, "Super Glue?"

He considered it. "Would it work for that?"

"Highly doubtful," Ida interjected, her attention on Quinn's choice of classes. Those he had chosen surprised her. "You've marked a lot of science and health related classes."

For a second, he thought he had done something wrong. He gazed at her, wide-eyed. "Yeah. So?"

"I'm impressed, that's all."

Stephanie remarked, "He knows some medical terminology. What was that word, Quinn? The one that meant *bruising*?"

"Purpura."

To her mother, she said, "He also knows all about the spinal column and what everything there is called and what parts of the body they control."

Both of Ida's eyebrows shot up at this unexpected revelation. "Are you thinking of becoming a doctor, Quinn?"

"I don't know yet."

"Have you thought of volunteering at the hospital?"

"What for?"

"To see what doctors do… you know, all of that."

His expression grew dark. "I've spent half my life in hospitals. I know what doctors do. Most of them don't know their ass from a hole in the ground."

"That's unfair, Quinn."

"Tell that to my mother. First, they fried her with radiation, and then they took what little she had left with their useless chemo treatments. Then they told her she was cancer-free. One month later, they told her, 'Sorry. It's spread. Have fun dying. Here's some painkillers and a hospice worker.' So, am I being *unfair*? I disagree."

In a flat tone of voice, Ida gently told him, "You're shaking."

"I know I am."

She draped her arms around him, rested his head upon her shoulder. "I'm so sorry, Quinn. I'm sorry you lost your mother."

Her compassionate gesture, the way she gently held him to her heart, reminded him too much of his mother. His eyes burned with unspent tears at the memory. His throat ached with repressed rage at the fact she left him before he was prepared to release her. His memory of her cold fingers clutching his hand nearly overwhelmed him at that moment, and he saw her face, pale and dry, her eyes begging him to let her go, and then the moment her eyes told him she was letting go because she had to go. It was too much. Quinn felt a hard sharp pang in his belly, felt his throat tighten, and felt the heat of enormous grief emerge from his soul into his cheeks. Yet, he did not try to release himself from Ida's comforting arms; for those few moments, he wanted to remain there in her protection.

"I didn't lose her," he said, his voice distressed and sorrowful, "She gave up and chose to die. I don't blame her."

"She didn't *choose to die*. She faced the reality of the situation. Your father told me all about it and how brave she was."

Quinn's face abruptly reddened, his eyes narrowed, and his tone deepened with scorn. "Did he also tell you how many bottles of whiskey he went through? Most of the time he was too drunk to even hold her hand. *I* was the one holding her hand. *I* was the one that monitored her meds. *I* was the one who changed the sheets when she pissed herself. *I* was the one who told her lies to keep her from worrying. *I* was the one who was there. *I* was the one holding her when she died." Quinn then raised his head and peered intently at Ida. His chest was heaving with each furious breath. "You wanna know where my precious dad was at that moment? He was passed out on his recliner in his precious den! A coward, that's him. The only thing he was honest with you about was the fact that my mother died bravely. *She* was the brave one."

Ida cupped her palm under his chin, stroked his light blond hair, and caressed his cheek. "You're the brave one, too. God bless you, Quinn. God bless you." She lightly kissed the crown of his head and guided his cheek to rest again upon her shoulder, an impulsive maternal action she gave no thought to before or after. Yet, to Quinn it was everything in the world.

15

Stephanie decided it was impossible to predict Quinn's ever-changing moods. One moment he was excited and exuberant, the next angry and dour, and then a moment later excited and exuberant as if the angry and dour moment had never happened.

Now he was again excited and exuberant, his map spread out on the hood of Gene Blackwell's giant truck as he pointed out various locations to Caleb who leaned over his shoulder to view the map.

"We can't screw this up," he told Caleb, "This is our only chance to get this right."

"Got'cha," Caleb replied confidently.

"Have you ever done this kind of thing before?"

"Gene has. He helped at the old cemetery in Reyton. That's where he got the equipment from today – borrowed it from them. Who owns this place, anyway?"

Quinn stood upright, unconsciously puffed out his chest. "I do."

Caleb squinted doubtingly, "*You* own it?"

His chest deflated. "Well, my family does. We've owned it for over a hundred years. My third-great-grandfather was not only the town's only doctor but also the town mortician." Quinn then pointed backward at his house with his thumb, "He used to store and prepare the bodies in the basement. I haven't told Steph about it because it might creep her out."

Caleb laughed silently, his shoulders bouncing. "In that case, you never told me, either."

"Thank you, my good man."

Stephanie did *not* hear any of their conversation due to the noise Gene was making removing the small crane from the bed of his truck. Yet, the conversation didn't matter to her. What mattered was the smile on Caleb's face and the way his cheeks turned pink when he laughed. It was the first time she had ever seen him drop his guard. This entirely relaxed demeanor lent an almost irresistible magnetism to his appearance and persona.

Tapping his forefinger upon the precise location on the map, Quinn told Caleb over the rumble, "Tell Gene I want to start with Isaac Iversen's headstone and the ones beside it—the Tarantinos. This is for Stephanie, you know."

As the work progressed and the men had restored half of the toppled headstones to their proper places, Maria, drawn by the commotion, bounded down the hill off the side of the Vanderfield property into the cemetery.

Maria immediately caught up to Quinn and gripped his arm. "What on earth is going on here, Quinn?"

He replied offhandedly, "We're cleaning this place up."

"You can't just take it upon yourself to do this!"

"Why not?"

"It's not your property."

"Yes, it is. My family owns it."

"Does your father know about this?"

"No, he doesn't, and you're not gonna tell him."

She brought her palm flat against her forehead. "Oy! Dios Mio! Why are you doing this?"

He placed his hands firmly upon his hips, looked her square in the eye, and yelled defensively at her, "Because it needs to be done. It needs to be done not only in respect to those buried here but also because it was a goddamned fire hazard before I started cleaning it up."

"Oh, Quinn... You should have told your father."

The volume of his voice only increased. "He doesn't give a shit. And, you know what? The only thing he would've given a shit about is the idea that somebody might get hurt here and then he'd be sued. So, that means I've done the old lush a favor, but he'd never see it that way. He never pays attention to anything but his money, his booze, and his shop—in that order. This place now, thanks to me, is no longer a potential lawsuit should some bum or vandal get hurt or killed in here. This is my project, and he doesn't need to know about it."

"And, who's footing the bill for all this?"

"No one." Quinn gestured with a sweep of his arm to Stephanie, Caleb, and Gene who had ceased working to listen in on the conversation. "Everyone here is doing this for *free* because they *want* to do this."

Caleb and Gene, listening to Quinn's emotional diatribe, had stopped their work and considered Quinn suspiciously. Caleb motioned Gene to stay put while he approached Quinn and pulled him aside. "What's the truth?" Caleb inquired sternly, "You told me you wanted to surprise your dad, and now you're telling Maria you're doing this to prevent a fire or prevent someone from getting hurt, and your father doesn't give a shit. Which is it?"

Quinn ducked his head, tried to make sense of his conflicting thoughts and feelings. "It's kind of... both," he finally answered.

"Both?" Caleb demanded. "How can it be both? If your dad doesn't give a shit, and you're not really doing it for him, how can it be both?"

Maria chimed in, "Stop lying about everything, Quinn!"

"I'm not lying!" He gazed at both of them helplessly. "I just needed to do it, that's all. I was afraid he'd try to stop me if he knew. And then I was gonna show it to him when I was done. Once it was done he couldn't do anything about it. I just *needed* to do it!" He waved his arms to direct their attention to the results of his work, "How could all of this be wrong? How can it be a bad thing? What have I done wrong?"

Maria softened. "Oh, Quinn..."

"You roped us into this!" Caleb raged through his teeth.

Quinn wailed, "I'm sorry!"

Gene approached him and snugly wrapped one meaty arm around the boy's shoulders. "You ain't done nothin' wrong, young man." He regarded the others lightly, his eyes glinting with humor. "Y'all lay off this boy. Caleb, you stop yellin' at him. He didn't mean no harm."

Caleb silently mouthed the mother of all cuss words and walked away. Maria subtly shook her head and sighed, frustrated at both Quinn and Gene.

Gene blurted to Maria, "This boy's got more balls than the entire school football team!"

Caleb whispered to Gene, "Jeez, Gene; you don't say that to a woman."

"Well, I'm defendin' the boy, ain't I?"

Caleb spat. "Well, I'm not defending him. He lied to us."

"Not exactly," Gene countered.

Caleb waved up his hands. "God almighty..."

Gene spied Stephanie. She had been standing apart from them in a state of commiseration for Quinn and a hefty dosage of guilt for her part in the charade, "What about you, girl? Are you gonna defend this boy or what?"

"I helped him knowing full well he didn't want his dad to know," Stephanie answered softly. "So that makes me just as guilty—if, in fact, we did anything wrong. I don't think we did anything wrong. We wanted to do this for the people buried here more than anything else." She eyed Quinn, "Isn't that right? That's how it all started. Right, Quinn?"

"Yeah," Quinn stated, "That's really how it started. This is my family and Stephanie's family, and a whole bunch of other people resting here."

"It's a crime it got to this point," Stephanie said to Maria. "We were just trying to right a wrong. Stop picking on Quinn." She glared at Caleb, "That goes for you, too, Mr. High and Mighty. Quinn's got the biggest heart in the world, and you've got no right to break it."

Caleb stepped away insolently, "Great."

Stephanie told him, "You go ahead and walk away. We'll finish this ourselves."

Gene intervened. "I'll make sure this gets done. You with me, Caleb?"

"I don't know."

He narrowed his eyes at Caleb. "What would Ms. Grace, God rest her soul, advise us to do?"

Caleb rolled his eyes. "Finish the job."

Gene smiled jubilantly. "And that's what we're gonna do."

Caleb resignedly approached Maria, "A few more hours and we'll be done. Although I don't fully forgive their deception, I think Quinn and Stephanie have done a fantastic job here."

Caleb and Gene replaced all fifty-two gravestones by sunset, while Stephanie and Quinn documented the information on each stone and verified their placement via the plot map.

As the last cerulean vestiges of the evening surrendered to the dawning starlit black of night, the woman and child mourned for the ones below; the ones unknown and undiscovered.

* * * * *

Many of the stones were so dirty and coated with lichen as to be almost unreadable, and this particularly tugged at Stephanie's heart. She set about collecting soft brushes, rags, towels and buckets from the utility shed the next morning while

Caleb was pruning the rose bushes. His voice startled her when he stepped to the shed doorway to see what new project she was planning.

"I'm going to clean the gravestones," she replied, placing two buckets outside the door.

"Is Quinn there already?"

"He's on restriction."

"Oh, crap. Maria finked on him, huh?"

"She had to. Quinn doesn't pay her salary, you know."

He picked up one of the buckets, standard plastic household buckets, regarded them with a blatant expression of disapproval. "Are you planning on carrying water all the way over there?"

"I guess."

"You need buckets with lids. I have two. I'll carry them over for you."

"Are you sure?"

"I'd be glad to help if you don't mind."

Comforting warmth filled her with the realization he was finally beginning to cast his introversion aside. She believed yesterday's camaraderie during the graveyard restoration encouraged him, and she was glad for him.

"I'd love your help."

Once there and ready to work, Stephanie began at Isaac's gravestone, which did not surprise Caleb, who worked alongside her at Lottie Tarantino's stone.

They had no idea the wispy woman had settled across from them at the head of Isaac's grave. Mistaking Caleb as Isaac, she tried many times to touch him but was frustrated in her efforts as her hands passed through him. Tears slid down her white cheeks as she attempted to overcome her muteness to talk to him. Her frustration boiled over after numerous attempts to get his attention, and she pounded her fist upon Isaac's headstone, pounded repeatedly until her energy waned. She grudgingly accepted they could not see or hear her but she could hear them... and maybe that was enough. She gathered the folds of her dark blue dress over her bare legs and feet and made herself comfortable upon the warm dirt at the head of her beloved's grave.

Unaware of the woman's presence, Caleb and Stephanie had little conversation at first, just instructional snippets from Caleb about the proper way to use the brushes upon the granite of Isaac and Lottie's stones. Stephanie listened and followed his guidance, and sometimes paused to silently appreciate the delicate manner in which he went about his work. He was so careful, and his expression revealed his deep respect for the people buried in this once forgotten place. She suspected this came from a loss of someone in his own life, and she summoned her courage to inquire.

"Did your parents pass away, Caleb?"

He abruptly paused, the soft-bristle scrub brush in mid-swipe. The conflict of whether or not to share such private matters showed in his troubled expression.

"You don't have to tell me," Stephanie said, "It's not my business."

"My dad died in a car accident when I was four," he finally said in a flat tone of voice. He didn't look at her.

"I'm sorry." Yet, she noted the doubt below the flatness of his voice.

"It's okay." He then met her gaze sympathetically, "Your mom says you were very close to your dad. I know it hasn't been that long. Are you doing okay?"

She sighed forlornly before she answered. "Yeah. I'm okay. Mom says we will never get over it, but we will get *through* it. That's what we're both doing. There're still times when I talk to him, you know, and sometimes I overhear Mom talking to him, too. You know what's just as hard, though?"

"What?"

"When we left L.A. I thought all my friends would keep in touch with me. I spent the first couple of months here calling them on my phone, trying to stay current with everything. But they didn't—oh, I don't know. It seemed like we had nothing in common anymore, and they didn't really miss me that much, and I was the one always calling them. I don't call them anymore. I guess they weren't my friends."

"That sucks."

"When you were still in school, did you have some friends? Quinn said he thought you pretty much kept to yourself."

"I didn't socialize much. School was for learning. Learning was, and still is, important to me."

"Didn't you make *any* friends?"

"Do I seem like a social butterfly to you?" He said this with a self-effacing grin.

"You are kind of quiet." Stephanie chuckled to herself and added, "People used to get on me for talking too much. Since Dad died, I've found it easier to keep my mouth shut. And then... there's the fact that my so-called friends didn't miss me at all after I moved up here. Pisses me off, you know."

"You deserve real friends. You're a good person, a likable person. You didn't deserve to be hurt like that." He saw her blush at his words. He chose to ignore it. "Screw them. They don't matter. You're better off without them. I'm glad you found Quinn. He genuinely likes you."

"It's mutual. He's better than he thinks he is. I hope you'll be his friend, too. I think he needs a guy for a friend—for guy stuff. I don't think he's ever had that."

"I like him. He's all right."

"He sure likes you."

"I guess it's because I'm older."

"I think it's because he knows you won't beat him up. Yesterday you were so mad at him I thought for sure you were gonna smack him one. But you didn't. And he knew you weren't gonna hit him, even though I thought you would. That says a lot about you, and a lot about his instincts when it comes to you. Did you ever get into any fights?"

"No."

"That's amazing."

"Why?"

"Well, most of us get into a least one fight in our lives. I got into a fight with a girl back in L.A. We both got suspended. Gym class… tempers, you know."

"I try to stay away from violence. Life is hard enough without that." He became silent, resumed cleaning the headstone.

Stephanie did the same, and they worked silently for a few minutes. All the while, her mind was full of curious questions. She relented to her need to know more about him and hoped he would be forthcoming. "Why did you come to live with my grandmother?"

"I worked for her. It was easier."

"But, I overheard Mom mention to Gene that you were only fifteen or so. Didn't your mother care?"

Caleb gave her a stern look. "I don't want to talk about that."

She regretted stepping on his bad nerve. "I'm sorry."

"My mother had problems. Ms. Grace saved my life. It's ancient history I don't want to revisit."

"Okay." Her eyes welled with remorseful tears. "I'm sorry. Every time I open my mouth I piss someone off."

"No harm done. Now I have a question for you. What is it about," and here he gestured at Isaac's gravestone, "this Isaac guy that's got you all interested in him?"

"He was only seventeen when he died."

"It wasn't uncommon for folks to die young back then."

"He was murdered. That bothers me."

At Stephanie's comment, the wispy woman sat forward and sadly nodded in agreement.

Caleb asked, "Did they find who did it?"

"Not really. They had a suspect; some guy named Jacob Sheers."

The wispy woman drew her hands to her mouth in sorrowful recollection.

"Who was Jacob Sheers?"

"A schoolmate of Isaac's."

"So, what happened?"

"There wasn't enough evidence to convict him, so they let him go. His father sent him off to the East Coast not long after."

"Sounds suspicious."

"Yeah."

"So, what happened to this guy after he went east?"

"He went to law school. That's all I know."

"Do you think he did it?"

"I don't know. Mom says it doesn't matter anyway. They're all dead now."

The wispy woman dropped her hands. She gazed incredulously at Stephanie, now understanding the condition of her existence but at a loss to remember when or how it happened. She realized then Caleb was not Isaac, was not her beloved returned from the grave, and perhaps she would never be reunited with him. The information and confusing emotions that followed overwhelmed her. At this point, she let go and evaporated away from the cemetery into that limbo place of dreamless sleep.

Stephanie paused with a thought, decided to share it with Caleb. "You look so much like Isaac. I can't believe how much. It's kind of eerie."

Caleb set the brush on the bucket lid and settled on his rear on the dry soil, spied the surname "Iversen" on Isaac's stone.

My dad's last name begins with an "I." Could it be? I have to look at my birth certificate.

"My mom can help you," Stephanie said.

He emerged quickly from his contemplation, "What?"

"If you have your birth certificate."

Amazed, he peered intensely at her, and demanded, "How'd you know I was thinking that?"

She sighed very quietly and peered at Isaac's gravestone, "Sometimes I see images in my mind of things people are thinking."

"Your grandmother used to do that."

She knew about her grandmother, but she wanted to stay on track with Caleb's issue. "My mom can check it on the Internet for you. She can find out about your dad, too."

"How'd you know?"

"What?"

"That I don't believe my mom."

"I felt something when you mentioned your dad, that you didn't really believe it."

"Do you ever sense the presence of spirits or anything?"

"I thought I felt Isaac's spirit once. I think it was more wishful thinking than anything else. Do you sense spirits?"

"No."

Again, she heard a twinge of doubt in his voice. "Are you sure?"

"I thought I heard someone talk to me once, but I think I was mistaken."

"What did they say?"

He responded with an outright lie he felt compelled to say, only because he didn't want to believe the truth was really true. "I don't remember. It was nothing, I'm sure."

Stephanie knew he was lying, and she suspected he had a good reason to lie. "My mom is between projects right now. She has the time to help you find the answers you need. Talk to her, okay?"

* * * * *

Stephanie and Ida gaped in both surprise and delight when Caleb presented his birth certificate to them. Indeed, Caleb's father was named Robert Iversen, and he was the third great-grandnephew of Isaac's father, William Iversen. Ida's further research into her online family history revealed Caleb's branch of the Iversen family had settled in Georgia fifteen years before the Civil War. The northern branch, young Isaac's branch, had settled in Pennsylvania at that time before traveling southwestward to Kansas after the war.

"So, I'm directly related to Isaac," Caleb mused, "That explains everything."

"Why did your mother give you her last name of Anders?" Ida inquired.

As he folded and returned his birth certificate into the envelope, Caleb replied, "Because my mom and dad never married, I guess."

Stephanie smiled broadly. "We're cousins!"

Ida said quickly, "*Distant* cousins. This is a most amazing surprise. Welcome to the family, Caleb."

Caleb examined the page on the monitor that displayed his lineage. He pointed to his father's name, noting the death date, and asked Ida, "Can you tell me how my father died?"

Ida brought up Robert Iversen's profile page. She then clicked on a link to a newspaper article she had attached to his profile. The Baton Rouge newspaper article headline said *Head-On Collision Takes Life of Local Teacher*. He had died in his Ford Pinto when the driver of a gasoline rig fell asleep at the wheel and crossed the yellow line late one night. The fuel tanker pinned Robert Iversen's Pinto into a guardrail where the small car exploded in flames. The driver of the rig bailed and escaped with minor injuries.

"Burned to death…" Caleb whispered, the sickening reality heavy in his voice. "She never told me that part. I didn't even know he was a teacher."

Ida remarked, "I'm sure she didn't want you to know the details of his death. It was her way of protecting you."

Caleb laughed sardonically, "My mother? *Protective* is not the word I'd use to describe her."

Ida placed her hand firmly upon his wrist. Her voice gentle and just above a whisper, she said consolingly, "I'm sorry."

He shrugged and replied with forced resilience, "It's all right."

Like her mother, Stephanie detected the pain below Caleb's casual reply. She could only imagine the depth of his loneliness since the death of her grandmother who had been his only truly caring maternal figure. She hoped he now found solace and some form of kinship with her and her mother. Just in case he had not, she told him, "We're your family now. Oh, wait… we've been your family all along, only none of us knew it till now." Then to her mother, she asked, "Do you think Grandma knew?"

"I fully doubt it," Ida replied quickly.

Caleb added, "I never showed her my birth certificate. There's no way she would have known. I appreciate what you've done here for me, Ms. Ida." He smiled and squeezed Ida's hand, a glint of warmth and gratitude in his eyes. He then turned to Stephanie and briefly hugged her as he happily thanked her, "This was a great idea, Steph. Thank you so much! You have no idea..." He paused, unable to come up with the right words, and stammered, "Aw, damn it. I... I just gotta let this settle in, I guess."

Stephanie subtly lifted and dropped her shoulders. "I'm just happy. Happy for all of us."

Once her mother shut off the computer and Caleb retired to his cottage for the night, Stephanie went up to the attic to reflect upon all she had learned about Caleb and his surprise genetic link to her ancestors.

She reclined in the rocking chair with the carved geese on the backrest, observed the old furniture and wondered about all the people who had once used it every day long ago. She pictured them sitting about. In particular, she pictured Isaac studying his schoolbooks at the little round table beside her chair. Undoubtedly he had sat in the very same chair she was seated in now.

I wonder what he'd say if he was to meet Caleb. What would he say when he saw Caleb's face was his face? *I wonder if their personalities are the same; their voices, their mannerisms—are they the same, too? God... I wish...* She lifted Isaac's photo from the table and held it tenderly, gazed at the young man who had died too young. "I wish I could talk with you, Isaac. I wish you could know you're not forgotten. I wish you could know a part of you lives on."

Uh-hmm...

The utterance, soft, seemingly drenched in a waterfall, came over her right shoulder to her ear.

She whispered, her voice wavering, "Isaac...?"

Silence.

16

John Vanderfield settled into the black wicker rocker beside Quinn on the terrace. He sipped his bourbon on the rocks. He then opted for a substantial swig before he set the glass on the black wicker end table. "Do you understand why I put you on restriction?"

Quinn had been sulking in the companion rocker for the past hour. He deemed his father's inquiry as insulting and not worthy of his reply. He silently peered straight ahead at the clear starry sky that framed the treetops beyond their rear property line. It was a perfect night, the temperature in the low seventies and the air as still as Mt. Shasta's peak in the distance. He caught sight of a meteor plummeting behind the peak, plummeting as if aiming for the mountain. It reminded him he had missed the Perseid meteor showers earlier that month, a display he had watched annually for the past seven years.

His father gasped, gazing at the sky, "Did you see that?"

"Yeah. That was cool."

"We used to wish on those when I was a kid. Every year I wished for a bicycle. I finally got one for Christmas when I was eleven. It was a red Schwinn. I loved the damn thing. Rode it everywhere."

"What happened to it?"

"It got stolen from the bike rack at school. Son of a bitch cut the lock chain."

"Did you get another bike?"

"I got a used V.W."

Quinn laughed. "What happened to that?"

"I crashed it doing donuts in the parking lot at the strip mall. Hit a light pole. I was very drunk. Your grandfather told the police to make me sober up in the cell at the station. The hippie in the next cell kept insisting he was Jesus Christ—did that all night—yelled and screamed that he was Jesus, and it was illegal to put Jesus in jail. I didn't touch another drink until I went to college. By then I had saved up for a third-hand Pontiac Bonneville. It was a tank—that's what I called it. Guzzled gas like you wouldn't believe. But, damn… it was roomy. And it was perfect for the drive-in. Your mother and I had some great times in that car." John waited for a response from Quinn. The boy said nothing. They fell into silence for a few moments while John finished what remained of his tumbler of bourbon, and then he returned to his original reason for joining Quinn there on the terrace. "If you had told me you wanted to restore the old graveyard, I would have been all for it. You didn't have to hide it from me. Why didn't you tell me?"

"I thought the place was off limits. I thought you'd be mad."

"What compelled you to do it in the first place?"

"Curiosity. And then I worried about fire, you know, all overgrown like it was. The weeds and stuff were climbing up the hillside toward the side of the house. It made me nervous."

"I never thought about it. I never noticed it. Too busy all the time, I guess."

Too drunk all the time, Quinn said in his mind.

"Well," John continued, "I didn't put you on restriction because you restored the cemetery. I put you on restriction because you hid it from me." He fell silent again for a few moments, thinking about everything. Finally, he assured Quinn, "I'm proud of you for what you did there. You took it over, got help, and supervised everything like a goddamn corporate executive." He chuckled to himself, "You amaze me, Quinn. Thank you for doing what you did there."

Quinn did not fully believe him, "You mean that?"

"Yes, I do."

"Am I off restriction now?"

"I suppose." John's eyes were beginning to close from the effect of the bourbon, his third tumbler that evening. Undisguised envy accompanied his next statement. "Your grandparents would have been proud of you."

Quinn gazed at the sky again. He decided he would make a wish on the next falling meteor, should it appear. He would wish his father would find peace.

* * * * *

The school year of 2001-2002 got off to a good start for Quinn. One of only three boys in the Big Band Blast dance class, he quickly found himself the most desired dance partner due to his knowledge and skill. The girls in the class flocked to him, not the teacher, for advice and additional practice sessions. Eventually, the teacher, Mrs. Standish, a woman in her late fifties, enlisted Quinn as her official Teacher's Aide, which earned him extra credit.

By the end of their first week of class, his two fellow male students requested him as their tutor, which kept the three of them, plus Stephanie, after school practicing in the cafeteria while the janitors cleaned up the place for the breakfast hour.

Hearing the commotion and music on his way to the school parking lot that first Friday, bug-eyed Farley Larson peeked in the door. He observed Quinn teaching the boys while Stephanie did her homework at one of the long tables. At first, Farley didn't know what to think as he watched Quinn instruct the boys step-by-step in one of the routines. He watched quietly, unobserved, while Quinn recruited Stephanie to partner with the unabashedly effeminate Jeff Franco, another of the *Fermented Four's* victims of occasional harassment. But, Farley's eyes were not on Jeff (who he had shoved face-first into a mud puddle once), but on Stephanie. He had been waiting for an opportunity to become better acquainted with her, especially since he was enrolled in the same first period Civics class as her and Quinn. Farley knew Quinn had seen his curious glances at her, and he knew Quinn was fiercely protective of the girl. However, it seemed to him Stephanie and Quinn were not "an item," but close friends. If ever there was an opportunity to convince Quinn his intentions were benign, this was it. He waited until Stephanie and Jeff finished the number, and then he snuck in and took a seat at one of the tables away from the double doors.

Quinn at first was too focused on teaching Calvin Lathrup, the school brainiac and fellow social outcast, the basic steps to the West Coast Swing. Although a bit clumsy at first, Calvin persevered under his tutor's patient guidance and was finally getting the steps and the rhythm in sync. After some time reviewing the steps, both of them opted for a break. As he watched Calvin take a seat and was just about to signal Stephanie to dance with him, Quinn spotted Farley watching, and glared at him. "This is a closed tutoring session."

Farley took no offense. He smiled subtly, "I heard the music. I had no idea you could dance like that, Quinn. I'd like to stay and watch."

Quinn turned off the c.d. player and planted himself atop the table opposite Farley, his feet dangling over the edge. From this position, he loomed over Farley who was seated casually in a metal chair facing away from the table across from him. It made Quinn feel powerful to be above his nemesis where he had a perfect view that afforded no surprises. Quinn crossed his arms in front of his chest, a combative expression on his face and in his voice as he spoke. "Why? To give your buddies another reason to fuck with me?"

"No," Farley spoke sincerely. "I've never seen anyone who could master those dances like you do. Did you know my mom teaches dance at Parks and Rec? She tried to teach me, but I just couldn't get it."

"Well, obviously, you're better with your fists," Quinn said.

Jeff moaned, "Aw, Quinn! Don't piss him off. I don't want my ass kicked again."

Farley laughed dryly. "I don't wanna kick anyone's ass, Jeff. I just wanna see how you guys learn this stuff."

Quinn stated stubbornly, "No, you don't."

At this point, Calvin gathered his backpack and headed for the door with a quick, "See ya Monday, Quinn!" He was out the door before any of them could say goodbye.

"Sonofabitch…" Quinn grumbled. He looked sharply at Jeff, "I suppose you're bailing, too."

"Uh…" Jeff reached for his backpack and then changed his mind, and then changed his mind again. He decisively grabbed the backpack and headed for the door. "I gotta practice my violin."

"Shit…" Quinn said under his breath.

Stephanie interceded. "I tell you what, Farley. If you're sincere about this, it's okay with me if you stay. Quinn and I can both teach you some steps if you want."

Quinn immediately shot her a disbelieving, exasperated grimace, his eyebrows practically meeting his hairline. She shrugged it off unconcernedly.

Farley sheepishly replied to her. "I just don't want the other guys to know."

Now it was Quinn's turn to laugh. "Afraid they'll kick your ass, huh?"

Smiling, he spread his arms, palms up. "No."

Raucous laughter and familiar, unwelcome, voices sounded outside the door. It was Farley's crowd: Bruno, Harry, and Marcus—tough-ass bruisers who had no sympathy for anyone.

Quinn saw Farley nervously ducked a little as their shadows paused at the window in the door. "What's going on, Farley?"

His eyes widened with forced innocence. "Huh? Nothing."

"Nothing, my ass. I hear your posse out there."

Farley's eyes narrowed as he stated in a volume so low only Quinn could hear him clearly, "They ain't my posse."

"Since when?" As Quinn received only silence in reply from Farley, he continued, his voice bitter, "I know damned well you're setting me up."

"No, I'm not. I'm not." He almost whispered the words as his eyes darted back to the shadows upon the little window. The shadows finally moved away, and a square of sunlight spilled upon the floor.

Quinn remained fixed on his misgivings. "Then get the hell outa here."

Farley glanced cautiously at Bruno's unmistakable shadow crossing past the window en-route to the school parking lot, heard the hulking linebacker holler at his friends to let him catch up. Farley took a deep breath, rubbed his sweating palms against the material of his jeans. "In a minute."

Quinn observed Farley's uncharacteristic behavior with suspicion. "You're setting me up!" He pointed his index finger close to Farley's slim little nose, "Don't fuck with me, Farley. Got it? I ain't that same punching bag you knew last year. You're gonna be beyond sorry when I get through with you."

Farley gazed with surprise at Quinn's tough, no nonsense, demeanor and the way Quinn glared at him, unblinking, with his teeth gritted and his lips narrowed. For the first time since grade school, the boy believed Quinn was serious. "I'm not setting you up, man. And, keep your voice down." Farley then looked at each of them in turn, looked them straight in the eye, his own eyes revealing his fear.

Quinn bent forward, his face close to the other boy's slightly perspiring face. He could hear Farley's breath speed up. In all of his life, Quinn had never seen this guy afraid of anything, and it both puzzled and amused him. He couldn't resist the urge to taunt him. "Trouble in paradise with the boys? What'd you do to get on their shit list?"

"Nothing."

"Oh... it must have been a big nothing for you to be this scared."

Stephanie stood tensely, "Quinn... don't."

He ignored her, focused entirely on his enemy, this pop-eyed bully who had made his life hell since the first grade. "What happened?"

Farley stated evenly, although with a hint of anger in his voice, "I'm through with all that shit. Those guys are nothing but losers. I almost ended up in juvie because of them. I'm not gonna risk my chance for a college scholarship on those assholes. I'm though with'em. I'm waiting here until they're gone."

Quinn did not change his position; he was still in Farley's face. "I'm not buying it."

Farley stood and lifted his shirt. "Alright, asshole. Buy this. This is what they did to me when I cut ties with them." He allowed Quinn to examine the scars on his chest, ribs, and back. They were cigarette burns, some still scabbed-over.

"What the hell…" Quinn murmured. "Do your folks know?"

"Hell, no, I'm not telling them." He pulled his shirt down as he added, "And you're gonna keep your mouth shut." Turning to Stephanie, he demanded, "And that goes for you! You never saw this."

They waited. Eventually, they heard Bruno's and Marcus's trucks rev up. Farley sent Stephanie a timid glance, humiliated at his obvious, unsuccessfully subdued terror of the young men he once considered his friends. She approached him and wordlessly placed her hand over his forearm. Her eyes met his with understanding, compassion, and trust. He melted under her gaze.

"What are you gonna do now?" Quinn asked him.

"I'm gonna buckle down and earn that scholarship."

Stephanie told him, "I'm sure you'll have no trouble with that."

"Thanks." He subtly cast Stephanie a shy grin. Stephanie responded with a flattering smile.

Quinn caught their two-second flirtation and wasn't willing to approve of it. Yet, he said nothing; there was plenty of time later to warn her not to get involved with him. Besides, he was having too much fun watching Farley sweating, shaking, licking and biting his bottom lip, and damn near ready to have a heart attack. Seeing him like this gave Quinn a whole lot of satisfaction and a delicious sense of power. He savored the moments as the two trucks passed away from the cafeteria and onto the blacktop, their engine sounds becoming softer with distance.

* * * * *

Caleb had no idea Jake was nestled in the passenger seat of his truck as he drove home from a remodeling job over in Sunset Hills. It had been a long day that began at six that morning, and a particularly difficult day because Gene had messed up his back again and couldn't lift the sheetrock. Caleb didn't mind, though; the work was good for him, a great workout, and he observed his body, which was naturally sinewy, was more muscular than it was last spring. He loved having a strong body, not for the attractiveness of it, but for the strength it gave him. No more would he be the object of ridicule and beatings; now he could fight back, and God help the fool who decided to toy with him.

It crossed his mind that he would love to return to his mother's little shack of a house on the outskirts of town, return for the express purpose of beating the shit out of her boyfriend Richard. Richard had it coming. He'd had it coming since Caleb was eight years old. Caleb imagined the scenario, imagined the violence and the victory. Yet, the short fantasy brought him no pleasure, only a feeling of emptiness.

I don't need to prove anything.

"No, sir, you don't," he said aloud to the road ahead as he spun the steering wheel to the right onto Gadfee Lake Road.

Jake found Caleb fascinating, especially when the young man talked to himself, which was often. He remembered Isaac used to do that, too. Funny the things one remembers after nearly one hundred years have passed.

Caleb whispered to himself, "It's all better now." He took a Winston from the open pack in his shirt pocket and lit it with the truck's lighter, took a long satisfying drag, cranked the driver's side window down all the way. The warm air tousled his naturally unruly brown hair. He liked the way it felt when a breeze caressed him, especially a warm breeze. As the road curved westerly, he used his middle finger to push his sunglasses up on the bridge of his nose, and then he flipped down the visor to block the setting sun. Even with the sunglasses on, he still found himself squinting when the sun hit his eyes, for the light often hurt his eyes.

Caleb's mind wandered as he drove the sparsely populated rural highway. He thought briefly of his mother and the fact her eyes were brown. He decided then he must have inherited his pale blue eyes from his father. He wondered what the man was like as both a person and a father. Eventually, this led to Caleb realizing he would never have the opportunity to know him, and it filled him with sadness and a sense of being robbed. His thoughts then returned to his mother.

"What was she like before he died?"

Jake stared at him amusedly, his sparkling black aura emanating and swirling about the cab of Caleb's truck. He had been with Caleb all day, like a fly on the wall, observing the young man and occasionally searching his soul and spirit for Isaac's hiding place. Isaac was in there, all right, and Isaac was sleeping. It was a fitful sleep because he sensed Jake's presence. Jake watched and waited patiently; after all, he had all the time in the world – had been pursuing this opportunity for decades, had searched every Iversen descendent from east to west until he found the one who carried Isaac's energy in his bones.

"Well," Caleb continued aloud, "For all I know she drove him crazy, and that's why he was working late that night—to get away from her. I bet that's what happened. It's her fault. That wouldn't surprise me in the least."

"Yeah," Jake said, knowing Caleb couldn't hear him. "It's her fault. All women are crazy. Ask my mother. Now, there was a bitch." He laughed to himself before adding, "Isaac can tell you all about it. By the way, Isaac… I know you're in there. Still afraid of me, huh?"

Unconsciously, Caleb remarked, "I'm not afraid of anybody. Not anymore. No sir. Not anymore." He took another drag off his cigarette, held in the smoke, and then let it out slowly. "I'm stronger."

When Caleb arrived at the driveway to Ida's house, he had to wait behind the city bus that was dropping off Quinn and Stephanie. He found this unusual, for the bus continued on to the lake with no stops between. At the same time, Jake dispersed himself into the bus to avoid Quinn. Once the bus continued on its way, Caleb pulled up next to the two teens and lowered the passenger side window.

"How'd you two get door service from the City?"

Quinn replied smugly, "I passed him a five-dollar bill."

Caleb laughed, but he noticed Stephanie rolled her eyes in response, turned away, and walked toward the house. She walked quickly, her shoulders slumped, her backpack dangling from one hand and scraping the concrete.

He shut off the engine. "Is Stephanie okay?"

"She's pissed at me."

"Why?"

"She likes someone I hate."

"A guy?"

"Yeah. She's got no sense."

"Who's the guy?"

"Farley. I got scars from that bastard."

"Oh." Caleb took a few seconds to remember. "Oh, yeah. He's that fish-eyed guy that hangs out with that big bald guy with all the tattoos."

"That's the one."

"He was always nice to me."

"The bald guy?"

"No. Farley."

Quinn surmised, "That's probably because you were quiet, and Bruno wanted to figure out your story. I bet he sent *Fartly* out on a mission to find out about you."

Caleb's laughter at the nickname, *Fartly,* snorted out his nose before he said, "Well, in that case, *Fartly* had nothing to report. They left me alone."

"Hey, Caleb…" Quinn lifted his chin thoughtfully, "You know what you look like with those shades on?"

"What?"

He grinned and chuckled, "You look like a mosquito."

Caleb had to hold his belly, he laughed so hard. He took off the sunglasses and peered at Quinn. "Better?"

"Yeah, man. Put those baby blues to work for you and go get laid."

"What the hell, Quinn?"

"You oughta have a girlfriend. Why don't you?"

"I've got enough going right now. Me getting laid is none of your business. But, thanks for the tip, buddy."

Quinn leaned through the passenger side window, "You got an extra cigarette?"

Caleb handed him one. "Need a light?"

Quinn retrieved his lighter from his pocket and lit the cigarette. "Wanna come over to my house for dinner? Maria's cooking barbecued chicken tonight."

"Naw… Ida's already made me promise I'd eat with her and Stephanie tonight."

"Steph'll probably tell you all about *Fartly* and what a bastard I am."

"Is she your girl, Quinn?"

"What? I don't know."

"Have you kissed her?"

"No."

"Then she's not your girl."

Quinn got very quiet, the wheels turning in his head, his face crinkled in serious contemplation. Finally, he replied, "I never thought of that."

"Do you want her to be your girl?"

He answered quickly, not wanting to give it enough thought to learn his true feelings and then face those feelings. "I don't know."

"Well, if you don't know, she doesn't know either." Caleb continued gently,

"That means she can date Farley if she wants to, so long as her mother okays it."

"But, I don't trust Farley, and I'm gonna tell her mother that."

"Stay out of it, Quinn. Trust me."

Quinn stared disconsolately at the ground. The idea of Stephanie spending all her free time with Farley instead of him filled him with the same grief he felt at his mother's death. It was almost unbearable, and the depth of his pain astonished him.

Caleb was not prepared for Quinn's disturbingly emotional reaction. At first, he wasn't sure what to do or say. However, once Quinn's face began to redden and his lips started to quiver, Caleb felt compelled to deliver him some words of consolation and hope. "Hey… It probably won't work out anyway. Give it time and see what happens."

Quinn felt his eyes burn, felt tears forming. As hard as he tried to prevent it, one slipped down his cheek and he brushed it away with his fist.

Caleb leaned over and patted Quinn's arm. "Just give it time, buddy. If you want to talk some more, you know where I live."

Quinn nodded and walked away. Caleb watched him, observed his slouched shoulders and slow gait as the boy made his way up the hill toward his house. He had never seen one so dejected, so miserable, and so utterly alone in the world. It was something Caleb knew well, and his soul ached at the sight.

* * * * *

Quinn's sadness turned to coolness toward Stephanie as the next week progressed. Farley frequented Quinn's tutoring sessions in the cafeteria after school, and one day Farley let it slip that Stephanie had been teaching him dances on those days Quinn did not hold tutoring sessions.

Channeling his anger into retribution, Quinn removed Isaac's small headstone from the cemetery and carted it home where he hid it in his room. Late that night when his father and Maria were asleep, he stole his father's keys to their boat, stole Maria's keys to her worn-out Ford Escort, and headed for the lake.

As usual, the parking lot and docks were dimly lit and, since it was a Wednesday night, the deadest night of the week at the lake, there was no security guard on duty. Quinn parked the Escort behind a neglected overgrown oak tree near where his father docked his boat, and Quinn carried the heavy granite headstone to the gate. Once he unlocked the gate with his father's key, he lugged the headstone onto the boat, a small motorboat that seated six. After disengaging the boat from the mooring, he started the motor and gently coasted the thing out a ways from the docks and the lake edge.

There was just enough moonlight to guide him to deeper water within eyeshot of his "parking space" at the dock (God forbid he returned the boat to the wrong space). Satisfied with the spot he chose, he turned off the motor and dropped the anchor.

He sat there in the pilot's seat for a long time contemplating the violation he was about to commit, contemplating the serious trouble he'd be in if discovered, and then contemplating the pain it would cause Stephanie—that two-timing bitch, once she discovered the headstone missing. Would she suspect he did it? No doubt. Could she prove he did it? Not likely. Would God curse him for this? Most likely. Did he care at that moment? Not a lick.

Quinn took the headstone from the passenger seat and set it on his knees. He rubbed his fingers gently over the stone, felt the smoothness of the granite, thought it amazing that it was still in one piece considering the many seasons of bad weather and the fact it had escaped all the episodes of vandalism over the years.

He traced the lettering with his fingertips, stopped when he came to the phrase engraved in italic capital letters, "BELOVED." A pang of jealousy stabbed and then twisted his gut.

Murder. He was murdered. Quinn pondered this. What had Isaac done to incur such wrath in his killer? Quinn's next thought came with a mean smirk. *He was probably a total asshole who deserved it.*

He muttered, "Fuck you, Isaac. Fuck you, especially, Stephanie!"

And he dropped it over the side.

17

Caleb awoke from a nightmare in which he was drowning. He sat up in bed panting for air, his heart pounding so hard he could feel it thumping against his ribcage. It took a minute for him to get his bearings, for his heart to slow, for his eyes to adjust to the illuminated red numbers on the clock.

1:37 AM

He cussed and threw the sheet and light bedspread off his sweating body. A soft warm breeze entered the open window beside his bed, soothing him. The songs of crickets and frogs in the creek brought him fully into consciousness, and he listened for a few moments, slowly re-entering the real world.

Now I'll never get back to sleep…

He lit a cigarette and trudged to the bathroom where he emptied his bladder, and then he drew on his jeans and went out on the little porch of his cottage where he sat on the steps and smoked, contemplated the nightmare. It made no sense to him, and he could only muse that it was a manifestation of his inner fear of someday drowning because he had never learned to swim. Recollecting, it occurred to him he had avoided bodies of water all his life, had no desire to visit the lake or even the place in the heart of downtown Providence where Riddling Creek, a portion of which meandered laconically behind his cottage, ran deepest and widest. On the heels of that thought, he recollected the violent winter storm of two years before that gave everyone hope the drought had finally ended. The accompanying torrential rains continued for three successive days. The creek overflowed its banks to within four feet of the rear steps of his cottage. Unnerved by the roaring noise of the deluge tumbling and rushing through the creek like a ravaging monster; he sought refuge with Ms. Ida in her house. Ms. Ida had laughed unconcernedly and told him Riddling Creek had seen more turbulent days than that in the "Old Days" when a series of stronger storms had targeted the area.

Caleb accepted his aversion to water as just another thing to overcome someday. Tonight, it didn't matter. He relegated the nightmare to the "Irrelevant" section of his memory where it would slowly die.

Aside from the chirps and croaks from the creek, it was a quiet night, the kind of night he loved best. The temperature was in the low seventies, the sky a black dome of vividly sparkling stars, the only lights the porch and driveway lights from Ida's house and Quinn's house across the road a little way up.

Desiring a better view of the sky without the trees in the way, he walked barefooted to the edge of Ida's driveway and continued a short distance along the road away from the lights of the houses. Here he had a better view. He smoked and watched the night sky, listened to the night sounds. The memory of his nightmare escaped the *Irrelevant* place in his brain. Again, he tried to clear his mind of the terror that awoke him.

At his left, someone blurted, "*You'd better wake up.*"

Caleb nearly jumped out of his skin. He turned and looked in all directions for the source of the voice, a voice full of a lifetime's worth of battles; the cynical alcohol-fueled voice of a man. There was no one.

His heart accelerating, yet controlling his first instinct to defend himself, he called out in a whisper, "Hello?"

An owl hooted from an oak tree across the road.

Okay. Now I'm hearing things.

Just to make sure: "Who's there?"

No reply.

Still, on alert, he called out louder, "Hello?"

Again, no reply.

He listened carefully to all the night sounds, tried to separate the layers of the sounds, listened for breathing, the rustling sound of clothing rubbing against clothing, the sound of footsteps upon the dry grass along the road, the movement of brush, anything that would indicate another human was near him. Still, he could hear, feel, and sense nothing. He even sniffed the air for any hint of human fragrance. There were only the usual scents of grass, trees, hay and alfalfa, and the horses and livestock at the ranch near the junction.

Caleb discounted the sweet scent of burning tobacco, for he could see it was his as he took a drag and exhaled it. There was silence as he finished his cigarette, bent, and snubbed it out on the blacktop.

Then, from inside him, a desperate, high-pitched, male voice cried out—from inside him but yet from far away; it filled his ears, and his heart almost stopped at the sound and the words…

"…*in the water!*"

He shot into a standing position, at once ready to fight and at once thought he was imagining things. *Oh, God, I'm going crazy.* Minutes passed with no further surprises. He decided the voices he heard were nothing but auditory hallucinations brought on by fatigue.

The hum of a car engine grew faintly from beyond the crest of the hill from the direction of the lake. Traffic on this road this late during a weeknight was rare. Caleb turned toward the sound and waited for the car to top the hill as the sound of it drew nearer. Finally, the light from the headlights shown over the crest, and the light suddenly extinguished once the car paused at the top of the hill. The motor sound died a few moments later. When his eyes adjusted, Caleb recognized Maria's Ford Escort at a standstill, sitting atop the crest of the hill below the white illumination from the fancy carriage lamps lining the Vanderfield's front yard. The motionless vehicle impressed him as some kind of giant silver insect frozen in fear.

He wondered what had brought Maria out this late at night, and why she was returning from the lake. Surely, that's where she had been; there were no stores or anything else in that direction. He thought maybe she couldn't sleep and simply went out for a drive, or maybe she or John had left something in John's boat and Maria went to retrieve it. Yet, it was strange to him why she would stop on the crest of the hill, shut off the engine and the lights, and just sit there.

Caleb observed from the partial cover of a bush, saw the Escort's interior light spring on as the driver's side door opened. He saw the blonde hair of the driver, but, thinking it was Maria, assumed the yellow interior light had cast the gold upon her dark hair. It wasn't until the driver stepped out that he saw it was Quinn. He watched as Quinn leaned his weight upon the open car door and, with one hand controlling the steering wheel, coasted the vehicle quietly into the Vanderfield driveway, then hopped in and parked it. A few moments later, Quinn got out and soundlessly eased the door shut and locked it with the key. After that, Quinn entered the side gate and disappeared in the darkness.

It was all too suspicious. Caleb waited curiously for a while to see if the boy would re-emerge. Quinn apparently had snuck back in for the night. As he returned to his cottage, Caleb assumed it was just a case of teenage rebellion, Quinn going out for a joyride behind his father's back. He decided then it was none of his business, and he would not mention it to anyone, not even Quinn.

All boys had their secrets.

And I am hearing voices...

18

Quinn denied everything when Stephanie confronted him at his front door after finding Isaac's stone missing.

"Who else would do it?" she demanded.

"Maybe Farley mouthed off about it to his posse," Quinn offered coldly. "They probably did it as a joke."

"I never told Farley about it. I've kept my promise to you to keep the cemetery a secret. Now, put it back before I tell your father."

"I didn't take it."

"You did, too!"

"No, I didn't!"

They argued this way for many minutes until Stephanie gave up and returned home in a fit of temper and with every intention to file a police report.

Caleb pulled into the driveway and observed her angry gait, bent shoulders, and tightly clenched fists. He rolled down the passenger side window and hollered out to her, "What happened?"

"Quinn stole Isaac's headstone. I know he did it."

"Why would he do that?"

"To get back at me."

"About Farley?"

"What other reason would he have?"

Quinn's late-night excursion now made sense to Caleb. "Do you want me to talk to him?"

"I'm gonna let the police talk to him."

"Don't."

"Why not?"

"The cops have bigger things to deal with, that's why. Is your mom home?"

"She's visiting Mrs. Larson at her dance studio. I keep telling her I don't want

176

to enroll. God damn it, Caleb! Why doesn't anybody ever listen to me?"

"I'm listening." He leaned and opened the passenger door. "Hop in. We're going over to Quinn's."

She took the seat beside him. "He'll never admit it."

"Oh, yes, he will."

* * * * *

Quinn spent his allowance to rent the rowboat he anchored as close to the spot where he had dropped the headstone. He was both humiliated and angry at being caught, but at the same time, he found himself impressed with Caleb's understanding of why he had done such a spiteful thing. Caleb had used gentle persuasion spiced with a generous dose of compassion, plus his eyewitness testimony to extract his confession, while Stephanie sat seething across from them in the Vanderfield den. It was only out of respect for Caleb that Quinn found himself out on the lake. He considered his friendship with Stephanie ruined beyond repair, and he convinced himself he didn't care, although he cared a great deal, and a part of him grieved the loss.

Stephanie and Caleb watched from the dock as Quinn stripped to his underwear in the boat.

Stephanie giggled. "Boxers..."

Caleb mused, "Keeping the future Vanderfields happily unrestricted."

Stephanie spit laughter. She embraced Caleb's waist and rested her cheek against his shoulder. He casually tugged her to him as he chuckled with her.

It took Quinn twenty minutes and just as many dives to find the headstone twelve feet below. He used a rope he had brought to lift the thing out of the water. Then, on the journey home, just the same as on the journey to the lake, Caleb relegated him to the bed of his truck amongst the tools and leftover construction materials. Quinn knew Caleb meant this seating arrangement as a warning of what would happen to their friendship if he ever pulled another stunt like this one.

* * * * *

September rolled in with pristine cloudless blue skies and temperatures in the high seventies. Providence High was abuzz with fresh promise and seasonal activities: the Cougars football team determinedly into practice, the Glee Club and the marching band in rehearsal for the homecoming show, the Drama class in rehearsal for their first production, and Big Band Blast in preparation for their first show scheduled for November.

Farley enrolled in the Big Band Blast class at Stephanie's request, which made the teacher happy to finally have another boy in the female-dominated register. This did not sit well with Quinn, although Farley made every effort to atone for his past sins against him. Quinn would not forgive and would never forget.

Farley had gotten into the routine of giving Stephanie a ride home after their practice sessions. On this particular day, he offered Quinn a ride, too.

"I'll walk it," Quinn said, packing up his c.d.s into his backpack.

"It's five miles," Farley stated.

"I like walking."

"Jeez, Quinn. Take the ride home," Stephanie said.

"I didn't ask you," Quinn retorted.

"Look," Farley told him, "Bruno and those guys were talking about going to the lake after school. If they see you walking up that road, you know what's gonna happen."

Quinn sneered at him. "So now it's your job to protect me? Screw you. I can handle them."

"Three of them?"

"Screw him," Stephanie moaned, "Let him walk."

"No!" Farley faced her sternly, "He's not walking. I heard they're after him because of me."

Quinn scrunched his face in disgust. "Oh, yeah? Since when are you and me fast friends? The only reason I'm teaching you dance is because I get extra credit for it. So, just go and tell your ex-friends I'm still the same asshole I've always been. Oh… and also be sure to tell them I'm not that same wimp I was last year, and I can take them on anytime they want."

Farley had not failed to notice the amount of hard muscle Quinn had developed over the summer, and the boy had no difficulty lifting the girls for some of their dance routines.

"I believe you can. But you can't take on all three of them at once. Even I couldn't take on all three of them. You saw what they did to me. C'mon, Quinn. I'll drop you off at Steph's. It's just a damned ride."

Stephanie urged him, "Don't be so hard-headed."

Quinn relented grudgingly, and he took the back seat in Farley's blue 1997 four-door Cavalier. "Nice car," he remarked, as he got comfortable.

"It was my mom's," Farley replied, "She gave it to me for my birthday."

Quinn griped, "Shit. All I got out of my parents was a bicycle!"

Stephanie volunteered, "My mom's taking me for my learner's permit this month. Once I get my license, she's giving me my grandmother's car."

"Cool," Farley said, smiling at her. "What kind of car is it?"

"A Honda Accord."

Farley laughed. "That's a grandma car, all right."

She protested, laughing with him. "It's in perfect condition! What the hell."

Quinn stewed in resentful silence as Farley drove out the lot and through town toward the outskirts that led to Quinn's rural neighborhood and the lake. By the time they approached the junction at Gadfee Lake Road, he was sick of Farley and Stephanie's playful banter between themselves. To him it was like he was not there at all or that he was just as important to them as the school backpacks they had tossed dismissively beside him on the seat.

Farley brought him out of his resentful thoughts. "Say, Quinn. Have you noticed Mae Murray's been giving you the eye lately?"

He didn't believe it. Mae was one of "popular" girls on campus, the product of a very wealthy family and groomed in all the nuances of social etiquette. The boys practically tripped over their own feet to get next to her. What would she want with a loser like him who didn't even have his own car yet?

Quinn replied to Farley's inquiry with typical dry humor, "Giving me the eye? What makes her think I need an extra one?"

Stephanie groaned at his bad quip.

Farley didn't find Quinn's remark worth a response. "She likes you."

Quinn scoffed, "Bullshit."

"Okay then. Don't believe me. But I overheard her telling Nancy she would say yes if you asked her to be your date for the homecoming dance."

"I'm not going to the homecoming dance."

"Suit yourself, asshole."

"Yeah… I'm an asshole." He met Farley's eyes in the rearview mirror; saw Farley regarding him with a mixture of frustration and amusement. That rankled his ego and only fed his resentment. "I suppose you and Steph are going together?"

"We're planning on it." Through the rearview mirror, Farley maintained eye contact with Quinn, patiently awaiting his response. "It'd be dope if you had a date, too, and we could all go together."

Stephanie turned and faced Quinn. "You really should ask Mae."

"I told you I'm not going."

Her lips narrowed over her gritted teeth, a sure sign to Quinn she had spent her patience. As he expected, the tone of her voice dropped an octave as she challenged him. "Don't be such a dickhead. Lighten up for a change. And stop being so pissed-off at me."

"I'm not pissed-off at you."

"Sure could've fooled me."

"Now, now, kids," Farley drawled, "If y'all don't stop your bickering I'm gonna stop this car and make y'all walk."

"Fine with me," Quinn muttered.

Farley's eyes immediately filled with fear as he glanced at the rearview mirror. "Oh, shit!"

Quinn and Stephanie exclaimed at the same time, "What?"

"We're being followed. Shit…"

Quinn looked out the rear window, saw two familiar vehicles racing up to them. The one in front, Bruno's big gray monster, spit exhaust as it neared the bumper of the Cavalier and then swerved into the oncoming lane and passed them. The second vehicle, Marcus's giant red 1992 Ford Extended Cab truck caught up and closely paced Farley's car. It was clear to Quinn Marcus did not intend to pass them.

"Just be chill," Farley said.

At first, it crossed Quinn's mind that Farley had set him up. However, Farley would not do that with Stephanie in the car with them. He watched Farley's tense expression through the rearview mirror. This was not a set-up. Farley had no idea this would happen, and he was genuinely scared.

"What do we do?" Quinn asked him.

"Just be chill."

"Marcus and Harry are on our bumper."

"I know."

Ahead of them, Bruno swerved into the right lane and slammed on his brakes, causing Farley to hit his brakes. The Cavalier skidded to a halt inches from the fat bumper of Bruno's truck. Bruno and Marcus killed the engines of their vehicles. The Cavalier was now sandwiched between the two giant trucks with no room for

Farley to maneuver his car out of that position. He sat indecisively with his foot on the brake and the engine running, his face turning pale as he assessed the situation.

Stephanie took her cell phone out of her purse. Farley covered it with his hand, "What are you doing?

"Calling nine-one-one."

He emphatically shook his head, "No!"

"Why not?"

"They're only messing with us."

"I think we should—"

"Not yet."

From the back seat, Quinn observed Bruno in the truck ahead talking and laughing on his cell phone. He turned and looked again at Marcus and saw he was also on his cell phone. Quinn knew what they were planning. "This is not gonna be good." He then addressed Farley in a louder voice. "You got a weapon on you?"

"A pocket knife. Worthless."

There was fear in Stephanie's eyes, "I wish I had some pepper spray."

"A wish ain't gonna help us," Quinn responded.

Farley glanced at each of them in turn, his expression confident, but his voice revealing a trace of nervousness. "Just be cool."

To Quinn, the option of playing it cool bitterly clashed with his growing anger at his tormentors' unrelenting desire to constantly victimize and humiliate him. The fact that Stephanie was now in danger only fueled his need to take action to end this situation. He regarded Farley's advice as ludicrous, "They're laughing at us!"

Stephanie cussed under her breath and rubbed her forehead with a trembling hand. Farley caressed her shoulder, "I'm not gonna let anything happen to you."

Quinn sat forward between their seats, "I won't, either."

Stephanie giggled nervously. "Ah, such brave men!"

"Well, Farley," said Quinn, "How are we gonna handle this?"

"Wait them out. See what they're gonna do."

Quinn was already imagining what they were going to do, and it had everything to do with them hurting him and possibly hurting Stephanie, all to send a message to Farley. He needed to come up with a plan quickly. "I know Bruno carries a knife. What about Marcus? I've never seen him with anything."

"Marcus doesn't need to carry."

"What about Harry Richter? Does he still carry?"

"Not since his dad became Mayor."

"Oh, yeah…" Quinn smirked, "Mayor Rectum."

Farley and Stephanie snorted, their bodies jiggling with their faint wheezy laughter.

Bruno flipped on his hazard lights. They flashed red upon the hood of the Cavalier.

"Oh," Quinn's tone rose with his contempt, "Now he's sending us a warning. Piece of shit." He opened the back door and set one leg out, "Well, I've had enough of this. Whatever happens, get Stephanie home."

Farley's bug eyes bugged out even more. "Don't do it, Quinn!" At the same time, Farley opened his door to step out, but paused long enough to instruct Stephanie, "Keep the doors locked."

Against Farley's advice, Quinn was already out the rear side door. His fury quelled his anxiety as he strode purposefully up to the driver's side door of Bruno's truck. "Hey, asshole!"

Bruno lowered the driver's side window, poked his shaved head and mockingly grinning bulldog face out. Quinn, being tall, had no trouble meeting his enemy face-to-face from his position. Without warning, and before Bruno could voice a comeback, Quinn brought up his fist and smashed the bulldog's nose with one rapid and very powerful blow. Blood spurted and went flying. Bruno's hands went to his destroyed nose, and his vibrating eyes regarded Quinn with surprise and shock. In the next few seconds, the big bruiser's head bounced sideways on the window ledge and then lay still as death.

Quinn felt the tremor of pain race through his knuckles all the way down his wrist to his elbow. The thought that he had broken his hand formed for a millisecond in his mind, followed by the thought the injury was worth it. However, Quinn was not finished. He dodged Farley's attempt to rein him into the Cavalier as he strutted with even greater intent to Marcus's vehicle where Marcus was leaning out his window watching Quinn with abject disbelief.

When Quinn approached him, Marcus exclaimed, "What the hell?"

"Wanna be next?" Quinn offered ominously. After Marcus responded with vengeful silence, Quinn shifted his menacing gaze to freckled, red haired, Harry Richter cowering wide-eyed in the passenger seat. "What about you, Rectum? Step out. I'll bust your face, too!"

Harry silently shook his head, his fear obvious in his stunned expression.

Marcus ducked into the cab, started the engine, and swiped the gearshift into reverse. "You'll pay for this!"

As Marcus reversed the vehicle, made a U-turn and raced toward town, Quinn yelled after him, "I'll be waiting."

Empowered by his victory, he jutted his fist into the air and emitted a savage roar of triumph on his way back to Farley's car. As he settled excitedly into the back seat, Farley and Stephanie regarded him admiringly, their mouths agape. Quinn grinned the biggest grin he'd ever grinned in his entire life. It felt so damned good to be the object of respect for a change.

"Dude!" Farley blurted, laughing approvingly.

Stephanie scolded him half-heartedly, unable to suppress her smile, "Are you out of your mind?"

"Totally." Quinn unfolded his fists, discovered he had clenched them so tightly his palms were covered with his fingernails' indentations. He accepted the discovery as just one more indication that he had reached his breaking point. "I've had enough of this shit. Let's get out of here before Bruno wakes up."

Farley backed the car up and then drove around Bruno's truck. As they passed, he slowed the car enough to get a good look at Bruno's head laying askew out the window, and the thin streaks of blood dripping down the door.

"Damn…" Farley marveled, "You knocked that bastard out cold."

Stephanie looked upon Quinn as one would a hero, "Who woulda thunk it?"

Quinn reclined proudly in the seat. If only they knew everything he had gone through over the summer: the battles with his father, his encounters with the dead, his deft control of crazy Jake. They were all small victories that strengthened his self-confidence. This current victory was the biggest and most important to him, the sweetest of the sweetest because he had regained Stephanie's friendship and earned Farley's respect in the process.

He examined his swelling knuckles, flexed his fingers, flexed his wrist. Everything worked fine, just a little painful. Nothing broken. He considered it a good injury, minor damage earned in the heat of battle, the good pain that comes with victory. It never occurred to him before this that pain could feel so exhilarating.

* * * * *

Jake was waiting for him in his bedroom, sitting casually on the chair at Quinn's desk when he returned home. Jake's aura energy bounced off the walls, the colorful shards exploding upon impact. Quinn perceived the aura was not as dark as usual and more translucent, which gave him a clearer view of Jake's handsome but timeworn face. Jake's expression told him this would be a serious meeting; Jake was not happy with him.

Jake stated as Quinn closed the door, "You're not holding up your end of our bargain."

"I've been busy with school. You know that." Quinn shivered and sat at the end of his bed. "You're making my room cold."

"I can't help that." He sat forward and pushed his face close to Quinn's. "Isaac's waking up. Deliver him to me."

"I'm still trying to figure out how."

"He's been talking to Caleb. Caleb doesn't know it. Caleb's an idiot."

"I need more time."

"I'm sick of time. If you don't find a way to bring Isaac out of Caleb, I'll go inside that boy and drag him out. You know what'll happen if I do that?"

Quinn's eyes widened. "What?"

"Caleb will go bat shit, and then he'll die. He'll die from me being inside him, eating him from the inside out like a parasite. That's what happens. I've seen it. I've seen it at the crazy house. Ain't pretty, either."

Hiding his alarm, Quinn replied stoically, "I said I would handle it. I need more time."

"I'll kill the girl."

Quinn thought to repeat his threat to kill himself but immediately realized Jake no longer needed him now that Jake discovered he could possess another person's body. At this moment, all Quinn could do was plead for Stephanie's life. "Don't touch her, Jake. She's done nothing to you."

"Then get off your ass and deliver Isaac to me."

"Give me more time to figure out how. I'll spend more time with Caleb; try to draw Isaac out without him knowing. Just give me more time."

"I'll be watching you."

"That doesn't surprise me."

Quinn had no idea how he could keep his promise. All his bravado from his victory earlier that day melted away. He found himself trembling in fear again, feeling powerless again, feeling angry again. Comeuppance was a real bitch.

19

Like most of their fellow students, Quinn and Stephanie did not listen to the radio or watch television before boarding the bus to school on the morning of September 11, 2001. At the Vanderfield home, John Vanderfield had left for his store at five-thirty that morning, and Maria cooked breakfast for herself and Quinn to CDs of Mexican music. Ida Norris tuned in the classical station that played a pre-programmed loop on her way to the gym. Routine and blessed obliviousness of world affairs ruled the lives of most Americans this day and previous days. No one expected the horror unfolding in New York City and Washington, D.C., but as the morning progressed on the West Coast and the images filled cell phones, computer monitors and televisions across the country, initial confusion followed by shock followed by rage spread from coast to coast and beyond. The first Quinn and Stephanie heard about it was when a girl on the bus found the video online and alerted her fellow students.

The television was on in their first period Civics class as the two took their seats in the rear of the classroom. Quinn and Stephanie's desks were across from each other, and Farley's desk was behind Quinn's. The students became silent as their teacher briefly explained what had happened and announced there would be no class work this day, but the school was on lockdown for security reasons. From their desks, they watched and listened attentively to the CNN reporters broadcasting what little they knew from blocks away from what would be called Ground Zero. They watched mostly in silence save for the occasional gasp or angry murmur from a few fellow students when the footage of the Pentagon came on. At this point, the extent of the terror attack was still not clear to any of the young people, as they had tuned in at the tail end of the NYC report that segued instantly to the damage and evacuation at the Pentagon. Following the Pentagon coverage came footage from a DC elementary school of a government official informing President Bush of the situation. Brows plunged as the Providence High School students tried to make sense of the unfolding events and how they were connected.

Farley tapped Quinn's shoulder, whispered his inquiry. "Bombs on some planes? They're bombing us?"

Quinn turned to him and replied in a soft but distressed tone of voice, "I think they're using the planes as weapons."

At last, the replay of the first tower collapsing filled the wide screen television in all its diabolical horror. Stephanie felt a silent scream rise and then pause halfway up her throat. This hit too close to home for her. She saw her father pinned under the rubble, although it was not the rubble of the tower in Manhattan, but the burning rubble of a dilapidated four-story apartment building in a rundown section of East L.A. Her body filled with heat, sweat popped from every pore, her heart sped up to breakneck speed, and every bone and muscle began to tremor. Finally, her scream escaped her throat. She stood and pounded her hands on her desk, eyes round with hysteria, the words, "*Daddy, Daddy, Daddy!*" accompanying the vicious percussion of her palms upon her desk. "*No, no, no, no, no, no, no!*" Spit dribbled from her mouth as she wailed. It was the wail of an irreparably broken heart.

Quinn and Farley shot up from their desks as all eyes focused on Stephanie. Quinn reached her first and scooped her into his arms. He told Farley, "Get our stuff," as he carried her up the aisle.

The teacher, cell phone in hand, alerted the school nurse's office as she pushed the door open for Quinn. Stephanie's wailing echoed through the hallway.

* * * * *

Ida gently laid the comforter over her daughter and sat at the edge of the bed. It had taken an hour, but Stephanie was finally quiet, lulled into a state of dull oblivion by her mother's Valium washed down with a tablespoon of sherry in a small glass of water.

"It was only a matter of time," Ida told Quinn who stood worriedly at the foot of Stephanie's bed. "She never fully grieved for her father."

"What can I do to help?" Quinn whispered.

"Stay here today. I'd like you to stay."

"Will she be all right?"

Full of sadness and concern for her, Ida stroked her messy dark hair that was matted with sweat. "I hope so." As an afterthought, she added, "When we go downstairs, please keep the TV off."

They heard the familiar sound of Caleb's truck coming to a halt in front of the open garage. Quinn looked out the window. "Caleb's home way early." He watched silently as Caleb exited the vehicle and hurried to the front door.

In a few moments, Caleb's voice drifted up the stairs. "Ida? Ida, did you hear what happened? Ms. Ida?"

She met Caleb at the bottom of the staircase. "Yes. I know. Why are you home so early?"

"The clients canceled the job today. Lines are already forming at the gas stations and the banks. I guess you know all planes have been grounded. It's a mess."

"Please keep your voice down."

The pain in her eyes and the fatigue on her face finally registered. "What is it?"

"Stephanie had a breakdown at school. She's sleeping now."

He gazed at her as if her pain was his own. "Oh, no."

"She'll be all right."

"Can I see her?"

"I guess so; but she's asleep. Don't wake her."

They entered the room quietly. Quinn sat on the edge of the bed, stroking the girl's hair with one hand, holding her hand with the other. He briefly lifted his head to acknowledge Caleb, and then he returned his attention to his slumbering friend.

"I want her to sleep," Ida whispered. "Let's leave her alone for now. Come with us, Quinn."

Quinn hesitated. He bent and tenderly kissed Stephanie's cheek, reluctantly rose and met them at the door. Ida soundlessly shut the door, and she followed the two young men downstairs.

Although normal life had come to an abrupt halt that day, the earth itself continued its revolution westward, towing the sun with it. Night descended upon an unusually quiet town, a town full of people cocooned in their homes and glued to their televisions.

Ida slept beside her daughter. Quinn offered reassurance when Farley called, then he phoned his father to tell him what happened to Stephanie and that he was spending the night at the Norris house. After that, he and Caleb made grilled cheese sandwiches and watched the news footage in the family room with the sound turned low. By now, every news affiliate was broadcasting the same reruns of the towers falling, the destruction at the Pentagon, the obliterated crashed plane in a Pennsylvania field, and President Bush's address to the nation. Interspersed came new footage of gatherings in New York City: people examining walls and windows covered with photos and notices of the missing, mournful gatherings alit with candles, mournful voices singing for the dead.

No matter how many times he watched the footage of the towers collapsing, Quinn saw the unfortunate souls—the thousands—rising up and disappearing into the smoky sky. Most appeared confused, many bravely accepting of their fate, and many enraged at the realization their time on earth had ended. Finally, his gut churning at the sight, Quinn asked Caleb to shut off the television.

Beside him on the sofa, Caleb thumbed the remote. "It's too much," he said softly.

"Bastards…" Quinn muttered. At the same time, he expected many of the dead would wander the streets of Manhattan. They would wander the streets, trying to make sense of it all. How many Quinns were in that place to help them move on?

"*Evil rules the world.*"

Quinn recognized Jake's voice, but Jake was not visible. Beside him, Caleb's body emitted deathly coldness.

Caleb stated dazedly, "Yeah. Evil rules the world."

* * * * *

The house smelled like freshly baked cookies as Stephanie descended the stairs and entered the sunny kitchen. She watched Caleb remove two pans of cookies from the oven. He saw her and smiled at her, set the pans on the breakfast counter to cool. He poured her a cup of coffee, added her customary amount of cream and sugar, and set it before her as she wearily settled upon the stool.

"Feeling better?"

She gazed at him silently, her eyes lifeless. She pulled her robe closer, tightened the belt, then slouched forward with one elbow on the counter and rubbed her cheek. Her sight focused on the tray of cookies and then returned confusedly to Caleb.

He kept his voice low, his tone gentle. "Is your mom awake?"

She shook her head. Her hair drooped in matted strands framing her face. She made no effort to tuck it all out of her way.

"I made your grandmother's recipe. Chocolate chip cookies with walnuts, easy on the sugar."

She whispered hoarsely, "Those are the best."

"Have one."

After a sip of coffee, she selected one from the pan, took a small bite, chewed and subtly smiled. "Good."

"It was our Saturday ritual. I still miss her. I'll miss her for the rest of my life."

Her eyes sympathetically met his. "Does it still hurt?"

"Sometimes."

"Will it ever hurt less?"

"Gene said so."

"How long does it take?"

"I don't know. I guess it's different for everyone." He used his thumb to wipe the single tear that slid down her cheek. "Don't be afraid of it. Allow yourself to feel it."

"More advice from Gene?"

"Yeah."

"How do you handle it when you miss my grandmother and it hurts so bad?"

The corners of his mouth rose slightly. His pale blue eyes filled with the warm glimmer of fond reminiscence. "I bake cookies."

* * * * *

Ida kept Stephanie out of school the remainder of the week. They spent much time at the lake where Ida shared her memories of Ned Norris. She showed Stephanie all their favorite places at Gadfee Lake, the coves where they anchored their rowboat for a little private romantic time, the arcade where Ned won her a small black teddy bear, and the ballroom where they held their wedding reception. She talked with humor about their high school shenanigans and the time Ned shoved John Vanderfield off a pier in a fit of temper, and the time Bernice Talmadge got so drunk on senior prom night she puked all over John Vanderfield's rented blue tux. In those days, they called themselves "The Fabulous Four," although no one else thought of them as fabulous; they simply referred to themselves as fabulous as a kind of affirmation of future success in life. They were young and energetic and full of dreams, and their troubles were the same troubles as Stephanie's generation.

She took Stephanie to a spa where the girl received her first full body massage, facial, manicure, and pedicure. Afterward, they enjoyed lunch at a fancy restaurant along the river. They talked intimately about many things, including sex (it was time, after all). They visited the DMV the next morning where Stephanie got her learner's permit, and Ida proceeded to give the eager girl her first driving lesson in the vacant parking lot of a defunct department store.

Ida concluded their "mini-vacation," as she called it, with a visit to Oakview Cemetery where they placed bouquets on the graves of Grace and Rudy Tarantino and Ned Norris. They told Ned all the latest news and told him how much they missed him. And then right there on the soft green grass of Ned's grave, Ida laid out their picnic lunch, which included a serving of wine for two, and they broke bread in his honor after saying a prayer for him.

Despite Ida's efforts to raise her spirits, Stephanie continued to battle an unrelenting bout of depression that worried those close to her. She returned to school only because she had no choice in the matter, sat stone-faced and uncomprehending through her classes, and she even skipped Quinn's twice-weekly after-school dance practices.

Farley took her for drives along the river and into the foothills. He introduced her to one of his hobbies, collecting quartz crystals, and they searched together for more to add to his collection and for her to begin her own collection. The fresh air and exercise temporarily revived her, as did Farley's respectful affection towards her, but her melancholy mood held fast which only increased her despondency. She spent more time alone after school in the attic where she revisited the old photo albums, held one-sided conversations with Isaac, and too often fell asleep on the old sofa below the window. Her mother treated her with tenderness and infinite patience with the expectation only time would heal her wounded spirit.

Quinn demonstrated far less patience. He tried the "tough talk" approach with her that only served to enrage her and create a widening chasm between them. What Quinn didn't comprehend was that he was emulating the same hopeless approach others had unsuccessfully tried on him; inwardly he was just as miserable as Stephanie but hid it better. His frustration and concern for Stephanie led him to seek Caleb's advice. Although Caleb could offer no immediate advice to Quinn, they had many discussions in the woodworking shed while painting birdhouses. Their friendship deepened while Stephanie continued to distance herself from Quinn and everyone.

Finally, it was Caleb who lifted Stephanie out of her abyss. He joined her in the yard one day when she was planting spring bulbs. He revealed what he felt safe revealing about his past and the misery he had experienced, all the years of deep despair brought on by beatings at home and ridicule at school. And, with unashamed tears, he explained to her that he would not be alive had it not been through the loving efforts of her grandmother, Grace Tarantino.

He had meant his revelations to be an icebreaker with her. Instead, Stephanie consoled *him*, which was not what he wanted, "If my dad was still alive, he would love you as much as Grandma Grace loved you."

Caleb adopted her statement about her father as an alternative "in", for she seemed willing to talk about him. He brushed her hair away from her eyes and peered lovingly at her, "That's what your mother said. She told me a lot about him. She also told me you wanted to be just like him, right down to being a firefighter." He became silent for a few moments as she scoffed at herself for wanting to be a firefighter. After she cleared her throat and looked away from him, he told her, "But he's gone now. Let him go, Steph. It's okay to hold onto your memories of him, but it's not okay to hold onto him. Hold on to those of us who are still here with you. We love you just as much as he loved you. Embrace the living: your mom, me, and Quinn."

She twisted her mouth distastefully at the mention of Quinn. "Quinn's an ass."

Her hard opinion angered him, and his anger lay just below the surface of his voice when he reprimanded her. "Do you have any idea how devastated Quinn was when you broke down that day? He didn't want to leave your side. I could see the helplessness in his eyes as he held your hand while you slept. If anyone understood what you were going through, it was him. And now you've hurt him by pushing him away."

"Well, he was telling me to *just move on*. What the hell is that? Like I'm supposed to toss my dad aside like he was nothing to me!"

"That wasn't what he meant."

"Quinn doesn't know everything."

"He knows more than I do about these things."

"He wants everyone to think that."

"Let's forget about Quinn for now. Let's talk about you."

"I don't want to."

"Well, I want to." Caleb then took one of the daffodil bulbs and set it into the hole Stephanie had dug for it. "This is you right now; a creation full of promise but suspended in the midst of a long cold winter. However, with winter comes the rain that nourishes both the soil and the bulb, which begins the transformation and growing process. Without the winter cold and rain, the bulb could never produce

Hell Is In Me

flowers. It would be nothing but a bulb, never changing, never growing, never producing anything of beauty for the world to see and enjoy. We have to have winters in our lives, don't you see? Through all the cold, all the wet, all the darkness, and all the pain, the *You* rooted in all of this gains strength and rises and breaks through into the sunlight, a transformed creation full of beauty and promise. This is what's ahead for you, Steph. Accept the rain. Can you do that?"

She scrunched up her brow at him, "Where'd you come up with this?"

Her response embarrassed him. "It comes from something Gene and I were talking about when we were planting stuff in his garden."

"Gene again… And I'm a goddamn daffodil bulb."

He drew soil over the bulb and patted it down. "I guess I'm wasting my time."

"No…"

"My heart hurts for you, Steph. It kills me to see you like this."

Her eyes filled and she let the tears fall. "I get it. I'm just afraid that I'll forget him."

"You'll never forget him. By letting go of your grief over him, you're honoring him and releasing him in peace. It's just like I had to do with Ms. Grace. Now when I think of her, those thoughts make me happy, and everything she taught me I put to use every day."

Her nose and cheeks reddened. Her voice strained to escape her tight and painful throat, "The beauty and promise…" She fought to keep her composure, to rein in the painful waves of emotion surfacing.

All Caleb wanted to do at that moment was take her in his arms and provide her a safe place to surrender her grief. He tenderly caressed her cheek, gazed into her flooding eyes with deep compassion. His voice came as an echo of his own suffering and yet as a testament of hope, "Yeah."

At that point, Stephanie finally broke. Caleb held her as she emptied the ocean of grief from her soul, and by holding her close against his chest he was salving his old wounds, the wounds and scars of every injustice done to him, every brutal slap and kick, every spirit-killing condemnation that he was no good and would never be good. The pain broke upon him and washed over him like a torrent. He was not prepared for the onslaught for he had thought it resolved a long time ago. Now he realized a remnant of his past torments would linger just below the surface, and he felt himself grieve for that little boy who would forever struggle to stand tall despite it all.

Stephanie felt his tears wet her forehead. She glanced up into his face, saw not the face of Caleb the strong and resourceful man, but Caleb the despondent abandoned child. His tears created salty wet trails that seeped from under his tightly closed eyelids and stained his cheeks. It was then through the lens of her own sadness she recognized the profound roots of his compassion and empathy, the lingering misery of a child denied love, nurturing, and encouragement, a child denied his childhood. Oh, yes, he understood grief; he understood it well.

He murmured, "You'll be okay."

She understood he meant that for himself as well as for her. She tightened her arms around Caleb, and they held each other for a long time.

20

The shade spread throughout the grove as the sun settled upon the western horizon. Pale yellow light dappled the dry soil laden with dead leaves and decades of spent acorns and walnut husks. Gradually, the little sprinklings of yellow diminished, and the trees and bushes became silhouettes against the clearing. The few upright headstones in the graveyard stood as black sentinels in the dawning night. The birds quieted and the insects began to sing. A gentle lazy breeze cooled the evening air. The myriad scents of the trees and bushes and wildflowers rode upon the air, and their combined fragrance filled Caleb with a sensation of tranquility.

He could not feel his feet press the littered soil as he trudged among the headstones. His body felt weightless and free of the dull pain of psychologically induced muscular tension that had dogged him for years. He enjoyed the relief of his pain-free body, yet he found it vaguely disturbing, as if his core with all its scars of past trauma had taken flight and left him with a numb empty shell.

Compulsion drove him onward, wandering among the black sentinels. They seemed to be waiting for him, inviting him to stay awhile.

The friendly voice of a young man called in his ear, "This way. Just ahead to your right. I'm waiting. Come see me."

Caleb obeyed, veered to his right, and crossed over the graves in his path.

His mother once remarked, "It's bad luck to step on a grave."

In his mind, Caleb replied, *You're my bad luck.*

He feared just thinking of her would bring her to his side. She would spoil everything. She would erase every good thing in his life, every good thing he had attained purely through his own efforts.

Get lost. Get out of my head. Get out of my world.

She appeared before him, blocking his way. Her face was full of sores and aged far beyond her years. Her teeth were gone; their absence made her lips fold inward, drew her cheeks into shadowy cavities. Her hateful eyes drilled into his. His gut flip-flopped in response. He looked away from her, away from this walking corpse.

This time he screamed at her, "Get lost. Get out of my head. Get out of my world. I ban you. Do you hear me? I ban you!"

She dissolved into a ball of crimson light. The light danced in the air and then plummeted to the soil, evaporated into nothing.

Feeling victorious, Caleb resumed his journey, followed the voice that urged him, "This way. Over here."

Now there was only a sliver of light at the horizon beyond the graveyard. He thought it strange he could see the horizon behind the silhouetted trees that stood before it. He accepted the phenomena, his new ability to see what lies beyond what obscures.

The voice called again to him, "I'm here. Over here. Right here. See me."

He stopped and gazed astounded at the owner of the voice.

It's me. I'm calling to myself.

But the "self" was dressed in a dark suit. The open jacket and white shirt beneath it revealed black suspenders attached to the trousers. The young man sat casually upon an upright gravestone, a smile on his face, his bare feet dangling. He waved Caleb closer. Caleb approached him. They regarded each other with the silent welcoming acceptance of two old friends once separated now reunited.

He told Caleb, "You must release me."

"I don't understand."

"He'll kill you."

"Who'll kill me?"

"Jake."

Without taking a moment to comprehend how he knew the *Jake* identified was Jacob Sheers, and that he, Caleb, somehow intimately knew Jacob Sheers, Caleb questioned the young man upon the headstone, "Why?"

"Because I live in you." At that, he vanished.

A loud shrill buzzing tore through the cemetery. The gravestones vibrated, shattered, then collapsed in fragmented heaps. Caleb startled at the intrusive noise, marveled at the exploding gravestones.

He forced his eyes open and saw the bright red numbers, the time on his digital clock—6:00. He pressed the alarm button, and lay in his bed in the semi-darkness, the silence at once heavy and satisfying.

He replayed the dream in his head, tried to interpret its meaning. After a while he concluded it had something to do with his mother and the terrors of his past, the terrors he thought he had overcome.

Stop haunting me, you bitch.

Suddenly, his left cheek stung as if someone had just slapped him. Then, clearly—*clearly*—he heard a very harsh male voice yell at him, "Do what you're told!"

Half stunned and with shaking hands, he reached for the crucifix on a chain and draped it around his neck. He lay there for many minutes cupping the crucifix in the curl of his hands as he waited for his racing heartbeat to slow.

While he lay there, a realization came to him:

Quinn knew more than he let on.

* * * * *

The hum of an airplane caused Caleb to react with apprehension at first. He looked up and discerned it was a commercial aircraft, but it was too high up for him to identify the airline. His tension eased immediately as he recalled the government had finally reinstated air travel.

Gene stood erect upon the roof of the hilltop home that afforded a generous view of the valley and semicircle of mountains in their colorful autumnal glory. The plane entered and then exited one of the puffy clouds that dotted the pristine sky. Unlike Caleb, he experienced no post-traumatic reaction to the sound of its engines, but he recognized the initial fear in the young man's face.

"Heading west," Gene said. "Probably off to Hawaii where I'd like to be right now."

Caleb resumed laying shingles. "Hawaii's nothing but an overpriced tourist trap."

Gene laughed. "Like you've been there."

"Have you been there?"

"Once."

"Did you like it?"

"It was okay."

"If it was only okay, why do you want to go back?"

"Because winter is too friggin' cold here."

Caleb humorously chided him, "Weenie…"

"How are things going over at Ida's place?"

"Stephanie's doing a lot better."

"That's good. Can't believe it turned out you two are cousins. Small world."

"Yeah."

"I guess this means you get that cottage for life."

"I don't know about that."

"You're *family*!"

A troubled expression crossed his face. "I guess."

Gene saw Caleb's expression, nonchalantly began to refill his coil nailer. "What's going on, boy?"

"Promise not to laugh at me, Gene?"

"Yep."

"I think the cottage is haunted or something."

"What?"

"I've been having weird dreams, and sometimes I think I hear somebody whispering." He handed Gene his coil nailer. "Here. Refill this one, too."

"Maybe it's just Ms. Grace lettin' you know she's okay."

"No. The whispering is a man's voice."

"Maybe it's old man Tarantino."

"I'm surprised you believe me."

"I've never known you to come up with stories, Caleb."

"So… Do you think it's haunted?"

"I couldn't tell you unless I heard it myself."

"There's more, Gene. Someone or some *thing* I couldn't see slapped me this morning and yelled at me. They yelled at me, 'Do what you're told.' I swear I heard it as clear as you and me talking right now."

"Jesus H. Christ, Caleb! That's definitely a haunting! You're not thinkin' of movin' out, are ya?"

Caleb delivered his answer emphatically, "No."

"Good! Don't let them win."

"I won't. But I don't know what to do."

"Find a psychic to clear the place."

"Where the hell am I going to find a psychic around here?"

Gene shrugged. "The phone book?"

"Get serious…"

"I am serious."

"Well, I could use Ida's computer for Internet, but I don't want her to know."

"Use the library's computer. They got'em set up there."

Caleb considered it. However, he again thought of Quinn. Why was the boy so insistent about him wearing the crucifix all the time? What did Quinn know?

"Come to think of it," Caleb said slowly, "I might know somebody after all."

* * * * *

Two-dozen home-baked chocolate chip cookies proved the perfect bait to lure Quinn to his cottage that evening. Quinn arrived with an unexpected surprise in his pocket, which he took out and offered to Caleb.

"Have a smoke with me?"

Caleb eyed the joint disapprovingly. "Naw. I don't smoke that."

"Okay if I light up?"

Caleb knew from experience that weed tended to suppress inhibitions and loosen the tongue. His goal was to loosen Quinn's tongue to learn the truth. It was perfect. "Not in here. We can go down by the creek. I don't want the smoke getting in here."

Quinn smiled mischievously, "Bring all the cookies. Got any beer?"

"I have root beer."

"That doesn't work with cookies."

"Otherwise, I have ice water."

"Better than nothing." Quinn pulled open the back door and waited on the little porch while Caleb gathered the cookies into a bag and grabbed two bottles of water from the fridge. As they trudged down the dry weedy bank to the creek side, he teasingly told Caleb, "I had no idea you were such a square."

Caleb found a clear spot to sit. He replied to Quinn as he settled beside him, "Being a square is my personal choice. It works for me. So, where'd you get the pot?"

"I stole it outa my dad's stash. He smokes it every night, says it helps him sleep." Quinn paused long enough to light the joint and inhale a robust toke. He held it in for a few moments before he exhaled it. "Him and my mom both smoked it. They drank, too. They drank every night. I guess you could say they were alcoholics, although you'd never convince them of that. My mom, during her final days, smoked a lot of pot. She said it was the only thing that eased her pain."

"Does it ease *your* pain, Quinn?"

He grimaced. "Don't ask me shit like that."

"What did your mother have?"

"Breast cancer. It metastasized. She went quick. I don't wanna talk about it."

"But she was a real mother to you. She took care of you and loved you, and you loved her, right?"

"Of course. She was the best." He took another toke, closed his eyes and thrust his head back, released the smoke slowly.

"At least you had that, Quinn. Here, have a cookie."

Quinn took one, but didn't take a bite. Instead, he examined it. "You know, you could bake these with some pot in them. That'd be righteous."

Caleb laughed and replied, "No, I'm not lacing my cookies with pot!"

Quinn giggled at him. "Party pooper." He became silent while he took more tokes off the joint. In the interim he studied the terrain and the creek, noted the creek had very little water in it. After a while he commented, "They're talking about rationing water again if we don't get rain this winter. We've been in a drought for how many years now?"

"Five, I think."

"Do you think we'll get rain?"

"I'm not a fortune teller."

"Damn... Not only are you a square, you can't tell the future either. You're really boring, you know." Quinn said this with a lopsided grin. His eyes were already turning bloodshot from the pot. When he spoke again his voice came dreamily. "I like this time of day during this time of year. The shadows are long with the sunset. Have you ever noticed that?" After Caleb nodded, Quinn continued, "The air feels lighter. Do you know what I mean?"

"Uh-uh. I never thought about it."

"The air is heavy in summer. Didn't you ever notice that?"

"That's just the heat."

"Heat is heavy."

Caleb thought it was nonsense. Quinn was already good and stoned and getting philosophical like all the other pot smokers he knew. It was something he bore with patience back in The Day.

Quinn took one more puff and snubbed the remainder of the joint out to enjoy later. He put the stub into his pocket and casually observed the digger pines on the opposite bank. "Cold is light. That's why the air is lighter in fall and winter. That's my theory, anyway. I'll take some more of those cookies now." He stared off again, this time studying the play of sunlight on the trees and shrubs. The setting sun cast a rust-color glow upon the pale green pine needles and the slowly dying leaves of the shrubs. "I love the colors this time of year. Autumn has some of the best sunsets, too. Look at the colors on the pines, Caleb. I call that 'sun painting.' That's what I call it. Old Mr. Sun spitting fire paint on everything as a going away present. That's what it is. Maybe I should call it 'fire paint.'"

"Yeah. Fire paint. That's a good idea."

Quinn shoved an entire cookie into his mouth and chewed it up before he replied. "Fire paint. Brought to you courtesy of Old Mr. Sun. Man! These are good cookies. Can I take some home?"

"You can take all of them home."

"You really baked these yourself?"

"Yes, I did."

"Damned good. Yessirree. Thanks for inviting me over. Why'd you invite me, anyway?"

"I was just wondering how you've been doing. I know Stephanie's been hard to deal with these days, and now that Farley's in the picture, it's gotta be hard on you."

"I don't care. Stephanie's getting better. That's what matters. I don't mind if she hates me a while longer."

"What about Farley?"

"Farley's cool. Did he tell you I knocked Bruno out cold? Did he tell you about that?"

"I haven't had the opportunity to talk with Farley. What's this about Bruno?"

"He was screwing around with us on the road, trying to scare us. I walked right up to him and socked him. Broke his nose, knocked him out cold. Man, oh, man! I never felt so good in my entire life."

Caleb assumed it was another one of Quinn's stories. "No way, man."

"Yes way! Ask Steph. She was there. She'll tell you." He looked at Caleb arrogantly. "No one messes with me anymore."

"Don't you think they're gonna come after you? Y'know, Bruno's friends."

"That's the word. So far, they've done nothing. I'm not scared."

"Take my advice. Always be just a little bit scared."

"Why?"

"It keeps you vigilant."

"Did that work for you?"

"Yes, it did."

"But you were more than a *little bit* scared. You were a coward. You never talked to anyone. You disappeared as soon as school let out. You avoided everybody and everything."

"I hope that's just the pot talking."

"That's *me*, Quinn, talking."

"You don't know anything about my life."

"Does this mean you want your cookies back?"

Caleb chortled and shook his head.

Quinn continued his stream of thought. "Now, me… I can take it and I can dish it out. You don't know anything about my life, either. You don't know nothing about the things I've seen and the weird things I've experienced. Most people would be crazy by now, but I just keep puttering along. They must know I'm strong because they keep coming to me."

"Who?"

"Oh…" Quinn contemplated the cookies in his hand. He took another one and ate it. "Can you make some with raisins next time?"

"Sure. Who keeps coming to you?"

He laughed nervously. "Uh… I can't say."

"Which means you're full of bullshit. Why do you have to lie about everything?"

"I'm not lying."

"If that's true, maybe you're not the only one they keep coming to."

Quinn looked at Caleb confusedly, "Who?"

"The cottage is haunted. Is that the '*they*' you're talking about?"

Quinn rubbed his chin while he considered this. "Have you seen them?"

"No. But I've heard them." Caleb then told him everything. Quinn listened raptly, his bloodshot eyes and dilated pupils fixed intently upon Caleb's penetrating eyes. Quinn's complete attention confirmed Caleb's suspicions.

In conclusion, Caleb produced the crucifix from under his shirt and showed it to Quinn. "That's why you gave me this, isn't it? You're trying to protect me from them."

Quinn leaned across Caleb and grabbed one of the water bottles. "I'm thirsty."

Caleb persevered, "I need you to level with me. It'll stay between you and me."

"Are you scared of them?"

"One of them slapped me."

"Fuckin' ay! I got an idea who that was. Oh, shit…" He forlornly swung his head from side to side.

"You'd better tell me everything, Quinn. And I mean *everything*."

Quinn's emotional account lasted until the sun set and only crumbs remained in the cookie bag. The pot had worn off by the time they trudged to the cottage and continued their conversation. Now sober, Quinn wondered whether he had done the right thing by telling Caleb the whole story.

Caleb had only one more question, a question Quinn was at a loss to answer:

How does one release a soul trapped in a minute fragment of one's DNA?

21

Quinn did his best to ignore Jake who was sitting upon one of the tables in the school cafeteria. Jake had made it a habit to follow him at school for the past week. He never said a word; he simply watched Quinn with an aim to intimidate him. It didn't work the first two days, but on the third day in the boys' bathroom, with no one to see or hear, Quinn told him, "I'm still working on it."

Quinn maintained his routine despite Jake's creepy presence. This day the students in Quinn's tutoring session complained about the lack of heat in the cafeteria as they practiced their dance steps. The most persistent complainer was Mae Murray, who didn't need any dance practice but had joined Quinn's tutoring sessions simply to be near Quinn.

"I'm sure it's just a central heating malfunction," he told her casually, "If you can't handle it, go home."

She protested, "But I need the practice! Mrs. Standish said she's partnering me with you for the finale, and you're a much better dancer. I'll look like an amateur if I can't dance as good as you!"

Having Mae as his partner for the finale, *Sing, Sing, Sing*, was news to him; he had planned to have Stephanie as his partner. He immediately suspected Mae's parents, who were intimate friends with Mrs. Standish, had arranged this, just like they arranged for Mae to star in all the Drama class school plays which Mrs. Standish also taught. Mae was a mediocre actress and a mediocre dancer. The only thing she had going for her was her beauty and high-class family background. On the surface, Mae was congenial and charming, but below the façade, she was selfish and insecure. All she cared about was how she would appear to others, and no one in her small circle of friends had the heart to inform her she was nothing but a privileged rich kid who not only had no talent but was also dumb as a post.

"I had planned to partner you with Calvin," Quinn replied coolly.

"It doesn't matter what you planned." She gathered her curly blond hair into a ponytail and secured it with a rubber band, cast him a supercilious gaze as she did this.

He wanted to smack her. It took every ounce of self-control for him to maintain his dignity and patience. "Calvin is a very talented dancer, Mae. You and him will look good together." He then addressed Calvin who looked surprised. "You'd like to have Mae as your partner, wouldn't you, Cal?"

Calvin's eyes grew wide with pleasure. "Uh... sure."

Mae insisted with a slight whine, "But I want to dance with *you* in the finale,"

Over at the table against the wall, Jake giggled and shouted to Quinn, "She's wet for you, boy!"

Quinn almost reprimanded him but remembered at the last millisecond the others could not see or hear Jake. Gathering all the patience he had left, Quinn addressed Mae politely. "Well, we'll see. For now, let's practice. Let's see where you're having trouble."

She brightened, all her perfect teeth on display with her happy grin.

He stepped over to the c.d. player that Farley was manning, all the while considering what number would give Mae the confidence to partner with Calvin instead of him. He instructed Farley, who was trying hard to stifle his amusement, "*I Double Dare You*." As the music began, he spread his arms out to Mae, "Okay... Let's see what you got."

It was an easy Fox Trot dance number that required no acrobatics such as that typical for The Jitterbug. Quinn started her off easy and then added a few Swing steps that he knew she could handle. The entire time she was gazing into his eyes, daring him to challenge her abilities. He ignored that and kept it as simple as possible while bolstering her confidence with encouraging platitudes.

She whispered in his ear, "Take me to the homecoming dance."

He whispered back, "I'm working at my dad's store that night helping him with inventory."

"You can get out of it."

"No, I can't."

The whine again, "Why not?"

"Because he needs me."

She pouted. "Bummer."

"I'm sure plenty of other guys want to take you."

She squeezed his well-developed biceps, "They don't have your muscle."

"That's a lie and you know it. By the way, you're an excellent dancer. You don't need tutoring."

"Really?"

"Really. As a matter of fact, I think Cal will excel under *your* tutelage."

"Really?"

"I mean every word. You two will bring down the house."

Jake taunted him from across the room, "Liar, liar, pants on fire!"

Quinn's bolstering of Mae's ego worked. Two days later, at Mae's request, Mrs. Standish assigned Calvin Lathrup as her partner for the eight-minute finale in which all the students would have a chance to shine. Farley had her for an early number in the show, and then he had Stephanie for a steamy number in the second half that was a Tango. As it stood, the four boys in the class did triple duty to give all the girls enrolled their moments in the spotlight. In the end, Quinn triumphed with Stephanie, the best dancer of all the girls, as his partner for the finale. Quinn, now with more pressing and urgent business to attend to in his life, cut his tutoring sessions to once per week on Wednesday afternoons.

* * * * *

Now fully awake and not understanding, but aware of his situation and the threat Jake posed to Caleb, Isaac continued to feed his memories into Caleb's dreams as a way of building a telepathic bridge to eventually unite them.

Tonight, he sent Caleb one of his fondest memories in hopes Caleb would recognize the importance of this recollection.

He was in the woodshed applying the final coat of varnish to his gift for Uncle Frank. The rocking chair with the flying geese was a special project; one Isaac did in secret. Oh! How Uncle Frank's eyes would glimmer when Isaac presented it to him on Christmas morning 1912.

Uncle Frank had taught him how to make simple things such as tables and chairs. The artistic embellishments came much later when Isaac discovered his once untapped talent for carving. Soon, he was making and selling jewelry chests, silverware chests, and elaborate hope chests from oak, cedar, and rosewood. Uncle Frank admired his work and gave him praise, commented about how he wished Aunt Lottie were still alive to see what an artist her young nephew had become.

Isaac heard the familiar ringing of bells, the slow trot of horse hooves, the girls' mischievous laughter as they turned the surrey through the open gates and up the path toward his house. He stepped outside the shed into the light rain and waved to them as Sarah brought the mare and vehicle to a halt.

Sarah smiled at him and thrust a towel-covered basket to him. "Good afternoon, Isaac, and we hope you have a Merry Christmas. I made a fruitcake for you and your uncle."

Beside her, Emily Vanderfield said, "I swear you must spend every waking moment in that shed of yours. What are you working on now?"

"A secret project," he whispered with mock conspiring.

Emily played along. "Oh! A secret. Why, I bet you're full of secrets. Tell us what it is. We won't tell."

"If I tell you, it will no longer be a secret."

"Oh, be that way!" She blushed as her eyes met his.

He averted his attention to the mare. "Miss Sarah, this girl needs a drink of water. Have you been visiting all over town today?"

"Delivering fruit cakes… yes."

"Well, this horse is worn out. She needs a rest."

"My goodness," Sarah exclaimed, "I had no idea. May I tie her by your well for a little while?"

Isaac led them across to the well where he filled a bucket of water and set it before the mare. The mare lapped it up greedily.

Sarah regarded the horse sympathetically. "Oh, my goodness. I forget how old she's getting. Thank you for your kindness, Mr. Iversen."

Still holding the basket in one hand, he crossed his arms in front of his chest; his heart was beating fiercely. "While she's having her rest, would you girls like to come in for tea or coffee?"

Emily gave him a shy smile. "Why, Mister Iversen, you know that wouldn't be proper, what with your household consisting of only you and your uncle."

"To the devil with propriety."

She flirted with him shamelessly and playfully, with every intention to win his heart. "My goodness, Isaac. You shock me."

"Shocking you wasn't my intent."

"I have an idea," Emily said brightly, "Sarah and I were going to have tea at my house after she brings me home. We're on our way there, and you're our last stop.

Perhaps the three of us could ride over and Daisy can rest in our barn. Jonathon wants to show you his new rifle, too. It was an early present from Papa."

Sarah interrupted apologetically, "It's getting very late, Em. I'd like to get home before this storm increases." To Isaac, she remarked, "The Farmer's Almanac says this will be a harsh winter coming. Did you know that?"

"Yes, I know."

"And, Daisy," referring to the mare, "Is getting wet, and she hates being wet. Poor thing. Jake will have to towel her down. Poor *Jake*. You know how he hates anything that resembles work. Well, we have to be on our way. I'll see you at school. Say hello to your uncle for us."

"Thank you for the fruitcake, Sarah." He wished Sarah had come by without Emily; certainly, she would have accepted a beverage and visited for a while.

Daisy drank all the water in the bucket. Sarah clicked her tongue against her teeth and undulated the reins, waved one black-gloved hand to him as the mare turned the surrey toward the road. He waved back to her, his heart finally calming, the saliva returning to his parched mouth. Her brown hair had come loose under her wide hat, and the strands bounced upon her shoulders as Daisy picked up speed. He imagined the softness of her hair entwined in his fingers.

He returned to the woodshed where he finished varnishing the rocking chair and then he put away his tools. His thoughts were of Sarah, though, and he decided he would use the leftover wood to make a trinket box for her for Christmas. He pictured the pattern he would carve on the lid, a single rose. Yes, she would like that.

Caleb turned over in his sleep. "Sarah…" He sighed and turned over again. "The chair's in Steph's attic."

Isaac spoke to him telepathically, "Help me, Caleb. Help me."

Caleb didn't hear him.

* * * * *

Jake screamed in his ear, "Up and at'em, Caleb, you shit head!"

Every nerve in Caleb's body jumped; he convulsed under the covers as he awoke and then sat up in the semi-darkness. Was it a dream? The hard slap to his cheek answered his question, and he yelled a string of expletives at the invisible culprit.

Jake screamed at him again, "Do what you're told!"

Caleb's temper boiled over, "Shut up!"

"I will eat you alive from the inside out!"

"I'm not afraid of you." No sooner had Caleb said that did he find himself thrown across the room into the kitchen. He landed hard with his back against the refrigerator. Winded and shocked, he could only sit there and wait for the next assault.

The chairs at the kitchen table flew onto the bed. The table tipped over and slid, came to a stop when it made impact with the back door.

Caleb covered his head with his hands, "Oh, Jesus! Help me!"

"Jesus is dead!"

"He's alive."

"He's a fraud!"

"No! I've been reading. I know he's real. His blood saves me, and his blood protects me."

"That's bullshit."

"You're not welcome here. Leave this place."

"Only if your precious Jesus drops in. Fat chance of that! He never helped me when I called for him, and he ain't gonna help you. I think I'll make myself at home." Jake then added, "Quit your shaking, asshole; you're rattling the fridge."

"What the hell do you want from me?"

"Give me Isaac."

Baffled, Caleb demanded, "What?"

"Do as you're told!"

"It's impossible."

"I'll tear your heart out."

Those words strangely calmed Caleb yet, at the same time, filled him with sadness. He could not fathom why he wasn't frightened until he recognized the threat was only a threat. Experience taught him when a threat was only a threat; all his wounds, all the agonies he still carried, had been delivered without warning. The wounds and the agonies had already rendered his heart half-numb, and he often wondered if all the true demons that had tortured him since childhood had already torn it out without his knowledge. And now this dipshit, mean-ass, psychopathic phantom thought he could tear out what no longer existed? The thought made Caleb laugh at the irony.

Jake puzzled at his reaction. "You think this is funny?"

Caleb shook his head, still laughing. "Someone already beat you to it."

Jake squatted in front of Caleb, shoved his face close enough for Caleb to get a whiff of his rotten chemical and booze odor. "You're a real piece of work."

"So are you."

Exhausted and fading from all his energy-draining activity, Jake left him with a promise, "See you again soon."

Caleb felt the warmth leave his body as if someone had siphoned it away. He sat there on the linoleum shivering in only his underwear. Overwhelming fatigue set in with his shivering. The shock of the experience began to ebb, and he found himself wondering if this had actually happened or if it was another nightmare. He reasoned he could have tipped over the table and thrown the chairs while sleepwalking during the nightmare. Yet, Jake's odor still lingered, and Caleb couldn't explain that away.

I need to talk to Quinn…

* * * * *

Big Band music drifted faintly to his cottage. Caleb awakened slowly; saw the time on his clock was 12:15. He had returned to bed and slept sporadically, awakened with a start at every sound. He finally fell into a deeper sleep sometime after ten that morning. The only fragment of a dream he recalled was something about swimming. He was swimming through murky water in search of something—what, he couldn't recall.

The music stopped. Quinn and Stephanie laughed and teased each other. Caleb couldn't discern the words, but he understood they had settled their differences and were now pals again. He was glad for Quinn; the boy had been hurting tremendously over Stephanie's anger with him – this Caleb knew, for Quinn was no expert at hiding his pain.

He found them reclining in the plastic lounge chairs on the Norris terrace, soaking up the weak October sunlight. Stephanie arose and gave him a gentle hug when he approached them, and he draped one arm across her shoulders and kissed her cheek.

"It makes me so happy to see you smiling again," he told her softly.

"Thanks to you." She unfolded one of the spare lounge chairs for him and set it in place. "Join us. Would you like an orange juice? Mom just made fresh-squeezed a while ago. We're up for seconds."

"I'd love that," he replied, smiling fondly at her. He settled into the lounge chair and watched her hasten toward the house. He couldn't help but be amused by the duck walk she unconsciously adopted when she was hurrying.

Quinn watched her, too, and then he gazed at Caleb with a smart remark playing upon his lips. "You'd better be careful. She could easily fall in love with you, and then, being you two are cousins, you'd be the proud father of gargoyle children."

Caleb's laughter welled up unfettered. It was not only what Quinn said, but also the goofy grin on his face after he delivered his words of wisdom. Caleb responded, still laughing, "That ain't gonna happen, my man."

"You'd have to fight Farley for her, anyway. He's taking her to the homecoming dance, and she's all excited about it. Ida's taking her shopping for a new dress today."

"Have you got any plans today?"

"Not a thing."

"I need to talk with you. I had a very unwelcome visitor this morning."

"Jake?"

"I'm sure it was him."

"Did you see him?"

"No. But we had a conversation—sort of. He yelled a lot, and I yelled back. The bastard slapped me again. He threw stuff around trying to scare me. As a matter of fact, he threw *me* against the refrigerator. He wanted me to give him Isaac—like I could do that. What the hell is his problem with Isaac?"

"He said Isaac can tell him what happened."

"What happened when?"

"He doesn't remember killing Isaac."

"Do you think someone else did it?"

"No. I'm positive Jake did it. He's crazy. I think he was always crazy."

"Why do you think he targeted Isaac?"

"I have no idea. Maybe Isaac was an asshole. Who knows?"

Ida stepped halfway out the sliding glass door. "Are you going to join us for brunch, Caleb? I made quiche Lorraine."

"I will never turn down, quiche Lorraine, Ida."

Quinn raised his hand and said, "Me neither."

"Well, you two come in, then." She shivered and brushed her hands briskly over her arms, "It's awfully cold out."

After she closed the door, Caleb returned his attention to Quinn. "What are we gonna do about Jake?"

"I don't know."

"Do you think he's all talk and no action?"

Quinn sat up from his reclined position, pressed his palms upon his bent knees, his expression serious. "I wouldn't underestimate him. He threw you against the fridge, for cryin' aloud."

"Yeah. Hurt like hell, too. Maybe we should get a priest or something."

"They only do that in the movies."

"So, what can we do? I'm sick of losing sleep."

"Losing sleep? That's all?"

"Alright already… yeah, I'm scared. Okay. I admit it."

"Are you wearing the crucifix I gave you?"

"Except at night."

"You're gonna have to sleep with it on."

Caleb shook his head dourly. "I can't. It makes me feel like I'm choking."

"Well, hang it on the wall behind your bed, then. It's got to be where he can see it."

"How do you know it'll work?"

"I don't."

"Then, why'd you give it to me?"

"Because I had nothing else."

"Shit…"

"I tell you what. Give me a ride into town later. There's a store—I'm sure it's open on Saturdays—that sells special oils and sage and stuff. We can bless the cottage with the oils and say some prayers, and then we'll burn the sage. They say sage is great for getting rid of evil spirits. We can try that. It wouldn't hurt."

"I've never heard of such a thing."

Quinn stood and patted Caleb's shoulder. "Just trust me, man."

22

Caleb did not put much trust in Quinn's latest remedy, but he went along with it because, as Quinn said, "It wouldn't hurt." Caleb felt like a bystander as Quinn took over their mission at *Guiding Light Books and Gifts* in the old part of downtown Providence as Quinn presented a list of needs to the middle-aged hippie-throwback woman at the counter. Her long tie-dyed dress, beaded necklace, and matching earrings reminded Caleb of a late 1960's photo of Grace Tarantino. The woman took a basket and led them through the aisles, collected the vials of "blessed" rose oil; a slim palm-size cross carved out of olive wood (the sticker said "Made in Israel"); a bundle of dried sage and the requisite abalone shell to go with it.

Upon return to the counter, the woman tossed in a complimentary book of matches with their purchases and inquired as to the nature of the spirit or spirits they were attempting to banish. Before Caleb could even think how to describe Jake, Quinn gave her his well-rehearsed succinct account of the violent haunting. He omitted the information about his ability to see and converse with the dead.

Yet, once Quinn finished his spiel, the woman gazed straight into his eyes and said, "You're a Medium." Then, as Quinn stood there speechless with his mouth half-open, she produced a short piece of paper and set it on the counter. "These are the prayers you must say as you use the oil to paint the Sign of the Cross on every door and threshold. The prayer at the bottom of the page is the closing prayer after you have saged the home."

She abruptly shifted her attention to Caleb, and she took his hands in hers as she told him, "This spirit is using your past troubles to manipulate you; be mindful of that. But that's not all. There is a second spirit that attached to you in the womb. That spirit is becoming active inside you. He's been trying to communicate to you through your dreams. He's trying to protect you." She grimaced and shut her eyes. Her grip on Caleb's hands tightened as she added, "So troubled… some kind of injustice done to him and someone else. Much sadness… He wants to right things. Oh…!" At this, she released his hands, "You two must be very careful. There are many involved."

"Many spirits?" Quinn inquired uneasily.

"Yes. I can't say any more. They're draining me."

Quinn did not believe her. If the dead were there, he would see them. "They're here?"

"They're appearing to me, but hiding from you. Please go now."

Once they returned to Caleb's truck, Caleb sat troubled behind the wheel. He made no attempt to turn the key in the ignition.

Quinn nudged his arm, "Are you okay?"

He gazed ahead at the store's windowless stucco wall that faced the parking lot. "What if this doesn't work?"

"It *will* work."

"What if it doesn't?"

"Don't doubt. They feed on fear and weakness. Be strong. Believe."

"Easy for you to say; you can see the bastard."

Quinn helped himself to a cigarette from the pack on the dash. "That same bastard threw you against your fridge and sent stuff flying around your cottage. You have to face this or he'll win."

"What will he win?"

"He'll take your sanity – Jake will. Do you want to live the rest of your life in a nuthouse or wandering homeless on the streets? That's what'll happen."

Caleb cussed to himself, took a cigarette and lit it. He inhaled a long drag and pushed it out with vicious force. His cheeks reddened as he considered Quinn's warning. The cigarette trembled between his fingers. Quinn strained to hear him when he stated dejectedly, "I need a case of beer."

Quinn stated firmly, "We need to be sober for this." When Caleb offered no reply, Quinn added, "That's Jake trying to weaken you. He knows all about your past. He knows you've inherited your mom's weakness for drink and drugs."

"I never told you about that!"

"You didn't have to."

"I've never touched either because I saw what it did to her and all her so-called friends."

"Then, don't start now. I'm here for you, Caleb. You're not alone in this. You've gotta trust me."

He slammed his palm upon the steering wheel. "Why the hell was I born?"

"To right the wrongs of the past; to break the cycle. Maybe even go on to do great things with your life. You have it in you. You're stronger than you think." Quinn turned sideways in the seat. He faced Caleb directly, his expression sincere and compassionate. "Despite everything you went through you kept it all together, worked hard to rise above what you were born into. You inspire me. Don't you know that? You inspire me."

Caleb felt his eyes sting. He looked away from Quinn, looked out the side window, wondered how much Quinn ascertained about his past battles. Did Quinn know about the worst of it?

Quinn offered no indication about any of that; his mind was set on the present. "So, let's do this."

Caleb turned to him and smiled subtly. He put on the sunglasses that made him look like a mosquito and turned the key in the ignition. "Let's do this!"

* * * * *

By the time they finished saging, clearing and blessing the cottage, only one thing was clearly evident to Caleb: he was allergic to burning sage. His eyes itched, he sneezed repeatedly, and his lungs protested. It would take at least the rest of that day and night for the smoke to disperse. He considered it would be worth it if Jake and all the other spirits dispersed in the process.

He easily accepted Quinn's offer of the guest room for the night at the Vanderfield home. There, Maria doted on him as if he was royalty, which Quinn considered both hilarious and touching. It had been years since the opportunity arose for her to play hostess, and she made an event out of it by cooking her favorite dishes, plus flan for dessert. She set out the best towels and a mug of hot chamomile tea in the guest bathroom and, learning Caleb had only a shower stall in his cottage, encouraged him to soak in their antique claw foot bathtub as long as he wanted. The experience was truly a luxury to him, and he soaked for well over an hour in the hot water, Epsom salts, and jasmine-scented bubbles. For the first time in months, he felt the nagging soreness leave his muscles, felt the ever-present tension leave his body and mind.

When he returned downstairs after ten o'clock to join Quinn and Maria in a game of Tri-Ominos, John Vanderfield, stinking of weed, was killing his second bourbon on the rocks while taking part in the game. John greeted him with enthusiasm and offered him a glass of bourbon, which he politely refused. The four played until eleven-thirty during which time John emptied two more tumblers of bourbon. The man was red-eyed and bleary-eyed, and more than a little clumsy by the time they called it a night. Although the sight of John like this upset him, Caleb gracefully excused himself and retired to the guest room where a large bed with a feather filled mattress cover and down filled pillow awaited him.

No sooner had he settled in then Quinn tapped on his door and asked to come in. Caleb welcomed him, and Quinn moved the upholstered chair from the vanity table to the side of Caleb's bed.

"How do you like your accommodations?"

Caleb gave him two thumbs-up and intoned happily, "Bliss!"

"You can stay over any time you want to, you know."

"Thanks. I appreciate it. I want to take this bed home with me."

"All of the furniture in this room dates to the late eighteen hundreds," Quinn said proudly. "Emily carved her name on that vanity table over there. I think this must have been her room at the time."

Caleb found the name familiar, but couldn't fathom why. "Emily?"

"Uh-huh. My great-great-aunt. She was friends with the Tarantinos. My whole family was." He paused suddenly in thought as if something important just occurred to him. "Damn! I forgot all about it! Her photo album is in that chest of drawers over there. I need to get that out for Stephanie."

"Why?"

"There are some pictures of the Tarantinos in there. Back in the old days, us Vanderfields threw a lot of barbecues and stuff. The Tarantinos were always invited."

"No kidding...?"

"Yeah. There are a lot of photos of Isaac. Steph'll want to see."

To Caleb's knowledge, Stephanie had turned her attention to Farley and was less interested in the mystery surrounding Isaac. He immediately thought it was a bad idea to re-ignite the girl's obsession with Isaac.

"You shouldn't do that," he advised Quinn.

"How come? She's been bugging me to find more old photos of them all."

"Ida wants her to find other interests. You've gotta admit Steph was starting to get a little crazy over that Isaac business."

"Oh, yeah... I forgot."

"But, *I'd* like to see the pictures."

As he removed the album from the drawer and brought it to Caleb, Quinn said, "My great-great-grandfather Jonathon was the shutterbug in the family. He took almost all of the pictures, so there isn't many of him in here. He looks just like my dad. But, wait'll you see Emily. She was beautiful."

"She must have had a lot of boyfriends. She married well, I bet."

"No. She died of pneumonia at eighteen. You re-set her headstone down in the cemetery, remember?"

"Oh. That's why the name *Emily* rang a bell with me."

"Yeah." He referred to the album on Caleb's lap, "Open it up and let's see."

They examined the photos together, Quinn identifying the subjects. They found many photos of Emily and agreed she was indeed a beauty. Caleb was amazed at the resemblance between himself and Isaac Iversen. He and Quinn both found it curious that Isaac was in so many of the photographs, often accompanied by Emily alone.

"They must have *really* liked each other," Caleb remarked confidently.

Quinn didn't see it as anything deeper than friendship despite what Caleb's tone suggested. "Well, they grew up together."

As they progressed through the album, something puzzling became apparent; many photographs had been removed, leaving blank spaces on the faded black pages. Quinn presumed someone had removed them to put them in frames or into a different photo album. "They're probably of the Tarantinos and up in the attic at Stephanie's."

Caleb felt fatigued. He closed the album and told Quinn, "My eyes are beginning to cross. I'm gonna get some sleep, buddy."

"You can look at the rest tomorrow."

As Quinn stood to leave, Caleb inquired, "Do you think my cottage is clear?"

"We'll know tomorrow."

* * * * *

Maria served a huge breakfast the next morning: bacon, eggs, sausage, hash browns, English muffins, fruit, and menudo. Because she expended so much effort to cook such a feast, Caleb ate more than he needed or could comfortably hold. Quinn had no trouble at all going for thirds. Caleb was astounded at how much the boy could eat.

With their bellies full, they returned lethargically to the cottage, both fighting the urge to take a long nap. They found the sage smoke had deteriorated enough for Caleb to tolerate what little remained, although it made his nose itch. The first thing he did was open the windows and doors.

Quinn stood in the kitchen that opened to a full view of the sleeping area, surveyed the scene and tried to read the energy there.

"Well, Caleb. How does it feel to you?"

"Quiet."

"But, how does it *feel*?"

"Peaceful."

Quinn gave him a triumphant half-smile, "I think it worked. Put a small nail on the wall behind your bed to hang your crucifix on at night."

"Why? They're all gone."

"Insurance, dude."

Caleb blew out a long impatient sigh, "Whatever."

"You know, we should join Maria at church this morning."

Caleb made a face, "Uh… I don't know."

"She made us that big breakfast and everything. Plus… we should go there just to let God know we appreciate His help with this. Plus… I want to take Communion."

"I never would have taken you for a churchgoer, Quinn; not with all the cussing you do."

Quinn giggled at that.

Caleb said over Quinn's giggling, "Besides, I don't have any good clothes. I've got jeans and tee-shirts and stuff, but nothing appropriate for church."

Quinn flipped his hand dismissively. "Nobody cares. Do you think Jesus and all the disciples had fancy wardrobes?"

"I wasn't there to see."

"Smartass…"

"I'm tired. I'm staying home." He dug in his pocket and removed a ten-dollar bill from his wallet. "Here. Give this to the donation basket for me."

"A guilt offering?"

"No! A thank offering."

Quinn took the money and put it in his pocket. "Okey-dokey. Have a nice nap."

"Later on I might go shopping for one of those feather filled mattress pads."

"In that case, bring plenty of cash!"

"I don't care what it costs; I want one. I want one of those bathtubs, too. I guess I'll have to get Gene to help me add on a new bathroom to hold it." He grinned, amused with himself and his newly discovered love of luxury.

Caleb slept well that clear and cloudless Sunday morning. When he awoke early that afternoon, he recalled no dreams, but only a vague memory of the distant sound of a baby crying. Now awake and able to think about it, Caleb assumed what he heard in his sleep was likely an argument between some visiting stray cats from the ranch at the junction.

He had absolutely no idea a gentle young woman in a long sapphire-blue dress had rested beside him with her tiny baby nestled between them.

23

Stephanie's knee length dress for the homecoming dance was merlot red with a sprinkling of rhinestones at the rim of the sweetheart neckline. Her mother splurged on matching high-heel shoes and a necklace for the event, a little gold heart pendant on a fourteen-karat gold chain. When Stephanie put on the whole ensemble and viewed herself in the full-length mirror, she saw a young woman instead of the gawky soon to be sixteen-year-old girl she was accustomed to seeing. She couldn't wait to see Farley's reaction, and she could hardly wait for the event itself, her very first date.

Her mother viewed her with admiration, "You are absolutely beautiful, Steph."

"And, you'll help me with make-up?" Stephanie inquired anxiously.

"Of course. Not that you need a lot."

The girl blushed. "He wants to know what color my dress is so he can match the corsage. How do you explain 'merlot'?"

"I already talked to him. Your corsage will match perfectly."

"When was that?"

"This morning."

"Oh, thank you, Mom!"

"And don't come flying downstairs the moment you hear the doorbell. You don't want him to think you're in a rush. I'll open the door, have some small talk with him, then I will *inform* you your date is here."

"Is that how it went with Dad when he took you to the Prom?"

"Exactly."

"Why?"

"Men enjoy feeling they are the pursuers. You don't want to be easy to catch, do you?"

"But, it's Farley. He's already caught me."

"Oh, Steph. Please trust me. This is a special occasion. And don't forget to compliment him right away on how handsome he looks. That counts for a lot. And don't take the corsage from him. Let him pin it to your dress."

"It's a wrist corsage, Mom."

"Well… let him slide it onto your wrist."

"Okay."

"Kissing is fine, but make sure he keeps his hands to himself."

"This is an awful lot of rules for a simple dance."

"Honey, you in that dress – oh, maybe we should have chosen something else."

"Maybe I should wear sweatpants and a sweatshirt. Will that make you relax?"

"I like Farley, and I trust him, but boys are boys. Please set the boundaries and don't allow him to cross them."

"I bet you and Dad had lots of kissing and beyond on Prom night."

"I set the boundaries. He respected them."

Stephanie doubted it was true.

Ida said with a guilty smirk, "Don't give me that face."

* * * * *

With Caleb now safely on his way to the cottage, Quinn turned away from the front door and stepped quietly up the stairs. He felt all wound up. He followed the increasing strength of the vibration through his house until he entered his bedroom where the sensation was strongest. Now he was at the French door that led to his little balcony. He stepped out and leaned over the balustrade, peered out over the grove and the partially hidden cemetery, his eyes scanning the scene for the shimmering black aura that radiated tiny sparkles of multi-colored light. It did not take long for him to see it and to see Jake's form within it.

Jake was kneeling at one of the graves, facing away from him, rocking back and forth. The sight reminded Quinn of the black-draped Iraqi women he had seen on the television news that were mourning their children killed in the war. Jake remained like that for many minutes, rocking, rocking. He moaned a long, drawn out, sorrowful moan. The black expanded and shimmered. The sparkles of light shot skyward and receded into the black in a few second's time. Jake stood unsteadily, shook his fists at the deep amethyst sky. His cry of profound despondency and rage cleaved the air.

"Just let me talk to him! Let me talk to him!" Jake exploded into black shards and soaring sparkles of bright colors that burst and fluttered like a million psychedelic starlings.

When that happened, the air turned frigid. There came a gust of cold wind from Quinn's right. It slammed against him and chilled him to his bones before it continued off to his left. He watched the trees and bushes bend to the force as the wind passed. It seemed to him the air was running as if by command to join the erratically dancing fragments. As the torrent met its target the shards and colorful sparkles died quickly. The air immediately warmed.

After a few moments of sudden silence, a mockingbird uttered, "*Talk to him talk to him talk to him talk to him…*"

Quinn sunk against the doorjamb, utterly stunned by the violence.

Was that Isaac's grave? How can Jake not know Isaac isn't there? Who was he yelling at? God?

A shrill scream sounded in the distance in the direction of the cemetery, grew louder. Quinn felt the piercing noise dive painfully into his head and travel into his ears where it pulsated with a stabbing sensation upon his eardrums. He squished his eyelids shut, covered his ears with his hands, folded his body forward, and ducked his chin almost to his chest. The position offered no relief. The pain was unbearable. He gritted his teeth and murmured a guttural cry that rose up from a forgotten primitive ember in his soul, that smoldering ember where eons of terror try to die but can not die, that ember surreptitiously touched and stirred in Quinn's moments of cowardice by Lucifer himself.

Stop it! Stop it! Get out of me!

Quinn's desperate cry of pain and fear united with Jake's despondent scream. The sounds harmonized and slowly subsided, relieving Quinn's pain. All that remained was a pulsation in his ears from the rapid and strong beating of his heart. Heat filled his body. His pores released a torrent of icy sweat that dampened his clothing, soiled the material with the pungent odor of spent adrenaline. He remained in his folded position, eyes tightly shut, hands to his ears, his open mouth panting.

Hands gripped his upper arms, squeezed them tightly. The smell of formaldehyde and stench of vomited whiskey assaulted his nostrils.

No, Jake!

Jake's raspy voice came angrily yet softly. "Don't spy on me."

Quinn opened his eyes; clearly saw Jake's misery laden face behind his thin gray veil of strengthened energy. Quinn immediately understood Jake had been gradually acquiring power from his earthly surroundings, and soon he would be dangerously formidable.

"I felt your presence. I wasn't spying on you."

Jake's eyes glistened with a mixture of misery and shame. "Even God has abandoned me."

"I don't believe that."

"Then, why am I trapped here? I must have done something horrible to deserve this. That's why I need Isaac. He knows the truth. And, here I am so close to finding out. You promised you'd bring him to me." Still gripping Quinn's arms, Jake angrily shook him. "I'm tired of waiting!"

Quinn did his best to remain calm, to prevent any type of reaction that would fuel Jake's temper. Jake's hands felt hard and icy upon his skin, like the hands of someone at the precipice of homicidal rage. This was bad, bad, *bad*, and all Quinn could do was remain silent in hopes Jake would interpret his silence as submission.

"If you don't give me Isaac..." It was both a warning and a plea.

The pleading tone beneath the threatening tone in Jake's voice gave Quinn the opening he needed. "If you do anything to hurt Caleb or anyone else, Jake... I won't help you."

Jake shook him again. "Then I'll kill you."

"And then I won't be here to help you."

"You'll be stuck here like me!"

"No, I won't. I have no reason to stay. I'll be glad to leave this place."

"You'll stay to protect your friends."

Quinn kept calm. "No, I won't. You know why? Because you and I both know if you hurt them, your chance of settling things, finding peace and finally crossing over will be completely obliterated. You'll be stuck here for eternity, and we both know you don't want that. You need me. We have to work together. Now, calm your ass down."

Jake shook him again, "Then, give me what I want!"

"Maybe what you want isn't what you need. Hasn't it ever occurred to you that the reason you're still here has nothing to do with Isaac?" Compassion arose in Quinn's spirit. "Tell me what happened to you. Tell me how you died."

"What? Why?"

"I've learned from the others that sometimes it's the way they died, or the circumstances, that kept them earthbound."

"It wasn't dying that hurt me; it was living. Living was like being dead and sentenced to hell."

"Let go of my arms – it hurts."

Jake released him and inquired in a childlike manner, "Do *you* like living?"

Quinn answered honestly without taking a moment to consider it. "Sometimes… but a good deal of the time, no."

Jake abandoned his squatting position and rested on his rear under the doorframe connecting the balcony to Quinn's bedroom. Now they were sitting together facing each other like two kids on either side of a campfire.

Jake scrutinized Quinn's face, "Your mouth looks like Emily's."

"Emily Vanderfield? My great-great-aunt?"

"She was kind to me. She understood things."

"Did you love her?"

Jake lowered his head with uncharacteristically self-conscious shyness. "I guess I did. Love… it's got many different flavors when you're seventeen. I never got to taste any of it, though."

"So, she never knew."

"She never knew. It's like you with Stephanie."

"I'm not in love with Stephanie."

"Keep telling yourself that."

"This is about *you*, Jake. Tell me how you died."

"I don't remember. They fried my brain. Do you know I walked right outa that place?"

"What place?"

"The madhouse. A bunch of them rioted one night. I snuck into the orderly's locker room while the staff was busy beating the shit out of the rioters. I put on somebody's street clothes and walked right out the back door into the alley, walked right out to freedom. You should've seen all those big tall buildings and the wide sidewalks full of people. And the noise! The racket of automobile traffic, sirens, and crazy music coming out of bars and clubs just about deafened me. And the lights! All the blinking lights everywhere. It plays with your brain, you know? Organized chaos. It was hard getting used to the noise and all the lights. But I was free. I didn't know where the hell I was, but I was free."

"What happened after that? What did you do with your freedom?"

Jake took a lengthy reflective pause. His voice became bitter and somber when he continued. "I saw the cops put my body in a wagon. I remember being in a drawer at the morgue – somehow I knew that. It was dark and cold, and I could hear the men's voices. They were talking about '*stiffs*' and autopsies and embalming – stuff like that. When they had to work on a body, they called them by their drawer number – that's how I knew I was in what they called a '*drawer*'. They had their own language for everything. Then I was out in the lights again on a table. They were cutting me up, and there were men up in this collection of seats, you know… like up in the balcony at the movie house – they were watching. They were watching these other men cut me up, and the men were describing the pieces of my body and… fuck… I was naked! Fucking bastards had me on display like some kind of freak show. I watched the whole thing, watched them cut me up and talk about me, talk about me being a drunk and full of disease and shit." He choked up and began to sob. "And when they were finished they sent some guys in that tossed all my parts into a big bag on this rolling cart thing. And… then I remember the next thing was this big huge furnace. I saw somebody toss the bag with what was left of me into that." Tears ran in steady streams down his face. His mouth and chin were trembling so hard he had difficulty expressing the words that followed, "That was it. They didn't even know my name. No funeral, no grave, no nothing. I didn't even get my name on a death certificate to show anybody I existed. What the hell! I heard of people giving dogs better than that."

Jake's revelation pained Quinn's heart as if they had experienced it together. Overcome, he gently placed his hand on Jake's trembling shoulder.

Jake abruptly stopped sobbing, regarded Quinn with a mixture of humiliation and grateful wonder. "What…? You're touching me."

Quinn did not pull his hand away. He set his empathetic gaze upon Jake's flooding eyes, offered no reply.

Jake said shakily, "I haven't felt the touch of another person in decades."

Quinn gently squeezed his shoulder. "You said living was like being dead in hell. From what you've just told me, being dead isn't much different—for you, in your experience."

"I want it to stop."

Tingling similar to that from an electrical current traveled up Quinn's fingers from Jake's shoulder. Nausea and weakness welled up inside him. Quinn pulled his hand away as he realized Jake was gradually becoming solid from feeding upon his life energy as well as the earth's energy. If this progression continued… Quinn couldn't imagine the consequences. He had to find some way to send Jake out of the dimension of the living and into the dimension of…

He gently questioned Jake, "How can we make it stop?"

"It rained so hard."

"What?"

He sang softly, "The itsy-bitsy spider…"

Quinn hung his head in frustration. He had never dealt with a spirit whose thought process ricocheted like a pinball.

Jake continued singing in a whisper, "…washed the spider out. Downspout… up the downspout…"

"You're tired," Quinn said, "Find a place to rest."

"There is no rest."

"Close your eyes and imagine a safe place that makes you feel peaceful. Do it, Jake. Close your eyes and go to that place."

Jake closed his eyes. His body gradually dematerialized and became what appeared to Quinn as a thin wisp of gray smoke. It swirled in the air and slowly disappeared.

Quinn had not expected it to work, but was glad that it did. He wondered if it meant Jake had crossed over, wondered hopefully if this was all it took.

* * * * *

Providence High School was not known for having a huge budget for festivities. Someone on the decorating committee thought they would save money by stringing white Christmas tree lights in a starburst pattern from the auditorium ceiling, and someone else draped all the tables with pale green paper table covers, and someone else decided small plastic bowls full of jelly beans would suffice as table centerpieces. The long snack table, borrowed from the cafeteria, had no cover at all, and was stocked with the usual giant bowl of red punch, tiny plastic glasses, plastic utensils, plain white paper plates, three pre-packed grocery store meat, crackers, and cheese trays, and three pre-packed grocery store veggie trays with little bowls of ranch dressing in the middle of each.

Stephanie and Farley looked upon the snack table with disappointment.

Farley said apologetically, "Last year we had barbecued chicken wings and potato salad, plus two different kinds of green salad and a cake in addition to all of this."

Stephanie took a moment to observe the small turnout mingling around the snack table and seated at the guest tables. "Well, so far there aren't many here to eat this food."

"It'll pick up later. Would you like some punch?"

"Sure."

He handed her a paper plate before he grabbed a glass for the punch. "Load up now before it's all gone."

Stephanie took only a little from the unimpressive culinary offerings. Farley did the same.

They chose a table near the exit doors at the advice of their mothers. Mothers thought about safety first. Farley's mom reasoned, "Best to be the first one out if there's a fire."

The subject of fire and escaping first out the door was not Farley's choice for conversation. Instead, after relieving Stephanie of her coat and pulling her chair out for her to sit, he told her, "I'm glad you dressed up for this. You really are beautiful."

She beamed up at him, her cheeks reddening beneath the light amount of rouge she had applied. He was the first boy to ever call her beautiful. The sincerity of his compliment made her feel beautiful.

He had also dressed nicely for the occasion: slate gray trousers, a light blue shirt and striped tie, and a dark gray sport coat. The combination of colors enhanced his slightly protruding eyes, which to Stephanie did not resemble "bug-eyes" or "fish-eyes" or "pop-eyes" as so many had commented behind his back.

She told him, "I think you look great, too."

He squeezed her hand before he took his seat, "Thanks."

"I can't believe you used to hang out with Bruno and those guys. You're not like them at all."

"We all connected in elementary school. I don't remember how it even happened; it just happened. I guess it was easier to be *with* them than *against* them." He shrugged his shoulders to indicate the subject was now irrelevant.

More students strolled in, many in small groups. They were all wearing casual clothes, but for one exception: Mae Murray sashayed across the auditorium in a sparkling dark green full-length halter-top gown. She carried a black fake fur stole draped over her left arm. Her date, the casually but nicely dressed Calvin Lathrup from their Big Band Blast class, carried two plates of food in one hand and balanced two glasses of punch in the other as he followed her to her chosen table at the front near the stage.

Farley rested his chin in the palm of his hand and laughed softly. "Poor Cal!"

Up on the stage the D.J. tested his equipment and made adjustments, then went through his four shoeboxes of CDs and chose one.

"Oh, shit," Farley moaned, "Not this guy again!"

"What?"

"He plays the worst music."

"What kind of music?"

"You'll have the displeasure of hearing it in a minute."

The shoeboxes contained Rap, Hip Hop, Grunge, and Urban Funk, most of it not dance-friendly. As a result, the area reserved for dancing hosted only a few couples at various times for various sort-of-danceable numbers. The exception once more was Mae Murray. She abandoned Calvin Lathrup after he refused to dance, took to the dance floor solo and feverishly exhibited her best moves and gyrations to every crappy song the ogling D.J. played.

Farley fastened his big blue eyes on Stephanie's, an impatient expression on his face, "Let's go someplace else."

She nodded happily, "Yes! Let's!"

Behind the wheel of his Cavalier, Farley inquired, "Where do you want to go?"

"I'm still new to this town. You choose."

He relaxed in the seat and thought for a few moments, and then he sat forward and turned the key in the ignition. "I know just the place. Good food and good people. I don't know about you, but I only had a light dinner."

"Me, too."

"Okay. You'll like this place. And, what the hell – we're dressed for it." He grinned and winked at her.

As Farley turned the car onto Providence Road, Stephanie asked, "Where are we headed?"

"Have you been to Riddling Creek Marketplace yet?"

She recognized the name *Riddling Creek* from her historical research related to Isaac. This sparked her curiosity. "There's a market out there?"

"Ten years ago the City Council voted to turn that area into a shopping and recreation area. It used to be nothing but an overgrown weed patch that was full of litter and stuff. Anyway, they beautified the area, put in a walking and biking trail along the creek, put in shops and restaurants; it's really something. There's a bridge over the creek that connects to the trail. Everything is all lit up all night for security reasons. The restaurant we're going to is in that complex."

"How much do you know about this town's history?"

"A little bit. Why?"

"Did you ever hear about a murder victim found at Riddling Creek back in the early nineteen-hundreds?"

"Everyone's heard about that. They never found the murderer. There are rumors the creek is haunted. I believe it. My dad is one of the people that saw a shadow figure on the bridge just this summer near sunset one evening. Said he almost… well, you know. I'm not trying to scare you. You're not afraid of ghosts, are you?"

"There's not much that scares me, Farley."

He laughed softly. "I figured that the day I first met you out by the junction."

"How many other people have seen this shadow figure?"

"I'm not sure. Maybe six or so. The sightings only started this summer. You must have read about it in the paper, huh?"

"We don't get the paper."

"So, how do you know about the kid that was murdered?"

"He was one of my ancestors."

"What? No shit?"

"Do you have any idea what part of the creek they found his body?"

"Right by the bridge. He washed up on some rocks. The paper said the year it happened the area had experienced record rains and the creek was at the highest it'd ever been. It flooded over a couple of times that year."

"Can you show me exactly where they found him?"

"Yeah, I guess. The bridge is lit up all night, so you'll be able to see it just fine."

"Can we go there before the restaurant?"

"The restaurant's right next to the bridge. No problem." He steered the car left at the four-way stop. A sign on the road with a straight-up arrow advertised the *Riddling Creek Marketplace and Recreational Trail*. The lights illuminating the area were visible in the distance. Farley obeyed the speed-limit sign and eased off the accelerator. "Would you like to go biking with me on the trail sometime?"

"So long as Bruno and those other two aren't around."

"They wouldn't be caught dead on bicycles."

* * * * *

Caleb rewound the cassette tape and listened to his pronunciation of a passage from a book on elocution he found at a thrift store. He could hear a hint of his Louisiana drawl but was mostly satisfied with his progress. His dictionary lay open beside him on his bed, a handy reference to teach him the proper pronunciation and meaning of unfamiliar words. He had been using this method for a few months, ever since a new client of Gene's who happened to be a television news anchor opined, unaware Caleb was within hearing range, that Caleb had a very attractive speaking voice but needed to work on his diction. Caleb had noticed this same woman, a single-by-choice career woman in her late twenties, often glanced his way in an interested fashion while he was installing crown molding in the living room of her new hilltop home. She looked at him like a hungry child looks at an ice-cream sundae, which Gene thought hilarious. Although it was a boost to his ego, Caleb pretended not to notice. He didn't need or want the inevitable complications should he reciprocate. However, her comment about his voice and diction re-ignited his desire to shed all hints of his low-class upbringing and improve his social skills.

He pressed the "record" button on the cassette player and read the elocution exercise once more, this time paying more attention to his breathing and pacing as he vocalized. Upon review, he found this third effort most encouraging, and he decided he could call it a night. He set the tape player on top of his bookcase, returned the dictionary to the far left on the first shelf and the elocution book to its place on the first shelf beside *Basic Etiquette for the Socially Inept* and *Manners Still Matter*. Every book on the first shelf covered the subject of self-improvement. The second and bottom shelf contained manuals about general construction, woodworking, and electricity, plus some books about gardening and landscape design.

Never stop learning. Thank you, Ms. Grace.

She would be pleased with his progress. He wished she were still alive to see how far he had come since that day she first brought him home with her, a dirty, defeated and frightened boy. The first thing she did was exchange one of her dusters for his filthy ill-fitting clothing and ordered him into the shower while she tossed his rags into the washer. After his shower, she drew a bath for him and ordered him to soak himself until he felt completely relaxed. He cried silently there in the tub, and he knew she knew he was crying. She never mentioned it to him when he finally presented his scrubbed and exhausted self to her dressed in her pink duster with a pattern of giant daisies on it. Grace fed him, bandaged his sprained wrist, and then she cut his hair, "So the world can see this handsome face of yours." After that, she put him to bed in Ida's former bedroom upstairs, covered him under the crisp sheet and soft cotton blanket, and tenderly caressed his forehead.

This is your home now, Caleb. No one will hurt you ever again.

He would never stop missing her, yet he was glad she was at peace. Of this, he was certain because Quinn would have seen her if that was not the case.

Quinn was correct that saging the cottage would clear out the bad energy and prevent Jake from returning. Since that project, Quinn had become an almost daily visitor. Caleb had come to look forward to seeing him at the end of the day, for the boy usually had something interesting to talk about, and the breadth of his knowledge about obscure subjects both fascinated and impressed Caleb. Quinn's wacky sense of humor often had Caleb in tears from laughing, and Caleb found he was able to return the favor until they were both bent holding their guts.

Earlier that evening they had watched Stephanie and Farley leave for the homecoming dance, both marveling at how gorgeous the girl was in her new dress, and both guffawing from the shelter of the cottage window at her *duck in a hurry* walk as she tried to keep pace with Farley on their way to his car. Caleb would have felt awful about it if the couple had heard them, but Quinn didn't care. The way Quinn saw it if a person couldn't laugh at themselves then it was their own fault for being so insecure.

They dined at Quinn's house where Maria expressed her delight that Quinn had developed a closer friendship with Caleb. She made certain they both had enough to eat before they left the dinner table. There was never a shortage of food at the Vanderfield home, nor a shortage of antiques for Quinn to show off his knowledge. The design, intricate details, and luxury of the old Victorian provided endless fascination for Caleb as Quinn took him on a tour of its hidden rooms.

The windows on the unused third floor offered a stunning view of the valley and Gadfee Lake Recreation Area, plus the golden domed roof of the Gadfee Lake Ballroom. They settled at the west facing window seat on the third floor with the best view of the ballroom and lake. Only a sliver of sun highlighted by a crest of bright yellow light remained behind the dark jagged peaks of the mountains. Below that, the parking lot lights at the lake popped on according to the timers. The lights cast an otherworldly sheen upon the domed ballroom. Quinn pointed it out to Caleb and described what it was like inside that grand and glorious place in the days before America became cynical. He talked about the music and the bands, told Caleb about his dead trumpet playing friend Buzz Lester and how Buzz had gotten him interested in Jazz. With a healthy dose of black humor, he told Caleb how Buzz drowned at Gadfee Lake after a woman cold-cocked him with her purse and he fell unconscious into the lake. From there, he talked about the heydays of Gadfee Lake when there was an illegal casino there run by mobsters, and a cluster of little cabins frequented by the prostitutes and their johns. The more Quinn described it, the more Caleb saw the strange wistful light in the boy's eyes, and he realized Quinn subconsciously found that long ago world more appealing than his present-day world.

Curled up there on the window seat, remembering Buzz, Quinn became lost in his memories of the many visitors he had assisted into the Light. "I learn a lot from dead people."

"Do you think you'll always be able to see and talk to them?"

Quinn took his time, his expression contemplative and serious before he answered, "I suppose."

"Don't you ever get scared?"

"Of what?"

"That someone evil might latch on to you."

He chuckled darkly. "Well, I got that now."

"Jake?"

"Bingo! I'm still trying to figure out how to get rid of him." Then Quinn immediately became quiet, spaced-out, as if he heard or felt something. He massaged his left hand, still spaced-out, his attention diverted and subsequently driven inward. "My dad'll be home soon. I promised I'd clean my room before he got home." He gazed trance-like into a distant hidden world of shadows and mist. "Yeah… I gotta clean. He's…" Quinn finally broke from his stupor and encouragingly told Caleb, "I'll see you tomorrow, bud."

Confused by and concerned about Quinn's sudden strange behavior, Caleb did not know what to do. He stood and waited for Quinn to rise and accompany him downstairs. "I have some reading to catch up on, anyway. Thanks for having me over."

Quinn walked Caleb to the front door. He gave Caleb a weak smile and a

Hell Is In Me

three-fingered wave before he gently closed the door. Caleb sensed something was wrong, and that something involved Jake. He wanted to turn back and knock on the door, convince Quinn to allow him in to help him confront Jake, but his intuition told him Quinn was resigned to handling the dead on his own.

That incident was on his mind now. He wanted to phone Quinn but reconsidered when he saw the time was ten o'clock, the time John Vanderfield returned home. He decided he would wait until tomorrow to learn what had caused Quinn to suddenly shut down.

For tonight, Caleb had only one thing left to do before he went to sleep, and that was to take a shower. His energy ebbing, he didn't spend as long under the water as usual. He toweled off quickly and got his toothbrush from the medicine cabinet. He glanced at himself in the mirror as he grabbed the toothpaste off the counter with his free hand.

Something about his reflection seemed strange. He froze in place, toothpaste in the left hand, toothbrush in the right, two Calebs staring at him from the mirror. The toothbrush jumped out of his hand and did a swan dive into the toilet.

What the f...?

The two Calebs merged into one.

Okay... That's it. I'm going to bed.

His reflection moved his right hand to the glass, pressed his fingers there. Caleb stared at the reflection of his fingertips now white with the pressure against the mirror. He looked away from the mirror, discovered his right hand was resting palm down upon the edge of the basin; the toothpaste was still in his left hand at his side. His reflection had discarded the toothpaste onto the marble vanity.

Maybe I have a brain tumor from all the times they kicked me in the head.

His reflection replied, "I don't know what a tumor is, but I'm certain you don't have one."

Caleb startled, lost his balance and fell backward against the towel rack.

His reflection spoke again, the face expressionless, "Get a hold of yourself."

Caleb could hardly hear his own voice over the pounding of his heart. "Am I going crazy?"

"We could, but we won't. You must help me."

Caleb caught his breath, willed himself to slow his breathing, still his panic, assess the situation. He scrutinized the *Self* watching him through the mirror.

This can't be a ghost. Quinn cleared the place.

He felt the cold pressure of the towel rack against his naked back. It was beginning to hurt. He slowly pulled himself erect and took two steps forward and placed his hands on the mirror, traced the face regarding him impassively. He could see the reflection of the undersides of his fingers upon the reflected face, and he thought at first that he was only seeing his own reflection, that something misfired in his brain to make him think his reflection was a separate being.

Until his reflection Self tilted its head to one side and then straightened up again.

"Oh… shit…"

His reflection glanced downward for the briefest moment, looked up again at Caleb with sympathetic eyes. "I'm sorry, but we're running out of time. He's getting stronger."

"Are you talking about—?"

"Jake. Yes."

"So, you must be…"

"Yes."

"And, I'm gonna wake up any minute now."

"We're both wide awake. Time's wasting. I have to do this, Caleb."

"Do what?"

"Leave you."

A lump formed in his throat. His mouth went dry. When his voice came it sounded to him like the voice of a terrified child, "What…?"

The reflection that Caleb understood now to be Isaac gazed at him sadly. "Quinn's dying."

Caleb gripped the rim of the basin with both hands, "No… No!"

He awoke hours later against the wall beneath the towel rack. The back of his head hurt, and he felt the area and discovered a small lump had formed there. He grabbed the slightly damp towel off the floor and wrapped his shivering body, tried to estimate how much time had passed since he lost his balance and fell and hit his head on the towel rack. He sat up slowly and saw it was still dark outside the small bathroom window. The tube of toothpaste was on the floor against the base of the vanity. His toothbrush lay still on the surface of the water in the toilet.

His only recollection was stepping out of the shower and reaching for his towel. He half smiled, slowly shook his head and chuckled to himself, "Klutz."

* * * * *

There was not enough light for Stephanie and Farley to safely work their way down to the spot where Isaac came to rest so many decades before. Disappointed, she had to be satisfied for tonight with the shadowy view from the stone bridge that spanned the creek.

Farley tightened his grip on her hand as they leaned over for one last look. "We'll come back during the day."

She rested her head against his shoulder, "Do me a favor and don't tell my mother about this."

24

Quinn felt like hell. His health had been deteriorating for two weeks, and now he was at the point where he could barely make it out of bed each morning. Getting through an entire day of school was a battle he was gradually losing.

The culprit was not an infection or a virus; it was Jake. Jake was now dogging Quinn on a daily basis; sometimes behaving belligerently, and often times clinging to the boy as if they were best friends. Quinn could never predict Jake's mood, and that only added constant stress to his mind, and that stress further weakened his immune system. Conversely, Jake was becoming stronger, and his form was becoming visible as attested by the various eyewitness reports of a "Shadow Man" wandering the Providence High School corridors, the Riddling Creek Marketplace and Recreation Trail, and the many rooms inside the Vanderfield home.

Bernice Vanderfield's treasured Royal Doulton china collection suffered due to Maria dropping a plate or serving dish every time Jake entered the kitchen on an energy-collecting mission. Like Quinn, Maria began to experience chronic fatigue and debilitating headaches. Quinn's consistent denials of ever seeing anything unusual only added to the woman's frustration and fear. A chance to escape her duties and the newly oppressive atmosphere at the Vanderfield residence arrived like a gift from God in the form of her niece's upcoming wedding in San Jose. She approached John Vanderfield to secure time off for the wedding, and she also informed him of the supernatural occurrences she had been witnessing in the home which made her not only afraid for her own safety but Quinn's as well. John considered Maria's hysterical accounts of a "demon spirit" in the house as pure nonsense brought on by overwork and too much time alone. He had not witnessed Jake's presence because he spent little time at home, and was too loaded to notice anything when he was home. Deciding she was long due for a break, he generously gave Maria three weeks paid leave and even purchased her round-trip airfare.

Although glad to be rid of Maria for a while—only because he needed privacy to deal with Jake, Quinn stewed over his father's generosity to her. *Where is that damned car you've been promising me for two years*? To which John retorted, "You don't even have your learner's permit yet. Shut up about the car." They went round and round about it, and it ended in a stalemate with Quinn slamming his bedroom door and retiring to his bed for the rest of the day and night. His resentment and anger fueled his underlying depression. His depression became worse, and that only added to his physical debilitation.

Tonight brought him an almost insurmountable challenge: the Big Band Blast performance at Providence High. He had no idea how he would get through it, and it was obvious to Stephanie and Farley as they searched through the Drama Department costume racks in the school basement.

Stephanie dug through her purse and produced a small tin. "I have some aspirin, Quinn."

He laid a pair of trousers against his waist to see if they would fit. "It won't help."

"You really should see a doctor."

"Have you seen any suspenders down here?"

Farley pointed to a shelf that held small boxes of odds and ends. "There's some in there, in the black shoebox on the top shelf. I can sub for you in the fifth number if you need to rest for the finale."

Now preoccupied choosing a white shirt, Quinn didn't smile or show any gratitude for Farley's offer, "We'll see."

"There must be something going around," Stephanie said, "Caleb's not well, either."

Aware Caleb had been moderately ill for about a week now, Quinn finally gave her his full attention. "He's not any worse, is he?"

"I saw him leave for work this morning. But…" She direly shook her head, "He looked bad."

Farley's eyes showed his worry. "I hope to God we don't get it, too."

Overlapping Farley's comment, and deftly concealing his alarm about Caleb's illness, Quinn told Stephanie, "I need to borrow that fedora from your attic."

Her suddenly cross and baffled expression to his abrupt dismissal of Caleb's worsening condition bothered him. However, Quinn didn't want to pursue the subject of Caleb's health or his own declining health. His concern would worry her and cause her to question him in front of Farley, and it was none of Farley's business.

He relaxed when her expression softened a little and, still puzzled, she answered his request about the fedora, her voice full of forced reassurance, "I brought it out for you. I'm gonna wear the red cloche hat in the second number."

Quinn frowned at her. "That's wrong for the era. Don't wear a hat at all. I'll be lifting you and twirling you. You'll just lose it. We don't need any complications."

She shrugged obligingly and said tepidly, "Well, as usual, you're the boss."

* * * * *

The previous week, Ida hunted in every secondhand store in the area for a WWII Army Private's uniform that Farley required as his costume for the third number in this evening's Big Band Blast show. She lucked out at the sixth store, a little hole in the wall on Masonville's *Antique Row* near the Interstate, lucked out twice in fact because it was exactly Farley's size. Feeling triumphant, she took her find directly to Farley's mother at her dance studio that same day. Mrs. Larson, absorbed as usual in her own self-centered interests, gave the uniform and Ida's enthusiasm scant attention. Citing her busy studio as an excuse, she immediately relegated the rest of the costume project back to Ida. Although miffed at the Larson woman for her apparent disinterest in her son's stage debut, Ida felt curiously satisfied to have the project fully in her hands. Ned sometimes kidded her about her control issues when it came to things like this, but she took it much better than when he brought her minor OCD to her attention. *I do not have OCD. I just like to have things a certain way!* And she was determined the uniform, all wrinkled up and smelling like mothballs, would not grace Farley's muscular body in that condition. *No sirreeeee, no way, no how... can't have that, no sir.* When she retrieved it from the cleaners that morning, it looked and smelled brand new—enough to make any soldier proud. It was worth every penny of the sixty dollars it cost her to purchase and clean it.

Why... that bitch never even offered to reimburse me!

She draped the uniform still on the Dry Cleaner's hanger and in the customary protective plastic wrap over the backrest of one of the matching recliners in the family room. It was almost five o'clock. Stephanie, Quinn, and Farley were due home at any time to have a light dinner and be off to the school by seven for curtain time at eight.

She considered the storm forecast to come in close to seven-thirty and wondered if they should leave earlier, just in case. With that in mind, she flipped on the television to the local news that commenced with a weather update when a storm was imminent. The excited meteorologist talked about heavy rain, thunder, lightning, gusty winds, and the possibility of hail. The temperature had peaked at seventy-five degrees by four-thirty but had dropped by four degrees as of five o'clock. The meteorologist mentioned something about the warm temperature battling the colder temperature up in the atmosphere and something else about "convection" or "convergence" or something (Ida couldn't make sense of it), and the fact the storm front had entered from the Pacific and had gained momentum when it hit the warmer valleys between the mountain ranges.

California in early November… you never know what to expect when it comes to the weather.

As the meteorologist droned on while pointing to his maps and charts, Ida took in the view of the rear of the property through one of the tall windows in the room. It was already getting dark. Puffy black clouds sailed and tumbled into and over each other, gradually obscuring what remained of the blue sky that had ruled the day. She opened the door to the patio and stepped out. The stifling humidity, which had begun early in the day, had increased, and she could smell the rain that was already beginning to fall in the west. A brief gust of warm wind impressed her as a warning that made her uneasy.

But what was that sound? It made her think of her father, and then she knew why. But why was Caleb letting the truck idle? He never did that. She listened for a minute more. The idling continued. She returned inside, crossed through into the living room and the foyer, opened the front door and looked out. There was the truck sitting in the driveway idling away. Ordinarily, he parked on the gravel in front of his cottage door. The only time he had ever left his truck in her driveway was on September eleventh.

Something is very wrong.

As she neared the driver's side she saw the window was down and Caleb was sitting up in the seat, his head slumped to one side, his eyes closed. His hair was plastered to his forehead and cheeks with sweat. He didn't move as she pulled open the door and leaned in to wake him. Her voice drew no response. She could tell he was breathing as she unfastened the seatbelt and let it roll itself out of her way. His sunglasses were on the passenger seat, the ear rests open, a half-full pack of Winstons on the dash, and his coffee thermos in the cup holder.

He moaned and mumbled something as Ida framed his face in her hands and turned his head to look at him. His skin was cold, wet, and pale.

Her heart pounded. "Caleb... wake up. C'mon, Caleb."

He opened his eyes halfway and peered at her. "Ida... what?"

"Let's go in the house, honey."

"Gotta go work."

"You already went. You're done for the day."

"Gonna storm." He let his eyes shut again.

She leaned in further and wrapped her hands behind his shoulders, forced him to sit forward. "Come inside with me. Can you walk?"

His eyes fluttered open again. He gazed confusedly at her, "I'm gonna drive."

Ida gently patted his knees to draw his attention to his legs, "I need you to walk with me into the house. Can you do that, Caleb? Can you walk?"

He smiled weakly, "Miles and miles, Ms. Grace."

"It's Ida. I'm Ida."

"My legs hurt. Everything hurts."

She pulled him, "Let's go inside, Caleb. I can't carry you. You have to walk with me. I'll help you the best I can."

"Cookies on Saturday."

"Yeah. We'll do that." She hugged his torso and pulled him forward again, held him in position until he got the idea.

His gait was slow and unbalanced as if he was drunk. Yet, she smelled no alcohol on him. His sweat, however, gave off a pungent acidic odor through his damp clothing, and she had to periodically turn away from him to avoid inhaling the stench. Mostly through Ida's determination and that mythic surge of strength mothers summon to lift a car off their trapped child, they made it into the living room where she released him sideways upon the sofa. He collapsed in a partial fetal position, his feet splayed upon the carpet.

Ida observed him worriedly, lifted his feet onto the sofa, straightened his legs and began to remove one of his boots. He protested her action as if he was being assaulted. He finally allowed her to finish the task once he recognized her voice and her words of reassurance registered in his muddled brain.

Stephanie and the two boys hurried through the open front door just as Ida dropped his remaining boot on the floor. Stephanie immediately saw her mother seated at the edge of one end of the sofa, and Caleb prostrate, semiconscious, and pasty faced over the length of it. Her jaw dropped with an alarmed gasp, and as she bolted to the sofa the boys spoke over her, the three of them anxiously inquiring. Ida quickly explained as they threw more questions over her explanation.

Finally, Quinn sternly requested quiet from all of them, and he set himself beside Caleb and, with complete knowledge of what he needed to do, took his weak and slow pulse, noted the rancid sweat that dampened his cold skin.

"Does he seem confused?"

"Very," Ida answered.

Quinn stated authoritatively to Ida, "He needs electrolytes, and he needs them now. What have you got in the fridge?"

"Gatorade."

"Get it."

She couldn't help but notice Quinn's pale and exhausted appearance. "It looks like you need some, too."

Her comment hardly mattered to him. "Just hurry."

Stephanie and Farley were already on their way into the kitchen. Ida sunk to the floor beside the sofa, eyed Quinn speculatively. "What's wrong with him?"

"I've seen this at the hospital in the ER– people overcome by the heat."

"I'll call an ambulance."

"He'll get pissed at you for that. Let's see if the electrolytes help first. Do you have a blood pressure kit and a thermometer?" When she shook her head at the blood pressure kit, he scowled at her, "You must at least have a *thermometer*!"

He made her feel like a bad mother. She called out to Stephanie, "Get the first aid kit."

Quinn made no effort to hide his impatience with her lack of emergency preparedness. "Every family should have a blood pressure kit and an oximeter."

She pressed one fist to her hip, "Well, excuse me, but I'm not a nurse!"

He lightened up, remorseful about upsetting her. It crossed his mind to get her the supplies and teach her how to use them once things settled. For the moment, he could only teach her by example. He pointed at the toss pillow that had fallen on the floor, "Put that under his feet. You've got to elevate his legs."

Farley delivered two bottles of red Gatorade as Stephanie raced up the stairs. Quinn opened one and lifted Caleb's head, put the bottle to his lips and urged him to take a few sips at a time. To Ida's surprise, Caleb responded willingly to the gentle bossiness in Quinn's voice.

Ida observed and was impressed by Quinn's confident assessment and control over the situation.

As Caleb slowly began to recover, Quinn, aware Caleb had already been sick a few days, questioned him just in case there was a complicating factor he should know about: *When was the last time you drank some water? Have you worked with any new chemicals or solvents on your job over the last week? Does your throat hurt? Do you have a headache? Were you bitten by anything? Have you lost your balance recently? Have you been throwing up? How long have you been this sick?*

The answers came weakly: "This morning; No; No; Yes; No; No (Caleb forgot about the towel bar incident); No; Since this morning and got worse later."

Then, in a moment of lucid reflection, Caleb slurred, "He wants out."

Ida was all confusion, "What?"

Quinn understood. He concealed it. "He's just mixed up. Where the hell is Stephanie?"

"Oh, she probably can't find it…" Ida followed Farley up the stairs.

Now with some welcome privacy, Quinn again felt the coldness upon Caleb's skin, saw the faint white shimmer of another spirit in the process of emerging. He had no doubt as to the identity of the spirit, and he whispered tensely, "You have to slow down, Isaac, or you'll kill him."

The words came through Caleb, but the words were Isaac's. "Jake's killing you both."

"I can handle him. Slow down."

"You must listen to me."

"You have to slow down and let Caleb regain his strength."

"The storm…"

"What about it?"

"He's feeding on it."

"Who?"

"Jake."

This was no surprise to Quinn. "He's been feeding on everything."

A quivering sigh and then, "Oh no… can't finish. He's fighting me."

"Who's fighting you?"

"Caleb."

"Stop fighting back. Let him rest. You rest, too. Do what I say. I mean it." He took Caleb's hand and held it in his own, "I can't tend to Caleb if you're in our way. Do you get it? Do you understand? Bring Caleb back so I can take care of him."

"Hurry before the lightning comes."

"Sleep, Isaac."

The faint shimmer receded. Caleb's eyes showed alertness when he looked at Quinn. "Drink more…"

Quinn set the bottle to his lips, "You can have the whole bottle, buddy."

Caleb's temperature read in the normal range, which made it easy for Quinn to convince Ida it was just a simple case of heat sickness brought on by dehydration. At that news, everyone but Quinn relaxed. He wanted to skip tonight's dance performance not only to protect Caleb but also because he himself was becoming weaker and sicker by the hour.

Ida took over Caleb's care while Stephanie made sandwiches and the boys assembled and packed their costumes. Quinn downed a second Gatorade with two aspirin and hoped for the best. He opted to eat his sandwich in the living room so he could keep an eye on Caleb and be near Ida should she need his guidance. She was all maternal instinct and relying on the little bit of standard first aid procedures she recalled from high school.

Still, Quinn worried. He worried Isaac would attempt another escape that would be disastrous for Caleb. He worried Jake would make an appearance to confront Isaac. He worried about the storm that was dropping light rain ahead of schedule; he could hear the thunder moving eastward with the strengthening winds. Jake would use the electricity in the storm to further bulk up, and then he would be visible to everyone. How would Ida handle that? How would she react to that crazy bastard appearing in her house looking like death warmed over—which he was—and spouting all his ricocheting pinball brain process nonsense to her? Additionally… how would Isaac react to Jake's presence, especially if Jake had, in fact, murdered him? Oh, if only there was some kind of repellent to keep Jake away!

Oh, wait… oh, wait! Quinn checked for the crucifix beneath Caleb's shirt. He found the chain, pulled it up, and draped the crucifix over his t-shirt, out in the open.

When Ida saw him do this, she recalled the night Quinn had given it to him. The expression on her face told him she had no idea Caleb had been wearing the crucifix, and it was plain to her Quinn wanted it out where it would be visible. "Why did you dig it out and place it there on his chest like that?"

"It was blessed by a priest, and it just makes me feel better to see that he's wearing it."

Ida subtly smirked. "Are we expecting vampires?"

Quinn was just about to voice a bitter retort to her, but Caleb who was half conscious told her, "Quinn knows what he's doing."

This puzzled her, and she fell silent.

His comment surprised Quinn. All this time, Caleb understood what was happening to him. The realization gave Quinn comfort. "I want you to stay here and take it easy."

Caleb fought the urge to sleep again. "We were all set to go and watch you dance tonight."

Thunder rumbled in the distance. Ordinarily, Quinn loved nothing better than a spectacular thunder and lightning storm, but tonight's storm brought with it ominous energy he could feel just the same as when the dead were near. He expected the copious rains would arrive about the same time Ida would be driving toward the school, a treacherous journey on those long, dark, and poorly marked rural roads.

"Ida, you two should pass on this tonight. We'll have another show in the spring. Stay here and keep him hydrated. We'll be home as soon as we can, and you know Farley's a careful driver, so don't worry about us."

* * * * *

The trees and bushes along Gadfee Lake Road were swaying in the wind as the three headed toward town. One strong gust slammed the Cavalier like a battering ram. Farley gripped the steering wheel tightly to keep the car in his lane. As they turned south on the Masonville Highway toward Providence, the winds grew fiercer; sending broken twigs, branches, and leaves across the road and against the car. At one point Farley braked for a bale of hay that sailed over a barbed wire fence and tumbled to a stop directly in his path. He promptly apologized to Stephanie after she shrieked and braced her hands upon the dashboard.

In the back seat, Quinn tried to ease the tension with his typical humor, "Hay!"

Farley giggled, but Stephanie turned hotly to Quinn, "Not funny!"

"Oh, lighten up." He nudged Farley's shoulder, "Say, Farley. Are your parents coming to our show tonight?"

"No. They don't come to school stuff."

"Why not?"

"Mom's busy with her new boyfriend."

"What? Your mom's got a boyfriend?"

"My dad lives in Vegas. They've been divorced for years. They get along better that way."

"And your mom thinks her boyfriend is more important than you?"

"I don't care." He eyed Quinn through the rearview mirror. "Is your dad gonna make it?"

"I never told him."

"Why not?"

"He'd just embarrass me, that's why."

Farley laughed, "I totally get it, man. Same reason I'd rather my mom not come."

Stephanie remarked, "That's really sad… both of you—that's sad."

"That's okay," Quinn said, "We're adopting your mother."

Stephanie already knew that, and she considered a reply unnecessary. Instead, she looked out the side window at the view in the west where a black funnel-like cloud formation with a massive swirling mushroom shaped head appeared to be feeding upon itself and growing. It reminded her of a hydrogen bomb explosion she had seen in a film during American History class.

"Say, you guys, is that a tornado?"

Quinn replied, "Nah, it doesn't have a tail like a tornado. It's just a big storm cloud that's spinning rain into hailstones."

Her eyes were wide with amazement, "Hail? Oh, shit… Once we turn on Providence Road we'll be heading right for it."

All Farley was concerned about was the dents the hailstones would leave on his pristine car. "It'd better not hail!" He veered the Cavalier past an oak tree branch that lay crosswise on the white line between the lanes. "This wind is something else. The radio said it might peak at seventy miles per hour."

They went west on Providence Road just in time to see a giant flash of lightning whiten the dark gray sky. Thunder rumbled loudly a few seconds later as the sky darkened.

"Heading into the mouth of the beast," Farley remarked with mock trepidation.

Quinn half heard Farley's words; he was distracted thinking about the lightning, thinking about Jake gaining energy from the lightning, and wondering why

Jake had not come to visit him that day.

"You know," Stephanie said, "I wonder if anyone will show up to watch the show."

"Most of the parents will," Farley replied. Another flash of lightning, this one a jagged bolt accompanied by a crisp cracking sound, caused his mouth to drop open in astonishment. "Wow! That was cool! Hey, Quinn… Did you know Harry Richter's dad was struck by lightning once when he was out golfing with his buddies?"

"Nope. I never heard that."

"True story. He ended up in the hospital."

"Was that before or after he *sired* Harry?"

"Before."

"No wonder Harry's such a flaming asshole!"

Farley and Stephanie howled laughter.

Satisfied, Quinn slouched against the backrest. As horrible as he felt at that moment, he was proud of himself that his sense of humor was still intact. He closed his eyes and listened to the rolling thunder and roar of the wind, secretly prayed tonight's show would be canceled so he could return to Caleb and Ida.

At the outskirts of Providence, the traffic lights were out and the Trucker Burger joint was dark. Farther along at the edge of town conditions were the same. The Cavalier's headlights illuminated the wind driven leaves, twigs, and branches dancing upon the road. Farley didn't see until the last second an overturned white plastic lawn chair that went skidding down a residential driveway and across the blacktop. He kept his cool as he steered the car past it, his timing perfect. One block ahead, lightning hit a telephone pole in front of the Scrubs & Suds; the pole exploded into flames and sent shards of charred wood into the air.

"Damn!" Farley exclaimed over Stephanie's startled screech, "What the hell!"

Stephanie moaned, "I want to go home."

In the heart of Providence, the power was still intact. The streetlamps surrounding Providence High School cast muted yellow light upon the adjoining parking lot. There were no vehicles parked in the front lot, nor in the rear lot behind the gymnasium and auditorium where Farley pulled in. He parked the car in the space closest to and facing the auditorium door. The headlights illuminated a big white cardstock poster attached to the double doors.

Tonight's Show Postponed

Due to Storm

Quinn gazed up, his hands clasped in grateful prayer, "Thank you, Jesus!"

Stephanie's cell phone chirped; her mother told her Mrs. Standish had cancelled tonight's performance. Stephanie told her they knew, and assured her they were heading home. That plan immediately changed when sudden heavy rain sheeted the windshield and blurred their view of the sign. Stephanie added quickly to her mother, "That is, after this cloudburst passes. It won't be long."

Deciding he could manage through the heavy rain, Farley turned the wipers on and shifted the vehicle into drive. They made it as far as the driveway out to the street when hail began dropping with popping sounds onto the car. Farley cussed as the hail increased in amount and size.

Stephanie pointed to the self-service carwash up the road on the opposite side of the street, "Park in one of the bays until this passes, Farley."

He went for it. "That's what I was thinking."

They sat in the car under the cover of the wash bay as peach pit size hailstones pelted the town for nearly ten minutes. In the meantime, Quinn unbuckled his seat belt, removed his jacket to use as a pillow, and lay across the seat to rest his sore and weakening body. He quickly fell asleep, the percussion of hailstones playing inharmonious tones from a world too far away to reach his somnolent mind.

* * * * *

The cake had been cooling on the counter for over four hours by the time Ida got around to swirling white vanilla frosting over it. She had planned it as part of a post-debut performance celebration for Stephanie and the boys who had worked so hard practicing their steps.

The wind had picked up during the last hour, sometimes gusting with such ferocity that it shook the house. The hard unceasing tapping of rain and airborne debris hitting the windows on the west side caused her some concern when she heard a snapping sound from the family room across from the kitchen. Upon investigation, she found one of the windows had been hit with something heavy enough to produce a short jagged crack in one corner of the glass. She covered the crack with clear packing tape to prevent the crack from spreading, hoping it would do but expecting it might not. While there, she turned on the outside lights at the side and rear yards, peered through the window at the flying debris and swaying trees. Everything was drenched. Water had already accumulated in the lower areas of the yard, and the puddles grew into ponds that expanded and deepened as she watched.

Damn! If this keeps up, the kids'll need a boat to reach the house from the road!

That thought made her worry about them traveling the dark rural roads in this kind of weather. Yes, Farley was supposedly a careful driver, but how much experience had he driving through a monsoon? It only added to her worry when it occurred to her forty-five minutes had passed since Stephanie told her over the phone they were returning right away. Under normal conditions, it took fifteen minutes to drive home from town. Of course, it would take longer during a storm, but would it take this long? Ida tried to recall the storms during her childhood and teen years when she was growing up in this house, but could only remember one storm this bad. Her father had to stay in town for two days until the roads were open again while she and her mother remained in the house and baked cookies and made paper Valentines out of colored construction paper. Ida trusted Stephanie would call and tell her if the roads were closed and they had to stay in town. If they had to stay in town, she and Quinn would likely bunk at Farley's house.

Maybe I should call Mrs. Larson. Nah... forget it; she'd just get worried.

Ida tried the local radio station again; they were still playing a prerecorded loop. No one answered the phone there when she called for information twenty minutes before. They had bailed and gone home. It wasn't like the old days when people in communications considered it their duty to remain at their posts in an emergency. Nope. Nowadays, people bailed. After shutting off the radio, she tried the television again. The local affiliates were broadcasting regular programming.

She called Stephanie's cell phone. The girl finally answered after four rings.

"Where are you, Steph?"

"We're at the car wash."

"What?"

"We're parked in one of the bays waiting for the rain to ease up. It was hailing earlier. You wouldn't believe how big those hailstones were!"

"How bad is the rain there?"

"It's coming down in sheets! The street's flooded, and there are hailstones all over the place, plus blocking all the storm drains, and the electricity just went out down here. Farley wants to wait until this part of the storm passes. Better safe than sorry, right, Mom?"

"I guess. Promise me you'll keep in touch with me. I'm worried."

"We're fine. How's Caleb doing?"

"He's sound asleep on the sofa. Oh, my God! We just had a huge bolt of lightning across from the creek! I've got to get off this landline. Call my cell phone later."

She found her cell phone in her purse upstairs and brought it to the kitchen where she added musical symbols with red decorating icing on top of the cake. A sudden boom of thunder followed by a long rumble sounded directly over the house. Its concussion was enough to make the coffee cups tremble where they hung by their handles on the mug rack. The red icing squirted out of the tube in Ida's hand as she tightened her grip on it when she jumped at the noise. The icing landed in the shape of the letter "J" on the cake. She made it work by adding the letters, "azz" after the "J"

"Now, that's a happy accident," she murmured.

Soft singing drifted from the living room. She recognized Caleb's voice, and she paused and listened, recognized the lyrics he sang were in Italian. She had no idea he knew Italian or what prompted him to begin singing so softly to himself. She assumed he sensed she was tense because of the storm and he wanted to calm her. His tender intonation soothed her, and she strolled into the living room entrance, stopped under the archway and looked at him in the dim light.

Looked at *both* of him.

Caleb was sitting on the sofa, cradling his face in his hands, his feet firmly on the floor. The second Caleb was at the window looking out at the rain. This duplicate Caleb's form was shimmering white, and the white obscured any clothing he might have been wearing. Yet, she could see his face clearly as he turned and saw her, a smile of warm greeting upon his lips.

She gasped and fell against the side of the archway. Her throat closed and prevented her scream from escaping.

Caleb heard her gasp. He dropped his hands from his face, turned to her. "It's okay, Ida. He won't hurt you."

She gathered her courage and forced her throat open, "What the hell is going on here?"

"It's Isaac."

"You mean all this time the house was really haunted? Mom was right?"

"No. The house was never haunted."

She gestured at Isaac who was watching her and appeared to be analyzing her. "Then, what's *he* doing here?"

"He's setting things right."

"Setting what right?"

"Quinn will tell you."

"Quinn?"

"Quinn knows all about it."

Aside from some frustration at Caleb's remarkable calmness, she felt numb about the reality her dead cousin was standing in her living room. Perhaps it was shock, but not enough shock to allay her need to understand what was going on in her house.

"How and why does *Quinn* know about it?"

"He'll explain that to you himself."

Every working light in the home dimmed and then returned to full illumination. Isaac's form shimmered and flashed brightly as he absorbed the electrical energy that strengthened him. In those same moments, he stepped away from the window and gazed affectionately at Ida as if he had known her forever. "You look so much like Betty."

She recalled the photographs up in the attic. "That's what Stephanie said."

He grinned fondly at her mention of Stephanie, "I've heard her talking to me."

At that moment, Ida was glad Stephanie was not home to see this, even though she could not imagine how the girl would have reacted. How would anyone react to the sudden appearance of a walking, talking, and yet deceased relative in his or her house? It didn't matter if that relative was nice—as nice as Isaac conducted himself, anyway. It was just too weird. Even weirder was the fact Isaac apparently gained strength from the electricity in the house and the lightning outside.

As they stared at each other, Ida realized, although Isaac's mouth moved with the words he spoke, the words seemed to come from some other source, a telepathic source. His form was not solid but wholly comprised of ever-moving energy, an energy that seemed to recharge itself through constant activity without the need for a body containing lungs or other organs. The few details visible in his form, such as his face, were only remnants of the body he resided in during his distant lifetime when he was dependent upon his physical body and all its internal organs that made earthly life possible.

His expression changed to curiosity. "It's all different here. Where is Uncle Frank's chair?"

"What chair?"

"The chair I built for him—with the geese."

"It's up in the attic."

That hurt him. "Why?"

"Stephanie's made the attic into a private retreat for herself. She loves that chair. It's safe there."

After considering it, he took it as a compliment, "That's fine, then."

Ida shifted her attention to Caleb who was still sitting on the sofa. His calmness sharply contrasted with her jittery nerves. Partially in envy to his self-composure, she announced facetiously, "I need a good strong drink."

He cast her a cautious gaze, "It's better you don't."

"There's a dead guy standing in my living room!"

"Yeah… I know." Caleb shivered and wrapped his arms in front of his chest. "Please don't drink. I may need you, Ms. Ida."

"You're still sick…"

"Yeah."

Isaac told him, "I'm sorry. I'm trying to take as little as possible from you."

Ida sent Caleb a reproachful expression, "You mean it wasn't really heat sickness?"

"Well, yes it was. But it was because I passed out in the truck."

"For crying out loud…!" She directed her next question to Isaac, "How and why are *you* here?"

Isaac had to stop and think about it, try to remember, try to make sense of it. "I think it's for Jake. He found me and woke me. I wasn't supposed to be here inside Caleb. I don't know why that happened, but there must be a reason. Just don't ask me to explain it. I don't understand anything about these things. The last thing I remember is a bright light and being lifted into it. That's all I remember until I got woke up by Jake."

She squinted at him, her patience ebbing, her sanity wavering. "Who's Jake?"

A smile played on his lips, but the smile quickly transformed into a frown of grief. "He's my friend. He's Sarah's brother."

General situational befuddlement combined with menopausal short-term memory loss prevented her from recalling all her conversations with Stephanie about the suspect in Isaac's murder. "I have no idea who you're talking about."

Caleb said, "Quinn will explain."

Ida looked sharply at Caleb, "I want you to explain."

"I can't."

"Can't or won't?"

He raised his brows, a helpless expression in his eyes, "Can't."

"What's Quinn got to do with this?"

Caleb sighed wearily, "Let Quinn explain. Please, Ida… I can't."

Again, she directed her question to Isaac, "And, what about you?"

He raised his palms up and spread his hands apart. "I'm just as confused as you are, ma'am."

Thunder broke over the house, shook the house. The rain increased, it's fat drops pounding the roof with a cacophony of dull thumps upon the shingles. Lightning flashed widely over the property, and the house lights dimmed and returned to life.

Isaac lifted his head and uttered an ecstatic moan along with a sigh of distress. "Oh…" he whispered loudly, "It rained and rained and rained. Oh, how it rained."

25

Stephanie and Farley were making out in the front seat as Quinn stirred lethargically from his sleep. He jealously watched them for a few moments before he sat up and leaned between the bucket seats. "Come up for air!"

It was only because Stephanie chuckled that her lips parted from Farley's.

Quinn lightly slapped Farley's shoulder. "Hey! The rain's let up. Let's get the hell outa here."

Farley answered casually, "Not until it moves farther east, or we'll be driving right into it."

"I don't care."

Stephanie brushed Quinn's cheek with her fingertips. "Go back to sleep, Sicklyhead."

He sensed something bad would happen if they didn't leave right away. "I don't want to stay here."

"We're safe here," Farley said.

"I'm sick and I wanna go home!"

"We'll leave soon."

"I'll puke all over your seats."

Farley shook his index finger at him. "Don't puke!"

"Then, get me home!"

Farley sat up and gave him a hard stare. "You know, Quinn… this is why we beat the shit out of you. You're such a spoiled little dickhead."

His statement angered Stephanie. "Hey, Farley – don't ever say that! Quinn's been sick a long time, and if he pukes in your car, it's your fault. Get us home."

Farley shrugged his wide shoulders and raised his eyes skyward. "I'm just sayin'…"

Stephanie sneered at him. "Well, *stop* sayin'!"

He chuckled at her, not to make fun of her, but in appreciation of her spunk.

"Damn, girl. I should count myself fortunate if you feel as strongly about me."

"Damned right." She couldn't help returning his smile.

He turned the key in the ignition. "All right, Quinn. You win."

Quinn glared disapprovingly at Stephanie. "Button your blouse."

Embarrassed, she obeyed him. "Sorry. We thought you'd be asleep for a while longer."

"That's no excuse."

She dismissed him as overprotective. "Oh, stop it, Quinn!"

Farley eyed him peevishly through the rearview mirror. "Dude! Lighten up."

"Keep your hands to yourself, Farley. You'll treat her with respect or I'll kick your ass—when I'm better, that is."

Farley cast him an impatient frown. "I don't want to fight with you. Jeez, Quinn…" After a thoughtful pause, Farley added sincerely, "I'm glad you look out for her."

Quinn settled back wearily. "Just get us home."

Lightning flashed again in the distance, followed by a loud roll of thunder that vibrated through the car. The wind picked up behind them, and they all felt the rear of the car lift a little with its fury. Quinn's stomach twisted inside him, and a strange low-tone humming filled his ears.

Jake…?

Jake's mocking voice came, "*Hitchin' a ride in your body, Quinn. Surprise, surprise! By the way, she's got nice tits.*"

At the same time, Farley was just sitting there letting the car idle. Quinn ignored Jake and tried to hide the urgency in his voice as he asked Farley, "Why aren't we moving?"

Farley shut off the headlights. "Trouble."

"What trouble?"

He cut the engine. "I hear something."

Quinn practically whined it, "Now what?"

"Hey, Farley! Afraid to get your car wet?"

"Aw, shit…" Farley said slowly, "Fuckin' Bruno!"

A second voice, "Hey! We wanna bang her, too!"

Quinn shot to attention, his sickness forgotten, "Marcus! Jesus, Farley! Get us outa here!"

Stephanie locked her door, sent Farley a frantic look as he followed her lead and locked his door. Her eyes remained pinned on Farley as she asked Quinn, "Is your door locked, Quinn?"

"It is now."

Farley turned the key, hit the lights, set the gear in drive, and pressed the accelerator. The vehicle lurched forward and stopped as the engine abruptly died. Farley cussed.

Bruno stepped in front of the car at the mouth of the bay and spread his arms wide. "Go ahead, you traitor! Run me over!"

Quinn positioned himself between the front seats where he could get a better look at Bruno. The bulldog's nose was still swollen up and bruised; it looked like an old light bulb covered in a layer of dirt. It almost made Quinn laugh, but he was too scared to laugh. The words, *fight or flight* played repetitively in his brain.

Bruno chuckled and said, "You can only go forward."

The three turned and saw Marcus's truck parked sideways behind them at the other end of the bay.

"How in hell did he do that?" Stephanie hissed.

"They coasted it," Farley growled.

Bruno stepped forward, leaned and pressed his palms upon the hood. "Hey, Quinn! We got business to finish. Get your pathetic ass out here."

Quinn said nothing. He was too sick to fight and he feared one word from him would only encourage the big bulldog.

Marcus came up from the side and stood beside Bruno. He had a tire iron in each hand, one of which he handed to Bruno. They waved the tire irons in the air, and Marcus called out, "Get your ass out here, Quinn, or we'll destroy Farley's beautiful car!"

Farley's hands went to his head and his eyes widened with alarm, "Oh, shit. Oh, fuck! No. Not my car!"

Marcus continued, "And then we'll bust open Farley's head, and then we'll bust open your head, and then you'll both bleed to death right here while we pleasure your little girlfriend. Hey, girlie! Looks to me like you enjoy double-dipping!"

Quinn felt his gut twist. Now he had no choice but to fight. It wasn't Marcus's threat to bust his head with the tire iron; it was his threat to assault Stephanie.

Farley's face reddened with rage at Marcus's threat. He gritted his teeth and damned Marcus to hell.

Under her breath, Stephanie cussed shakily, absolutely terrified. She reached into her purse for her pepper spray, which she had remembered to bring with her since that day Quinn broke Bruno's nose. Farley, out of the corner of his eye, saw her bring it out. She surreptitiously hid her actions below the curve of the dashboard where Bruno and Marcus couldn't see.

Still fuming, Farley promised Stephanie, "No way will I ever let them get close enough to touch you!"

She realized at that moment she was visibly quivering at Marcus's threat, but Farley's pledge to protect her gave her some comfort.

Quinn patted her shoulder, almost making her jump. "That makes two of us, Steph. No matter what it takes, those bastards won't get anywhere near you!"

Jake's voice rattled through Quinn's brain, "*Fight or flight. What'cha gonna choose?*"

Telepathically, Quinn answered, *Fight.*

Jake responded proudly, "*That's my boy!*"

Fuck you, Jake. I don't need you to coach me.

Quinn thought if he could distract them, Farley would have a chance to get Stephanie to safety. As for his own safety, he considered the least they would do to him was put him in the hospital, and the worst they could do was kill him. He didn't think they wanted to kill him, though; they just intended to punish him severely, and he could handle that after so many years of injuries at their hands. Quinn unlocked his door and stepped out into the bay, his legs trembling partially with fear and partially with weakness from illness.

Farley released his seat belt and turned to Stephanie. "Do you think you can drive my car?" She nodded, although the idea of it gave her pause. He said tensely, "I can't let Quinn take them on alone. As soon as I'm out of here, hop in my seat and start the engine. I'll get Bruno out of your way so you can drive forward. Keep driving. Drive home."

She took her cell phone out of her purse and pressed the call button. "I'm calling the cops first. I'm not leaving you two here." The light went on the screen with a message: *No Service.* "Oh, no… The storm must have damaged one of the towers. Oh, Farley!"

He gazed at her with both confidence and desperation, "Then, drive!" He opened the door and stepped out quickly, pressed the lock button as he shut his door.

Quinn pushed him against the car, "This is *my* fight!"

Farley's voice reflected his rage, "This is *our* fight. You forget what they did to me!"

Bruno and Marcus grinned as if they were just on the verge of getting laid.

Quinn hollered to them, "No crowbars! No weapons. This is gonna be a fair fight. Put'em down!"

Marcus's mouth flew open. He narrowed his eyes at Quinn, challenging him.

"Too chicken to fight fair?" Quinn demanded, adrenaline kicking in.

Bruno howled and tossed his crowbar aside. He waved his arms at Quinn in an inviting manner. "You're mine, boy!"

"I accept!" A second later Quinn regretted his impulsiveness. Bruno tackled him and knocked him to the wet pavement. Quinn landed flat on his back, the air blown out of his lungs, and big Bruno on top of him with his full weight on Quinn's chest, his knees pinning Quinn's shoulders down.

Snarling, Bruno folded his impressive fist and drew it up in preparation for delivery. Drops of beer laced spit accompanied his warning, "Payback, shithead!"

The crack of bone and the searing pain came first as Bruno's fist made good his promise. Quinn saw stars, lights, and flying prehistoric neon-colored spiders. The sound that followed filled his ears with something similar to a dog's scream of agony, and he did not realize that sound came from his own throat. With his arms pinned down by Bruno's knees, he could do nothing but cringe in expectation of the next blow. But that blow did not come. Bruno alighted from his chest and triumphantly stood over him, and then he gripped Quinn's shirt collar, lifted him in the air, and threw him on top of the Cavalier's hood. Quinn sprawled there on his back gasping and swallowing blood, the stars and lights and flying prehistoric neon-colored spiders swirling and colliding and exploding inside his eyes.

Stephanie, now in the driver's seat, didn't dare turn the key. She stared catatonically at Quinn, who appeared to be convulsing. Her sight then shifted to Bruno who chortled as he surveyed the damage he'd done to Quinn. His smile abruptly disappeared. He nodded to himself, indicating he had made his point, delivered payback, and now they were even. Still on edge, Stephanie watched him abandon Quinn to turn toward Marcus and Farley at the edge of the light of the Cavalier's lamps. She saw what Bruno saw: Farley on top of Marcus viciously and unmercifully pummeling his face. Farley, consumed with temper, was perched on Marcus's chest delivering blow after blow. She felt no concern for Farley since he was the superior opponent in that battle. Her sight darted once again to Bruno as he observed them for a few moments, seemingly understanding the roots and depth of Farley's rage toward Marcus. Then Bruno yelled at Farley to stop and ran to separate them.

Quinn's pathetically whining moan drew her attention back to him. Expecting and then attempting to escape further damage from Bruno, Quinn scrambled onto his belly and gripped the cowl of the hood with both hands, his fingers digging in painfully. He lifted his head and made eye contact with her, agony and desperation contorting his face, blood streaming from his nose to his chin and throat.

Stephanie had to do *something*, anything, to help Quinn before Bruno returned. All she could think of was the pepper spray she was still clutching. Deciding to take action with it if necessary, she pressed the master lock switch that unlocked all four doors, and then she swung her door open and hurried out into the bay. As soon as she reached the hood, she unlatched Quinn's fingers from the cowl, seized his arm, and pulled him toward her at the front fender. He allowed her to drag him off the hood and around the open driver's side door to the rear side door. Supporting him by his waist, she deposited him quickly into the back seat.

Stephanie slid into the driver's seat and turned the ignition. She gasped at the sight of Bruno attempting to pry Farley off Marcus.

He's gonna try to cripple Farley!

Leaving the engine running, she immediately exited the car and rushed toward Bruno. Her voice resounded deep and threatening as it exited her throat, "Hey, Bruno!"

As he turned to her, she aimed the pepper spray at his eyes and pressed the spray button. She closed her own eyes and turned her head away as the caustic mix seared his eyes. His wail told her she had hit her mark. He stumbled in her direction, his hands over his burning face and eyes, and fell forward on his belly, moaning miserably and angrily.

Adrenaline guiding her actions, Stephanie jumped over Bruno and reached Farley. What she discovered brought her to a halt. At this moment, he was not the same sweet and gentle Farley she knew. He straddled Marcus's chest while he viciously beat the boy's face. Droplets of blood soared into the air each time his bloodied fist made contact. A disgusting sucking noise accompanied the dull popping

Hell Is In Me

thump of each impact. Although Marcus was unconscious, Farley continued to beat him. Stephanie's gut wrenched with that telltale flipping sensation that was always a warning of danger ahead, yet she disregarded it, only wanting to rescue him from his uncontrollable actions.

"God damn it, Farley," she screamed at him, "You're gonna kill him! *Stop!*"

Recognizing her voice, Farley finally became conscious of his actions. He stopped pummeling his nemesis and dazedly viewed the damage. Marcus's face looked like a bloody rare rump roast that had been pounded by a meat tenderizer mallet. He sent Stephanie a mortified expression, and then he dismounted Marcus's chest that was almost imperceptibly rising and falling with his wheezy breaths.

Stephanie looked away from him to Marcus, viewed hopelessly and grievously Marcus's destroyed face and twitching body. She feared Marcus would die or at least end up brain dead for the remainder of his life. She didn't take her eyes off Marcus as she stated in a choked and tremulous voice, "Farley, we've got to go."

They hurried into the Cavalier, and Farley wasted no time exiting the car wash. Stephanie didn't want to think about what he did to Marcus, yet she couldn't stop thinking about it. A welcome distraction presented itself when she heard Quinn's labored breathing behind her in the back seat. She turned halfway, enough to see him. He was slouching, breathing out of his mouth, his broken nose too full of dripping blood to allow air intake. He had both his hands cupped under his nostrils to catch the blood. The skin below his left eye was discolored and beginning to swell. His eyes were closed and his brow was puckered with pain.

She thrust her hand between the bucket seats to reach his knee where she rested her fingers to get his attention. "Quinn?"

Farley briefly spied Quinn's miserable reflection in the rearview mirror. "Quinn! You okay?"

Quinn could only make rasping sounds in reply.

Farley told him, "Hold on." The sudden cloudburst of rain came down heavily, obstructing his view. He utilized the windshield wipers to clear the rain off the glass. "Just a little way and we'll pull over. Okay?" When no answer came, he repeated, "Okay?"

Quinn managed a grunt that sounded more like a snotted-up sob.

Stephanie turned in her seat onto her knees and instructed him, "Use your shirt to stem the blood flow."

Farley added, "Put your head back."

Quinn reclined and put his head back, but he could not coordinate his arms and hands to remove his shirt.

"Oh, my God..." Stephanie whispered.

"Calm down," Farley softly told her, "It looks worse than it is." He then remarked to Quinn lightheartedly, "Hey, Quinn... try not to bleed on my seats."

Quinn lowered his head and gave Farley a mock glare, along with *The Finger*, and a mush-mouthed, "Fuhh you." He appreciated Farley's attempt to lighten the mood. Now, if only the bleeding and throbbing pain would stop. The next thing that entered his mind was how he would explain this to his father.

"We'll think of something," Stephanie assured him.

"Shhh....thop readin' by bine...." he complained, the consonants mangled by the blood clogging his busted nose.

She winked at him, "Shut up and put your head back."

Farley pulled in to the parking lot in front of the Scrubs & Suds and joined Quinn in the back seat. He gently took Quinn's face in his hands and examined the damage under the illumination of the interior light. "Broke your nose, dude."

"Again..." Quinn uttered sullenly.

Farley gingerly pressed his cheekbones with his thumbs, which made Quinn wince. "Your eye's gonna be black."

"Again..." Quinn sighed.

"The nose is a clean break. Easy fix." Farley removed his over-shirt, which was already splattered with Marcus's blood, and pressed it against Quinn's nostrils, tried to absorb some of the blood with it. Without warning, he gripped Quinn's nose through the material and snapped the bone into position.

Quinn screeched and slugged Farley's shoulder, "Bastard!"

Farley grinned at him, "All fixed."

"Thanks," he managed as tears resulting from Farley's resetting of his broken nose rolled down his cheeks.

"My uncle's an Army Medic."

"Uh-huh..." Quinn was still breathing out of his mouth, trying to be subtle about it. He wondered if Farley's uncle being an Army Medic automatically made Farley assume that qualified him to be an Army Medic, too.

"Any other injuries?"

"By pride." He found it frustrating he could not pronounce the letter "m".

Farley smiled at Quinn like he was the most adorable puppy he'd ever seen. "Home or hospital?"

"Hobe." There was a new fondness and respect for Farley in his eyes.

Farley slapped his palm upon Quinn's shoulder, "Tuff bastard…"

The clouds seemed to vomit a month's worth of rain in the following minutes, enough to thoroughly wet Farley as he returned behind the wheel. He caught an expression of gratitude in Stephanie's eyes when she glanced at him, and it briefly puffed up his ego.

He reassured her about Quinn, "He's okay."

She didn't trust Farley's opinion. "We should take him to the hospital."

Farley's eyes grew wide as he exclaimed, "No!"

"He needs a doctor."

"He already said he wants to go home. I'm going by what he wants. It's not the first time he's had a broken nose. I fixed it. He's fine."

Quinn mumbled through his stuffed sinuses, "Ibe okay. Let's go."

Farley put his hands on the steering wheel. It was then he saw the blood on his hands and the blood on the steering wheel. He mentally retraced his movements since they left the car wash and realized how many things he had touched in the car since then. In the interior light he had not switched off yet, he discovered Marcus's blood upon the interior door handle, the gear shifter, and the wiper control. His face blanched.

"Get that package of wipes out of the glove for me."

Stephanie handed him the little white plastic box of pre-moistened wipes. He took a few out and began cleaning his hands. He used the entire box to wipe down the steering wheel, door handle and wiper control. As he did this he remembered Quinn still had his shirt, stained with Marcus's blood, pressed against his nose. Now it was stained with Quinn's blood, too. Who would suspect it wasn't all Quinn's blood? And then Farley recalled he had opened the back door to attend to Quinn's injuries. He quickly exited the car with the used wipes bunched up in his hand, and found one remaining wipe that wasn't very soiled to erase the evidence on both the exterior and interior surfaces of the rear door handle. Quinn watched him and assumed the blood was from his broken nose; he even apologized to Farley. When Farley was done, he deposited all the bloodied wipes down the nearest storm drain where the heavy rain would carry them away.

Stephanie had been observing his actions with a vague feeling of revulsion and distrust. When he returned to the driver's seat and tossed the empty wipes box onto the pavement, he gave her an anemic smile. She decided not to tell him about the blood spatters on his neck and upper chest, but she returned his smile as a feigned expression of alliance.

The winds picked up again and sent ferocious gusts through the valley and foothills. Trees and debris of all kinds lay across the flooding country roads leading to Gadfee Lake. Farley drove carefully, steered around the hazards. He cautiously judged the depth of the water on the lower areas of the roads based on his memory of the terrain. He crossed the narrow bridge over the bend of Riddling Creek slowly and continued until a large pine that entirely blocked Gadfee Lake Road ended the journey.

Swallowing the remaining blood that had dripped down his throat from his sinuses, Quinn leaned between the bucket seats. The action caused his nose to throb with a faster percussion and sharper pain. He spoke slowly, put a lot of effort into pronouncing his consonants correctly, "We're only a half mile from Steph's house. We can walk it from here."

Farley turned on the brights and tried to see through the rain sheeted windshield and the fast-flipping windshield wipers that couldn't keep up. "How are you two gonna get over that?"

"Carefully. Are you game, Steph?"

"I'm game."

"You can both stay at my house," Farley offered.

"No," Stephanie answered, "You don't have a landline at your house. Without cell service to call my mom, she'll be worried all night. I don't want to put her through that. We can get through. Do you have a flashlight we can borrow?"

Farley popped open the glove box and handed her the flashlight. "You're gonna get soaked out there."

She tested it and found the light good and strong. "It's only rain. I've got my umbrella. We'll be okay."

Quinn laughed at her as he zipped his tan leather jacket. "That wind will have you flying like Mary Poppins."

"Oh... yeah." She chuckled at herself for thinking her umbrella would be any use.

Farley rubbed his forehead and stared defeated at the toppled pine. "I hate to leave you guys here. Damn…"

"It's only half a mile," Quinn reminded him. Yet, the thought of having to scramble over the soaked pine with all its dripping branches and needles going in every direction gave him a reason to hesitate. His body ached and felt weak, and he could feel Jake stirring inside him. He wondered if Jake would offer any kind of help to them or if he had the ability or desire to help them at all. As daunting as the challenge appeared, Quinn found himself opening the door and stepping out into the pounding rain and chilling wind. The wind hurt his sensitive face the moment it made contact, and he winced at the pain. "Let's go, Steph."

Stephanie opened her door, "Are you up to this, Quinn?"

"Hell, yeah. Shut off the brights, Farley."

Farley obeyed him without question. "I'll wait here until you're both through." He then took Stephanie's hand and pulled her to him. "Hey, babe. One more kiss for the road." They shared a kiss, he expressing more passion than she. It lasted longer than Stephanie could stomach. When she pulled away, he observed her, a perplexed and wounded expression on his face. "What'd I do wrong?"

Stephanie did her best to hide her revulsion from him. She cast a glance out the window at Quinn in order to buy some time to think of a benign response to his question. It occurred to her she could tell Farley the truth without giving him a clue that it was about him.

"I'm just worried about everything, that's all."

He assumed distastefully, "You mean Quinn."

"Oh, Quinn'll be okay." With a forced grateful smile she tagged on, "Thanks to you."

That stroked his ego real good. Relieved, he told her, "You be careful. Call me as soon as the cell service is up again."

She gave him a fake smile so full of drummed up fondness she considered it worthy of an Oscar. She followed that with a second kiss. Continuing her performance, she replied to him in her sincerest voice, "I promise. Thanks for getting us this far."

26

Quinn made it halfway through before he lost his balance between two branches and tumbled between three lower branches that lay upon the flooded pavement. He landed on his outstretched hands, felt pain race up his left palm and wrist. His hips and legs, following by momentum, curled and sent his body into a flip before he finally landed on his rear. He froze in a sitting position, momentarily in shock, his body rattling from the impact.

With one large branch to climb over before she cleared the obstacle of the fallen tree, Stephanie heard Quinn's startled cry as he landed. She turned back and squinted to see him against the glare of the Cavalier's headlights.

"Quinn?"

The roaring wind and cacophony of falling rain muffled his angry exclamation, "Aw... shit!"

Stephanie scrambled over the branch she had just cleared, then climbed over the mess of smaller branches and drowned pine needles, plus one additional big branch sprouting new branches before she finally reached him. Her palms and fingertips stung from fresh scratches as she gripped his arms and tried to see his face.

"Are you hurt?"

"I don't know." Everything hurt. He couldn't discern yet what pain was from temporary minor injury and what pain was from long term serious injury.

Stephanie saw Farley's silhouette against the headlights. He clambered over the obstacles, cussing loudly and concurrently calling to them. When he came to a stop beside them in the hollow formed amidst the fallen branches, he immediately addressed Quinn.

"Are you okay?"

Quinn could not reply at first. His shock had not fully diminished. All he knew was that he was not okay, that everything hurt, that he felt dizzy and weak, and that he could not will his body to stand.

Jake's laughing voice taunted him inside his head, "*You clumsy dipshit!*"

Quinn pressed his fingers to his temples and harshly whispered in reply, "Shut up, Jake!"

Farley saw Quinn's mouth move, but couldn't hear the words. "What?" When Quinn gazed at him confusedly, Farley demanded to Stephanie, "Shine that flashlight on him!" When the light revealed the damage to Quinn's nose was no worse, Farley framed Quinn's wet face in his hands and looked intently into his eyes. "Talk to me, Quinn. Are you hurt? Did you break anything?"

"I think I'm okay." Feeling invaded, he added, "Get your hands off my face."

Farley dropped his hands away, but kept looking at Quinn's eyes, which displayed his shock. "Your eyes look kind of glazed over."

Quinn snarled and stated, "Yours would, too, if you somersaulted and landed on your ass!"

Farley thought that was hilarious. It took all his effort not to laugh aloud.

Stephanie yelled over the wind, "We've got to help him over this, Farley! He's just too sick."

"I can do it." Quinn unsuccessfully tried to stand. He bounced onto his tailbone, producing one more pain to add to the others before he surrendered. "Aw... fuckin' ay..." Humiliation caused a different kind of pain that was just as bad, and he would have broke down crying if he wasn't so angry.

Farley draped his arm around Quinn's waist and pulled him into a standing position. He paused to ask Quinn, "All right?"

This time, his legs supported him. "All right."

With a serious tone that suggested he would abide no argument, Farley told him, "I'm gonna help you over this. I'm not leaving until I'm sure you're both through."

Quinn drew in a wavering breath. Under normal circumstances when he was in tiptop condition, this tree would not have defeated him. He resented the wave of hopelessness in his voice when he answered Farley, "Okay, okay."

At the same time, Stephanie said, "Thanks, Farley."

Stephanie led the way. Once they cleared the toppled pine, Farley gently set Quinn upon the wet blacktop. "Just lay there and catch your breath," he instructed him. The car's headlights illuminated the side of Quinn's face and the slow stream of blood oozing from his left nostril. Farley suppressed his alarm as he informed Quinn, "Your nose is bleeding again. Where's that shirt I gave you for that?" An upsetting picture of it laying on the back seat came to his mind.

Quinn tucked his hand down the front of his jacket and slowly unrolled the bunched up bloodstained shirt until it was entirely liberated from its hiding place. With a smirk, he told Farley, "I didn't leave it. You said not to get blood on your seats." At that, he folded a corner of it and pressed it gingerly against his leaking nostril.

The rain increased, and dumped fat, cold drops that dripped from their hair down their necks and under loose collars to settle into their clothing. They were thoroughly soaked. Quinn shivered and curled himself into a fetal position to conserve what warmth remained in his core.

Stephanie knelt beside him and leaned over him, tried to see his face. She couldn't see much because the fallen tree interrupted the light from the Cavalier. She touched his forehead and judged he was a bit feverish, but she kept silent about it and lovingly stroked his wet hair. "Can you make it the rest of the way?"

He veiled his irritation at her insulting question, for he knew she did not mean it to be insulting. Yet, he wanted to scream at her, *I'm a man. I'm not some helpless child. Of course, I can make it*! Instead, he replied gently, "Just give me a minute. I'll make it. I'm okay."

She had to strain to hear him, but she heard him. "Okay. We'll wait."

"By the way, Quinn," Farley said hesitantly, "And, this goes for you, too, Steph… Tell everyone you broke your nose when you fell trying to get across this tree."

It made no sense to Quinn; he hadn't seen what Farley had done to Marcus. Puzzled, he questioned Farley, "Why?"

"We never saw Marcus and Bruno tonight."

Quinn became even more confused. "Why?"

Farley was losing his patience. "Just trust me."

Quinn gazed at Stephanie for an explanation that made sense. She answered Quinn's silent inquiry after a blazingly resentful glare at Farley. Yet, she understood Farley's reason for covering his crime, which any judge would rule was far beyond self-defense. "It's better no one knows about the fight."

"But Bruno's gonna brag to everyone about it, anyway."

Farley stated confidently, "No, he won't."

"Why wouldn't he?" Quinn tried to sit up, and he made it halfway. Stephanie positioned herself behind him to lean against her as his pillow. She wrapped her arms around his chest to secure him against her body. Her small and automatic effort to comfort him at first took him by surprise and made him feel vulnerable yet protected. He understood then she was indeed trying to protect him, not from the elements, but from Farley. He spied Farley suspiciously. "What else happened? What did you do?"

Farley looked away from him and stared into the blackness ahead. "It's better you don't know. Let's leave it that way."

Although no one could see it in the darkness, Quinn's face twisted into a myriad of expressions ranging from confusion to rage. "What?"

"This is the story," Farley continued slowly, "We left the carwash as soon as the hail stopped and I drove you as far as our friend the tree here. We didn't see anybody else tonight. You got that?"

Quinn was through with it. "Yeah, yeah, yeah. Whatever."

Farley reiterated, "You broke your nose trying to get over that tree."

Impatiently, Quinn replied caustically, "I got it, asshole. Now, shut up before I deck you."

"Hey!" Farley growled, "I helped you! I helped you, didn't I? If it wasn't for me, you'd still be stuck in that tree. The least you can do—"

Quinn was too tired and in too much pain to argue. "All right, already."

Stephanie whispered in his ear, "We're okay, Quinn. Just rest."

The three remained there in the rain and wind for a few minutes until Quinn sat up and assured them he could finish the journey. They had no idea how much pain he was in, and how much sicker he had become in the interim. Regardless, Quinn was determined to make it because of his strong intuitive sense that there was trouble at Stephanie's house. A flash of lightning near the home only served to strengthen his resolve to get there no matter what it took out of him or what he had to suffer. He forced himself to stand. He stood still to rule out dizziness, test his balance and coordination, and be certain he had no serious injuries to his lower limbs. Although pain remained from his hips down to his toes, it was not severe enough to indicate anything was broken. His left wrist, however, was a different story. He hoped it was only a bad sprain.

Stephanie and Farley stood with him and watched him concernedly.

Quinn announced with forced confidence, "I'm good."

Stephanie could not see his face in the darkness, but something below the tone of his voice caused her to doubt the confidence he displayed. "Are you sure?"

He did not appreciate her doubt when he needed her to root for him. "Damned right, I can make it!"

She briefly caressed his hand as a show of support. "Okay."

Farley was not convinced. He offered to walk with them until they reached Stephanie's house. Quinn stubbornly refused, and reminded Farley he had left the driver's side door of his car open, which meant the interior would be soaked from the wind driven rain. That was enough to encourage Farley to return to his car. Quinn and Stephanie watched him ascend and descend the splayed wreckage of the fallen pine until he reached the blacktop and his car. Farley blinked the headlights twice to tell them goodbye, and then he maneuvered the auto around and headed back toward Providence.

Quinn muttered to Stephanie, "He loves that damned car more than he cares about you. I hope that's obvious now."

It had already crossed her mind, and it hurt to believe it. "Shut up, Quinn."

"And he'll forget all about you once he starts college next year, you know."

That had also already occurred to her. "I know."

One more checkmark against Farley fell out of his mouth, "And, whatever he did back there at the carwash must have been pretty bad…"

Stephanie thought it was beyond *pretty bad*. Still, she had to keep Quinn ignorant of the details in order to protect him. "Nothing happened at the car wash. We parked there to get out of the hailstorm and, once it was over, Farley drove us as far as that tree."

"So the story goes."

Stephanie replayed the scene in her memory. Farley's savageness had frightened her, but she had ignored her fear in her haste to remove him from the situation. Now that she had time to think about it, she wondered if he would turn into one of those men who shed their tempers upon the women in their lives. Maybe he was already one of those men.

Moreover, she couldn't help replaying her memory of him cleaning the evidence of Marcus's blood from his car. This replay presented an additional impression of him: Tonight was not the first time Farley had destroyed the evidence of a crime.

Yes, he just might be one of those men.

Quinn interpreted her silence as stubbornness. "Don't say I didn't warn you."

Although she knew he was right, she was angry and didn't want to discuss it with him, "Shut up already. Just leave it alone."

Her tone of voice indicated she was already thinking about it, and that was good enough for him. His most urgent need to reach Stephanie's house took precedence over her doomed romance with Farley.

"Well, let's get going." He stared at the road hesitatingly, took a few painful steps. His body screamed with pain. "Do me a favor, Steph."

"Why? I'm so pissed at you right now, I'm ready to leave you here."

He made no effort to rein in the heartbreaking resignation in his voice, "I need you to help me support my weight, or I won't make it."

"Oh, Quinn…" Her tears were in her voice. She wrapped one arm tightly around his waist, drew her body securely to his side. She pressed the button on the flashlight, and they slowly began the journey home.

He said into her ear so she would hear him clearly, "I'll always love you, Steph. No matter what."

"Same here." Her tone was casual.

"No, I mean it."

"I didn't say you didn't mean it. Now, let's keep moving."

He gave up, sighed heavily and kept plodding forward. The fact she loved him enough to support his weight at this moment was little consolation. Obviously, she only *friend* loved him. Now that he realized how deeply he loved her, her *friend love* could never be enough.

They continued silently up the road.

* * * * *

Isaac found the electronics and appliances inside the home that he lived in almost one hundred years ago fascinating, especially the television Ida had turned on to get the latest information on the storm. The news anchor on the local station reported the bad news of sporadic power outages, fallen trees, blocked and flooded roads, and reports of looting downtown.

Seated anxiously forward upon the sofa in what used to be the summer porch (according to Isaac) but was presently the family room, Isaac questioned Ida who was sitting beside him about the technology, "How do they do that? It's amazing!"

"It would take me half a day to explain," she replied.

"I'd heard of *radio*, but we could never afford one." He paused with a thought and giggled. "If we could have afforded one all we could've done was look at it because we didn't have electricity either. But, godawmighty…! This teevee thing is something of a marvel!"

Caleb, on the other side of him, said, "The world has changed a lot since you were last here."

He rubbed his transparent hands together gleefully. "I like it."

Over the past hour, Ida and Caleb had showered Isaac with questions, trying to understand why Isaac was there. Isaac had no answers to offer. However, he had many memories of the house when he lived in it, and he toured the rooms with them in order to identify what the rooms used to be and who slept in which bedroom. When he saw his chair and table up in the attic, saw how Stephanie had polished both to a sheen, he was overwhelmed with gratitude. He expressed his desire to meet Stephanie so he could personally thank her for taking such good care of his creations. Ida kept her opposing desire to herself.

Isaac's wispy form had been steadily warming since he first left Caleb's body. Caleb was aware of it and silently wondered if Ida had noticed it as well. He felt the strength returning in his own body now that Isaac was drawing energy from the lightning that had increased over their area.

Ida leaned across Isaac and tapped Caleb's knee. "Do you want another Gatorade?"

He was just about to answer when a house shaking roll of thunder sounded directly above them, accompanied by the biggest flash of lightning he had ever seen in his nineteen years. The house immediately became dark and silent.

"Oh, dammit…" Ida hissed.

"Is it all off forever?" Isaac questioned.

"Until the power company can get out and repair everything." Ida reached for the flashlight nestled between her hip and the arm of the sofa. She turned it on and stood. "Guess it's time to light the candles."

"I'll do that," Caleb offered, preparing to stand.

"No. Stay here with Isaac." She didn't want to tell him in front of Isaac that the boy's ghostly presence still made her uncomfortable. Polite cousin or not, she wanted to get rid of him before Stephanie, Quinn and Farley arrived. The need to light candles gave her the perfect excuse to create some distance from him while she tried to calm her jumpy nerves.

She took her cell phone into the kitchen where she lit some candles, and then she tried once more to reach Stephanie. The cell phone service was still down.

Disappointed and worried, she went into the formal living room that Quinn adored, and lit a few candles grouped together on the coffee table.

They should have been back by now.

Outside, the wind chimes sang. One made an irritating, nerve rattling noise of breaking glass as its hanging chain broke and sent it crashing to the porch surface. Many had succumbed to the ferocious wind over the past hour. Ida hoped the one set of chimes Bernice Vanderfield had made for her mother had yet survived. She recalled then how Quinn, knowing his mother made it, always tickled the chimes to make them sing whenever he approached the front door. It would sadden him deeply to find it didn't survive the storm. She decided to rescue it.

The wind assaulted her when she opened the front door to step out to the porch. Rain pelted her face when she leaned out, but she suffered it long enough to let her eyes adjust to the darkness as she surveyed the driveway that sloped down to the road. The lower half of the driveway was a lake at that moment, too deep for Farley's Cavalier to cross, but not so deep the kids couldn't wade through it to reach the house.

Oh, where are they…?

Then, something blacker and icier than the night lifted her off her feet, slammed open the door, carried her into the foyer, and threw her violently against the wall. She saw dancing pinhead size exploding stars and fell unconscious before she could release her scream of terror.

* * * * *

Jake's voice startled Quinn, "*That fucking bastard!*"

Telepathically, Quinn asked him, *Who? What's going on?*

"*My father!*"

What?

"*Gotta go!*"

Before Quinn could register what "*Gotta go*" meant, he suddenly dropped from Stephanie's arms and hit the blacktop. His stomach immediately surrendered the sandwich and Gatorade he had consumed earlier that night.

Stephanie knelt beside him. "Oh, no… Quinn!"

He helplessly continued to vomit until it was all spent upon the sleek road. The rancid mess followed the slant of the road to the shoulder where it rested in a puddle unseen in the darkness. He didn't care where it went so long as he didn't end up with his face in it. His body shivered with sudden exhaustion; the wet cold air blowing through his drenched clothing only added to his shivering. He collapsed sideways and curled up, his energy spent.

The fear in Stephanie's voice only served to increase his fear as she asked him, "What can I do to help you? What do you want me to do?"

"Tell Caleb to come get me in his truck."

"I don't want to leave you here alone in the road."

"We're less than a quarter mile away. Run and get him."

* * * * *

The black full body shadow form of a man found Isaac instantly. He and Caleb had just stood to investigate the loud noise from the foyer when the shadow man appeared and lifted Isaac off the floor by his throat. A flash of lightning illuminated their figures at the same time.

Pale blue eyes bulging at the assailant he recognized and feared, Isaac screamed, "No, no, no, no, no!"

Caleb immediately tried to peel the shadow man away from Isaac, but his hands went through the black form that he had mistaken as being solid. He could only watch helplessly as the intruder lifted Isaac by his throat and carried him, dangling and kicking, to the sliding glass doors. The glass exploded outward, and the shadow man with his prey disappeared into the turbulent darkness.

* * * * *

A painfully violent vibration rattled Quinn's body and brain from the inside out. He screamed in agony as his body writhed under its own volition.

Jake suddenly appeared before him, standing and brushing irritably at his shimmering black aura that was shooting crimson sparks into the air. "God damn! That hurt!" He finally noticed Quinn, noticed the boy was experiencing his own distress. He squatted and tousled Quinn's drenched hair. "Sorry about that, kid."

Quinn narrowed his eyes at him, "Is that all you've got to say?" The writhing stopped, and the pain lessened to the level it was before Jake made his grand exit out of Quinn's body; not that the level it was before offered much relief.

Jake mirrored Quinn's resentful expression, "What the hell do you want me to say?"

"Say you're sorry like you mean it!"

"I mean it just as much as you meant it when you told Stephanie you love her."

"You heard that?"

"I heard everything. You're right about Farley. What an asshole he is! She knows it, too. When are you gonna kiss her, you idiot?"

"What the hell, Jake? You're starting to sound like you care about me."

"I do."

"Serious?"

"You've kind of grown on me—like a *wart*. Ha-ha!"

"Can you help me?"

"Help you what?"

"Get back to Steph's house."

"I ain't got time. The shit's hittin' the fan."

Quinn recalled the song he made up just before Farley and Bruno kicked his ass behind the Scrubs & Suds. He mumbled to himself, "The fan's splatterin' shit…" Then it hit him what Jake meant: *the shit's hittin' the fan at Stephanie's house.* "Jake, can you get there in time to stop it?"

"I'm gonna try." With those words, he vanished.

* * * * *

Stephanie, out of breath from running, stood fuming at the lake that had formed halfway up the driveway. The water had overflowed the roadside ditch and rose over the pavement connecting the driveway to the road. Panting, she directed her complaint directly to God, "Are you serious?" Needing the time to catch her breath, she assessed the situation. "Well, I'm already soaked through from head to toe. I guess I can try to wade through it. Aw, damn it… I'm talking to myself again."

She stepped one foot into the water and promptly removed it. "Jeez, that's cold." Her waterlogged shoe squeaked and spit when she set her foot back on the pavement.

Her last memory of Quinn lying sick and exhausted in the road formed a compelling picture that caused her to realize her loyalty and love for him. *I've got to do this!* She bravely hopped into the water with both feet and endured the cold. "All right, Quinn… for you." The water went up to just below her thighs. The level would lower the farther up the drive she went. With that in mind as additional encouragement, she began to wade through it.

* * * * *

Inside the house, Caleb helped Ida to her feet and guided her to the sofa in the living room. Her body trembled with fear and shock. He continued to hold her to him as they sat.

Her voice came as a gasp, "Did you see it?"

"Yeah. It took Isaac. Grabbed him by his throat and took him outside."

Pain and disbelief rose in her voice as she whimpered, "*What*? Why?"

"I don't know." He nodded toward the destroyed sliding glass door a little ways behind and beside the sofa, "He busted the glass there by just looking at it. That's how it seemed, anyway."

She turned and looked. Anger replaced her shock. "What? Son of a bitch!" And, just as quickly, her shock returned. "Why is this happening?"

"Like I said, Quinn's the only one who can explain this."

"Why? Why Quinn? How could he possibly understand this?"

"If I tell you, I'll be breaking an oath."

"What oath?"

"The one I made to Quinn."

She raised her head from his shoulder and sent a furious gaze to him. "God damn it, Caleb! Tell me. You better tell me."

He couldn't help grinning at her, what with all the profanity she had used in the last minute or so. "Why, Ms. Ida, I do believe you were a drunken sailor in your last lifetime."

She slapped his arm, slapped it hard.

"Ow…" he whined, although his mother and Richard had routinely hit him much harder.

"Tell me about Quinn," she demanded in her *Mom-Has-Had-Enough* voice.

"You're probably not gonna believe it."

"Try me."

"Quinn can see and talk with the dead."

"Bull!"

"Truth." He then gave her a condensed version of his own experiences and what he knew about Quinn. He didn't want to waste any more time. Isaac was out there somewhere with the shadow man, and God knows what was happening to him. "And, now that you know the truth, you and I have to go out there and help Isaac."

"How on earth can we help him? And why is that… *thing*… after him?"

"I think that *thing* is his murderer, Jake Sheers."

"What does this Jake guy want to do? Murder him twice?"

"Do I have to say, *I don't know* again?"

274

Hell Is In Me

Impatiently, she spat, "Oh, Caleb!"

Caleb stood and told her, "You stay here and wait for Steph and Quinn. I'm going out to help Isaac."

"You're not well enough to do anything."

"Actually, I'm feeling better now than I've felt in a long time. I'm going out there to help him."

She placed her hands over her face, began to rub her eyes, smearing her mascara. "This is insanity. This is insanity. You can't help him, Caleb."

Regardless, Caleb was already outside.

* * * * *

Quinn covered his head when the giant flash of lightning accompanied by an earth-trembling roll of thunder lit up the sky. The wind picked up from the west. The rain that had decreased for a few minutes, increased again. Quinn glumly surmised the wind had carried it to dump it specifically on him. A loud cracking sound made him cringe. The blacktop gently trembled as another tree toppled behind him.

What's taking Stephanie so long?

He tried to stand, but his legs would not support him. Accepting this, he began to crawl on his knees, using his forearms to pull himself forward. The effort increased the pain in his left wrist. Adapting his technique, he put most of his pulling power on his right forearm. It worked well enough. He hoped Caleb would arrive before his body failed him.

Then he saw something so astounding it caused him to stop in awe of it.

White flashing lights beyond the grove of walnut trees sent jagged branches of lightning into the clouds. A strange and terrible scream resounded within the flashing lights.

Quinn's blood turned cold in his veins.

The phenomena were coming from Stephanie's house.

* * * * *

Stephanie had just made it to the top of the driveway when bright electrical discharges from inside her house sent jagged luminescent bolts into the sky. She froze in place at first, panicked.

Mom's inside! Mom's inside!

It was enough to propel her onward. She raced up the porch and found the front door off its hinges as if someone had taken a battering ram to it. Electricity assaulted her from her toes up to her head the moment she set foot in the foyer. Someone suddenly gripped her from behind, lifted her and tossed her onto the carpeting in the formal living room. She landed facedown, unable to conceive who had saved her until Caleb came to mind.

Expecting to see him, thank him, and then tell him about Quinn, she rolled over and sat up facing the foyer only to find her rescuer was something shaped like a man but encircled in an aura of shimmering colors. He ignored her and flew—*flew*—toward the family room at the rear of the house as if he was on a life or death mission.

Stupefied, she sat where she landed and watched the table lamps and ceiling fans with their teardrop-shaped bulbs flash on and off, on and off. Voices on the radio in the kitchen and the television in the family room popped in and out with the same intermittent timing as the flashing light fixtures. The wind whipped through, extinguishing the candles on the coffee table, and scattering papers and lightweight knick-knacks. Stephanie had to hold her hair away from her face in order to see the show of flying and tumbling stuff.

She called as loudly as she could, "Mom! Mom! Where are you? Mom?"

She heard Caleb's voice, muffled and seemingly coming from the back yard, "I can't find him. I'm gonna keep looking. Take the truck and get out of here. Here are the keys. Catch!"

Her mother's voice, "I can't leave you here!"

"Ms. Ida, stop arguing with me! Get the hell out of here! *Now*!"

Stephanie got to her feet and ran through the family room to the sliding glass door. The wind seemed to be coming from there, but it didn't make sense to her. Out of habit, she unlatched the lock, slid the door, and stepped out into a sea of shattered glass. At last, it made sense, but what didn't make sense was the fact the glass was shattered from the inside out. Had her mother and Caleb broken the glass to escape the house?

And… who was Caleb looking for?

Her mother almost collided with her on the veranda in the darkness. She gripped Stephanie's arm and led her inside the house and toward the foyer, "We've got to go. We've got to go. Let's go, Steph. Where's Quinn?"

"Quinn's sick on the road. We have to get him!"

"How far?"

"About a quarter-mile. Will the truck clear the flooding down the driveway?"

"Yes, if we take it slowly."

When they reached the edge of the foyer, Stephanie tugged her, causing her to stop. "The floor there will shock you. I almost got electrocuted."

Ida tested it with the toe of her shoe. Nothing happened.

She jerked Stephanie's arm, "It's safe. Let's go." She pulled her daughter along with her, despite her frightened protests.

* * * * *

Now that the surge of adrenalin subsided after helping Quinn and Stephanie, and after his initial rage directed at Marcus, Farley felt the pain in his hands for the first time. His fingers were so stiff he could not release his grip on the steering wheel. He knew his hands were injured, the right far more than the left, and he knew how they got injured. The image of his fists pummeling Marcus's face played repeatedly in his memory. The image of Marcus's blood splattering off his knuckles with each vengeful blow sickened him. The hideous squishing sound of his fists striking pulverized tissue and broken facial bones played in his ears as if he was there in the moment, trapped in the moment. Farley couldn't recall Marcus fighting back. He couldn't recall Marcus uttering a sound after he delivered the first blows that broke Marcus's front teeth. All he could remember was his rage and his desire to punish him. Had Marcus survived? If he had survived the injuries would be serious at the least, perhaps enough to cause permanent disability. If Marcus had died…

Farley stopped the car at the approach to the bridge that crossed Riddling Creek where it curved toward downtown Providence. The headlights illuminated the water overflowing the bridge. Farley sat still and peered through the swiping windshield wipers and rain-sheeted glass at the deluge. The wind blew the creek water into undulating currents upon the narrow old wood and steel bridge. The bridge had been clear thirty minutes ago when he had crossed it going in the opposite direction to drop off Stephanie and Quinn. He decided to wait a few minutes to see if the water would subside with the weakening of the storm.

He gingerly released his grip on the steering wheel and painfully pressed the interior light button. His hands were swollen from his fingertips to his wrists. Bruises were already developing over his knuckles. Scabs had formed on the knuckles of his right hand over the cuts from Marcus's broken teeth. Closer examination revealed dried blood under his fingernails.

He wondered if Bruno had taken Marcus to the hospital, or if he had fled the scene on foot, leaving Marcus and his fancy truck behind. He expected Bruno had split, snuck home to be with his parents who were probably stoned out of their minds by this time of night, as they were most nights. Bruno would make sure to interact with them so they would swear to the cops he had been home with them the entire night. It had worked every time in the past. Regardless of Bruno's actions, Marcus was either critically injured or dead at this moment. Farley's injuries would convict him once the police came around to investigate.

Farley sunk despairingly in the seat. He whispered, "Oh, what the hell did I do?"

He saw his college scholarship flying away in a whirlwind; saw himself entering a prison cell. The images brought tears to his eyes.

Again, he whispered, "What did I do?"

His mother's voice screeched in his brain, "Just like your father!"

"No, no, no..." He laid his sore wrists upon the rim of the steering wheel, bent and gently rested his forehead upon the center of the rim. "Gotta figure a way out, or I'm screwed."

* * * * *

Quinn shielded his eyes from the bright yellow lights as he sat up. He felt rainwater roll down the back of his neck, and it caused him to shiver. The familiar sound of Caleb's truck filled him with relief as the driver, who he assumed was Caleb, steered the vehicle into a half u-turn and braked with the passenger side door facing him. The interior light came on as Stephanie opened the door and alighted hurriedly. At the same time, Ida opened her door and raced around the front toward him. He found it curious Ida was driving Caleb's truck. His next thought was she had hurried, for she was not wearing a coat to protect herself from the weather. The two reached him quickly.

"Can you walk?" Ida inquired loudly against the wind.

"If you can help me stand up," he answered with equal volume.

They each took a side, wrapped their arms around his waist and slowly lifted him to his feet. His head and his nose throbbed with pain. Vertigo overtook him. He wavered, his legs weakening.

"Stay up!" Ida ordered like a drill sergeant. "It's four steps to the truck. You can make it." She lifted his arm to rest upon her shoulder. "We'll support you. Come on."

They hoisted him into the passenger seat. Stephanie hopped into the bed and pounded her palm twice on the roof of the cab. Her mother turned the truck toward home.

"What's happening at the house?" Quinn asked, using the sleeve of his jacket to wipe a sudden stream of black snot from under his swelling nose.

Ida kept her eyes pinned to the road, veered into the oncoming lane to avoid the top one-third of another fallen pine. "I couldn't begin to explain it."

"Where's Caleb? Is he okay?"

"He's fine. Don't ask any more questions. Just take it easy."

Quinn persisted, "What were all the weird lights I saw, and what was all that screaming I heard?"

"I said, no more questions."

"Why?"

"That's a question, too."

"I know something bad's going on."

With a disgruntled sigh, she offered lamely, "The electricity is off and so is the phone service."

He sneered at her, "No shit, Sherlock."

"Don't get smart with me, mister."

"Why'd we just pass your house?"

"I said, no questions."

"Why do I feel like we're playing tennis in a parallel universe?"

"Don't get psycho on me, Quinn." She steered the truck into his driveway, accelerated a little to ascend the incline where she parked with the motor still running in front of his garage. "You and Steph are staying here tonight. No arguing with me."

"Why? I don't wanna go home. Why are you making us stay here?"

"Because my house isn't safe. It's a mess from the storm." She felt the truck rock slightly as Stephanie alighted from the bed. "The two of you are staying here. I mean it. Can you make it into the house with only Steph helping you?"

"I guess I can." As soon as Stephanie opened the passenger door and offered her hand to him, he told her, "Your mother is acting weird."

"Give me your hand," Stephanie said impatiently. "Let me help you."

Her sullen expression told Quinn she did not agree with her mother's demand. Quinn decided to go along with the program until he and Stephanie chose when to return to her house. He allowed her to assist him out of the truck. They waved goodbye to her mother and waited in the darkness of the front steps while the truck backed out into the road. They said nothing to each other as they watched the taillights move in the direction of the Norris house and then disappear behind the bushes as Ida steered the truck up the flooded driveway.

Quinn gingerly lowered himself upon the top step. "What the hell's going on?"

"She won't tell me anything. Caleb's out in the back somewhere looking for someone."

"A looter?"

"I don't think so." She settled close to his side, and spoke rapidly, "I saw something in the house. It picked me up and tossed me into the living room when the floor in the foyer sent an electrical shock through me. I think it was trying to help me. It was all these bright colors, and it was shaped like a man, only it flew. It flew away somewhere. Remember all the talk at school about the shadow man? I think that was him."

Jake came immediately to Quinn's mind.

Stephanie continued, delivering her words at high speed, "I think all the lightning stirred something up. I think we've got a ghost or something in our house. But, Mom won't talk about it. She won't talk about anything that's happening except about you. She's worried about you. I told her you broke your nose falling over that tree, and Farley – how he fixed it for you. But, gosh, Quinn; it's you being so sick that got her worried. That's why she wants us to stay here."

"So you can babysit me while she and Caleb go ghost hunting?"

Grimacing, she slipped off her sneakers and her socks. "My feet are soaked. You ought to get out of those wet clothes. I still have the flashlight in my pocket. We can use it while you unlock the door and go in. The electricity is off."

Quinn could tell by her fast and clipped speech pattern she was frightened to the point of panicking. He was determined to keep her on track before she fell apart, and the only way he could see to do that was to keep her talking. "What else did you see at your house?"

"The sliding glass door is shattered from the inside out. I couldn't guess what that's about. Let's go inside out of this weather."

"I'm not going inside."

"But you're sick."

He replied truthfully, "I've been through worse. Put your shoes and socks back on. While you're doing that, I'm gonna level with you about something important."

27

Caleb stumbled in the darkness over the broken branches littering the waterlogged yard. Attempting to regain his footing, he slipped on the mud and landed flat on his back. The rainwater flew up and returned to him as his body hit the saturated mud, drenching his clothing. Winded and stunned, he stared up at the expanse of white clouds in the sky, watched them part just enough to show him the full moon that the storm had hidden for hours. Its brightness hurt his eyes that had adjusted to the darkness, and he closed them to get relief from the sharp pain.

A man's voice called out in the distance, "Ollie ollie oxen free! Where can you be? Where can you be, you son of a bitch?"

Eyelids flipping up at attention, Caleb folded into a sitting position and peered into the darkness. "Hello?" At once he regretted saying anything; what if it was Jake coming after him?

A figure encased in shimmering colorful illumination appeared and leaned over him, and demanded briskly, "Where is he?"

Frozen, Caleb asked, "Who?"

"My father! My father and Isaac! I know they're here somewhere."

Caleb couldn't see anything except the multicolored outline of the man's form against the curtain of white clouds sailing in the night sky. "Who are you?"

"I'm Jake. No time for introductions. Where is that bastard?"

Caleb could only think of one reason why Jake was there, and he assumed Isaac had gotten away from him. "Isaac?"

"No, you asshole! My *father*!"

Caleb answered with the same rudeness, "Hell if I know!"

Jake stepped away from him. "Useless," he complained, "Useless!"

"What the hell is going on?"

"Retribution."

"What? Who… for…" Caleb stammered, "*What*?"

"I gotta help Isaac."

"*Help* him?"

"That's what I said, dumbass."

Caleb protested, "I'm trying to help him, too."

"You can't help him. I'm the only one." He flung himself into the air and flew toward the cottage. His action created a weak wind that caused Caleb to shiver with the icy cold when it caressed his wet clothing.

Could it be Jake was telling the truth? Vacillating between trust and doubt, Caleb scrambled to his feet. A flash of lightning lit the sky. The flash was enough to enable him to see Jake's form round the corner of the cottage and swiftly race in mid-air toward the creek behind it. Caleb felt a strong impulse to follow him, and just when he took his first steps, a hand gripped his arm and pulled him back.

"No!" Ida screamed at him. "We're getting out of here!"

Caleb tugged his arm from her grip and admonished her, "I told *you* to go."

"I'm not going unless you go with me."

Caleb yelled at her in the most threatening voice he could generate, "Get the hell out of here!"

"That voice doesn't work with me, mister! You forget I have a daughter."

"Damn it, Ida…"

"Damn it, Caleb…"

"What'll happen to your daughter if something happens to you?"

"All the more reason for you to go with me."

"I can't."

"Why not?"

He couldn't explain it. "I just can't."

"Then, I'm staying."

"No, Ida!"

"Has it ever occurred to you that you've gotten to be like a son to me? I'm not losing any more of my family, and you're family. So, if you're staying, I'm staying. We're in this together."

Before Caleb could express how deeply her statement touched him, Quinn's miffed voice rang at them from the veranda, "And, so are we!"

To which Stephanie added, "Damned right!"

Ida hotly approached them with long strides, wagging her finger at them. "I told you two to stay at Quinn's house!" As she reached them she could see Stephanie's arm was draped around Quinn's waist, supporting him. Quinn's stubbornness made her temper boil over. "What the hell do you think you can do here, Quinn? You can hardly stand up."

He quipped, "I'm getting better at it with practice."

"Then go practice somewhere else."

Caleb caught up to them, frustrated to the max with all three of them. "What do any of you think you can do?"

Ida retorted, "What do you think *you* can do?"

She caught him unprepared. He had not thought that far, had no plan, did not even understand what was happening or why. "I… I just want to help Isaac."

"How?" she inquired briskly, knowing he had no plan.

He surrendered, humiliated. "I have no idea. Do you?"

"Not a clue."

Quinn spoke over Ida's reply, "Where is Isaac?"

At the same time, Stephanie spoke over both of them, excitement and wonder in her voice, "Isaac's here? Where? How? Are you kidding?" To Quinn, she irately demanded, "Why didn't you tell me?"

"God!" Ida wrapped her hands around the crown of her head, her fingers entwining her hair, pulling gently. "I'm going crazy…"

Quinn inquired to Caleb, "Has Jake gotten here? Have you seen him?"

Caleb ignored Ida and Stephanie's curious utterances as he answered Quinn, "Yeah. He went out by the creek. Said he's the only one that can help Isaac."

Quinn stated firmly, "That's what I needed to know. I can take it from here." He pulled away from Stephanie and produced his hand expectantly to her, "Give me that flashlight."

As she produced it from her jacket pocket, she worriedly asked him, "You're not going there by yourself, are you?"

"It's the way it has to be."

Stephanie reassuringly informed her mother, "Quinn can communicate with dead people. He can see them."

Ida muttered gruffly, "Yeah… I know."

Quinn demanded, "How'd you know?"

Caleb answered ashamedly, "I told her." He expected Quinn would chew him

Hell Is In Me

out for that. When Quinn reacted with zoned-out silence, he knew something was wrong. "What is it?"

"He's close," Quinn answered, the vibration increasing in his body, traveling up from his toes to his brain. As the vibration met his brain, it exploded into a million pinpoints of color and a high-pitched oscillation that sent sharp pain into his eyes and ears. Wincing at the pain, he stated firmly, "He's got company. I have to go."

"I'll go with you," Caleb said.

"No. They wouldn't like that." He closed his eyes and waited for the sensations to subside as he pictured the three dead men's location. It was the same place he had sat the day he got stoned and ate a bag full of cookies while Caleb told him about the haunting at his cottage. It was the place where he and Caleb bonded in friendship.

Caleb vaguely heard voices quarreling in the distance at the creek. He had an idea of the location. The memory of Quinn stoned on pot and eating all the cookies briefly gave him a smile. His smile faded quickly at the realization Quinn was determined to handle the situation on his own. Quinn was in no shape to go down there alone to spar with the troubled dead – not this time.

At this moment that place was a battleground.

* * * * *

Quinn knew the others were following at a distance as he made his way in the darkness through the mud and wind-whipped debris down the bushy incline to the creek. His legs ached with the effort, and the windblown rain stung his face, particularly his nose that was still painful and throbbing from Bruno's fist. Still, he forced himself to continue despite his pain, convinced he was the only one who could send the restless dead on to their destiny. The closer he got, the deeper the water, which told him the creek had overflowed its banks and was continuing to overflow. He could hear the rush of the water tumbling over rocks and disengaged tree limbs. He could hear the splash of heavy rain upon the greenery as the storm sent an unwelcome cloudburst over the area. He pressed onward, soaked and dripping, his shoes and socks waterlogged, stumbling now and then over small obstacles hidden below the litter of dead pine needles. In his hurry, he tripped over something large and solid and automatically stretched his arms in front of him to brace for the fall. He landed harder on his already damaged left hand, which shot burning pain from his fingertips to his elbow. He clenched his teeth as the grandest cussword in the universe rose like gravel in his throat and died quickly with a pitiful whimpering groan that escaped through his poor abused nose. He gave in and sank upon his belly. He shut off the dying flashlight, watched and listened to the confrontation below on the flooded bank. He needed time to rest, and time to plan how he would deal with them.

* * * * *

Vernon Sheers absorbed the energy from the lightning that struck a quarter of a mile away, and the black aura surrounding his form flashed copper when the electricity entered and scattered through it. Even while that was happening, he kept his fingers around Isaac's throat as he roughly laid him upon the saturated mud at the flooded edge of the creek behind Caleb's cottage.

"You will not tell them!"

Isaac could feel the tightness of Vernon's hands around his throat, but since he did not need air to speak, he sent his voice out using the electricity in the air. "Tell who what? I don't understand!"

"Liar… you remember it all."

"Please, Mister Sheers. I don't know what you're talking about!"

His face, which was fully visible to Isaac, crinkled up into a vicious and sadistic expression as he yelled, "You took her away from us and ruined her!"

"Please…" Isaac managed to say as he struggled to free himself.

"She's gone forever! Why, you bastard, why?"

His memory was blank about most things, but his memories of Sarah lingered. "I loved her. I still love her. Please, Mister Sheers!"

"Where is she?"

"I can't remember anything. I don't know anything." He tried to pry the old man's fingers from his throat. "Why are we here? We don't belong here. Let me go."

"Not until I cast you into hell."

Another voice called out to them, "No, Father! *You* belong in hell!"

Vernon loosed his grip on Isaac's throat as he turned to look at Jake, his "*disappointment of a son.*" He told Jake sharply, "It's about time you got here."

"You taking over my soul just about killed poor Quinn, y'know."

"I don't care about him!"

"You made me crazy!"

"You were always crazy!" He tightened his grip on Isaac's throat and pulled him up into a sitting position. His eyes were on Jake as he demanded, "Are you going to help me with this, or what?"

"I hate you, Father."

Vernon gritted his teeth. "Are you going to help me?"

Jake stayed where he stood a few feet away. "You're the crazy one. And, no… I'm not going to help you. Now, let him go."

"Sarah's gone because of him!"

"Sarah *died* because of *you*!"

"I can't find her."

"That's because she doesn't want you to find her."

"Where is she?"

"I won't tell you."

Vernon's eyes practically bulged out of their sockets as he roared at Jake, "Do what you're told!"

Jake smiled out one corner of his mouth as he glared rebelliously at his father. He replied firmly, "No."

He shook Isaac, shook him by his throat while directing his threat to Jake, "In that case, I'll torture this bastard until he dies."

"You can't kill him twice."

"Then I'll—"

"And I won't let you torture him. I won't take any part in this like last…" He stopped talking as the memory of that terrible night returned to him, the night in their barn when his father struck Isaac with a thick six-by-twelve inch oak plank. The tears of remorse and bitterness stung his eyes as he told his father in a trembling voice, "It was you, Father. *You* crippled him. You did it *all*, and you let me rot in jail for it; and then you hid me in a crazy house. You've escaped hell long enough."

"No," Isaac interjected weakly and sadly to Vernon Sheers, "You didn't *escape* hell, Mr. Sheers. I remember it now. I forgave you the moment I went into the light. My forgiveness saved you from that. Hell will not accept you."

Vernon loosened his grip again. "You forgave me?"

"Yes, sir. As God is my witness."

Vernon treated that as an insult, "*Forgave* me?"

Confused, Isaac questioned, "Sir?"

"You deserved what you got! Now, where is my daughter?"

"I don't know. I don't understand." Isaac turned mournfully to Jake, "You said she died. Why isn't she with me?"

Jake pointed at his father Vernon, "He damned her, trapped her here with his hate."

"Oh... no, no..." Isaac said dolefully. He cast Vernon a heavy, spiteful, gaze. "Killing me wasn't enough for you?" Without warning, he struck Vernon's face with his fist. The old man tumbled backward. In a rage, Isaac stood, and he directed his fury at Vernon, screamed so loud and so long the cows at the dairy farm near the junction kicked at their stalls. But his scream was not enough to relieve his pain, so he pinned his blazing eyes upon Vernon Sheers, placed his hands roughly upon the old man's shoulders and began to drain the electrical energy from him into his own body. Sheers's spirit body convulsed as the energy left him and entered into Isaac. He screamed and struggled to free himself from Isaac's grip on his shoulders, but it was hopeless; Isaac's rage gave him astounding strength, and he would not stop until Vernon Sheers was empty of all he had absorbed from the earthly dimension.

However, Isaac did not consider the depth of rage Jacob Sheers carried against his father, and it caught him by surprise when Jake brought him to a halt by concurrently demanding, "Save some of that for me!"

Isaac maintained his grip on the old man as he considered Jake and recalled fragments of Jake's tumultuous life under Vernon Sheer's boot. He recalled the misery the controlling and sadistic man doled out to Sarah as well. Yes, he decided, Jake deserved a piece of him, deserved to have the final say and end this chaos. He sternly advised Jake:

"*Do what you will with him, but forgive him once you're done or you will never find peace.*"

Abruptly, Isaac's expression changed to one of confusion. He tilted his head up and to the side, listening intently to a voice only he could hear. His voice came tinged with a mixture of pain and discovery as he shouted out to the heavens, "Sarah? Oh... Sarah, Sarah! Yes! I'm here! I'm *here*!" He then looked fiercely at Jake and said, "Remember what I just told you. Choose peace."

* * * * *

Hearing and seeing all, Quinn marveled at the instantaneous vanishing of Isaac's spirit body. Now it made sense to him why Isaac had invaded Caleb's DNA. Maybe Isaac had no memory of it, but he had clearly used Caleb as a vehicle to reunite with his eternal love, Sarah. Quinn could not fault him for that; could not blame him for the turmoil and sickness his presence had inflicted upon Caleb; he was certain

Isaac was unaware of it until Caleb began to weaken and he became stronger. He had become strong enough to gradually manifest into a physical being once again as indicated by the fact that Quinn heard the impact of flesh upon flesh when Isaac struck Jake's father. The noise revealed the alarming fact the lightning they both had absorbed was solidifying their spirit forms. Quinn had never seen this before in all the dead he had encountered until Jake began to transform. Now there were three, although Isaac seemed to have somehow managed to restrain his new earthbound body and was able to transcend dimensions at will.

Did Jake and Vernon Sheers have the same ability?

As of that moment, Quinn could not discern the answer, for Jake violently attacked Vernon and began to beat him. Profanity and guttural noises accompanied each strike Jake delivered. The old man quickly succumbed to his son's violent assault, and he cringed at the words Jake screamed at him as he continued to beat him:

"I'm not afraid of you anymore! You made our lives hell, you sack of festering shit. I hope God impales you on a spit and roasts you slowly. That's what you deserve. And, I'm gonna give you the burden you placed on me all those decades ago. Wear *this*, you bastard! Wear it forever!"

Jake opened his mouth wide and vomited upon his father, vomited the decades of "punishment" that encased his spirit body in a shimmering black prison of relentless pain. The aura abruptly turned a bright red that seemed lit from within by a tempestuously swirling inferno. Sparks of various colors shot from it, lit the night sky like fireworks, and turned the rain into a downpouring spectacle of colorful wet lights. Jake's aura became smaller as he continued to purge his pain onto Vernon. The aura descended into Jake's body like water draining into an outlet and rose up in his throat from whence it exited in a foul-smelling torrent into the now powerless devil that was Vernon Sheers.

Their screams cleaved the air—Jake's screams of liberation, and Vernon's terrified screams of one damned.

From behind him, Quinn heard the accompanying shrieks and inaudible cries from Stephanie and Ida. He turned briefly away from the battling men just in time to see Ida push her daughter facedown upon the muddy embankment, lie over the girl and cover her head. Quinn locked his sight upon Caleb and saw he was shocked and sickened by the violence. When their eyes met, Caleb resolutely abandoned the women and ducked down beside him.

"We've got to get out of here!" Caleb shouted to him over the noise of screams, wind, thunder, and rain.

Quinn turned his attention again to Jake and Vernon as he replied stubbornly to Caleb, "I can't. You go. Take them to my house."

"You can't stay here," Caleb argued.

"I have to," Quinn insisted vehemently. "I can't let Jake do this. He's damning himself and he doesn't realize it. I have to stop him."

Quinn had gotten as far as his words, "I have to" when Jake completed transferring his torturous black aura onto Vernon and began to drag Vernon down the embankment through the deepening flooding water to the creek's edge. He knew what Jake planned, and he struggled to his feet and half-ran, half-slid to the creek to stop him. Caleb followed in the same fashion, cussing at Quinn while trying to grab hold of his arm to pull him back to safety. Quinn would not relent. He backhanded Caleb's shoulder, sending Caleb and himself off balance. He determinedly slid and rolled away from Caleb's reach until he came to rest in the water overflowing the creek's edge. He lay there on his back, his eyes taking in the turbulent sky for a few moments, amazed to discover he was floating.

The saturated mud suddenly gave way, and Quinn spilled into the creek with it, right into the flailing arms of Vernon Sheers who was crazed with the agony of the punishment he wore. Thinking Quinn was Jake, Vernon wrapped his arms around him and dragged him to the bottom of the creek. Quinn had no time to prepare to defend himself, and Vernon's hug was like a vice around his torso. The filthy water filled his nose and lungs instantly when he instinctively attempted to breathe. He struggled to free himself from Vernon, but Vernon held him tightly as the water undulated around them. Blind in the blackness of the deep water, Quinn continued to struggle until the blackness became light and peace replaced his panic. His final thought was that it was not so bad to die by drowning.

He heard Jake's voice order gruffly, "Take him there. Push him up. I got'cha, kid."

Then came Ida's voice, "Here, I've got his arm. Push, Caleb, push."

Stephanie's voice, "I got him. C'mon, Caleb! Grab that branch there and use it for leverage. That's it. We got him! We got him! Take him, Mom. I'll help Caleb. Grab my hand."

The voices impressed Quinn as coming from far away. They continued to shout over each other; he couldn't understand what they were saying because of it. The only thing he did understand was the sensation of hands upon him, pulling him, and then the sensation of rolling onto his stomach and something pressing hard and rhythmically upon his back. Fetid water rolled up his throat and spewed out of his mouth. He took a heavy breath and then another as consciousness returned and he found himself cradled against Ida's chest.

In a daze, Quinn looked back to the creek, saw Jake and Vernon were still warring. His fear that Jake would damn himself if he did not forgive Vernon returned to his memory. He struggled to find his voice, and it finally came. His voice feeling and sounding like gravel, he begged Jake to stop and forgive the old man.

Jake ignored him and only battled harder, determined to destroy the man who had made his life and his afterlife a hellish existence. Vernon was determined, too, to destroy his son, not only because of his hatred for him but just out of the sheer will to teach him who was boss. Their violence created its own bubble of chaotic energy that followed the two men below the water's surface as they sank into the churning black. Moments later, a massive bolt of lightning shot out of the water; it carried Jake and Vernon inside it to the surface where it rose up and met the air. The bolt continued its ascension until it exploded into a whirling ball of fire that dissipated in the cold raging wind until nothing remained of the fire or Jake and Vernon.

It was all for nothing, Quinn realized. He had failed Jake, and the picture in his mind of Jake burning in hell with Vernon grieved him as deeply as the loss of his mother. He struggled out of Ida's embrace and weakly crawled a few feet to a tiny clearing along the creek where he could see a small patch of sky between the swaying treetops. Upon his knees, his hands outstretched in supplication, he begged God to forgive Jake. He cried out to Jake that he was sorry.

Completely exhausted, overcome by his physical and emotional pain, Quinn collapsed and wept until all awareness subsided into oblivion.

28

Farley Larson had a plan, and he made a decision.

He arrived home to see the embers still glowing in the fireplace. He saw a depleted wine bottle, two empty wine glasses, and a mirror littered with the remnants of cocaine plus a razor blade on the coffee table. The rhythmic squeak of bedsprings and the moans of his mother and her boyfriend assaulted his ears.

This is what Farley expected to find upon arrival, and it worked into his plan perfectly.

As he showered, he thought about how much he hated his mother who had always treated him as if he was in her way. He thought about her selfishness, her giant ego, her bleached hair and fake boobs, her string of boyfriends, and her insatiable sexual appetite. He bristled at the memory of all his school sporting events and his glee club performances she could not be bothered to attend—ever. She always had an excuse, none good, and none honest. She was a bitch; she had never impressed him as anything else.

She worked into his plan perfectly. She worked into his decision perfectly.

He lathered up, paid special attention to his injured hands, especially the right hand, to clean Marcus's blood from under his fingernails. While he did that, he reminded himself to rinse his jeans and the cuffs of the shirt he wore that night under cold water to get rid of the splatters of Marcus's blood. Then he would store the items in his suitcase so he wouldn't leave them behind when he left for Vegas. Once out of the shower, he quickly accomplished that task and returned the suitcase to the floor of his closet.

Now, for the plan…

The bedsprings squeaked at a faster pace. The up and down weight of their sweating bodies vibrated the wood floor. He could feel it under his feet, and his anger grew.

Yes… I need to be angry. Shit… What is this NEED crap? I AM angry. It's perfect for the plan.

Squeak, squeak, squeak. Squeak squeak squeak squeak squeak squeak squeak squeak.

Her voice, "Baby! Give it to me! Give it to me! Yeah... Give it to me!"

She had no clue her son had returned home, or maybe she didn't care that he had returned home.

Leg-spreading whore!

He put on a fresh pair of underwear, and he sat at the end of the bed where he studied the plain white wall across from him. It was cheap wood paneling painted white over drywall. There was a sloppily patched hole there, evidence of his past show of temper a year before. The patch, although painted over in white, was lumpy and the edges were ragged. He had made the repair at his mother's insistence as punishment for his lack of self-control, and he did a bad job of it just to piss her off. That hole had cost him two broken fingers and a cracked wrist bone, although he felt no pain when he had put his fist through the wall.

Tonight, he anticipated pain, a lot of pain. Farley re-examined his bruised knuckles and the newly bleeding scrapes from Marcus's teeth. He flexed his fingers. They still worked, but they hurt like hell. Yeah, it would be painful, but worth it. Only this time, he would have to put both his fists through the wall to account for the lesser damage to his left hand.

Worth it.

Squeak, squeak, squeak. Squeak squeak squeak squeak squeak squeak squeak squeak.

"Give it to me! Give it to me! Yeah... Give it to me!"

Hate'erhate'erhate'erhate'erhate'erhate'er...

He released a loud gravelly roar through his gritted teeth that made clear his rage. He closed his eyes tightly and shot his fists through the wall. The pain elicited another roar followed by a cry of agony. Drywall particles and dust, and splintered fragments of the flimsy wood paneling flew through the air as he quickly drew his freshly bleeding hands to his side. His fingers and knuckles stung and throbbed with sharp pain. He let the blood drip upon the floor as he stood there shaking from the shock and from his rage.

His breath came in deep gasps when he heard his mother's exclamation that came to him not as words but as noise. He waited for her as his blood continued to gather in small puddles at his feet.

She was still tying the belt of her fancy silk robe as she burst through the open doorway of his room, her face white, and her expression a mixture of concern and anger.

"What the hell, Farley? Oh, my God! Oh, shit!" She lifted his left hand and examined it as he stood seething at her, and then she took his right and saw the more serious damage there, the two knuckles completely exposed by the skinned-off epidermis. She glared at him, "Why? Why? What the hell is wrong with you?"

"I can't take this anymore," he wailed, "I hate it here. I hate *you!*"

The boyfriend appeared naked in the doorway, a clean-cut, slightly overweight man Farley recognized as the owner of the local used car lot. The man inquired, "What happened?"

She spun on him impatiently, "Get me some towels." As soon as he disappeared in search of towels, she turned her wrath on Farley. "Now I have to take your sniveling ass to the emergency room again. Thanks a lot."

"I'm gonna go live with Dad," Farley replied with a sneer, "And I'm leaving tonight."

"You're gonna fix those holes in the wall first."

"My hands are busted, you dense bitch. I ain't fixing anything. Have your fat sack lay do it. I'm outa here."

Her boyfriend returned with two towels. "Are you all right to drive him to the hospital?"

"Of course I'm alright," she spat, "This isn't the first time he's done this."

"In that case, I'll call you in a few days." He lingered for a moment under her fiery gaze before he shrugged and returned to her bedroom.

Farley sunk at the end of his bed, pretended to be thoroughly psychologically and emotionally wounded. He even managed to produce some phony tears that enhanced his performance and elicited a scrap of sympathy from her as she wrapped the towels around his hands.

She stepped barefooted into a puddle of his blood and angrily tried to wipe it off her foot by swiping her sole against the floor. She only managed to smear it, which added to her irritation. Under her breath she muttered, "You stupid…" (Which Farley was not certain she meant for him or herself.) After a deep breath, she directly told him, "Your father deserves you. I wish you both luck."

Farley ducked his head and covered his face with his left hand so she could not see his satisfied grin.

Plan accomplished.

* * * * *

The sun greeted a pristine blue sky upon which there was only one puffy sugar-white cloud to hint a storm had come and gone. Sunlight-warmed steam rose from the saturated grass, plants, and bushes in the backyard where drops of dew and lingering rain clung to the leaves and branches.

Caleb swept the remaining fragments of broken glass into a dustpan and emptied it into a bucket. He set the dustpan and bucket off to the side of the sliding glass doorway where no one would trip over it, and he observed the ethereal scene in the yard with a sense of wonder and appreciation of its beauty. It was all so peaceful after the turmoil of the night.

Although he had had no sleep, all the things he needed to do kept his adrenalin up. He needed to go to town to buy some plywood to cover the sliding glass doors, but he couldn't get to town until the road was cleared of the fallen trees. So far, he had not heard the sound of chainsaws this morning, and he believed it was because the ranchers – their only other neighbors besides the Vanderfields, were too busy rounding up their escaped livestock and mending their fences. Caleb figured it was up to him as his next order of business to cut the downed trees with his gas-powered chainsaw and drag the pieces to the side of the road so traffic could get through.

The property was a mess from the wind, but it was still too wet to work out there without sinking in the mud, which he discovered when he tried to get to his cottage for a change of clothing. Complicating matters further were the two muddy cows sleeping on his cottage porch. He knew nothing about cows and wasn't about to risk being attacked for a change of clothes.

This morning he accepted a pair of plain gray sweatpants and a sweatshirt Ida loaned him that used to belong to her husband, Ned. She told him a secret about why she kept them: sometimes when she missed Ned, she would wear the items to bed. Caleb told her there was nothing wrong with that and she shouldn't be embarrassed. His words gave her a reason to smile, and he loved to see her smile, especially after everything that had happened and her resulting worry over Stephanie and Quinn. The woman was finally taking a nap on the sofa after adding another log to the fireplace to fend off the morning cold.

He and Stephanie had spent most of the night helping Ida take care of Quinn. They had attended to his injuries as best they could, using a saved wrist splint for his undetermined sprained or broken left wrist. The splint was a leftover from a time when Ida had developed carpal tunnel syndrome. She also found an icepack for his swollen black eye. Ida treated the boy's illness with a cup of chicken broth fortified with herbs from her kitchen window garden. Quinn alternated between combative protesting, appreciative surrender, and semi-consciousness until he eventually succumbed to deep sleep. In all of this, Ida told Caleb how Quinn had lectured her about having a properly stocked first-aid kit, and how surprised he would be when she showed him the big *all the bells and whistles* first-aid kit her mother had stowed at the bottom of the linen closet. When she was certain Quinn would not need her for a while, she took his muddy and damp bloodstained clothing, including the shirt Farley loaned him, to the fireplace where she burned them among the blazing logs.

Standing out on the terrace gazing at the glimmering and misty backyard recalling all these things, Caleb felt a strong admiration for Ms. Ida and for once felt proud of his genetic roots, for they were connected to hers. Now he understood the source of his strength, which certainly didn't come from his drug-addicted mother. He decided right then that as soon as the roads were open and businesses reopened he would go to the Social Security Office and change his surname to his late father's surname, Iversen.

Charles Caleb Iversen. He liked it.

The aroma of freshly brewed coffee and the dull clink of full coffee mugs diverted his attention. It pleased him to see Stephanie come out to him with two coffees, one of which she extended to him with a weak smile upon her pale face. The last time he had looked in on her, she had fallen asleep on the queen bed in the guest room with Quinn. Ida, although not fully condoning it, understood and let the girl stay there. Caleb viewed it as completely harmless but said nothing about it.

He accepted the coffee gratefully while Stephanie told him, "Thank you for cleaning up the broken glass."

"No problem."

"And thank you for re-setting our front door."

Caleb simply nodded. He made a mental note to add supplies for that project to his shopping list, for the door repair was only a temporary fix.

"And thank you even more for saving Quinn from drowning."

"I'm no hero. I was scared shitless the whole time."

"You still saved him, so don't knock yourself. I wanted to jump in there too, but Mom kept holding me back. By the way, she's still out cold."

"We'll let her sleep."

"I used Grandma's old stovetop percolator. Did I do it right? Does the coffee taste good?"

"It tastes exactly as good as Ms. Grace used to make it."

That made her grin, and she looked away from him to the yard. "It looks like another planet out here."

"Beautiful, isn't it?"

"Yeah." She said it in a detached way, her thoughts now on something more important to her.

Caleb didn't need to guess. "How's Quinn doing?"

"Still asleep. We need to get him to the hospital. The phones and electricity's still out, so we can't call for an ambulance or anything, and that tree's still blocking the road anyway, so what good would it do to call for help?"

"I'm gonna try and clear the road in a bit. Got my chainsaw in the back of the truck. Would you like to come with me? I could use your help moving the pieces off the road."

"I can't move the big pieces."

"No... just the light stuff. I can handle the heavier stuff."

She brightened up. "Okay."

"How are *you* doing? After last night, I mean."

"I don't know. I've never actually seen ghosts before, or ghosts fighting with each other, at that. Now I know what Quinn goes through. I mean... How would anyone be doing after that? I'm so worried about him. I've never seen him like this. Seeing him all freaked out like this scares me a hell of a lot more than those ghosts ever could. I don't know if he'll ever be all right after this."

"He's stronger than you think. He'll bounce back. You'll see."

Aching hopelessness muffled her voice. "He's been through too much."

"He'll be okay." Caleb waited for a reply from her, but she slowly shook her head and sat down on the white plastic bench under the patio cover. Her expression was sad and worried. She had spent most of the night at Quinn's side, had helped her mother tend to his injuries and soothed him during his short bouts of tears and despondency. The memory of her dedication to his recovery would remain forever with Caleb.

She finally responded to his statement of reassurance, "I hope you're right."

"I *am* right. You'll see."

She studied his face for a few moments, and her expression changed as if a light suddenly flashed inside her. "I only caught a glimpse of Isaac, and you guys really are twins! I wish he could have stayed under different circumstances so I could talk with him. Oh, Caleb, I guess you think I'm silly."

"No. I don't think you're silly. And, by the way, he said he was aware of you and he heard you talking to him. He wanted to thank you for preserving that table and chair he made up in the attic. That made him very happy."

"Really?"

"Yeah. Your mom was right there when he said it. You made him really happy. Those pieces meant something to him."

Her eyebrows met as she thought about it and then accepted Caleb's words as truth. Her nod and the accompanying vague lift of her cheeks indicated she was flattered.

* * * * *

Ida's cell phone chirped from the coffee table in front of the sofa. Her eyes blinked open on the third chirp when the sound finally infiltrated her thin barrier of sleep. She took the phone without sitting up, noticed John Vanderfield's name on the Caller I.D. As the phone chirped again, she considered how she would explain the events of the previous night to him, how she would explain Quinn's injuries and illness. The ghost issue was something Quinn had sworn them to secrecy about, so she could not tell John. However, she could tell him Quinn had been ill and how Quinn had gotten injured. Chirp five… she pressed the answer button before the message function took over.

"Hello, John."

He spoke over her, "Is Quinn at your house?"

"He slept over. He's still asleep."

There was fatigue in his voice, and his pronunciation was mildly slurred. "Oh, thank God. I've been trying to reach him on the house phone but the lines are down."

"We lost cell service, too. They must have just fixed it."

He spoke over her second statement. "I was stuck here in the store all night with my thirty-eight handy. There were looters, so I stayed just in case they wanted to break into my place. Let'em just try—the bastards! I was stuck here anyway because of the flooding and the road closures. So, if they thought of providing a little entertainment—what the hell… Target practice for me." He paused and chortled at his pathetic attempt at middle-aged bravado. His voice rose a bit when he inquired with little interest in her answer, "How did you fare during the storm?"

"Flooding and a shattered sliding glass door, and still no electricity or landline service. We're all okay, though."

"Oh, that's good," he said unconcernedly.

Ida resented his lack of concern for her and her family, plus that of his own son. She delivered her next words coated with chastisement. "Well, actually… Quinn is ill; a flu bug perhaps, and he hurt himself trying to climb through a fallen tree down the road. He may have broken his wrist. I've splinted it for the time being until we can get him to the hospital."

"What was he doing down the road in this weather?"

"Coming home from their dance show at the school."

"What dance show?"

She was flabbergasted he didn't know about it. "The dance show he and Stephanie were performing in. The show was canceled and they came home early. Farley's car couldn't get through, so he dropped them off in front of that tree that fell."

"Who's Farley?"

"For crying out loud, John… Don't you and Quinn ever talk to each other?"

In his defense, John blurted, "He said nothing to me about any of this! Is the road there still blocked?"

"Caleb checked a while ago and, yes, it's still blocked. He's going out there soon with his chainsaw."

"Well, I'm leaving the store in a few minutes. Some of the streets are still flooded, and the traffic lights aren't working, so I'll have to take the long way around. But I should see you in a half-hour or so. If Quinn wakes up in the meantime, keep him there with you."

"Of course. But – you know what, now that the cell phone service is up again, I can call an ambulance for him and have them meet us at the tree."

"No, don't do that. I'll take him to the hospital myself."

Ida thought her plan was better, but she wasn't about to argue with John when it came to his son. "Okay, John. Drive carefully."

Quinn was in that twilight state between sleep and awake when she sat down at the edge of the bed in the guest room. He turned slowly onto his side to face her as she lowered herself gently onto the edge of the mattress. His left eye was swollen and the skin purple-gray. His nose was in the same condition, but not as swollen as his eye. Surrendering fully to her motherly instincts, she caressed his temple and brushed his hair away from his pale face. He welcomed her attempt to comfort him. He closed his eyes and enjoyed the pleasure of her delicate touch.

"How are you feeling, Quinn?"

"Run over."

"Do you remember last night?"

"All of it." He grimaced at the recollection.

"We'll keep our promise to you."

"Thanks."

"Why don't you want him to know?"

"Because he'll think I'm crazy."

"We saw them, too."

"He'll think you're just covering for me."

"That's ridiculous."

"Don't tell him. Please."

"It's your call."

"Has Jake come back?"

"No. But maybe we can't see him anymore. Maybe it's like it used to be where only you can see him."

He fought tears. "No. He's gone. He's gone. I failed him."

"It wasn't your fault that he wouldn't listen to you."

Quinn sighed a wavering and despondent sigh. After a few moments. he smiled subtly and whispered tiredly, "Now you know why I'm so weird."

"I've never thought you were weird. In fact, I have always found you delightful. If I thought you were weird I would never have let my daughter be near you."

He squeezed her hand affectionately. "You're a special lady, Ida."

"I'll send Caleb over to your house to get you some fresh clothing."

"No hurry. I want to stay in bed if that's all right with you."

"Your father will be here in a while to take you to the hospital."

"Shit… I don't want to go there. Especially with *him*."

"Your wrist may be broken."

"It isn't. I was still able to bend it before you put this splint on it."

"Take it up with your dad, then."

* * * * *

Caleb and Stephanie had managed to clear one lane of the road by the time John Vanderfield reached what remained of the obstacle. He rolled down his window and inquired about Quinn.

Caleb approached the window and told him, "He's doing a little better." He abruptly stepped away from the stench of bourbon that made his stomach protest.

John leaned out the window and motioned Caleb to return. When Caleb kept his distance and took up his chainsaw, he hollered impatiently, "Does he still need to go to the hospital?"

"Ask Ida." Closing the conversation, Caleb revved the chainsaw. As soon as John passed them and continued up the road, he shut off the machine and walked to the side of the road with it where Stephanie was stacking branches. "He's drunk," he told her angrily. "Call your mother and warn her."

Ida smelled it the moment she opened the door. She had just thumbed off her cell phone and it was still in her hand as John, disheveled and stinking of *Eau de Boozer,* entered the foyer. Her eyes blazing, her voice deep with disappointment and simmering rage, she stated, "You're drunk. How dare you! How dare you do this when your kid needs to go to the hospital? Do you really think I'm going to let you drive him there?"

"Oh, fuck off, Ida. I only had one."

"One *bottle*, you mean."

He stepped around her and scanned the premises. "Where is he?"

"He's still in bed. You're not driving. I'll drive."

"I can drive him."

"No, you can't. If you insist, I'll call the police."

He halfheartedly swept her aside and wove forward, glancing around until he spotted the staircase and began to ascend.

Ida stopped him. "The guest bedroom is down here." She pointed to a room along the hallway beside the staircase. "I suggest you clean yourself up before you go in there. You look like hell."

He screwed up his face like a protesting toddler. "I've been up all night!"

"So have we." She pointed again to the hallway, "The bathroom is there. Comb your hair and wash your face. Straighten up your clothes. You look like a bum. Your son doesn't need to see you like this."

John flipped his hand up in an exaggeratedly foppish manner, "He doesn't care."

"Yes, he does care. And you will not take him out of this house."

He smiled innocently, "You're still a bossy bitch, Ida."

"You're still a drunk, John."

He sunk and planted himself on the bottom step. He compliantly looked up at her through his red-rimmed eyes and mumbled petulantly, "I know that. The kid knows it, too."

Quinn interjected from the doorway where he stood wrapped in the bedspread and obviously weak, "And I'm sick of it."

John stood at the sight of him, gazed wide-eyed at the boy's battered face. "Jesus… That happened from a fall?"

Quinn sneered at him. "It happened from the way I *landed*. And you're not taking me to the hospital. If I go, I'll go with Ida." His face reddened with his humiliation as he addressed Ida, "I'm sorry for the trouble I caused you."

"You didn't cause any trouble, Quinn." She hugged him gently, careful to avoid causing him further pain. "I'll take you in to have you checked out. After that, you can stay here until your dad sobers up." The next she directed to John, "At *home*."

Quinn chuckled sardonically and said, "He's never sober." He faced his father combatively. "Are you, Dad?"

John scratched his head and stared at the wood floor. He noticed the muddy footprints, many of them mixed together and smeared over each other. He saw the drops of blood, too, some of it also smeared. It gave him a hint of the ordeal they had endured through the night, the ordeal his son, especially, had endured. Every muscle in his face slackened with his shame.

Quinn added contemptuously, "You can't be here for me, just like you couldn't be there for Mom when she needed you. You're a self-centered prick, and I'm embarrassed to call you my father. You have one choice and only one choice if things are ever gonna change for us: get some help and be the father I need. If you don't do that, then I guess you've decided I don't matter to you—and I'm all you've got. You said it yourself, Dad. You said I'm all you've got. Now, go home. I don't wanna be seen with you."

Avoiding eye contact, his shoulders slumped, and his gait unsteady from inebriation, John silently left the house. Quinn drew a deep breath and leaned his back against the wall for support as Ida watched from the front doorway as John folded himself into his crookedly parked car and pulled out of the driveway. She anticipated by the fact he was driving in the oncoming lane that he would crash into a tree, but he narrowly avoided the collision by swerving into the correct lane and making a wide turn up his driveway. Expecting him to not stop in time and collide with the garage door, she waited for the sound of splintering glass and broken wood. That sound never came. Instead, she heard the racket of the garage door rolling up, then the sound of his car door closing, and finally the rattling noise of the garage door meeting the concrete. Relieved, she closed the front door and locked it, her hands trembling slightly from anger and frazzled nerves. She took a few moments to calm herself before she returned to Quinn.

To her surprise, he regarded her stoically as she approached him, yet the pain of years of battle was in his eyes as he looked at her. He gave her a lopsided smile and a thumbs-up, and said proudly, "I've been wanting to say that for a long time."

* * * * *

Quinn expected his father would not stop drinking and the man proved him correct. Over the following week, they existed in the big old Victorian under a tenuous truce supported by little conversation and their customary separate autonomy. During that time Quinn segregated himself to his bedroom where he slowly recovered from the turmoil of what he referred to as, "Storm Night", but his grief over his failure to save Jake still resonated heavily in his soul. So, although physically healing, his mind and spirit remained in a deep depression he had no will to fight. His father gave him plenty of space in the belief the boy's seclusion was caused by their fractured father-son relationship. Quinn was happy, in a sadistic sort of way, to let the man believe that and stew in his self-blame.

One night he heard the unwelcome voice of his father summoning him from the bottom of the stairs. Expecting to be in trouble for something, he entered the den cautiously and lowered himself slowly upon the sofa diagonal to *The King's Throne*, his father's recliner. He immediately noticed the half-empty tumbler of bourbon on the table beside the *throne*. His father's bloodshot eyes indicated he had already drunk more than he should have. Quinn also noticed the stack of unopened mail he had left on the table earlier that day, mail he assumed were the usual bills and business correspondence that had nothing to do with him. However, his father had opened one piece of mail that he clutched in his hand. Decisively, the man lowered the footrest and sat upright, then regarded Quinn impassively. Positive the letter was about some infringement he had unknowingly committed at school, Quinn looked at him sullenly and said nothing.

He told Quinn in a gentle tone of voice, "Maria's decided to stay in San Jose with her family. She's quit her job with us."

"I'm not surprised," Quinn said with a shrug and a bit of relief that he was not in trouble.

"She wants you to have her Escort, and the pink slip here says she sold it to you for one-hundred dollars." John smiled at Maria's smart little lie to save Quinn the taxes that would have been due had she simply transferred ownership of the vehicle. "That's invisible money, of course."

Quinn was hesitant to feel joy over this gift since he still didn't have a driver's license. He said composedly, "Cool."

"I've just got off the phone with Ida. She's agreed to give you driving lessons."

Without thinking, Quinn revealed arrogantly, "I already know how to drive."

John cast him a glare, "I'm aware of that. Do you really think I never heard that car starting in the middle of the night? Where did you take it, anyway?"

"To the lake."

"Why?"

"Because I like it there at night, and I needed to think."

"Think about what?"

"Things."

John kept digging, his tone surprisingly compassionate, "Your mother? Me?"

"Sometimes."

"And other times?"

"The way that place used to be back in the old days. The ballroom, the bands, the people that danced there. We don't have that kind of thing anymore. People are different now than the people back then."

"That's why it's no longer a ballroom, Quinn."

"Yeah, I know. People don't care."

John leaned forward and said in almost a whisper, "You can hear the music, can't you? That old music. You can hear it just like I used to be able to hear it sometimes."

That came as a complete shock to Quinn, and he blurted, "You? No way!"

"Yes. Only at night when your mother and I used to go there to make out before we were married. I thought I was crazy because she couldn't hear it. She couldn't hear it coming out of that old dark ballroom. But when you started collecting all those seventy-eights, I knew you heard it, just like I had heard it."

It was true. Quinn had heard the music coming from the ballroom late at night from the time he was four years old. It wasn't until the ghost of Buzz Lester began to visit when he realized the source of the music. Buzz had been there for a long time, keeping the music alive. But Quinn couldn't reveal his ability to converse with the dead.

He was careful with his words as he replied introspectively; "I'd heard it since I was four. I knew it was coming from that place with the gold dome for a roof. At least I know now that I'm not crazy. Do you still hear it sometimes?"

"No. Not anymore."

"Do you miss it?"

"No." John relaxed and sat back in his recliner, "You can have the car as soon as you pass your driving test and have that license."

"Thanks." His heart pounded at the freedom of driving his own car.

"I'll cover the insurance for the first year. After that, you'll have to get a job and be responsible for that. Deal?"

"Deal."

"How's that sprained wrist doing?"

"It's healing fast. It doesn't hurt much."

"Good. The swelling's gone down on your nose, too."

They looked away from each other in uncomfortable silence until John stated, "I'm going into detox next week."

Quinn didn't believe it. His voice came full of doubt, "Really?"

"Yes. I'm already registered. I'll be staying there for a month, maybe longer. You're to live at Ida's while I'm gone."

"I can do just fine here on my own, Dad. I'm not a child."

"Don't argue. I hate it when you argue with me."

"I hate it that you don't trust me. What do you think I'll do? Throw a party?

I only have two friends."

John laughed softly; Stephanie and Caleb were certainly not bad company. He thought it over for a few moments and realized he must trust his son if they were ever to resolve their problems. "Okay, Quinn. I'll call you from the detox place as soon as they say it's okay for me to make calls. If you're not here, I'll check for you at Ida's. Deal?"

"Deal." Quinn then added encouragingly, "I'm glad you're doing this, Dad. Just get well."

However, Quinn had little confidence his father would complete the program.

* * * * *

Marcus Stanley was the topic of conversation at Providence High. Still in the hospital with a fractured skull and fractured bones in his once movie-star handsome face, he had no memory of how he had ended up that way. The police decided, because the boy's wallet was missing, Marcus had been the victim of a robbery and, because of the viciousness of the attack, that he knew his assailant.

The police investigated his friends and acquaintances, specifically targeted Harry Richter, Bruno Ruiz, and Farley Larson as both sources of information and possible suspects. The police eliminated Harry Richter off the list once hospital records proved he was an inpatient sick with sepsis that night. As for the remaining two, Larson's temper was well known to the authorities in Providence, and Ruiz had priors for drunk and disorderly conduct. Ultimately, both young men were crossed off the list: Farley because his mother brought him to the ER after he punched holes in his bedroom walls which the police saw for themselves, and Bruno's parents swore he had been home with them the entire night.

Questioned separately, Stephanie and Quinn stuck to Farley's story they never saw anyone at the carwash the short time they were there, and that Farley dropped them off at the toppled tree in the road a half-mile from Stephanie's house. Quinn was not pleased when the police asked him to explain his injuries, and he later berated Stephanie for ignoring his warnings and dating Farley in the first place. The rift between them lasted a week until Stephanie apologized to him but reiterated it was better he not know the truth (although Quinn had already figured out the truth).

"Well, at least Marcus didn't die," Stephanie considered as they sat on the front steps of the Victorian. Her volume rose as she directly addressed Quinn, "And at least he got a clue what it feels like to get beat up. The way I look at it, he got what he deserved."

"No one deserves that," Quinn responded with unexpected sympathy.

"Are you kidding me? After all he did to you?"

"It was mostly Bruno and Farley. Marcus got a kick out of watching."

"But, what about what Marcus did to Farley? Remember all those cigarette burns?"

Quinn gave her a sideways glance of warning, "Be careful what you say. If the wrong person hears that, your man Farley might find himself in custody."

"He isn't my man, and he's living with his dad in Vegas."

"That doesn't matter. I'm gonna pretend I never heard that. Again, Steph… be careful what you say."

"You're right. As always." She watched him light his cigarette and exhale the smoke. "Those things'll kill you, y'know."

"I know."

"Do you want to die?"

"Of course not."

"You've been thinking about it. I can tell."

He chuckled casually and asked her, "How's that?"

"You've been avoiding us, keeping yourself locked up in this house. You hardly answer the phone. Caleb's worried about you, too."

"Tell him I'm fine. Do you all expect me to be Mr. Congeniality after all I've just gone through? I needed some time alone. No big deal. Don't any of you worry about me; I'm okay."

"I know you've been really depressed. It's worse now since your dad's in rehab."

"I'm not depressed. Besides that, why would I want to kill myself? How could I? How could I do that to my dad? How the hell would that be for him to come home from rehab and find me dead? I don't have to tell you what that would do to him. God…! I may hate him sometimes, but I'd never do anything like that to him."

"Or to the rest of us, I hope. You know we love you. Besides that, I don't want you to end up like Jake, walking the earth for centuries because you screwed up."

He responded hotly, "Jake didn't screw up, and he didn't walk the earth for centuries. It was his dad that screwed up, and he's paying for what he did to Jake."

"So, do you think you can't see Jake anymore because he's gone to heaven?"

"That's what I'm hoping. God wouldn't punish him for something that wasn't his fault."

"You kind of miss him though, huh?"

"Yeah, I miss him."

"Is he the first one you sort of became friends with?"

"No." He stared off for a few moments, thinking not only of Jake but also of Buzz and the young woman in the dark blue dress. He'd been thinking about the woman for days. She had not made an appearance for weeks, and he wondered if she was connected to the events of Storm Night. But why hadn't she appeared to him then if that was the case? Where had they all gone—the woman, Isaac, Jake, and Vernon Sheers? It was beyond his comprehension, yet he couldn't stop wondering about their fate.

He expected Stephanie wanted details, but she didn't ask. Instead, she viewed him with a strange expression in her eyes as if she had just discovered something in him for the first time, something wondrous and admirable, and perhaps even ethereal, that was stirring a delicious brew of love in her heart for him. It was far beyond, far stronger, than that *friend love* he had previously seen in her eyes. The insecure part of him warned him he was misinterpreting. A moment later, the newly confident part of him nurtured by all the battles and small victories of the past months assured him what he observed in her was true. His heart actually fluttered with the realization, fluttered and then recovered its rhythm, albeit a faster rhythm.

He slipped his hand in hers and entwined his fingers with hers. For a while, they didn't talk. They watched the brown maple leaves skip along the concrete walkway in the gentle breeze, and they listened to the birds call to each other as they claimed their perches among the trees and bushes. Soon the birdcalls became fewer as they settled in for the night. The sky slowly darkened from lavender to plumb above the horizon. Stephanie and Quinn relished the peacefulness of the dawning night, that exquisite quiet of dusk, as it settled into their beings and erased their concerns of the day. Quinn tightened his fingers between hers, offered her a fond smile.

Stephanie's cheeks reddened as she giggled briefly and inquired softly to him, "What?"

He paused, considering how to express his feelings for her. He found the words and replied haltingly, "I like being with you."

"Did you mean what you said that night on the road?"

"On Storm Night?"

She smiled subtly and answered softly, "Yeah."

"I said a lot of things that night."

"You said you would always love me, no matter what."

"Yeah. I meant that."

Her voice came shyly, "I... I think I'd like it if you kissed me."

The weight of his depression, failures, and worries lifted as if some giant magical hands took it all away. He tossed the cigarette sideways to the driveway where it rolled into the wet ditch alongside the road. As he did that, he thought about cigarette breath and regretted he could do nothing about it at that moment. He wished he had brought a stick of gum with him, but he wasn't expecting this, especially since they had been at odds all week. Additionally, Quinn had accepted his erroneous belief Stephanie only considered him as a friend. Now, here he was with cigarette breath and his lips tingling with the anticipation of meeting hers.

Aw... damn it...

He recalled Jake demanding of him, "When are you gonna kiss her?"

Right now.

She eagerly allowed him to gently hold her in his arms and then lift her chin with his fingers. He took his time meeting her lips with his. He wanted it to be right, not rushed. He tasted her gently at first, and when she offered no resistance, her lips lingering fully and receptively to his, she melted in his arms under the passion of his warm lips upon hers. He then kissed her firmly, demonstrating his dominance yet at once expressing his deep love and respect for her. To his delight, she tightened her arms around him and reciprocated likewise, both wishing the moment could last forever.

Marcus, Farley, the cops—they didn't matter anymore. All that mattered was that moment. That moment was what they would reminisce about for years to come.

29

Stephanie overheard her mother and Caleb confiding to each other the obvious fact after dinner that evening of her and Quinn's intimate glances across the table. Ida waited until Caleb accompanied Quinn back to the Victorian, before she joined Stephanie in her room for a mother-daughter talk.

They talked not only about the girl's relationship with Quinn, but about the intricacies of love and romance. This led to Ida speaking in a sentimental voice about Ned and how they had known since high school they were meant to be together through life although they had both dated others in the process at the insistence of their parents. She couldn't say if it would be that way for Stephanie and Quinn.

Her tone abruptly changed to her regular *Mom voice*, "Now, tidy up this room and strip that bed for me so I can put those sheets with the laundry. Don't forget to flip the mattress."

At this moment, she would do anything to please her mother. She got to it right away and took the linens downstairs.

Upon returning to her room, she regarded the mattress as a challenge. It was a full size mattress and very heavy. The last time she flipped it she had done it side-to-side. This time it needed to be flipped end-to-end, which was not as easy. Illogically, she decided the easiest way was to pull it fully off the end of the bed frame, lean it on one end against the closet door across from the bed and then flip it fully over onto the box spring from there and slide it into place. She got as far as pulling the mattress off the end of the bed onto the floor when something under the corner edge of the bed frame caught her eye and brought the mattress-flipping project to a halt.

On her hands and knees, she fished under the bedrail and brought out a brown suede-covered diary and one handmade wooden jewelry box. She gave an audible gasp at her discovery. Quinn must have unintentionally shoved the articles under the bed in his haste to return the other items into Emily Vanderfield's hope chest. However it happened, Stephanie considered it not as a fortunate accident, but the benevolence of someone on *The Other Side* who wanted her to find them. She controlled her urge to stop everything and start reading the diary, for she knew her mother would come up soon to check on her progress. Instead, she hid the objects in the roomy bottom drawer of her nightstand. She had all night to read the diary uninterrupted, and that's what she planned to do as soon as her mother went to bed.

It was hell waiting that long.

* * * * *

This Diary Belongs to: Emily Mae Vanderfield
Jan. 1, 1913

We stayed up until after three this morning. Mama played the piano for us and we sang many songs, some old and some new. We danced, too, but not as much as we sang. The men are not very good at dancing. Isaac and his uncle Frank brought homemade Italian sausage, and it was so good! Jake accompanied Sarah to our door, but he took the carriage home right away. It made me happy Mr. and Mrs. Sheers allowed her to join us overnight. (She is still sleeping, poor thing.) Isaac kissed her cheek when he said goodbye last night when they were out on the porch. She kissed his cheek, and they whispered something to each other, and then she rested her head on his shoulder for the briefest moment. She seemed a little sad. I am sad, too, for he treats me like a sister.

Jan. 10, 1913

I accompanied Isaac to town this morning for us to pick up supplies. His new woodworking tools and Frank's music disks finally arrived at the train station, and I was purchasing some items for Mama who is feeling poorly. Isaac tied his horse and wagon in front of the mercantile building just when Mr. Sheers came out of there. Well, that man gave poor Isaac the meanest look, and then he looked at me like I had sinned terribly by being friends with Isaac. As everyone knows, Mr. Sheers does not like Italians. He says they are dirty people. He really knows nothing. Isaac and Frank are very clean people and keep their home very tidy. Who would think men could be so tidy? Isaac, especially, is always neat and clean. Oh, his eyes drive me mad! What a beautiful creature he is! Sometimes I want to confess how I feel when he is near me, but I know he loves Sarah. She knows it, too. I think she loves him but is afraid of angering her family.

Jan. 21, 1913

Jake got in trouble for fighting with Andrew at school. It was Andrew's fault for making fun of him, but Mr. Sheers whipped him just the same. Sarah said Jake could not sit for a long time afterwards, but their father still sent him to school today. I felt sorry for him.

Feb. 6, 1913

The weather is terrible with much rain and wind. It is so cold it feels like it might snow. Poor Mrs. Gadfee's little newborn babe died yesterday morning. She was only six days old. Papa has a supply of only adult size coffins on hand. He asked Isaac to build a special coffin for the baby. Isaac brought it over tonight and refused to take pay for it.

Feb. 14, 1913

We exchanged Valentines at school. Tonight most of us attended the Valentine's Day dance at the grange hall. My heart almost stopped when Isaac asked me to dance. Of course I let him sign my dance card, which was almost full by the time he drifted over to me. His hands are very calloused, but I loved that they embraced mine if only for that one dance. I can still feel his hands holding mine. Sarah did not have a full dance card and spent much of the time sitting and drinking cider. I noticed Isaac never asked her to dance. I think that was because the Sheers family was hosting the dance.

Feb. 20, 1913

Heavy rain the past four days. The river and creek are flooding. The roads are impassible even for our poor horses. Papa is staying in town to be near his patients. We are low on flour, barley and coffee. Thank God our milking cows and chickens are still producing. Mr. Tarantino brought us some potatoes, walnuts, and goat's milk. He said he expects to earn a good deal of money at sheep shearing time, as the price of wool has increased from last year. He and Isaac only raise sheep for their wool because they have become more like pets to them and they could not bear to slaughter them for food.

Feb. 30, 1913

I have been ill for a week. Papa gave me medicine, but it does not help.

Mar. 5, 1913

More heavy rain, plus thunder and lightning. It is quite a sight at night. Papa is in town again, but he telephoned home to tell us there was word the trains are stopped because of flooding. Frank Tarantino and Isaac visited us and brought a bag of flour, a smoked ham, and soup. We are sharing what we have with each other until the roads are clear again. Thank God we all have chickens plus preserved fruits and vegetables!

Mar. 10, 1913

It was a beautiful day today. The hills are blanketed in green. I noticed some flowers budding along the road. Isaac said they might be snapdragons or narcissus. He took me to school this morning on his wagon since he was going into town anyway to pick up bales of hay and alfalfa, visit the post office, and then buy tobacco, sugar, and coffee for his uncle Frank. We had a very pleasant ride and talked the entire way. He is so full of good humor and always has a funny story. I love to hear him laugh. We sang a couple of songs, too. He is a better singer than I, but he was nice and said I could carry a tune quite well. He taught me some Italian words he learned from Frank, and he told me most of Frank's operatic disks are sung in Italian. Isaac also told me the Italian language is rooted in Latin. I never knew that! He knows so much about so many things.

Mar. 13, 1913

Mr. and Mrs. Sheers gave Sarah permission to spend the weekend with us to celebrate Jonathon's birthday. I am looking forward to fun with my best friend. We are planning a hike and a picnic together on Sunday. She wants Isaac to join us. That is fine with me.

Mar. 16, 1913

Our hike and picnic was very pleasant, although the weather was chilly and windy. Jonathon flew his new kite. Isaac told us his father was of Danish descent and that's where he got his light blue eyes. Sarah and Isaac went off by themselves for a little while to gather flowers. They were gone a long time and returned with a very large bouquet of wildflowers. Jonathon confided in me that he thinks Sarah and Isaac are "sweet on each other," (his words). Us Vanderfields would have to be blind and deaf not to have figured that out by now for, whenever she is here, Isaac finds an excuse to come visit, or she finds an excuse to go visit him. Sometimes it makes me angry, but how can I be angry with two people I love so? Shouldn't their happiness make me happy for them? Oh, Father in Heaven, please take away my resentment and instill in me a pure heart.

Mar. 20, 1913

Mr. Jordan's funeral drew most of the town today. Papa did his best to heal him, but he was too ill from Consumption. Papa is very sad. Mr. Jordan was his good friend for many years. Now we only have Mr. Kinley to play the fiddle at our gatherings, and he does not play as well as Mr. Jordan.

Apr. 6, 1913

Mama and Papa held a surprise birthday party for me today. They gave me the most wonderful gift: a hope chest they had Isaac make special for me. His personal gift to me was a music box he made. It plays Clair De Lune. He also gave me a pretty birthday card. Sarah gave me a poetry book. Jonathon gave me a very beautiful hair comb now that I am old enough to wear my hair up. Papa arrived late because he had two patients, one ill with a cough and fever, the second with a broken leg. He attended our party for only a little while because he had to return to the basement to embalm Mrs. Williams who died of heart failure. She was a nice lady. Papa didn't tell me about that until tonight.

Apr. 15, 1913

More rain! Sarah said maybe we should start building an Ark.

Apr. 18, 1913

Papa's new surrey arrived on the train today. Now we have two, and Mama and I no longer have to rely on Isaac and Frank to take us in their wagon when we need to get supplies.

May 4, 1913

We roasted a pig for Mama's birthday celebration. All of the women from her quilting circle attended the festivities and brought presents and flowers. Sarah and Mrs. Sheers gave her new lace gloves. They didn't stay very long, because Mrs. Sheers was busy at home. I think Mrs. Sheers gets spooked by the fact Papa does his embalming work in our basement. They left just before Isaac and Frank arrived with two bottles of wine. For once Papa didn't have to rush off to tend a patient or someone who had died. He was all smiles and laughter, especially after he and Frank emptied the second wine bottle. My goodness! They were so funny!

May 6, 1913

Jake had a terrible convulsion at school today. I overheard one of the boys tell the other boys he thought Jake was possessed by the devil. How mean boys can be! Our teacher, Miss Gray, was very compassionate to Jake and let him sit outside to rest a while before he returned to class. Poor Jake sits near the door at the back of the classroom because of his convulsions. Sarah told me he doesn't always feel it when they are coming on. She said she heard her mama and papa talk about sending Jake away. I think that is very sad. If Jake were my brother we would never send him away.

May 12, 1913

I am worried about Sarah. She has a bruise on her cheek she said happened when she fell at home. This is not the first time I have seen bruises on her.

May 14, 1913

Today Sarah implored me to let her stay the weekend at my home. She was very distraught and crying. She confessed she and Isaac are in love, and this is the only way they can see each other without her parents knowing. What else can I do but say yes? And what else can I do but release my dreams of Isaac some day being mine? Oh, how my heart hurts! I have been so silly to believe in the impossible.

May 18, 1913

Sarah, Isaac, Jonathon and I went fishing today. We caught seven fish. Sarah and Isaac fell asleep together on the blanket after lunch. Sarah slept with her head on Isaac's chest. They looked so content. Jonathon promised never to reveal Sarah and Isaac's secret to anyone.

May 26, 1913

The Constable and Mr. and Mrs. Sheers came to our home tonight looking for Sarah and Isaac. They said Sarah has been missing for three days, and they have not been able to locate Isaac to question him. Mr. Tarantino told them Isaac had gone up north to bring back a load of wood for his shop. I think Frank Tarantino knows the truth. I think Sarah and Isaac have eloped.

June 1, 1913

Isaac and Sarah returned late this afternoon and visited us this evening. They showed us their wedding bands. They were both glowing with happiness, yet very worried about telling Mr. and Mrs. Sheers. Sarah is especially afraid. Her father has a bad temper and she expects he will beat her and Isaac, too. They plan to live at Isaac's home for the present and maybe forever. I pray to God to protect them. I have seen what Mr. Sheers has done to poor Jake when angry with him. (Papa once tried to explain Jake's convulsions and episodes of violence were caused by when that horse kicked him in the head, but Mr. Sheers would never believe it.) I wish that horse had kicked Mr. Sheers in the head and killed him! (God forgive me!) I am so afraid for Sarah and Isaac.

June 4, 1913

Sarah and Frank are very worried. Isaac left for town yesterday and has not returned. Although Isaac said he was going to pick up supplies, Sarah is afraid Isaac went to talk to her father without her and tell him they got married.

June 5, 1913

They are frantic. The horse brought the wagon home without Isaac.

June 7, 1913

My heart is in pieces! Isaac was found dead in Riddling Creek this morning. Sarah is living again with her mother and father. Frank Tarantino is inconsolable.

June 8, 1913

Papa had forbidden me to go down to the basement. I stole down there anyway this morning around 3 o'clock. I just had to see Isaac's face once more – just once more, and kiss him goodbye. So foolish of me. I was not prepared for what I saw. His beautiful eyes were wide open, but they were no longer beautiful. His face was swollen, scraped and bruised, and his mouth was wide open as if in the midst of a scream. Oh! How horrible the sight! How terrible his death! I must have fainted from the shock, for I awoke on the floor, and Papa kneeling over me. Papa carried me upstairs. I don't know how many hours I cried, but Papa stayed with me. He gave me an injection of something – I don't know what kind of medicine. What good could it do? All I see before me is dear Isaac's terrified face.

Stephanie stopped reading, although Emily's diary contained much more in the pages to follow. She expected the next pages would include Emily's account of her father's findings from Isaac's autopsy and then the burial. But she reconsidered the autopsy part; Mr. Vanderfield would not have shared that information with Emily, would not have shared his opinion that Isaac had been murdered. The funeral, though, had to be a heartbreaking experience for the poor girl. It was simply too much to contemplate all at once, yet her curiosity about the aftermath of Isaac's death drew her back to Emily's diary.

Emily's tearstains on the next entry page were still visible after eighty-eight years.

June 16, 1913

Many from town came to Isaac's funeral. The Sheers family accompanied Sarah who was so overcome with grief she could not speak. Jake told me privately she had lost her ability to speak when she learned Isaac had died. Jake also told me he liked Isaac and was sorry that he had died. He had tears in his eyes as he told me. Frank Tarantino cried and cried, and he hugged Sarah and told her "You are still my family and I will be here for you when you need me." (Mr. and Mrs. Sheers did not like that at all, let me tell you!) Papa and Mama did their best to comfort Frank, as did I. That poor gentle man just seems lost without Isaac. However, his son, plus his daughter and her husband came for the funeral and to take care of him until he could get through the worst of this very tragic time. They loved Isaac, too. He was like a little brother to them, and they cried a lot. I cried a lot, too. The Gadfees spoke of Isaac's generosity when their little baby died, and about the beautiful little casket he made for her. Mrs. Gadfee said Isaac carved a little lamb on the lid and lined the inside of the lid and the box with a down filled blanket. He set a tiny white satin and lace baby pillow there to rest the precious little head. She said it was the most beautiful work she had ever seen. Mama kept watching me. I think she knows how I feel about Isaac. Mothers know these things. My eyes hurt from crying. I must close this entry now.

She added as an addendum:

God must have needed another angel or He would not have taken Isaac so soon to be with Him in Paradise.

June 20, 1913

The newspaper said Isaac was murdered. I asked Papa why they printed that he was murdered. He said someone must have seen the autopsy report. I had no idea Papa had performed an autopsy on Isaac. He said the constable ordered it. Papa refused to tell me what he found that pointed to murder. Why would someone want to murder Isaac who was kind to everyone? Could it have been a robbery committed by someone passing through our town? But yet the newspaper said the constable has arrested Jacob Sheers as the suspect. This I cannot believe! Jake was a fighter, yes, but he never had any problems with Isaac. I do not understand it.

June 23, 1913

Jake is still in jail. His trial has been set for July 15. His father, who insists Jake was home with him that night, has hired an associate to defend him.

June 25, 1913

I saw Mrs. Sheers's maid at the mercantile today. She told me Sarah is still in mourning and doesn't want to leave home. I think she is only telling me what Mr. and Mrs. Sheers told her to tell everyone. I then asked her about Jake, and she said she is not allowed to discuss him because of the trial coming up.

June 27, 1913

Today I visited Isaac's grave and left flowers for him. It is difficult for me to believe he is gone. I feel like I have been living in a fog since that terrible day they found him. I am angry with God for taking him. Oh, if only I could hear Isaac's voice and his laughter once more, then I would know there is a Heaven and he lives on in God's glory. Yet, I hear only silence. Tell me this, Father in Heaven... why the silence? Answer my prayers and let me hear his voice once more!

Stephanie paused to blink back the tears that blurred her vision, and to swallow the painful lump in her throat. She released a wavering mournful sigh in response to Emily's brokenhearted account of irretrievable loss.

June 30, 1913

Frank Tarantino gave me the jewelry box Isaac had made for Sarah last Christmas. He asked me to keep it for her, as he was certain Mr. and Mrs. Sheers would never let Sarah come see him. I have not seen Sarah since the funeral. Perhaps she is still unwell, or perhaps her parents have forbidden her to see me, too. I tend to believe the latter.

Stephanie thought back to the contents in Emily's hope chest: the jewelry box with the name "Sarah" carved inside the lid, and the little purple pouch containing a gold ring and pearl pendant necklace. The mystery of how Emily came into possession of the jewelry box was now solved, although Emily did not indicate if the box contained Sarah's wedding ring and necklace. Stephanie hoped to find the answer as she continued reading.

July 16, 1913

The jury found Jake innocent. It appears the Sheers's maid and their houseman confirmed the Sheers's testimonies that Jake was home during the estimated date of Isaac's murder. The prosecution had only one witness who claimed to have seen Jake near the area where Isaac was found, but he was unsure of the date and exact time (he gave a different story to the constable back in June), and is a reputed drunk.

July 19, 1913

Poor Mr. Tarantino is very ill these days. He did not attend the trial. His son Rufus is staying with him and tending to the animals, etc. His daughter Betty has returned to San Francisco to be with her husband. They are all devastated by this. I am angry most of the time and I cry myself to sleep—that is, when I sleep.

July 22, 1913

I left flowers for Isaac a little while ago and watched the sun rise. I think Isaac knows when I am there for he sent me a sign: Just when the sun rose to that spot between the trees behind Isaac's grave, its light fell upon his headstone and cast gold upon the word BELOVED.

July 24, 1913

Calvin Dempster, who works at the train depot, told me Mr. Sheers and Jake boarded the eastbound train to New England last night where Mr. Sheers plans to enroll Jake in Law School. Calvin doesn't believe this. He thinks Mr. Sheers is taking him away to put him in a hospital somewhere because of his convulsions and recent bouts of hysteria. He said Jake looked like he wanted to jump out of the train and run for the hills! I feel so sad about everything.

Aug. 1, 1913

We all slept on the summer porch last night due to the heat. I miss going swimming in the creek behind the Tarantino house. I miss Isaac. I miss Sarah.

Aug. 12, 1913

Little Andres Johansen died of a rattlesnake bite yesterday. Jonathon picked up two more bags of concrete today, and told me he plans to take extra care engraving Andres's headstone. Andres's sister, Inga, who Jon is courting, told him her mother wants an engraving on the stone of an angel flying to Heaven.

Sept. 14, 1913

This morning I heard Jonathon crying in his room. I found him sitting on the floor there, rocking himself with his face in his hands. While gathering his hiking gear for an outing with his friends, Jonathon found the compass Isaac gave him for Christmas last year. As far as I know, this is the first time Jon has cried over Isaac.

Sept. 25, 1913

I tried to see Sarah today. Mrs. Sheers wouldn't let me in. She said Sarah is ill with a cold and needs her rest. Liar. Liar. Liar!

Sept. 30, 1913

If not for the love of my family, my life would be nothing but a black hole.

Oct. 1, 1913

I put flowers on Isaac's grave today and said a prayer for him. I wish I could re-live that day when he took me in his wagon to school, that lovely morning when we sang together along the way and he told me funny stories. To only remember it is one *thing, for in remembrance he is only a memory. To re-live that day, he would be alive again and I would be alive again.*

Nov. 27, 1913

Frank Tarantino and his son Rufus joined us for our annual feast. Mr. Tarantino is not as gregarious as he used to be. Thanksgiving is not the same for any of us.

Nov. 30, 1913

Leaving church this morning, I overheard Mrs. Dempster tell Mrs. Halland that Mr. Sheers has returned home. Mrs. Dempster also said she heard Mrs. Sheers will be escorting Sarah to live with a family friend in Illinois. This is terrible news.

Dec. 12, 1913

Sarah arrived at our door at four-thirty this morning, cold, frightened, starving, and very dirty. In tears, she indicated to us that she still could not speak. She told us (by writing her answers for us) she devised a ruse to leave the train that was to carry her and her mother to Illinois. Her mother had stayed seated in the train, expecting her to return before the train departed. Sarah ran away just before the train left the station. It took her two days to walk here, walking only at night and sleeping in the woods during the day. She begged us to let her hide here because she is carrying Isaac's baby, and her parents planned to give it to an orphanage. Of course, we will hide her here. Papa insisted we shall guard this secret with our lives. He forbid us to tell Mr. Tarantino because Mr. Tarantino would fight Mr. Sheers to keep Sarah with him, and that is why Sarah did not go to him for help.

Dec. 18, 1913

Mr. Sheers arrived here with the constable this afternoon. Papa saw them coming and had plenty of time to hide Sarah in the electrical service space between the walls downstairs. They did not believe us when we feigned surprise and concern over Sarah's "disappearance," and thoroughly searched our home – including our basement that serves as Papa's embalming and preparation room – and every inch of our property. Papa and Mama promised they would inform them should Sarah contact us. Now it is our turn to lie, and we can be better liars than Mr. and Mrs. Sheers!

Dec. 25, 1913

We had a very quiet Christmas this year. Mrs. Dempster flapped her mouth after church again this morning with news Mrs. Sheers is remaining in Illinois.

Jan. 9, 1914

Sarah is still unable to speak. She cries in her sleep. Her middle is showing her condition. Papa and Jonathon built a hidden room for her connected to my bedroom.

Jan. 14, 1914

Mr. Sheers has made it a habit to drop in on us at odd hours. Mama and Papa actually hosted him for supper last night when he darkened our door while Mama and I were cooking. He often brags about how well Jake is doing at Dartmouth while, on the other hand, gets tearful when speaking about his missing daughter. Lately he has been asking questions about Frank Tarantino, noting he has seen Frank's son Rufus in town, but not Frank. He wanted to know if Rufus is planning to stay on at the Tarantino ranch to take over his wool business or take Isaac's former profession supplying Papa with coffins. It is true Rufus is now building coffins for Papa when needed, but why would that matter to Mr. Sheers?

Feb. 1, 1914

While Papa was in town today, he heard Mr. Sheers has closed his law firm. Papa said he went to see for himself and the office was closed. He then went by the Sheers's house and saw it was very unkempt on the outside. A neighbor told Papa Mr. Sheers had let his servants go and was planning to hire a new houseman and a gardener. It seems he is considering selling the house and moving to Illinois – that is the rumor, anyway.

Feb. 5, 1914

Sarah has been ill. Papa has ordered bed rest for her. I think it would be better for her to sit out in the sun for a while each day, but it has been raining steadily for a week and very cold. Mama has been keeping watch on her and is worried about the health of the baby, as well.

Feb. 19, 1914

Sarah is still unable to speak. She writes us notes and makes certain we burn them immediately.

Mar. 1, 1914

Sarah is having terrible back pains. Her face is very pale. Papa and Mama do what they can to ease her discomfort.

Mar. 14, 1914

Jonathon requested we not have a birthday party for him this year, so we had a quiet celebration at home with no guests. Sarah is too ill to take part in anything. The baby is due any day.

Mar. 15, 1914

Sarah gave me her wedding ring and the pearl necklace Isaac gave her for her birthday. She wrote me to keep them in her jewelry box that Frank Tarantino gave me. She had not worn her wedding ring since late January when her fingers started to swell. I asked her to keep her jewelry box with the ring and necklace with her, but she insisted I keep them in my hope chest that Isaac built for me. She is considering seeing Mr. Tarantino after her baby is born in hopes he will arrange for her to live with Isaac's cousin Betty in San Francisco. If Betty says yes, she will board the train at the Masonville station. There are too many eyes and loose lips here in Providence, as you know!

Stephanie set the diary facedown and open on her bed to save the page, and she further examined the jewelry. There was no engraving inside the gold wedding band except the notation of karat weight. She tested the pearl pendant with her front teeth, like she saw a jeweler demonstrate on television. The pearl was real. Isaac had no trouble parting with his money in the name of love. She took a closer look at the jewelry box, noticed a notch cut out at the interior bottom. Using a metal fingernail file, she pried the bottom up to reveal a hidden pocket. The pocket contained small photographs of Isaac and Sarah: two individual photos of each, and one of them together with their arms around each other's waist. They were dressed formally, he in a suit and hat, she in a long pale dress with lace ruffles at the collar and sleeves. Her hair was piled in a neat bun crowning her head; wavy shoulder length strands framed her face. Sarah was no beauty, but the purity of her soul lent an ethereal quality to her continence. Her expression, like Isaac's, was of ecstatic happiness.

The clock on the nightstand showed it was two in the morning. Stephanie's eyes were hurting and her back ached. She thought to tell Quinn what she found. The recollection of him frantically returning all the items into the hope chest and rushing it home gave her pause. These items did not belong to Quinn's family; they belonged to her family. They should stay with her, and she hoped he'd agree.

Despite the late hour and her fatigue, her curiosity drew her into what remained of Emily's account.

Mar. 18, 1914

How many times can our hearts be broken and still beat? Sarah died in childbirth early this morning and her baby—a darling little boy—never took a breath. We named him Isaac after his father who we loved dearly. Papa plans to bury Sarah and her baby next to Isaac's grave. He regrets he cannot place a headstone for her because we will be found out.

Mar. 19, 1914

Papa, Jonathon and I buried Sarah and Baby Isaac this evening. Papa placed a letter in the coffin identifying Sarah and her baby and the dates they were born and the date they died. Mama joined us while we covered the grave and put broken branches, etc. over it to hide it. We prayed for Sarah and Baby Isaac as the sun set.

Apr. 2, 1914

I will write no more. I simply can't.

The remaining four pages were blank. Stephanie closed the diary slowly, with great respect and even greater sadness. All of this time poor Sarah and Baby Isaac lay in an unmarked grave beside the final resting place of the only man Sarah ever loved. Stephanie reopened the diary and reread the passage describing the gravesite; it had to be the same spot to the right of Isaac's grave she had cleared while Quinn was recovering from Bruno and Farley's assault back in June. She recalled battling with all the twigs and branches that were tangled together, and all the layers below of rotten wood and wet foul-smelling dirt invaded by earthworms. That had to be the spot. It had to be.

There was also the matter of the hidden room adjacent to Emily's former room at the Vanderfield house. Did Quinn know about it? If not, would there be anything more to discover in there? And what about Emily whose heart was broken, not only by her unrequited love for Isaac, but also by his death and then Sarah's death?

Stephanie intended to give Quinn the diary in the morning. He had every right to possess this only remaining chronicle of his ancestors and their story. He would come to know his second-great-aunt Emily, his second-great-grandfather Jonathon, and his third-great-grandfather Dr. Wendell Vanderfield. Quinn would also learn about Isaac and Sarah and their struggles. Together she and Quinn would find where Sarah was buried. Sarah and Baby Isaac would finally have a headstone; they deserved that much.

30

Quinn lowered himself into the thin cavity between the wall of the grave and the slowly decaying coffin. He used his hands to carefully brush the remaining dirt off the damp splintering lid.

Alighting from the rented bulldozer, Gene Blackwell called out, "Well, Stephanie was right."

"I never doubted her," Quinn said. "But we have to be sure it's Sarah and Baby Isaac."

Gene scrunched up his face as if he'd just tasted an overripe lemon. "I wouldn't open it, Quinn."

Quinn replied stoically, "I know what dead bodies look like."

Gene swept his arm to draw his attention to the others in attendance: Stephanie, Ida, Caleb, and Quinn's father, John. They stood a distance away, watching silently with an air of curiosity combined with guilty revulsion because of their curiosity.

Stephanie stood ready with Sarah's jewelry box in her hands, steeling herself to endure the sight of the contents of the coffin. Gene considered her the most vulnerable of the attendees at this bizarre and illegally executed investigation. But he knew the girl was determined Sarah and Baby Isaac would be treated with respect. Gene indirectly referred to Stephanie as he cautioned Quinn, "Well, the rest of us don't, and we don't expect it to be a pretty sight."

Quinn answered him with a question, "How are we gonna know for sure it's her and the baby unless I lift the lid and look?"

John Vanderfield stepped forward and softly told Quinn, "Lift it just enough so only you can see. Be prepared for the stench, though."

Quinn removed the handkerchief from his pocket he had brought for the occasion. He held it upon his nose and mouth as he used his right hand to slowly lift the creaking lid enough to dispel some of the odor. Surprisingly he smelled only a light odor that reminded him of the earth after a heavy rain. For a few moments, he vacillated between lifting the lid enough to see the occupant of the coffin and closing it to give himself more time to man-up for the task.

Caleb inquired supportively, "Do you want me to help you?"

"No. I got it." His projection of self-confidence was one hundred percent fake and everybody knew it. He knew they knew it.

He returned the handkerchief to his pocket, took a deep breath and used both hands to lift the lid one-quarter-way, enough to see. The sunlight shimmered upon the sapphire blue dress that looked almost new after all the years underground. Desiccated bones lay within the dark blue folds. The curly tresses of her once dark brown hair had fallen from her skull, but some still rested in reddish waves over her shoulders and rib bones. He made it a point not to look at her face. He wanted to remember her as she had appeared to him in her spirit body instead of her earthly decomposed condition. Someone, probably Quinn's third-great-grandfather, had positioned her arms to where she was eternally cuddling her baby, now a tiny skeleton dressed in a white christening gown. Quinn saw enough to determine the identity of the woman and baby. He spotted a folded sheet of paper beside the woman's hip. He removed it, unfolded it and read the brief information. Quinn committed the information to memory, refolded the paper and returned it to its place beside Sarah Sheers Iversen. He closed the lid slowly and with the utmost tenderness.

Quinn allowed himself a moment to regain his composure that had slipped a little at the sight of the two bodies. When he looked up at the small group standing away off to the side of the grave, he almost laughed, for they all backed away as one unit the moment he closed the lid and cast his eyes upon them. Once more he had to take a moment to collect himself before he told them, "It's Sarah and Baby Isaac."

Ida spoke, a respectful inquiry, "Are you sure?"

"Absolutely. Do you want to see the letter? I can take it out again."

A chorus of "no" and "that's okay," answered him.

Stephanie bravely stepped forward with the jewelry box protected in a zip-loc plastic bag. She paused at the edge of the grave and offered it to Quinn. He took it and gave her a slight smile of admiration in return. Stephanie remarked in a voice just above a whisper, "It's only right. It all belongs to her and belongs with her."

Wordlessly, he lifted the lid again and set the jewelry box upon the folded letter beside Sarah's remains. This time he uttered softly, "Rest in peace, Sarah" before he closed the casket. A profound feeling of finality welled up in the core of his soul and with it he felt a twinge of grief at her suffering. However, he was satisfied he had given her the acknowledgment she wanted, which was to be identified as Isaac's wife and her son as Isaac's son. She was finally free.

Gene, who was an ordained minister by mail (to no one's surprise), opened his prayer book to the funeral rites section and commenced the service once Quinn joined the others. They concluded the service with a prayer for Sarah and Baby Isaac and wished them peace and happiness. After that, Gene returned to the bulldozer and began the process of reburial. They all stayed until it was done, and then Quinn and his father set the new flat granite headstone in place.

Stephanie and John lingered as the others left and Gene manned the bulldozer to return it to the rental store. He gave Quinn a congratulatory salute as he steered the machine up the path between the rows toward the path that led to the road. Quinn smiled gratefully and returned his salute as the man and machine passed him.

His father drifted away to Emily Vanderfield's grave. Quinn observed him reading the information and loving sentiments upon her elaborate headstone that had an angel in flight carved upon it. An image came to Quinn's mind then of his father as a child exploring this lonely place. It caused him to wonder if the man had indeed spent some of his childhood days examining the many headstones, not knowing what they were and what they represented. He intended to ask him about it later.

Stephanie's voice drew his attention to her as she told him, "I put a note in the jewelry box."

"You did?"

"I wrote that we set it there together for her because Isaac made it for her, and it belongs to her. I put today's date on it, too." She cast a tender gaze at him that gave him the impression all the love in her soul had risen up into her eyes. At that moment, his heart leaped in his chest, so great his desire to envelop her in his arms. Her gaze still holding him rapt, she added, "I hope they can both rest now."

"Me, too."

"You're really something, Quinn. You know that?"

"What do you mean?"

"Remember that day here when Caleb and Gene were helping us re-set the headstones and Caleb was mad at you because he thought you had lied about everything?"

"Yeah…"

"Remember I told him you have the biggest heart in the world?"

"Uh-huh…"

"Well, I meant that." Stephanie embraced him and rested her cheek upon his shoulder. "I'll stay with you if you want to stay here a while."

"Gosh, Steph. You keep this up I'll start getting the idea that you kind of like me." He held her tightly to him.

She teased him, "Yeah, I like you. Kind of."

Over her shoulder, he saw his father move to another grave to read the headstones of Emily's parents and her brother Jonathon who shared a double-depth plot with his wife Inga, who were his Vanderfield ancestors. John had never shown interest before, although it was common knowledge in the family he had been named after Jonathon who was his great-grandfather. It made Quinn curious to hear his thoughts on the matter. "I need to talk with my dad about something before he leaves."

"You'll still join us later for dinner, right?"

"Yeah." He released her and kissed her lips gently. "None of this would have happened without you, Steph. I hope you know that."

She regarded him thoughtfully. "You're the one. You're the one they counted on, and you delivered."

"*We* delivered."

She giggled and said, "If you insist." She pulled away from him and walked away, but stopped shortly, turned and waved her fingers at him. As an afterthought, she informed him invitingly, "Yams with raisins and toasted marshmallows." Without waiting for his response, she quickened her pace up the path and he watched her until the brush obscured his view.

His father strolled over to him and hugged him. "I'm proud of you, son." He appreciatively smiled at this son of his who used to hide his sensitivity and compassion behind a mask of bitter rebelliousness. John liked and respected this improved version, even found him somewhat inspiring.

Quinn treasured his father's love for him, love the man had once been unable to express. He wished his father had given him that love when he most needed it after his mother had died. His self-pitying wish that came in response to his father's love caused him to finally understand his own culpability in their battles. He understood, too, that he had never made the effort to know this man or to learn what compelled him to work such long hours and drink too much. Quinn mulled it over and the answer came to him.

Before he could voice his thoughts and conclusions, John beat him to it. "I know how bad you hurt, son. I do, too. We have to get through this. I want us to get through this."

"So do I."

"What you've done here; it still amazes me."

"Did you ever come here when you were a kid?"

"I didn't know about it until I was older. Even then, I never came down here to explore it."

"But, this is our family here. Our ancestors. Our family plot that they decided, quite generously, to share with the rest of their community at a time of need. Didn't you ever wonder about all the stories these people had? Weren't you the least bit curious?"

"I didn't care about it. My life was full of better things then. Your mother, for instance."

"We should move Mom here," Quinn stated.

"I don't know about that."

"Her ancestors are here, too. Did you know that?"

"Her parents are buried at Oakview where she's buried."

Quinn scoffed crossly, "She never got along with her parents. You know that! She should be here with us."

"What do you mean '*us*'? I don't plan to be buried here. I'm going to be beside her at Oakview."

"This began as our family plot, and we should all be here with our family."

The idea was ludicrous to John, yet the earnestness in Quinn's eyes stirred him to reconsider. "We'll talk about it," he replied hesitatingly.

"*I* want to be buried here."

"Please, Quinn…"

"Tell me you'll bury me here if I go before you."

"Don't be so morbid."

"I'm not being morbid. I'm telling you what I want."

John caved, but he could not hide his ambivalence. "I'll see to it. Just don't leave before me. I really don't want to be the one to bury you here. I want you to grow up to be an old man with a successful and happy life. I want you to have children that will piss you off as much as you pissed me off, but will love you enough to give you your final wish."

Quinn found that amusing.

John continued over Quinn's half-subdued sniggering, "I want your children to love you as much as I love you, which is immeasurably and eternally."

Quinn laughed aloud and replied, "That's a bit overboard, Dad."

"After all the shit you've put me through, if I didn't love you so much I would have snuffed you and walled your body up in the basement. '*He ran away from home,*' I would have told everyone. No one would've believed anything else." His eyes glistened with humor.

"Damn! You must have been close to that a lot of times!"

Following a playfully sinister chuckle, John said, "Nah…"

Nodding with mock worry, Quinn teased him. "Well, from now on I'm gonna watch my back."

With frustratingly bad timing, the vibration welled up in him, and he fell silent as the wave of it followed its usual course up to his brain where the explosion of colors and high-pitched humming absorbed all his attention.

Concerned by Quinn's abrupt trance-like state, John asked him, "Are you all right?"

Quinn emerged from inside himself at the sound and worried tone of his father's voice. It took him a few moments to invent an answer to John's question. He delivered his words with just the right amount of introspection, "Yeah. I just want to stay here a while by myself."

"Why?"

He glanced at Sarah's grave at the four spirits reading her new headstone. They glanced at him with expressions indicating their approval. Jake Sheers lifted his index finger to signal they were waiting to converse with him. Quinn had not seen them in over a month, assumed they had all passed over, and he missed them.

His father still did not know about his ability to see the dead. Quinn wanted to keep it that way. He answered him with a lie as to why he wanted to stay behind, "I just want to pray. I need privacy for that."

John was not a churchgoer, although he was a believer and had always respected Quinn's more intense devotion to God, which was encouraged by his late wife Bernice. "I understand. I'll see you tonight when I get back from my A.A. meeting."

In the back of his mind, Quinn expected his father would backslide as many alcoholics do during their first try, but he preferred to focus on the positive fact that at least the man was trying. "Keep up the good fight. I'm proud of you, too, you know."

John glanced at the ground, self-doubt playing hardball against his intention to conquer the bottle. Quinn sensed it clearly, even as the man meekly looked him in the eye and affectionately squeezed his shoulder to express his thanks.

The sun hung close to the peaks of the western range against the cloudless blue sky, sending long tree shadows upon the graveyard. Now that his dad had departed, Quinn looked again at his visitors. He noted the shadows, which lay everywhere else, did not lie upon them. Instead, the shadows passed through them to the flora and fauna behind their forms.

Sarah stepped forward in her sapphire blue dress, followed by Isaac who was holding their son's hand. The boy, now a child Quinn estimated to be five or six years old, was wearing a gray suit jacket and matching short pants. His spirit body glowed with a shimmering white aura like those of his parents and his Uncle Jake. He walked trustingly with his father and mother toward Quinn. The child gazed at Quinn with his pale blue eyes, gazed at him as if they were old friends reunited. Sarah smiled encouragingly at the boy as they stopped in front of Quinn.

She looked upon Quinn with an expression of unconditional and profound love. "Thank you," she said.

Quinn responded sincerely, "I'm glad for you, Sarah. God bless you."

"Oh, He has!" She wrapped her arm around Isaac's waist. Isaac draped his arm over her shoulders and kissed her cheek. They exchanged loving glances and admiring smiles that told the world both here and beyond of the depth of their love.

After a few more moments engaged in their mutual spell, Isaac turned his attention to Quinn and offered his hand to him. Isaac's hand was warm, which surprised him, and was encased in a vibratory glove of energy that produced an impression of solidity as their hands joined. They shook hands respectfully and sincerely, the way men do when they have emerged victorious after a long struggle against a common enemy. Isaac's eyes and voice were full of admiration and happiness as he said, "Thank you, Quinn. We'll never forget you. Tell Ida and Stephanie the same, and tell Caleb I'm sorry for what I put him through. Tell him I said he works too hard and needs to learn how to have some fun, too." He intoned the last remark with a wink and a mischievous grin.

Quinn answered, "I will."

Sarah said, "We have to go. Goodbye, Quinn. We love you."

The three faded away, leaving Quinn with the feeling they would not visit him again. He knew he would always miss them, yet he felt relieved at their departure, relieved because they had at last found peace.

Jake held back for a few moments before he approached Quinn, which he did with a strange reluctance as if he did not fully wish to part from him. Jake's appearance was different than it was before; he was a younger man, a healthier man, and his face expressed a condition Quinn had never seen in him before – inner serenity. Shimmering white energy replaced his former black aura that spat jagged shards of colors. Quinn noticed something else once Jake stopped and stood inches away from him: gone was the pungent odor of hard alcohol and chemicals. In its place, he emitted a faintly discernible scent Quinn recognized as that of ice flower, a shrub his mother planted at the south side of their house, which she referred to as "wintersweet."

Quinn joked about it, "So, what's with the wintersweet aftershave?"

Jake laughed a little before he answered, "There's a park with a huge arboretum where our house used to be."

"Oh," Quinn remarked, "I used to go there with my mom. So, that's where your house was, huh?'"

"Sarah thought it was quite an improvement."

"Of course." He paused while they gazed at each other wondering where to go from here. Quinn began with the obvious, "You look good, Jake."

"I feel good. For the first time in this long-ass existence, I finally feel good. I'm sorry for all the grief I caused you. But, it wasn't all me—"

Quinn interrupted, "Yeah. I know the old man possessed you. I know he was using you—speaking and acting through you. It wasn't your fault."

"Besides Isaac, you were the only other friend I ever had. I mean that, Quinn. Like I said, you kind of grew on me—*like a wart*." He laughed at his own joke, which caused Quinn to laugh. Jake continued after their laughter subsided, "Finding you was the best thing that happened to me. Leaving you is not the worst thing that ever happened to me, but it's high up on the list. I got no choice but to go."

"Where do the dead go?"

"I don't know. I won't know until I get there. I'm not afraid, though. I kind of feel peaceful about it. That's a good sign, don't you think?"

"Yeah. That's a good sign." Quinn felt his eyes begin to sting.

"Aw… don't go getting all weepy on me."

Quinn felt the tears slide down his cheeks. "I'm sick of saying goodbye to people."

"Someone always has to go first. Someday you'll be the one leaving and someone will be saying goodbye to you. That's how it is. I'm sure we'll see each other again. Not here, but there, where the dead go. That good place where there's no pain or sadness. That's what they promise, anyway."

"Who?"

"The ancient ones. I've seen them come for others. I've seen a lot of things. Like I said, Quinn—things you couldn't imagine, and I'm not talking about bad things like I was last time. The bad happens here in this dimension. Everything here is a two-sided coin. Can't have the good without the bad. But I guess I'm babbling again like I did in the crazy house."

"No, you're not."

Jake tilted his head sideways. His eyes glazed over as he listened intently to a message meant only for him. A few moments later, alertness returned to his eyes and he told Quinn, "They're calling me. This is it, kid." A thought came to him and he chuckled before he shared it with Quinn. "I find it kind of ironic that I'm leaving here from a cemetery, what with me never being buried and all."

"I found a photo of you in Emily's photo album. Stephanie added it to her family records. You will not be forgotten, Jake."

"Of all the things I've done in my life, getting through to you made all the difference. Sorry I made you piss your pants."

Embarrassed, but appreciating the humor, Quinn let loose with a cackling laugh through his tears.

"Now, that's the way I want to leave you," Jake said, "Laughing. I once read a quote that in essence said laughter is the elixir of life. Therefore, I advise you in your current vernacular to *'lighten up.'* Let go of what you can't control; embrace what makes you happy."

Unlike the others, Jake did not fade away. He simply disappeared instantaneously. No handshake. No goodbye. No nothing. Just… gone. Quinn figured he did it that way to save them both the pain of extending their parting any longer.

The shadows were fading in the waning sunlight. Tree frogs began to sing in the nearby creek. The cool temperature of the day dropped another degree.

Quinn zipped up his jacket and took one more look at Sarah's headstone. The plaque was a beautiful work of art, polished bronze, with spilling rose bouquets on each corner, and they got all the information correct; Quinn had made certain of that. He especially was taken with how the word, "BELOVED" glowed in the final golden ray of light that fell upon it before the sun descended behind the mountains.

THE END

Thank you for reading, "*Hell Is In Me.*"
*Independent authors rely on reviews to spread the word about their works.
If you enjoyed this book (or hated it), please leave a
review where your book was purchased.
If you would like to contact me directly, you can reach me here:*

On Facebook:
Colleen A Parkinson, Author

My Blog Page:
https://thefinesthat.jimdo.com

Email:
caparkinson.a2@gmail.com

Other books by Colleen A. Parkinson
The Finest Hat in the Whole World
Des Stewart sees himself as a loser in life and love. Haunted by tragedy, trapped in a dead-end job and responsible for the care of his elderly mother who is slipping into senility, he cannot envision a brighter future for himself. His life changes when he takes in his volatile and temperamental young niece. They have a special bond that has been unbroken since the moment of her traumatic birth. They are two troubled souls on a path of healing, heartbreak, and redemption. Set in the years 1917 through 1937, "The Finest Hat in the Whole World" is an unforgettable, award-winning story.